▼

LINDA HOGAN

SOLAR STORMS

A NOVEL

SCRIBNER PAPERBACK FICTION
Published by Simon & Schuster

SCRIBNER PAPERBACK FICTION
Simon & Schuster Inc.
Rockefeller Center
1230 Avenue of the Americas
New York, NY 10020

First Scribner Paperback Fiction edition 1997
SCRIBNER PAPERBACK FICTION and design are trademarks of
Macmillan Library Reference USA, Inc. under license by
Simon & Schuster, the publisher of this work.

Designed by Songhee Kim
Manufactured in the United States of America

19   20   18

The Library of Congress has cataloged the Scribner
edition as follows:
Hogan, Linda.
Solar storms: a novel / Linda Hogan.
1. Indian women—Minnesota—Fiction. 2. Indian
women—Canada—Fiction. I. Title.
PS3558.034726S58   1995
813'.54—dc20   95-24563
CIP
ISBN 978-0-684-81227-4
ISBN 978-0-684-82539-7 (Pbk)

For Danielle Marie. May you find your way
always to those who love you.

Acknowledgments

I WANT TO THANK Jean Fortier and my other friends who have listened to this story for so long a time; Marilyn Auer, Brenda Peterson, Connie Studer, Patricia Amman, Patrick Hogan, who lived parts of the story; Shelly McIntire, Lee Goerner, and Katherine McNamara, and my assistant, Wonshé. I am also so grateful to Leigh Haber and Beth Vesel for their assistance. And thanks to Michael Evans-Smith for providing information.

The Guggenheim Foundation provided financial support during the writing of this novel.

PROLOGUE

SOMETIMES NOW I hear the voice of my great-grandmother, Agnes. It floats toward me like a soft breeze through an open window.

"The house is crying," I said to her as steam ran down the walls. The cooking stove heated the house. Windows were frozen over with white feathers and ferns.

Bush said the house could withstand it. She had black hair then, beautiful and soft. She stepped out into the cold and brought in an armload of wood. I caught the sweet odor of it and a wind of cold air as she brushed by me. She placed a log in the stove. It was still damp and when the flame grabbed it, the wood spat and hissed.

I didn't for a minute believe the house could withstand it. I knew already it was going to collapse. It was a wooden house, dark inside, and spare. The floors creaked as she swept about. The branches of trees scraped against the windows like they were trying to get in. Perhaps they protested the fire and what it lived on.

Bush unjointed the oxtails and browned them in suet. She worked so slowly, you would have thought it was swamp balm, not fat and back-bone, that she touched. I thought of the old days when the oxen arrived in black train cars from the dark, flat fields of Kansas, diseased beasts that had been yoked together in burden. All the land, even our lost land, was shaped by them and by the hated thing that held them together as rain and sunlight and snow fell on their toiling backs.

The shadows of fish floated in the sink. Bush did her own hunting then, and she had a bag of poor, thin winter rabbits. She removed their fur the way you'd take off a stocking. She dredged them in flour. In the kitchen, their lives rose up in steam.

Day and night she worked. In her nightclothes, she boiled roots that still held the taste of mud. She stirred a black kettle and two pots. In her dark skirt, she cut onions. I didn't understand, until it was over, what it was she had to do. I didn't know what had taken hold of her and to what lengths she must go in order to escape its grip.

She folded blankets and clothing and placed them on the floor in the center of that one dark room. She took down the curtains, shook out the dust, washed them in the sink, and hung them on lines from wall to wall. All the while, bones floated up in broth the way a dream rises to the top of sleep.

Your mother entered my dreaming once, not floating upward that way, but crashing through, the way deer break through ice, or a stone falls into water, tumbling down to the bottom. In the dream, I was fishing in Lake Grand when the water froze suddenly like when the two winds meet and stop everything in their paths, the way they do in waking life, the way they left a man frozen that time, standing in place at the bank of Spirit River. In the dream I saw your mother beneath ice in the center of the lake. I was afraid of her. We all were. What was wrong with her we couldn't name and we distrusted such things as had no name. She was like the iron underground that pulls the needle of a compass to false north.

Whatever your mother was in that dream, whatever she is now, it wasn't human. It wasn't animal or fish. It was nothing I could recognize by sight or feel. The thing she was, or that had turned into her, pulled me toward it. I was standing, still and upright, drawn out that way to the terrible and magnetic center of what I feared. I slid across the glaring surface of ice, standing like a statue, being pulled, helpless and pale in the ice light. Old stories I'd heard from some of the Cree began to play across my mind, stories about the frozen heart of evil that was hunger, envy, and greed, how it had tricked people into

death or illness or made them go insane. In those stories the only thing
that could save a soul was to find a way to thaw the person's heart, to
warm it back into water. But we all knew your mother, Hannah
Wing, stood at the bottomless passage to an underworld. She was
wounded. She was dangerous. And there was no thawing for her heart.

Bush, the wife of your grandpa, had struggled with your mother's
cold world. She tried to keep you with her, to protect you from the violence that was your mother. There was the time she heard you crying
in the house when you were not there. I heard it, too, your voice, crying for help, or I would not have believed her. It was a chilling sound,
your soul crying out, and Bush turned desperate as a caged animal.
She fought for you.

In that battle with what amounted to human evil, Bush didn't
win, but she didn't lose either. It was a tie, a fragile balance that
could tip at any time. That was the reason she cooked the mourning
feast. That was why she baked the bread and soaked corn in lye
and ashes until it became the sweetest hominy, and who would have
believed such a caustic thing could sweeten and fatten the corn?
That was why she cooked the wild rice we harvested two years earlier,
and the rice was the most important thing because you had gone with
us that fall day. You were all wrapped in cotton, with netting over
your face so that the little bugs and dust wouldn't bother you as we
drifted through the plants, clicking the sticks that knocked rice into
the boat.

The last thing Bush did to prepare her feast in honor of you was to
open the jar of swamp tea, and when she did, I smelled it. It smelled
like medicine to me. It smelled like healing. It reminded me of the days
when the old women put eagle down inside wounds and they would
heal.

Bush is a quiet woman, little given to words. She never takes kindly
to being told what to do. So while she prepared the feast, I let her be,
even when she did a poor job on the rice soup. I knitted and sat in the
chair by the window and looked outside, straight at the face of winter.
There was a silence so deep it seemed that all things prepared for what
would follow, then and for years to come, the year you returned to us,
the years when the rest of us would be gone, when the land itself would
tremble in fear of drowning.

The windows were frozen over, so it was through ice that I saw them coming, the people, arriving that cold Sunday of the feast. Across ice, they looked like mere shadows against a darkening winter evening. Wind had blown snow from the surface of the lake, so in places the ice was shining like something old and polished by hands. Maybe it was the hands of wind, but the ice shone beneath their feet. I scraped the window with my fingernails and peered out. It wasn't quite dark, but Jarrell Illinois, gone now, wore a miner's headlamp and the others walked close to him, as if convinced that night had fallen. As they drew closer, I saw that their shadows and reflections walked alongside them like ghosts, or their own deaths that would rise up one day and meet them. So it looked like they were more. My breath steamed the window, I remember. I wiped it again for a better look.

Some of the people were wrapped in the hides we used to wear, or had blankets wrapped around them. They walked together like spirits from the thick forest behind winter. They were straight and tall. They were silent.

"Here they come," I said. Bush, for a change, was nervous. She stirred the iron pot one last time, then untied her hair. It was long and thick. Hair is a woman's glory, they say. Her glory fell down her back. The teakettle began to sing as if it remembered old songs some of us had long since forgotten. Its breath rose up in the air as she poured boiling water over the small oval leaves of swamp tea. The house smelled of it and of cedar.

"Look at that," I said. "They look beautiful."

Bush bent over the table and looked out the window as the people came through a path in the snow. The air shimmered in the light of the miner's lamp and a lantern one woman carried. Bush wiped her hands on her apron. Then they came through the door and filled up the crying house. Some of them stamped their feet from the habit of deep snow, their cheeks red with cold. They took off their boots and left them by the fire. They greeted us in a polite way. Some of them admired the food or warmed their hands near the stove. All of them looked at the pictures of you that sat on the table. After greeting us, they said very little. They were still uncomfortable around Bush even after all those years. She was a misplaced person. She'd come there to marry my son, Harold. They had never understood her and how love was the one thing that kept her there. To get them to her banquet, she'd told them this was her tradition, that it was the only thing that could help her get over her grief from losing you. There wasn't one among us who didn't suspect that she'd invented this ceremony, at least in part, but mourning was our common ground and that's why they came, not just for her, but out of loyalty for the act of grief.

Bush put a piece of each of the different foods in her blue bowl for the spirits, wiped her hands on her apron, and took the bowl outside. I could see through the doorway how heat rose from the bowl like a prayer carried to the sky, begging any and all gods in the low clouds to listen. The aching joints of my hands told me it was a bone-chilling, hurting cold, the worst of winters. Bush held up the bowl for sky to see, for the spirit of ice, for what lived inside clouds, for the night-wind people who would soon be present because they lived on Fur Island and returned there each night. I could barely make out her shape in the newly swirling snow, but when she came back in, she smiled. I remember that. She smiled at the people. It was as if a burden was already lifted.

One by one the people took their places, settling into chairs or on the couch that was covered with a throw I had made, or they sat at the long table. They hadn't been there before, and so they looked around the small, now-stripped house with curiosity. The wood and wallpaper were stained where rain had seeped through.

When Bush served up the food, it came to me that I didn't want to eat. I was a large woman then, I loved my food, but I must have known that eating this meal would change me. I only picked at it.

At first, we hardly spoke, just small talk, and there were the sounds of forks on plates, spoons in bowls. There were silences when the wind died down, and all you could hear was snow hitting against the wood of the house, dying against the windows, tapping as if it was hungry and wanted in. I remember thinking of the island where she lived, the frozen waters, the other lands with their rising and sloping distances, even the light and dust of solar storms that love our cold, eerie pole.

We had moose meat, rice, and fish. The room was hot. There were

white-haired people, black-haired people, and the mixed-bloods—
they wore such colorful clothes. Frenchie was there, dressed in a blue
dress. It was low-cut and she wore rhinestones at her neck, and large
rubber boots. We were used to her way of dress, so we didn't think it
was strange attire. We just believed she was one kind of woman on top
and another below the waist.

It was so damp and warm inside that the wallpaper, full of leaves,
began to loosen from the moist walls. It troubled my mother, Dora-
Rouge, who sat with her back against the wall. She was always an orderly woman and accustomed to taking care of things. And she wasn't
as bent as she is now, so when Bush wasn't looking she tried to stick
the wallpaper back up, holding edges and corners with her hands until
it became too much for her, and she gave up and went back to taking
the fine bones out of her fish.

Jarrell Illinois—he was a good man—took some tobacco out of the
tin and pinched it into his cheek and smiled all around the room.

In that one day it seemed that the house grew smaller. It settled.
The floors sloped as if they knew the place would soon be abandoned,
the island quiet and alone with just its memory of all that had happened there, even the shipwreck of long ago.

I don't know how to measure love. Not by cup or bowl, not in distance either, but that's what rose from the iron pot as steam, that was
the food taken into our bodies. It was the holy sacrament of you we ate
that day, so don't think you were never loved. It's just there was no
way open between us after the county sent you back to Hannah, and
however we tried, we never saw you again after that.

We ate from evening through to near light, or as light as it gets in
winter. The fire cast shadows on the walls as the old men picked the
bones, then piled them up like ancient tellers of fortune. They ate the
bowls empty, clear to the bottom. By then, people were talking and
some even laughing, and there was just something in the air. That
night, in front of everyone, Bush cut her long hair. The way we used to
do long ago to show we had grief or had lost someone dear. She said it
held a memory of you. She said that hair had grown while you were
living on the island with her. She said she had to free that memory.

When the dishes were all piled up, she went to the middle of the room where she had placed her earthly goods, then in a giveaway, she gave each diner present some part of her world. It was only your things she parted with unwillingly, holding them as if she dreaded their absence, and now and then a tear would try to gather in her eye, but she was fierce and determined. She gave away your handmade blanket, T-shirt, shoes, socks—gave one here, one there. Some of the people cried. Not only for her, but for all the children lost to us, taken away.

She gave away her quilts, and the hawk feathers that had survived both flood and fire. She gave the carved fish decoys my son Harold had made. They were weighted just right to drop through ice and lure many a slow and hungry winter fish. No one else had weights as good as those. She gave away her fishing poles and line, and her rifle. She gave away the silverware. At the end she stood there in her white sleeping gown, for she'd even given what she wore that day, the black skirt, the sweater.

With all the moisture of cooking and breath, the door froze shut, and when the people were ready to leave, John Husk struggled to open it until finally it gave. When they went through it each person carried away a part of her. She said it was her tradition. No one questioned her out loud or showed a hint of the doubt I knew they felt.

They came to love her that night. She'd gone to the old ways, the way we used to live. From the map inside ourselves. Maybe it reminded us that we too had made our own ways here and were ourselves something like outcasts and runaways from other lands and tribes to start with.

They left through the unstuck, pried-open door. Night had turned over. The white silence of winter was broken by the moaning, cracking sound of the lake.

I remained, but I watched the others walk away with their arms full. Going back that morning, in the blue northern light, their stomachs were filled, their arms laden with blankets, food, and some of the beaver pelts Bush had stolen and been arrested for—from the trappers who had trespassed the island. Anything that could be carried away, they took. Frenchie pushed a chair before her across the ice, leaving the track of wooden legs in shining lines. Beneath her coat, she wore Bush's black sweater over the dress and rhinestones. But the most important thing *they carried was Bush's sorrow. It was small now, and child-sized, and it slid its hand inside theirs and walked away with them. We all had it, after that. It became our own. Some of us have since wanted to give it back to her, but once we felt it we knew it was too large for a single person. After that your absence sat at every table, occupied every room, walked through the doors of every house.*

The people walked through the drifts that had formed when the wind blew, then they seemed to merge with the outlines of the trees. I was worried that Frenchie might fall into the warm spot where the lake never freezes. Others had fallen before her.

Bush went outside to get the bowl. It was empty and there were no tracks. Or maybe the wind had covered them. But a bowl without its soup is such a hopeful thing, and like the bowl, Bush was left with emptiness, a place waiting and ready to be filled, one she could move inside and shape about her. And finally, she was able to sleep.

The next evening, Bush said it was time for me to leave. "Go on," she said, handing me my coat and hat. I hesitated. She had little more than a few pieces of firewood and some cooking pots. She had given away even the food. She saw me look about the house at what wasn't there. I sipped hot tea. We'd slept near each other for warmth the night before, my bear coat over us. Once Bush sat up and said, "This coat is singing." I told her it was just the sound of ice outside the door. I must have looked worried. "I'll be fine," she said, holding up the coat to help me into it.

But I said, "What about me? It's getting close to dark." She wasn't fooled. She knew I walked late at night just to hear the sounds of winter and see the sky and snow. I was always a great walker. She handed me my gloves and hat. I left unwillingly. It was all I could do to go out the door. I felt terrible leaving her in all that emptiness. I guess it was her sadness already come over me. I wanted to cry but I knew the wind, on its way to the island where it lived, would freeze my tears.

I took my time getting home. Above me there were shimmering hints of light. I remember thinking how the sky itself looked like a bowl of milk.

Then one night, worry got the best of me. I laced up my boots and went back over the frozen water. She was thinner, but she looked happy, and she didn't argue when I opened this bear coat I've always worn and wrapped it around the two of us and walked her back to the mainland. The only sound was our feet on ice, the snap and groan of the lake. We were two people inside the fur of this bear. She said she could see the cubs that had lived inside and been born from this skin, and I said, "Yes."

▼

O N E

I WAS SEVENTEEN when I returned to Adam's Rib on Tinselman's Ferry. It was the north country, the place where water was broken apart by land, land split open by water so that the maps showed places both bound and, if you knew the way in, boundless. The elders said it was where land and water had joined together in an ancient pact, now broken.

The waterways on which I arrived had a history. They had been crossed by many before me. When they were frozen, moose crossed over, pursued by wolves. There were the French trappers and traders who emptied the land of beaver and fox. Their boats carried precious tons of fur to the trading post at old LeDoux. There were iceboats, cutters and fishers, and the boat that carried the pipe organ for the never-built church. The British passed through this north, as did the Norwegians and Swedes, and there had been logjams, some of them so high and thick they'd stanched the flow of water out from the lake and down the Otter River as it grew too thin for its fish to survive.

It was this same north where, years earlier, a woman named Bush had taken my mother, Hannah Wing, to one of the old men who lived along the Hundred-Year-Old Road. In dim lantern light he shook his head. With sorrow he told her, "I've only heard of these things. It's not in my power to help her." Nor was it in the power of anyone else, for my mother had been taken over by some terrible and violent force. It inhabited her, flesh, bone, and spirit.

The morning air was damp. From the ferry, as fog moved, I saw Fur Island, the place old people still call the navel of the world. It sat above the mirror of water like a land just emerged, created for the first time that morning.

As the ferry passed two islands several miles out from the mainland, I saw a woman adrift in a canoe. I leaned against the railing of the ferry and watched her. She, the floating woman, was very still, but I thought she watched me. The water that held her could have carried her toward tree-shaded places, toward a maze of lakes and islands that were doors to another wilderness, a deeper, wilder north we would one day enter together, that woman named Bush and myself.

She was the sole inhabitant of Fur Island, a solitary place, and she was one of the women who had loved me. Between us there had once been a bond, something like the ancient pact land had made with water, or the agreement humans once made with animals. But like those other bonds, this bond, too, lay broken, and that morning I paid little attention to Bush except to note how the canoe rose and fell with the waves of water and how, behind her, the islands looked like they floated above water.

As the ferry neared land, the ghostly shapes of fishing boats disappeared into the sky across water, and a soft mist rose up from the lake and the warming earth. Through fog, the pale trunks of birch trees stood straight; I was certain the dark eyes on their trunks looked at me. It was silent except for the call of a loon and the voices of other passengers as they called out to each other and prepared to disembark. I felt a last-minute panic, wondering if I should float on past this unfamiliar place that once held my life.

The ferry was early. As soon as it docked, the few passengers stepped off the boat into the rolling fog and soon, though I heard them talking, they were invisible.

I was among the last to leave. When I touched ground, my legs still held the rocking motions of water. It seemed to move beneath my feet. In every curve and fold of myself, I knew that even land was not stable.

It was Agnes Iron I was going to meet. She was my link to my mother, a blood relative who lived on the narrow finger of land called Adam's Rib. I'd found her name in a court record only weeks earlier and written her, saying, "Dear Mrs. Iron, I am Angela Jensen, the daughter of Hannah Wing, and I believe you are my great-grandmother." I wrote the letter several times to get it right, though it still looked like a child's handwriting.

In a shaky hand, Agnes wrote back, "Come at once." Along with her note, she sent fifty-five dollars in old one-dollar bills. They were soft as cloth and looked for all the world as if they'd been rolled, folded, counted, and counted again. When I opened the envelope, the smell of an old woman's cologne floated up from the bills. It was clear they'd been hard come by, those dollars, and that they must have been nearly all she had. But in the first few moments of my life in the north, with the sound of a loon breaking through fog, I had little courage. As I waited, all my worldly goods sitting near me in two plastic bags, I pushed my nervous hands into the pockets of my jeans jacket to wait for Agnes to arrive, for fog to rise or drift so I could see the stark place that held my people.

A cloud of fog lifted and I saw buildings, a sign that said, "Auto Parts, Boat Repairs." And then Agnes walked out of the mist toward me, a woman old and dark. I knew who she was by the way my heart felt in my chest. It recognized its own blood. She had a rocking gait. One of her legs was slightly shorter than the other. And she was stiff. She wore a blue-gray fur coat, worn in places, sloppy, and unbuttoned. It made her look like a hungry animal just stepped out of a cave of winter. It would have seemed a natural thing if leaves and twigs were tangled in it.

I watched her walk toward me, but my own legs refused to move. They were afraid. So was my heart, having entered this strange and foreign territory with the hope of finding something not yet known to me, not yet dreamed or loved. And Agnes, in her old bear coat, was part of it.

I wanted to turn back but she held out a cool, moist hand to me, then changed her mind and took me in both her fur-covered arms and held me, rocking me a little like the boat. She smelled like the dollar bills she'd mailed. I patted her back, wanting the embrace to end. She held me away from her to get a good look at me and I heard songbirds in the trees. I didn't meet her eyes, but I saw her smile. She took a handkerchief out of her sleeve and wiped her eyes, then bent over and lifted both my bags.

"I can carry those," I said. Because of her age, I reached for them. But she did not give them up. "They're light," she lied, already walking away up the road. "And you are probably tired."

I looked sideways now and then at her face, which was starting to sweat, and looked all around me at the foreign world I'd entered by way of a letter, an envelope, and a stamp.

It was a poor place, with the scent of long, wet grasses and the stronger smell of all towns that live by fish and by seasons. Walking uphill, we went past smokers and racks for drying fish. Rusted-out cars, American-made, wide and heavy, sat parked outside houses. It was called Poison Road, the road we walked. The French had named it "Poisson," after fish, because once it had rained tiny fish onto the earth along this road. They'd fallen from the sky. It was said they'd hatched in a cloud. But a few years later the road came to be one of the places where the remaining stray wolves and fox were poisoned to make more room for the European settlers and the pigs and cattle they'd brought with them, tragic animals that never had a chance of surviving the harsh winters of the north. Now it was called Poison and it was the only connecting passage on the hilly peninsula. Weary houses were strung along it in a line, and all of them looked dark brown and dreary to me. In a glance I was sorry I'd come.

The houses themselves were small, some patched with tar paper, pieces of metal, packing crates, or whatever else had been available. They had originally been built by missionaries some years ago and put together for the sole purpose of warmth. Inside them, in the long, deep winters, men went silent for months while lonely women, surrounded by ice and glacial winds, stood at windows staring out at the vast white and frozen world, watching for signs of spring: a single bud, a stem of green, as if spring were a lover come to rescue them from winter's bleak captivity.

As we walked with the warm sun on our shoulders and back, penned huskies and old sled dogs panted and barked in September's warmth behind makeshift fences.

Agnes had the face of a good-hearted woman, but she was sloppy about her appearance. A safety pin held her glasses together. Her gray hair was tied back but it was not neat even though it had been combed wet. In my memory I see, too, how on her dress, between her womanly breasts, she wore a silver brooch in the shape of a bear. It wasn't an expensive piece of jewelry. It was the Walgreen's kind, but it was pretty, with a black stone for an eye.

I wanted to talk to her but I didn't know what to say. I was full of words inside myself; there were even questions in me I hadn't yet thought to form, things not yet come to words. But I remained quiet. And Agnes was quiet, too, that day I returned to Adam's Rib on Tinselman's Ferry. She cried a little, and when her eyes filled up with tears, she'd stop walking, put my bags down, and wipe her eyes with an old, wadded-up hankie while I looked away, pretending not to see.

What a picture we would have made on that warm September day, Agnes and I, if any of those men and women had peered out through the little, streaked panes of glass. They would have seen a dark old woman in her blue-gray tattered fur, wearing practical black shoes and carrying the two plastic bags of my things, and me, barely able to keep up with her, a rootless teenager in a jeans jacket and tight pants, a curtain of dark red hair falling straight down over the right side of my dark face. Like a waterfall, I imagined, and I hoped it covered the scars I believed would heal, maybe even vanish, if only I could remember where they'd come from. Scars had shaped my life. I was marked and I knew the marks had something to do with my mother, who was said to be still in the north. While I never knew how I got the scars, I knew they were the reason I'd been taken from my mother so many years before.

But that day nobody peered out the windows. No one at all turned out to look at us. My return was uneventful, dull and common. And, unknown to me, it was my first step into a silence, into what I feared. I could have turned back. I wanted to. But I felt that I was at the end of something. Not just my fear and anger, not even forgetfulness, but at the end of a way of living in the world. I was at the end of my life in one America, and a secret part of me knew this end was also a beginning, as if something had shifted right then and there, turned over in me. It was a felt thing, that I was traveling toward myself like rain falling into a lake, going home to a place I'd lived, still inside my mother, returning to people I'd never met. I didn't know their ways or what they would think of me. I didn't know what I'd think of them.

And all I carried with me into this beginning was the tough look I'd cultivated over the years, a big brown purse that contained the remaining one-dollar bills Agnes had mailed me, the makeup I used, along with my hair, to hide my face, and a picture of an unknown baby, a picture I'd found in a one-dollar photo machine at Woolworth's. I used the picture to show other people how lovely I'd been as a child, how happy. I used it to feel less lost, because there were no snapshots of me, nothing to say I'd been born, had kin, been loved. All I had was a life on paper stored in file cabinets, a series of foster homes. I'd been lost from my own people, taken from my mother. One of the houses I'd lived in sloped as if it would fall off the very face of earth. Another was upright, staunch, and puritan. There was a house with cement stairs leading to the front door, tangled brambles all around it. There was one I loved, a yellow house in the middle of a dry prairie with two slanted trees that made it seem off-center. I'd sat for hours there listening to the long dry grasses as wind brushed through them. But so far in my life, I had never lighted anywhere long enough to call it home. I was the girl who ran away, the girl who never cried, the girl who was strong enough to tattoo her own arm and hand. An ink-blue cross on one knuckle, the initials of Lonnie Faro on my upper left arm. A cross on my thigh. And no one had ever wanted me for good.

In my life this far, there had been two places, two things that shaped and moved me, two things that were my very own, that I did not ever leave behind or allow to have taken from me. They were like rooms I inhabited, rooms owned, not rented. One, the darkest, was a room of fear, fear of everything—silence, closeness, motionlessness and how it made me think and feel. Fear was what made me run, from homes, from people. Moving made me feel as if

I left that fear behind, shed it like a skin, but always, slowly, a piece at a time, it would find me again; and then I would remember things that had never quite shaped themselves whole. And there was the fire-red room of anger I inhabited permanently, with walls that couldn't shelter or contain my quiet rages. Now I could feel another room being built, but without knowing it, I was entering silence more deeply than I had entered anything before. I was entering my fears head-on. I was about to stare my rage and history in the face. My hardness, my anger would not hold or carry me in that northern place called Adam's Rib.

I'd told myself before arriving, before constructing and inhabiting that new room, that whatever happened, whatever truth I uncovered, I would not run this time, not from these people. I would try to salvage what I could find inside me. As young as I was, I felt I had already worn out all the possibilities in my life. Now this woman, these people, were all I had left. They were blood kin. I had searched with religious fervor to find Agnes Iron, thinking she would help me, would be my salvation, that she would know me and remember all that had fallen away from my own mind, all that had been kept secret by the county workers, that had been contained in their lost records: my story, my life.

WE CAME to a worn path. "Here we are," said Agnes. At the end of the path was another boxlike house, dark brown and square, with nothing to distinguish it from the others except for a torn screen and a large, red-covered chair that sat outside the door. Like the other squat places, it was designed and built by Christian-minded, sky-worshiping people who did not want to look out windows at the threatening miles of frozen lake on one side of them and, on the other, at the dense, dark forest with its wolves.

Old smells were in the air of Agnes' house. The odor of fire smoke had settled in every corner, and there was a kind of stuffiness that dwells inside northern houses even in summer, the smell of human living, the smell of winter containment.

"You'll sleep here," Agnes said. She put my bags down next to a small cot. It was a narrow, dark living room. She hit the cot a few times with the palm of her hand as if to soften it, a useless gesture, I could already see. I could feel every lump in the mattress with my eyes. Already, my back ached.

I stood awkwardly for a moment. I felt large and clumsy. Then I sat down on the cot, as if testing it the way I'd seen people do in furniture stores. With a bend in the middle and terrible springs, it had been shaped by other bodies. Like my life, nothing at all formed by me, not skin, not shape.

THE FIRST WOMEN at Adam's Rib had called themselves the Abandoned Ones. Born of the fur trade, they were an ill-sorted group. Some had Cree ancestors, some were Anishnabe, a few came from the Fat-Eaters farther north. Bush, the woman who floated in the canoe near Fur Island on the day I returned, was a Chickasaw from Oklahoma. Others were from the white world; these, the white people, hadn't cared enough for their own kind to stay on with them.

The first generation of the Abandoned Ones traveled down with French fur trappers who were seeking their fortunes from the land. When the land was worn out, the beaver and wolf gone, mostly dead, the men moved on to what hadn't yet been destroyed, leaving their women and children behind, as if they too were used-up animals.

The women eked out their livings in whatever ways they could, fishing or sewing. They brought in their own wood, and with their homely, work-worn hands they patched their own houses to keep sleet, snow, and winds at bay. They were accustomed to hard work and they were familiar with loneliness; it lived in the set of their jaws, in the way their eyes gazed off into the distance.

When I arrived, there were but a few men, and you could count them on the fingers of two hands. There were a few fishers and boatmakers, and a man named LaRue Marks Time who lived at Old Fish Hook, a nearby settlement on another finger of land that curved like a hook into water and pointed accusingly at Adam's Rib, as if it had sinned. Rue, as we called him, was a taxidermist and a dealer in bones, pinned butterflies, hides, traps, and firearms. A man my heart would not like. He was a mixed-blood from the south, a Dakota, I think, and had only recently returned from Vietnam. He'd come in search of a refuge away from crowded towns or places that minded the business of strangers. What men were capable of, he hated, and his hatred included himself.

Three old men lived quietly along the Hundred-Year-Old Road with seven old women, all of them modest and solitary as bears. The women and the men were the oldest people, older even than Dora-Rouge. But they were rarely seen. They had been alive at the time of the massacre of Indians at Wounded Knee. They remembered, and they wanted nothing to do with the new world. Some said these people were keeping the Ghost Dance alive. Most everyone doubted this, but I came to believe it in a way, because in spite of the tragedies they'd witnessed, they all had the peaceful look of those who still had hope, those who still believed that their people and the buffalo would return. For them, time held no sway. Except for one man, that is. Wiley was his name and he had a very young wife. He rubbed his face with ice each morning to look good for his younger woman.

With the Hundred-Year-Old Road people lived a young man named Tommy Grove. He was a graceful young man with large, beautiful hands. There was no noise about him. He hunted and fished to provide the old people with food. Tommy was a year younger than I was, but in many ways, he was more like one of the elders. He spoke three languages, and because he lived with old people in death's territory, he did not fear it, which gave him a powerful strength.

The houses along the damp Hundred-Year-Old Road were even more decrepit and shabby than the others. These houses had not been built by missionaries. The old people would live in no construction of the Christians, neither physical nor spiritual.

All the rest of the people were women, mighty women, and it was to them that I returned when summer was walking away into the arms of autumn. It was 1972 and I was traveling toward myself, coming home to a place where I'd lived as an infant, returning to people I'd never met. I didn't know my own ways or what they'd think of me, but I was something back in place. I was one of the absences filled that autumn when the trees gave off a golden haze and smell, something back in place at Agnes' little dark, small-windowed house that had been designed by a missionary who did not want to see what surrounded him.

AGNES' HOUSE was cluttered and already crowded. It seemed there wasn't much room for one more. The kitchen was stained by leaks and had not been repainted. The table wobbled. Boots, waiting for winter, were lined up neatly against the wall, as if cold feet had just stepped out of them right into summer.

Agnes was a woman who stoked the fire and wore her coat even on warm summer days. Chilblains, she called it, complaining that her hands were like ice. But the day I came back, she removed her coat. "I'm warm," she said. I watched her as she absentmindedly ran her fingers through the blue-gray fur, touching it in the ancient, animal act of grooming that women's hands remember from long ago. She picked a piece of tree bark from it, a few wet grasses, then hung the worn-out coat on a hook beside other coats near the door, and suddenly she was as small as everything else in the brown house, a woman shrunk under the weight of a life the way a stone is made smaller by a river. Except that stones grow smooth, and you couldn't say that of Agnes.

Dora-Rouge, the mother of Agnes, lived in a small room off the side of the kitchen with its peeling linoleum, old and worn yellow. She was my great-great-grandmother by blood. She had a thin, old voice. She was the beloved old woman, the old and luminous elder of the house. All along, she had been the one who'd said I would return, and no one had believed her, but when she saw me on that first day, she called me by my mother's name. "Hannah?" she said. She spoke it as a question. It was only later, when I saw my mother, that I understood the mistake. I was the image of her, the woman I'd never seen, the woman who had scarred me. I had the same walnut skin and red hair as Hannah.

Dora-Rouge looked confused. It was this way with her. Some days her memory lived in a distant past, a time more alive and clear than the worn-out, fading present.

Agnes spoke loudly, "No, Mother. It's Angel, Hannah's girl."

Dora-Rouge fixed Agnes with her gaze. "I'm not deaf, you know." It wasn't that Dora-Rouge was hard-of-hearing. Her ears were fine. It was just that she had already begun to step over the boundaries of this world into the next. It was an intelligent world, she said, the next one. It was full of the makings of life, and it was where she conversed with her gone husband, Luther. From time to time it was difficult to bring her back the long distance from that world to ours. There was no map of the territory between the worlds, but I could tell something wonderful lived there, in that span we call "between." At times I could see it in her eyes. But Agnes was afraid. She feared her mother would get caught in a snare along the way and never return. That's why she yelled. She didn't want to lose her mother. She wanted to call her back to the world at Adam's Rib.

Dora-Rouge was the oldest person I'd ever seen, a white-haired creation thin as a key, who sat as if she had become bone already, with sunken cheeks and a confusion of snowy hair. Her eyes were joyous, dark and radiantly clear. When she turned her face toward me, I felt her light. When she laughed, both the house and I opened up a little. It frightened me to feel that way, as if now that I found her I'd have something to lose. She reached out for me. "Angel, is it? Come over here."

I hesitated, then took her thin, bony hand.

Dora-Rouge had no teeth and her toothless grin lent her an infant sweetness, in spite of the fact that her skin was old copper, her hands knotted with veins and human tributaries, intricacies a young woman like myself could not imagine. A red blanket stretched across her lap and her bony knees were sharp enough to cut their way through the wool.

And that first day as I sat on the edge of the springy bed, I studied her face, searched for traces of my own features, feeling like a small child. Dora-Rouge had an owl beak of a nose like mine. The same eyebrows, white and longer, though hers turned up a little at the edges, winglike. Her mouth might once have been full like mine, except that hers had eaten other foods, spoken another language, and kissed people who'd lived and died long before I was born.

"I always called you the girl who would return." Her eyes rested on me. "And here you are."

I tried to smile at her. I felt like a small child.

Antlers lay on a table in Dora-Rouge's room, and a grass rope, burned at one end. While the rest of the house was dusty and cluttered, her room was in order. She could not tolerate disorder.

"Open the window," she said to Agnes. "It's dark."

"It's open, Mother," Agnes said. "They are all open."

"Then you'd better close the door. The darkness must be getting in."

"I'm going to get her up," Agnes said. She lifted the red blanket from Dora-Rouge's lap.

"We're going to take her outside. She likes the morning sun. You take hold of her legs. I'll get the rest."

"I hate it, Agnes, when you talk about me as if I'm not here," Dora-Rouge said in a dry voice. She wore small, beaded moccasins, and her knees were drawn up and stiff. There was a yeasty smell to her skin, an odor of fermenting. She was tiny. She'd looked larger than she was, but her body seemed too light to contain a living soul. I think it was because her radiance was bigger than her body. Like the light of fox fire, it was the fire of life burning itself beautifully away. She was not a bit embarrassed at being carried. She smiled into my eyes as we picked her up. She said, with triumph, "I am gloriously old. I am ripening."

Agnes said nothing, as was her long-standing habit with her mother. Over the years, the two women had learned to tune out what they didn't want to hear from each other. In that way, they kept peace in the household, though not in their hearts.

Dora-Rouge leaned toward me. "Don't you know I remember when people lived below ground and were buried above?"

"Mother. You're not that old."

We carried her through the kitchen where the bear coat hung on its hook. She said, "That bear clutches at my heart every time I see it. I still don't know how you can wear it." This, too, had been said many times, I could tell.

With a movement of her hip, Agnes pushed the screen door open and backed out, her face red with exertion. Even her dress seemed strained. She was getting too old to lift and carry her mother, I could see that. And in that, too, I saw my opportunity. I was a strapping large girl. This is what I can do here, I thought, if I stay. If I stay, I can care for the old woman to earn my keep. I was sturdy. I could carry the delicate old woman by myself. In that moment I began to figure out my place in the house of old women with its worn-out linoleum and leaking roof. I wasn't sure they could afford me, but I plotted out the chores I could do even though up to that time I'd avoided work as much as possible. I thought I might even repair the torn screen. Me, the girl who would return. But I didn't know if I could hold myself there, tie myself to that place of dogs and fish and old people.

Outside, the sunlight rested on Dora-Rouge's hair like flame on a candle. She settled herself down in the chair and raised her face to the sky. "It is so good to sit in front of the fire this way." The insects were noisy around us. With her bony hand she took hold of my wrist and leaned toward me. "Don't you know I remember when we had to break the bones of the dead to let the souls take their leave."

"She's not that old," Agnes said. "You're not that old," she said to her mom, louder than she spoke to me.

Agnes straightened back Dora-Rouge's hair. "She's a character all right. And she's the source of both of us. We came from the Fat-Eaters of the north. Before cholesterol." She said this with a hearty laugh I wouldn't have suspected of her until that moment as she adjusted the cover about her mother's lap. When we went back inside, I felt a little more of the stuffy air in the house open up. It was cool inside. I swear that something almost happy walked toward me. In spite of myself, I smiled. It wasn't a wide smile; my happiness opened only a bit at a time, the way my story did.

THE BATHROOM SINK was stained red with the iron-rich water that made everything on Adam's Rib look and smell like blood. As I ran water, I looked at my face in the mirror. Half of it, from below the eye to the jawline, looked something like the cratered moon. I hated that half. The other side was perfect and I could have been beautiful in the light of earth and sun. I'd tried desperately all my life to keep the scars in shadows. Even then, before the mirror, I tried not to see them, and I wondered what Agnes saw, or Dora-Rouge, when they looked at my angular cheekbones and large eyes, the red hair so unusual above dark skin, and when they saw the scars. Maybe they felt the same surprise and fear I did when I looked at my face. Of what, I didn't know. My scars had no memory, were from unknown origin. There were others, as well, on my body.

The scars, I knew, were from my mother. They were all I had of her. For me, she was like air. I breathed her. I had to breathe whether I wanted to or not, and like air, she was invisible, although sometimes I thought I recalled her heartbeat from when I was inside her body. At those times, a distant memory tugged at me in a yearning way, and I felt something deeper than sorrow.

I looked like her, they said, that girl who'd washed up from stormy waters in 1949, washed in from a storm so fierce it blew fish onto the land. At that time she was ten years old and icy cold, the only thing blown in that had a spark of life remaining inside of it.

IT WAS STILL LIGHT when John Husk came in the back door that evening and placed two large fish on the counter and smiled broadly. I liked him from the first. Husk removed his hat. He had a fine face, skinny legs, no hips to speak of. The years of weather had eroded and etched stories on his face, all except for his forehead, which remained baby-smooth and pale from the constant wearing of a cap. He wasn't much over five feet five, and he smelled of soap.

Dora-Rouge was seated at the table, propped up by several pillows. "It's sweltering in here," she said, wiping her forehead. She complained about the heat from the woodstove. But I could see that she was concerned for Agnes.

Agnes was cold and tired. She not only tended to Dora-Rouge, whose skin had become thin as the parchment of birch trees and bruised easily, but there was also this man, John Husk, the man she cooked for. He was older than Agnes. He was closer to seventy, I believe, though I never knew for sure, and he was devoted to Agnes. The neighbors called him "her old man," but never to her face, because after many years, they were still curious about the relationship between the two. John Husk and Agnes hadn't married and they were seldom seen together in public, two things that cast doubt on their neighbors' speculations. Physically, Husk was young for his age and he was still sharp enough to fish and hunt, to play cards on cold nights and to tell people that "hell is cold, not hot." He knew this firsthand from the many long, fierce winters he'd endured, including two he'd survived in the near-arctic north when he'd once been forced to give up his values and trap for money. All these years later, he still felt guilt for having done this. There had once been a covenant between animals and men, he told me. They would care for one another. It was an agreement much like the one between land and water. This pact, too, had been broken, forced by need and hunger.

Husk fished and delivered groceries to people who lived out on islands, and he loved science. He kept stacks of magazines and books that divulged the secret worlds of atoms and galaxies, of particles and quarks. He'd read about the way bees communicate by dancing. His main desire in life was to prove that the world was alive and that animals felt pain, as if he could make up for being part of the broken contract with animals.

Agnes stirred the kettle with a wooden spoon. Without looking at Husk, she said, "What are you so happy about?"

He didn't answer, but there was a spark between them, I could tell. I was sensitive to sparks. But Husk said only, "Say, where's the iron? I need to press my shirt."

Agnes didn't remember where she'd last seen it. "They have permanent-press clothes now," was all she said. "Maybe you should get some."

Agnes, at the stove, wore thick hose and the heavy black shoes of an old woman. The kitchen smelled of stew. Dora-Rouge, propped up, was birdlike sitting there, but still she reigned over the table like a matriarch. Husk touched her hand. "How are you tonight, Miss Iron?" he asked.

"I want to go home to die," she said.

Agnes waved flies away as she cooked.

Husk nodded at Dora-Rouge as if he understood. She'd said it often enough. It was her hope, her one desire, to go back to the Fat-Eaters.

Husk rubbed his hand over his shaved chin, smiling broadly. His eyes followed Agnes as she placed dishes on the table. He was politely interested in me, kind to Dora-Rouge, but it was Agnes he watched with lively eyes, and in spite of his own careful grooming, he never seemed to notice her messiness, the safety pin she wore in her glasses, the slip that hung out from beneath her dress. He was that taken with her. It was clear that he adored her. Enough so that every day he showered at the docks before he came home, washed away the smell of fish that accompanied the other men up Poison Road. Husk's shoes were always clean and dry, without a sign that he had spent any part of the day walking in the skins, scales, blood, and innards of fish.

He was what they might have once called dashing, handsome, with a pencil-thin mustache, a full head of brushed-back gray hair, an ironed jeans jacket. He took pride in his appearance and was immaculate in his grooming. He was one for whom cleanliness was next to godliness. He did this for Agnes, who never noticed.

Husk and I made small talk, the where-do-you-live kind. I told him, Tulsa, mostly, and when I spoke, the trees and red dirt of Oklahoma entered the little kitchen at Adam's Rib. For a moment, I smelled the richness of nut trees and the thick-aired Oklahoma evenings. I felt a pang of loneliness for that land.

"Have you seen the salt?" Agnes asked. Then to me, she said, "See how he squints?" Meaning Husk. "It's because he had snow blindness once. In 1929." I could hear in her voice that she cared for him.

Husk was a light eater. He ate only a little bread and stew and a piece of the fried fish. Once, during dinner, while I savored the hot bread, Agnes looked at Husk, took off her glasses and cleaned them on her sleeve, then looked at him more closely. It wasn't until later, when I went to bed and tried, without success, to sleep, that I realized I had taken Husk's cot. It smelled of his soap.

That night, I lay down on the place his body had formed, and it came to me that maybe this was the first night they'd shared a bed in the old thin-walled house, and then from behind the wall I heard her tell him, "So, old man, you've got your way at last." He laughed out loud and so did she. Like they were kids. Already my presence there was doing some good, I thought.

Sleepless as always, I went outside and sat in Dora-Rouge's chair, listening to the insects and the wail of a loon.

The next morning, Dora-Rouge said, "You look much better, Agnes. It agrees with you to sleep with Mr. Husk."

BEGINNINGS WERE IMPORTANT to my people, as I would one day call them. It was why Agnes, on a warm, damp night a few days after my return, said, "Nobody knows where it began, your story." Behind her, white-winged moths and June bugs clung to the screens. "I've thought of it for years, where the beginning was." She turned toward the window, as if answers lived in the wings of moths and the snapping sound of bugs. "What happened to you started long ago. It began around the time of the killing of the wolves. When people were starving." In spite of the warmth, she pulled the coat tight around her and shivered. "I think and I think and still I don't know."

Dora-Rouge pointed her crooked finger at the cloud-colored coat. "It might have been that bear's revenge on humans."

"No. It was long before then."

She searched for words. As in Genesis, the first word shaped what would follow. It was of utmost importance. It determined the kind of world that would be created.

"There wasn't a single beaver that year. They'd killed them all. And they'd just logged the last of the pine forests."

I tried to make sense of what she said, but it was hard at first to put it all together. Harold, her son—my grandfather—was married to the woman named Bush, the woman of the island, the one I'd seen drifting in the canoe. But Harold left Bush, a slip of a girl, to go off with a woman named Loretta Wing, my blood grandmother, the mother of Hannah. Harold later vanished off the face of earth, Agnes said.

It was 1938. Loretta was older than Harold. You could see it. It showed on her face. She had dark circles and lines. Something, I think now, that might have been pain or secret sorrow.

She came here so suddenly, we thought she grew out of the land. Some people even say they saw her rise up all cold and blue from the water. But she arrived on a boat with a man and the very next morn-

ing he snuck off without her, and her hair was the only spot of color there was on that dark day when I first saw her. The birds were loud that day. They were migrating, so thick they looked like salt poured from a shaker all across the water and land and sky. But the country was dry. We'd had a drought and there was a windstorm; leaves blew about and the waves were high, so we knew, hoped, a great storm was coming at us from out on the lake. We needed rain in the worst of ways. We had not even a morning of it. Forests were what called down the water, the rain, but by then the forests were gone, and the clouds went away from us.

Harold and Bush were young. He brought her home from Oklahoma with him. He met her when he went to work there in an oil field. No one here accepted her. She was quiet and us women here are talkers. Now, I think we talk because what lives inside silence scares us. Maybe silence is where trees start to freeze and shatter, or where darkness and ice begin, and Bush seemed all of a piece with silence. She was timid and small and not very pretty, either, until you got to know her. Then she'd look beautiful.

The young men had a habit of getting together for beer at night. They would say to Harold, "You've had better women than that." I heard them say it. Harold, my son, was a weak man. I never knew why. He had a good father. But Harold listened to his friends. In his eyes, Bush began to fade and dim.

I COULD SEE the vision of my grandmother, Loretta, the catlike quality, the way men stared at her. Even women could not help themselves but to watch her. I could see this in Agnes' words. Loretta had long brown fingers and red lips, a too-tight blue dress.

Loretta smelled of something sweet, an almond odor that I couldn't place until years later. Her skin, even her dress, was thick with it. When I finally placed the odor, when I knew it was cyanide, I knew who she was, what people she came from. She was from the Elk Islanders, the people who became so hungry they ate the poisoned carcasses of deer that the settlers left out for the wolves. The starving people ate that bait.

Her people lived on Elk Island. About thirty miles to the east of here. Only a few remained.

Some said she was haunted. They said something terrible had come along with her. You could almost see it. But it was that very strangeness that attracted Harold and the other men. It made her more appealing to them, or maybe it was her sleepy way and the scar beneath her eye.

Overnight, my boy changed. He started to oil his hair with Wild Root and comb it back. Some men rubbed balm on their hands and faces. They wore their best shirts whenever they went out. But Harold was the only fool who followed her away. Like a hungry dog chasing a bone.

Some people said that what came with her was a bad spirit. Some said an enemy had thrown tobacco into the lake at midnight and laid a curse on her. But I've seen bad medicine. This was something else. It wasn't like any shadow under rocks or anything hiding from the face of light. The curse on that poor girl's life came from watching the desperate people of her tribe die. I saw the same thing once in a dog, retching and jerking from that same poison. How she'd lived, I didn't know. But after that, when she was still a girl, she'd been taken and used by men who fed her and beat her and forced her. That was how one day she became the one who hurt others. It was passed down. I could almost hear their voices when she talked, babbling behind hers, men's voices speaking English. Something scary lived behind her voice. I still feel bad about her. We judged her, you know. We wanted to blame someone like her. We wanted to hate her. But Loretta wasn't the original sin. It was just that something inside her had up and walked away and left the rest behind. There was no love left in her. There was no belief. Not a bit of conscience. There wasn't anything left in her.

I fought with Harold to keep him from going off with her. But he couldn't see it. None of them could. I guess he couldn't help it. "What about your wife?" I said to him, but Loretta gave me such a look, a chill came over me. It was a taste of ice I've never lost and just before they left I saw her through the window, near my house lighting a fire to some bunched-up old papers. It was dry outside, everything was kindling. I ran out screaming, first at her, then at Harold about what he was running away with. "You're my son!" I yelled after him. "Are you crazy?" I screamed at him about the fire, but the wind blew my voice away from his ears and the fire reached up the wall all at the same time, so I had no choice but to let them go while I tried to douse the flames.

The last I ever saw of them they were running to catch the ferry. Harold carried an armload of his things. I saw the sweat on the back of his shirt, even with all that wind. She ran on ahead of him, urging him on. I can still hear her voice saying, "Hurry. Hurry."

That was all I saw of them until I saw Harold's face and Loretta's red hair on your mother that day she came out of the water. She smelled of the same bitter almonds. It was a fainter odor, but it was still there all the same. We guessed her to be about ten years old. She had empty eyes I'll never forget.

No matter how we scrubbed, the smell never came off that poor girl. It was deeper than skin. It was blood-deep. It was history-deep, Old Man said.

By the time the shivering girl of your mother came out of the storm, Bush was a grown woman, strong but alone. Maybe she thought Hannah was a little bit of Harold come back to her. She loved Hannah, poison and all.

AGNES WENT to the sink. She was barefoot and her feet made a soft sound on the floor. I watched her back, memorizing it as if it were my own.

"I don't know where the beginning was, your story, ours. Maybe it came down in the milk of the mothers. Old Man said it was in the train tracks that went through the land and came out of the iron mines. I've thought of this for years. It might have started when the crying children were taken away from their mothers or when the logging camps started and cities were built from our woods, or when they cut the rest of the trees to raise cattle."

She looked out the window. I followed her gaze, half expecting to see the herds, but instead there were only the white-winged moths pressed against the screen, listening.

Dora-Rouge laughed out loud.

"What?" Agnes looked at her mother, brought back to the present.

"Luther says you'd have to creosote cattle to keep them in this weather. That's what Luther just said." Luther, my dead great-grandfather.

"What's creosote?" I asked.

Agnes was offended. "I don't believe Papa would say something like that."

Dora-Rouge, I thought, was something like the white-winged moths and june bugs that grasped the screen, held to the doorway of the next world with open wings and tiny fingers. She spoke this world to us. In it, in Luther's world, they took life less seriously than those of us in this world. Like they were Buddhists, Husk once told me, as if they realized life was pain and suffering and so they gave up all their resistance and started to enjoy themselves instead.

Agnes was disturbed by her parents' insensitivity and she finished clearing the table with quick, noisy movements. She hadn't appreciated her father's humor when he was alive either. Dora-Rouge confided this later. In fact, Agnes thought her mother spoke her own opinions and pretended they were Luther's. That way, she could say what she wanted without recrimination.

"What's creosote?" I said again.

T W O

DORA-ROUGE'S BONES were all sharp angles and she slept deeply and for long hours. I looked after her. I made it my work. At times I took her food while she was still in bed or as she sat outside in the morning sunlight. I carried her from table to bed, presented her to the sun. I felt protective of her fragile bones and thin skin. She seemed vulnerable. She became, in a way, my ward. But in spite of all this seeming frailty, the truth was that Dora-Rouge had fought gravity and won. It no longer held her as it held the rest of us. That was why she weighed so little and why she heard what no human heard and saw what none of us could see.

"Why is it you hardly ever sleep?" she asked me one day.

"I don't know." I couldn't tell her I was afraid to be held by night.

"Hand me the box under the bed."

I bent and pulled up the cover and saw the box.

"That's the one. Open it."

I did. It was full of small paper bags. In them were roots and dried leaves.

"How long has that been going on? Insomnia."

"As long as I can remember." I shrugged. I placed the box beside her. She reached inside and took out three bags. "Here, give this to Agnes. She'll cook them. It'll make you sleep."

The concoction was a mixture of roots, bark, and flowers. I was curious about the plants. There were unguents—ointments and balms—at their house, but it was the plants I wanted to know about.

"When you were a baby," Agnes told me, "all you wanted to do was look at plants. You watched the trees move when the wind blew. You listened to them and they leaned forward to tell you things."

I liked hearing this. It was the first time anyone had told me something about myself when I was a child.

One day while Dora-Rouge sat outside in the sun, and Agnes was gone to the lake, I opened one of the boxes in Dora-Rouge's room to see what it contained. It was a birch-bark box that had designs bitten into it by an ancestor's teeth. In it were some little bags, a few dried plants, and a piece of amber sitting in a bird's nest. In the amber was a frog, perfectly formed, stopped in time, its life caught in the tears of a tree. I quickly put the box back the way I'd found it. I was not going to steal out of this house. That's what they called it when I was forced to leave the yellow house for taking things. The social worker said, "Isn't this the same as running away? Isn't this another escape?"

No, I would try not to steal away from this house, dark and dreary as it was.

AT NIGHT, when I rested, I would smell the fresh air, feel cool breezes on my skin, and listen to the loons and the sound of water. All these things comforted me. And with Dora-Rouge's bitter sleeping potion, I slept. Mornings, I lay awake, thinking of the words of the women, Agnes and Dora-Rouge, and wondered what I was doing there in a life so different from what I'd known. At times I felt the old fear return, the need to shed skin, to leave everything behind and run, to keep these women out of my skin. But already they were my skin, so I willed myself to remain. I tried to figure out how I could earn some money. I didn't want to live off the old people. I'd asked at Tinselman's store for work and he said there was none. I asked at the Auto Shop, Boat Repair. They, too, needed no help. There were few options.

EACH EVENING AFTER SUPPER, Agnes walked to the place where the Perdition River flowed into Lake Grand. She went alone, to think, she said, and to be silent. Always she returned, refreshed and clear-eyed, as if the place where two waters met was a juncture where fatigue yielded to comfort, where a woman renewed herself.

One night, from the porch, I watched her coming back through the first shade of night. She didn't see me as she came up the road. She was half a world away in the first evening dimness. She wore the fur coat wide open and she walked with something like a dance step, even in her heavy black shoes, turning a little this way and a little that. I still remember how strong and wide her thighs appeared that night, her awkward movement. She was singing, too. On her upturned face, she wore a look—half-rapture, half-pain. She was singing. I felt the song and I wanted to stay there and listen, but it was a private act, I knew. I didn't want to intrude upon Agnes' inner world, so I slipped indoors quietly, before she saw me, put water in the kettle and waited for it to heat. But all the time I smiled at her passion, her rocking movement, her bent knees.

She was still singing when she came in.

"Oh, hi," I said. Sounding stupid. And guilty. I faced the stove, waiting for the water to heat.

But Dora-Rouge, from the next room, called out, "Say, where did you hear that song?"

"I heard it inside this coat."

"I've heard it before," said Dora-Rouge. "I remember it. It's the one that calls lost things out of hiding and brings them back. But it's from before your time."

"It's the coat, Mother. I've told you that." Still humming, Agnes put a tea bag in one of the cracked cups.

"It must have been the song that called Angel back to us."

I believed Agnes about the coat. I came to think of it as something alive. When no one looked I would touch the fur and put my ear against it and listen. It was old, with no shining left to it, and silent. At least with me, when I listened.

There were mornings I sat with Dora-Rouge in her little room with the antlers and turtle-shell rattles and the box I'd snooped in. We would breathe together the way wolves do with their kith and kin, the way they nurture relations by breathing. This breath was alive. It joined us as we were joined in so many other ways. One morning as I did this, Dora-Rouge looked directly into my eyes and said, "Agnes killed that bear, you know." She sat back against the pillow with a smile. Her thin hand touched her chest, fumbling at the button of her gown. "The one she wears, it was a glacier bear."

Then I brushed her hair while she talked. The brush was old, made of ancient tortoiseshell and boar bristles. I liked the feel of her hair.

The bear was the color of ice. It was the last of its kind. It still makes me sad. It wandered down to California. No one knew why it was so far from home. But it hid out and it lived. It was the mother, they said, of twin cubs.

There were tribes of bears in those days. They were around for thousands of years, clear back to when we lived by the laws of nature. A bear could only be killed at a certain time of the year and that was for meat and medicine and fur. Even then it was a rare thing when an Indian killed a bear, because bears resemble men.

There was a Frenchman. Beauregard. He went out west to find the last of the beaver. They were mostly gone here. But it was too late. Even in California they were gone. When he saw the bear he trapped it and took it captive. At first he used it to fight dogs. The men made bets on who would win. They kept it awake all year. That's against bear nature. Its poor mind was no longer sane. And its diet was bad, so it went weak, its teeth rotted out, and some of its fur fell out in patches. Then they tried to make money by letting men wrestle the poor creature. Finally, they charged people money just to come and see it. The last one. The last glacier bear. The last. They always loved the last of anything, those men, even the last people. I guess they felt safe then, when it was all gone.

Agnes was only twelve when they brought the blue bear here. She was plump and beautiful, my girl. She was round as fruit on a tree, and from the first minute she saw that bear, she loved it. It was a special thing, her and that bear. Every day she went to look at it. For a penny, they'd let her see it. A minute a penny. Some days she took thirty pennies.

When Beauregard saw how good she was with it, he hired her to feed it. He was afraid of it, you know. The other men, too. Afraid of that poor broken thing. When they went in the small cage, they kicked it away and pushed at it with their rifles. But Agnes was not afraid. She was a gentle girl. The bear liked this. It knew her, in a way. Through her eyes, I think. She stole good food for it, too, and its fur grew back.

In the afternoons, young boys would go around and poke sticks through the cage and Agnes would fight with the boys and come home crying.

Looking back on it, the boys, I think they were jealous of what's wild and strong. If the bear fought back, it was hated; if it didn't, they hated it for being weak. The bear was ruined in its heart. Even with Agnes' love. It sat with its back to the boys and let them poke it and call it names. Finally, they came to it with guns full of corn and they shot that poor bear to see if it had any fight left in its thick skin. Antagonizing it that way. Agnes cried and kicked at them. She chased after them. They called her crazy. "I'll shoot you," she said. "That's how crazy I am." She took a gun one day to keep them away. It was really just for show, the gun, but I really had to get after her for taking it. I hid it after that.

One chilly day alone, she went to the bear. She lifted her shirt and showed the bear her round, full breasts. Oh, it understood already. It knew she was a woman. It knew she had compassion.

Before she left the house that day I saw her crying. I had a bad feeling. I followed her. I watched how she entered the cage. She didn't even fear for her own life. She didn't have the gun. She only had a knife, so all the poor girl could do was cut the bear's neck and let it bleed. She did it fast, before I saw what was happening, before I could stop her.

The warm blood poured into the ground. It was a chilly day. You could see the steam rise from the wounds. Its eyes were grateful. I saw that. She stroked the big animal. I saw it with my own eyes. That bear put a paw on Agnes and stroked her in return. It touched her. It comforted her. I have never seen such a thing as that. I cried, too.

When all the life had flowed out of it, Agnes took the knife and slid it under the skin. I went to her. "What are you doing?" I said, but she didn't answer me. She knew I'd been there all along, and that I was crying. It was hard work to skin and quarter the bear. She removed the liver, the heart. She knew that bear inch by inch, where every muscle joined bone. "Don't just stand there," she told me. "Help me out." She was bossy like that, even when she was sad. "Go get the wagon," she said. "Hurry. Before they get back." The men, she meant.

I followed her orders. I rushed home. As I left I heard her singing a bear song no one had sung since I was a girl. An old, old song.

I did as she said. I went and got another knife and the bouncing wagon and when I went back, I helped pull the fur away from the flesh. I still remember the bones of the foot in a pool of blood.

Four wagonloads we brought back, bumping all the way.

That night, after dark, the Frenchman and his friend came knocking at our door. They knocked loud. They wanted the meat. Those men pushed their way into the house. "Get out!" I yelled at them. But I was scared of them. I fell back against the table. We were just women there. We had no men to protect us. They wanted the fur, too. It was a rare color for a bear. It would catch them a good price. Agnes had already pinned it. "Give me that," Beauregard said. He took it from her.

Agnes stood up to him. I couldn't believe my own eyes and ears. There were times I thought she was so stubborn, that girl, but this time I was proud of her. She stood up to him. She said, "It's all right. This fur belongs to me, but you go ahead and take it. I'll wait for you to die. You won't last long, but me, I have time."

Not even a year later, he died. While his woman grieved, Agnes stole into his house through a window and she threw the coat out onto the snow. I picked it up. She'd conned me into it, her crime, you see. I was under the window waiting. Even though I was afraid of what might happen if we got caught.

Agnes wore the nightmare. That's what I called the coat. First thing every morning Agnes brushed the fur, rocking it in the chair, her dark *hair around her plump shoulders. Like it was a baby. And talking and singing things—to this day I don't know where she got it all.*

By then, the land was settled. No bears were there to disturb the people. But at night in the woods, settlers heard branches snap. They heard the breathing in the forest. The bear lived there still, and it lived inside their own skin and bones. Everything they feared moved right inside them.

Agnes wanted to know, always, why some men will do what they do. She believed wearing its skin would show her these things.

Sometimes it happens that, at twilight, I see those eyes and that large paw brushing Agnes' back and I hear her sing and I get a feeling, just a feeling, Agnes is becoming something. Maybe the bear. Maybe she knows her way back to something.

DORA-ROUGE, I think now, was a root and we were like a tree family, aspens or birch, connected to one another underground, the older trees feeding the young, sending off shoots, growing. I watched and listened. It was an old world in which I began to bloom. Their stories called me home, but this home was not at all what I'd expected. I don't know exactly what it was I thought I was entering, but never would I have imagined a bear of a woman in an old, heavy coat, with bear-scratched trees outside her house, a woman who bent her creaking knees in a dance when she thought no one was looking, and boiled a kettle of the same stew nearly every night for a week, except Fridays, when she fixed macaroni and cheese in case a Catholic might stop by. Nor could I have dreamed Dora-Rouge with her handhold on the spirit world, saying grace each night by saying, "Give us our daily stew." Or the mixed-blood Cree named Frenchie who lived next door and had mincing steps when she entered the house at dinnertime, uninvited but always welcome, and sat down to dinner with us.

Each Thursday, several of the town's men played cards. The Thursday before they sent me to Bush and Fur Island, the men came to Agnes' house. Everyone knew Frenchie would show up. As she herself put it, she "had a thing" for Justin LeBlanc, an older fisherman and a regular at cards.

On that Thursday evening, Agnes looked at the clock and said,

"Frenchie's late." But as Agnes pounded some tough meat into tenderness, the door opened and Frenchie sailed into the stuffy, hot kitchen, wearing a pink chiffon scarf and carrying a platter of Russian tea cookies. "What's all the racket?" she said. "You building something?"

"Supper," was all Agnes said.

Frenchie was dressed for dinner, wearing a red dress and too much color on her cheeks. She smelled of face powder and wore a strand of pearls around her withered neck. Without bothering to untie her tennis shoes, she pushed them off her feet, then walked barefoot to the stove and peered inside the kettle. "Stew," she said, as if we didn't know.

Agnes' efforts to soften the meat had been in vain—the gristly meat was a failure and later, as Dora-Rouge sipped broth and marrow, she watched us trying to chew and said, "You make me grateful I don't have any teeth."

And just before the dishes were stacked and washed, Justin pulled up. Seeing his car, Frenchie ran to the bathroom to check her hair and spray lilac cologne on her neck.

The men all smoked pipes that year and before long the pipe smoke filled the house in a comforting sort of way. I was still uneasy there but I liked the men's voices as they talked and drank glasses of cola and ate peanuts. And I liked the smoke better than the perfume. I'd never heard men talk that way before, like friends. All the places I'd been, men didn't have friends.

For the first time—I met LaRue. LaRue Marks Time was his name, although some people called him "Done Time" behind his back. At other times, people shunned him, but he was a good hand at cards. He wore a gray shirt and his hair long, in a thin ponytail down his back. He was handsome, his hair beginning to gray at the temples, but for some reason I was uncomfortable in his presence. He, on the other hand, was eager to befriend me. "How about I take you fishing tomorrow," he volunteered.

"Okay. Sure," I sounded nervous. He didn't seem quite sincere. I didn't know then that he wanted to befriend me so he could get close to Bush. I didn't yet know I would soon live with Bush, the woman of Fur Island.

"Here, I have something for you." He reached into his pocket and brought out an arrowhead, warm with his body heat.

I studied his face. I looked at the arrowhead, then slipped it into my pocket.

"When are you going to the island?" he asked.

"What island?" This was the first I heard.

"You know, to Bush's." He straightened his collar, hitched up his jeans.

I was hurt, thinking that Agnes and Dora-Rouge were sending me away.

"I'll tell you about it later," Agnes said, seeing my discomfort.

Later that night the women retreated into the living room, but we could hear the sound of pennies sliding across the table, the shuffling of cards, and the warm sound of men's voices. Now and then Frenchie would walk through the door and offer cookies to the men, who never accepted. I could see her through the doorway. She smiled too much at Justin. He would pretend to be cranky and disturbed by her. "Are you telling them my hand?" he accused her.

"You know me better than that," she said with a gleam in her eye.

I listened, but still I thought of what LaRue had said, that I would leave the Rib. For the first time in my life I didn't want to go.

The men spoke in different ways from the women. Their conversations went something like this: "Have you ever caught bluefish? Those are something else. They go out, oh, about a hundred yards and you have to bring them back. They've got a lot of teeth. They look like tuna or something."

"Yeah, they give you a good battle."

Fish stories. And they talked loud.

"I fished until four in the morning," one would say. "And I couldn't catch a thing."

Now, I know this probably meant he'd caught so many he wanted to keep the place a secret. That's how they talked, in a circular fashion.

"Next time let's take some bacon. I heard they really strike at that."

"Yeah. Or salmon eggs. They like them, too."

"Where is Devil's Lake, anyway?"

"My uncle went there. He did real good."

"Red hots. I hear they bite at those, too."

"Is that the uncle that got struck by lightning three times?"

In the living room, which doubled as my bedroom, the teapot sat on the old gold-painted sewing machine and the women talked with one another. They talked about the deepest things, the most meaningful of subjects, about love and tragedy. Frenchie said she'd once loved a younger man. Agnes said she still thought of her son Harold and what had come of him. Dora-Rouge, propped up next to me on the cot, said, "I want to go home to die. It's my dream. It is so beautiful there. When I was young, the northern lights would dance, really dance across the sky. They were so close to us. When we saw them we'd say, 'Here comes sky on its many trails.'

"When I met Luther, he was just a boy. He came to sit with us. That's how it was done in those days. He'd just sit. A girl would ignore the boy who was coming to court her. She had to hide her smile. So would her family. And Luther'd come and sit. Then one day, I looked at him and smiled. After that, he started bringing meat to the house."

I cut a piece of cheese and handed it to her. She kept it in her mouth until it was soft enough to swallow. "Is that Wisconsin cheese?" she said. And that's how the talk went with the women. That is, until Frenchie pushed the plate of cookies toward me and said, "What happened to your face, anyway, dear?" She said it straight out. The forbidden question. No one had asked it in a long time. I had hit people for asking that question when I was younger. I had left schools for people's curiosity. I'd moved out of houses, run away as if I were running from ugliness or pain. It was what no one was allowed to say. Even I had stopped asking about it. At first I'd tried to find out what had caused the scars, but eventually I gave up. Now I was stopped dead cold, but it seemed I was the only one who heard Frenchie. Not even a moment of silence elapsed—the women kept chatting—but my heart raced with fear. I felt the color drain from my face. I sat stunned.

"Well?" Frenchie looked at me briefly, ignorant of her transgression, then said, "Maybe I should take some cookies to Justin." She rose from the chair to peer anxiously into the next room. Justin's back was toward her.

To hide my feelings, I tried to cut another piece of cheese for Dora-Rouge, but my hands shook and it slipped and I cut my finger, a deep bite off the tip.

Agnes stood up. "Come, let's fix that up." She was anxious. I think she noticed how my heart had fallen.

I pulled away from her. "It's okay," I said. I wrapped a napkin around it. "Really. It's fine." My eyes were beginning to tear.

"No, that's a worthless, rusty knife. Let's clean that wound."

I said, "No," but Agnes guided me into the washroom. Finally I let her. I nearly collapsed against her, as if the cut had been deeper, but it was the words that had hurt me, not the knife.

Agnes knew this.

She opened the medicine cabinet and took out gauze and adhesive tape and when I smelled that odor, something inside me began to move around, the memory of wounds, the days and weeks of hospitals, the bandages across my face, the surgeries. Or maybe it was the look of blood in the sink that hit me, the red, iron-filled water that had stained everything, even the insides of cooking pots. Whatever it was, I felt weak, my chest tight. I saw myself in the mirror, and suddenly, without warning, I hit the mirror with my hand, hit the face of myself, horrified even as I did it by my own action, that I would go so far as to break the mirror, the cabinet containing iodine, Mercurochrome, Merthiolate, Wild Root Oil. Glass shattered down into the sink and broken pieces spread across the floor, settling in corners. I heard a voice yelling "Damn it!" and it was me, my own voice, raging and hurt. There was an anger in it, a deep pain, and the smell of hospitals of the past, the grafts that left my thigh gouged, the skin stolen from there to put my face back together. That was all part of it, of what lay broken and sharp in the sink and on the floor. And I felt sick. I leaned over the toilet.

"What's going on?" yelled Dora-Rouge. And Frenchie was right outside the closed door. "Are you girls okay in there?"

Agnes called me honey and sweetheart and child. "Shhhh. It's okay." She held me. I sobbed helplessly. Me, the girl who never cried. When I stood up and looked, I saw that the sink was filled with cut, broken reflections of my face. I tried to clean up the glass, to pull myself together. "We'll get it later," Agnes said. "Let's go out and get some air."

"I'm sorry," I said. "I'm so sorry." I held on to her, my wet face in her shoulder. I didn't want to leave that little bathroom with its iron-stained sink and pieces of glass. I didn't want to face the others.

Then I said, "You don't want me. You're sending me to an is-land."

"It's all right," she said. "You'll be able to come back anytime you want."

"You didn't even tell me."

Agnes' voice was comforting, but it took all my courage to be willing to leave the room. I was still shaken and sobbing when Agnes opened the bathroom door and all the men stood outside it with their arms hanging lifeless at their sides, Husk in his white shirt and black suspenders. All of them looked at me, LaRue with his mouth open. Finally the silence was broken when Husk smiled and said, "Way to go!" He chewed on some peanuts, nodded at me, and laughed, then picked up a bottle of Coke from the table and toasted me. "Thatta girl, Angel. Those things are the source of vanity."

His words saved me from embarrassment. They were generous, quick-thinking words. The men smiled and turned and sat down to cards again, as if nothing had happened. "I'll raise you thirty cents," Justin said, hunched over like an old dark bird, squinting from the year when he'd been snow-blinded, 1942, when he was out on a trapline and injured his ankle.

Agnes and I stepped out of the bathroom and walked into the first of autumn darkness, together.

We sat side by side on a rock near the place where the river en-tered the lake, and I who had not cried as a child, not even at the taunting of other children, wept.

"She's like that, Frenchie is. It's her way. You get used to it."

Down on the lake, the light of a fisherman opened through darkness like an eye that peered at me and caught me without my face of toughness. I turned away, so nothing or no one could see me. Agnes put the bear coat over my shoulders, her arm about me, folding me in. "When I wear this coat, Angel, I see the old forests, the northern lights, the nights that belong to something large that we don't know."

That night after the card game, after the silent walk back up the road with Agnes, I was both relieved and heavy with weariness; I felt freed of something I couldn't name. Later, I undressed in the dark, close room of the house that breathed with the sleep of others and when I slept I dreamed I fell over the edge of land, fell out of order and knowing into a world dark and primal, seething, and alive as creation, like the beginning of life.

I BEGAN to form a kind of knowing at Adam's Rib. I began to feel that if we had no separate words for inside and out and there were no boundaries between them, no walls, no skin, you would see me. What would meet your eyes would not be the mask of what had happened to me, not the evidence of violence, not even how I closed the doors to the rooms of anger and fear. Some days you would see fire; other days, water. Or earth. You would see how I am like the night sky with its stars that fall through time and space and arrive here as wolves and fish and people, all of us fed by them. You would see the dust of sun, the turning of creation taking place. But the night I broke my face there were still boundaries and I didn't yet know I was beautiful as the wolf, or that I was a new order of atoms. Even with my own eyes I could not see deeper than my skin or pain in the way you cannot see yourself with closed eyes no matter how powerful the mirror.

My ugliness, as I called it, had ruled my life. My need for love had been so great I would offer myself to any boy or man who would take me. This was, according to women who judged me, my major sin. There was really no love in it, but I believed any kind of touch was a kind of love. Any human hand. Any chest to lean my head against. It would heal me, I thought. It would mend my heart. It would show my face back to me, unscarred. Or that love would be blind and ignore my face. But the truth remained that I was wounded and cut and no one could, or would, tell me how it happened and no man or boy offered what I needed. And deep down I dreaded knowing what had happened to me and the dread was equal to my urgent desire to learn the truth. Once, asking a foster mother what had happened to my face, there was silence. She and her husband looked at each other. "You fell," she said, and I knew she lied.

BUT I WAS LIKE Agnes had said: Water going back to itself. I was water falling into a lake and these women were that lake, Agnes, with her bear coat, traveling backward in time, walking along the shore, remembering stories and fragments of songs she had heard when she was younger and hearing also the old songs no one else remembered. And Dora-Rouge, on her way to the other world, already seeing what we could not see, answering those we could not hear, and, without legs, walking through clouds and waters of an afterlife.

▼

THREE

IT WAS A WARM DAY when two young men appeared at Adam's Rib in their canoe. When I saw them, I was at the water. They came from the south out of clear sky and the first autumn leaves floating on water. The sun was strong and it looked as if the shadow of the moon had never passed between it and earth.

Their canoe was yellow and they moved swiftly, as if they'd always lived on water, in canoes. They were lean. When they came to land, one of them jumped out of the canoe, pulled it forward a little, and held it for the other. They unloaded a few small packs, talking to each other. They seemed foreign here; they had different bodies, not American, not Canadian, but bodies still in touch with themselves and easy. They didn't rush. They appeared to know their place in the world.

They stood and talked a minute, undecided about what to do, then dragged the canoe out of water and turned it on its side in a grassy bank, putting some of their belongings under it.

One of them saw me. "Miss. Wait, please," he called. They were dark and slight, with intelligent faces. Both had straight black hair and beautiful eyes slightly slanted.

He spoke to me in a quiet and humble voice. I couldn't understand him very well except that he asked, "Where is Agnes Iron?"

"Just a minute," I said. "I'll go get her." I turned and ran to the house.

"Agnes!" I called out. "There's two men who want to see you."

She was in the middle of mending the screen door with needle and thread. "Where are they?"

I was breathless from running. "Down at the water."

"Where are your manners? Go get them. Bring them here."

Right away she put down the blue thread and went inside to cook.

I ran to where they sat in the shade of a tree. "Let me help." I took one of their bags, and led them up Poison Road. By the time we returned to Agnes', she had already sent for Tommy Grove and the Hundred-Year-Old Road people and pulled a meal together—eggs, bread, potatoes, and her terrible coffee.

Soon Tommy arrived. Some of the old people looked shaken from riding in the back of his red, faded truck, even though he'd built pine benches for transporting them.

I was uncomfortable with the two men and with the elders. I tried not to look at the four old women who came in Tommy's truck, but it was the first time I'd seen them and they were interesting to me. They were quiet, their clothing colorful but faded. An old cotton scarf on one woman, an apron, too. There were three old men, one with long, white hair and a clean shirt. One old woman dressed all in black sat in the living room on the cot and dozed, her dark gray hair braided, her eyes barely visible in her old, lined face. I waited on her, taking her a plate of potatoes.

After we ate, one of the young men began to talk. He was quiet and humble. He spoke softly but there was an urgency to what he said. They had heard about plans to build a dam, a reservoir. This year, he told us, the government and a hydroelectric corporation had decided to construct several dams.

I listened carefully. In the first flooding, the young man said, they'd killed many thousands of caribou and flooded land the people lived on and revered. Agents of the government insisted the people had no legal right to the land. No agreement had ever been signed, he said, no compensation offered. Even if it had been offered, the people would not have sold their lives. Not one of them.

Overnight many of the old ones were forced to move. Dams were already going in. The caribou and geese were affected, as well as the healing plants the people needed.

These men's people, my own people, too, had lived there forever, for more than ten thousand years, and had been sustained by these lands that were now being called empty and useless. If the dam project continued, the lives of the people who lived there would cease to be, a way of life would end in yet another act of displacement and betrayal.

These were my people. I listened carefully.

Without permission, roads had already been built. In order to determine what should be extracted before the land was drowned, mineral exploration was taking place. Then they would divert rivers into reservoirs. The effects would be seen even at Adam's Rib, as different bodies of water were changed around.

It was now a matter of how many communities, villages, and towns they could notify of the trouble. With winter coming, everything would slow down. Construction would end for the season. It was a break, a stay. It would give protesters time to reach the Fat-Eaters before the new projected wave of construction. It would give time to get the matter into court.

The young men asked for our help. Not for money, just for people to show up to stop the machines. Or, in the case of the Hundred-Year-Old Road people, a ceremony to assist them in reaching a good end.

Agnes set more black coffee and bread on the table for the Hundred-Year-Old Road people. I looked at the women's wide skirts. They ate hungrily. Agnes cooked more eggs, potatoes, and bacon.

This was the first time I spent with Tommy, and he was quiet and open. I'd seen him pass in the truck along Poison Road or at the store while getting supplies, but now I was impressed with how he spoke with the young men, my distant cousins, and with the elders. He spoke and then was quiet while they talked among themselves. He waited, listened, heard. Even at my young age, even without an ounce of wisdom, I respected this.

That day, with the two young men, I felt something in the air, that our lives were going to change, that nothing would remain the same, not the land, not the two young men, not the people present, not me. Change was in the air. It was palpable, a strong presence in the room.

FOUR

THE WOMAN named Bush, the one who tried to scrub the cyanide odor off my mother, the one who had taken Hannah to Old Man on the Hundred-Year-Old Road, the woman of the island five miles out in the lake, knew that I'd come back. That's what she told me after I moved into her house on Fur Island. It's why she was on the lake that morning of my return, the floating woman, still and watchful in her canoe.

On that first morning I arrived, she'd slept badly. It wasn't much more than the sound of water that she heard, or the loon, but something called out to her, and there was the familiar presence of a young child standing beside her bed in the first light of morning. It was a girl, about five years of age, wearing hand-sewn deerskin boots and a soft dress. The child looked like me. She had visited Bush all the years I'd been gone, but that morning the girl raised her hand in a wave of good-bye. That was how Bush knew I had come home after all her years of patient waiting. Twelve years had passed. Now was the time she had waited for.

ON THE DAY they sent me to Bush, Dora-Rouge called me into her room. "Hand me that box," she said. It was the one I'd snooped in while she slept on the porch. I thought at first she'd found me out. My face grew warm.

When she opened it, it smelled of cedar. She took out the amber I had already seen, the frog so small, so perfectly formed inside it, and she held it up and let the light shine into it.

"This is for you," she said. "It was found in water." Her old hands turned it over. Then she wrapped it in tissue and pressed it into my hand. "Those people from the south told our ancestors, 'Remember us when we are gone,' and they placed this into the hands of an old woman named Luri, one of my ancestors, one of yours.

"I know an animal-calling song," Dora-Rouge said. "I'm going to teach it to you. You might need it out on that island of Bush's." And then she sang.

Soon there were deer on the road walking toward the house in the first musky smell of autumn. Husk and I drove past them on our way to Tinselman's store to stock up on goods for Bush and for another person on his grocery-delivery route, then we drove to the dock. For a Saturday, it was quieter than usual. In autumn, when the fish were full of food, the fishermen were forced to travel longer distances, so when we reached the lake, it was still. There was no longer the drone of the boats, only of hungry bees in their last hold on life and the sound of crows cawing above the smooth water. The lake looked as if nothing had ever disturbed it except the reflections of the black birds.

Husk parked the old blue truck, then went to the truck bed and lifted out the black, half-full suitcase Agnes insisted I carry. It was more self-respecting, she'd told me, than a garbage bag full of my clothes.

I helped Husk carry the bags of groceries down the pier to the worn-out black boat he called The Raven. I took sticks of firewood out of the truck bed and helped load them. Winter would soon reach us. It was never too early to begin preparations. The wood smelled sweet and dry, the scent of what had been clear light through forests, and there was sap on my palms and the cool touch of changing seasons. All this along with the smell of leaves and firesmoke.

The engine made an urgent cutting sound that broke silence in half. Husk squinted through the gray cloud of exhaust. It was the way he had of looking at times. A squint something like Justin's, but from that winter of 1929 when he'd been stranded in minus-eight-degree weather with a dog team suddenly overwhelmed by a virus. Unlike Justin, who, according to Frenchie, had gotten hung up on a mass of ice, the squint made Husk look deep. I liked the look. Now, as the boat pitched forward, he looked as if he'd fixed his mind on unraveling some knotted tangle of thought and would find a way to pull it straight and clear as fishline. Even his lips were tight, concentrated. I liked to look at him, the man who used theories of science to confirm what he knew was true. On land, he wasn't much over five feet five, but in water Husk became large. It was his place, the swaying water. It was what he knew.

In the distance before us, several islands looked like rocky planets in a watery sky, and the world stretched wide open. Soon, the musky smell of autumn air gave way to the smell of fish and coolness, even a possibility of coming rain.

Behind us, in the wake of the boat, glaring water closed, hiding our path, and returned to stillness and secrecy. The houses on Adam's Rib vanished from sight, leaving only the thick shapes of trees, and then the trees, too, became nothing more than a dark blue line. Below us, I knew, fish swam in the awake darkness, green weeds bent with the currents.

HALFWAY BETWEEN ADAM'S RIB and Fur Island was the Hungry Mouth of Water. It was a circle in the lake where winter ice never froze. Young people, with their new and shiny beliefs, called this place the Warm Spot, and thought it was a geological oddity, a spring perhaps, or bad currents. But the older ones, whose gods still lived on earth, called it the Hungry Mouth of Water, because if water wasn't a spirit, if water wasn't a god that ruled their lives, nothing was. For centuries they had lived by nets and hooks, spears and ropes, by distances and depths. They'd lived on the rocking skin of water and the groaning ice it became. They swallowed it. It swallowed them. But whatever it was, none of them, young or old, would go near this one place. They all gave it a wide berth.

Every winter the Hungry Mouth laid its trap of thin ice and awaited whatever crossed above it. Young deer, not knowing the weaknesses of ice, fell through the thin roof of this trap, as did drunks who wandered away from their lives on land, forgot what they knew, and unwittingly offered themselves to this god. Once, a showman transported a sleek white beluga down from the mouth of Hudson Bay, taking it over the dry, rocky, and long portages with the help of logrollers. He even went so far as to hire Indian boys to keep the whale moist as it traveled. He showed it to people for a fee, calling out, "Come see the ugly beast!" And when it began to fail, he hoisted it up on chains and cast it outside his boat to die, into that hungry place, until finally it sank into the open mouth where it remained, an apparition from another world, in the warm circle of water. No one ever claimed to have seen the whale; no one dared to venture that close.

Alongside it were many thousand skinned carcasses of fur-bearing animals discarded by trappers. Without their pelts, it was said, they looked like human children, perfectly preserved, their eyes still open, dark and shining in water, peering through it. Two Skidoos had come to rest inside that mouth, as well as a shipwreck, hunters, and lost men who had believed they knew the waters. One of the faults of men, Husk always said, was that they believed they were smarter than they were. Nothing ever surfaced from that place, but some people said that if you dared close enough, you could see it all floating in there, each thing just as it had been the day it broke through or fell, the antlers of deer like roots unmoored.

I studied this place as we went around it. It looked no different from the rest of the lake, which made it all the more dangerous. Near this place was a current that would carry a boat north into the system of lakes, islands, and portages, all the way to places where remnants of old settlements and villages were now in ruins, and beyond that to rivers winding their way north. Islands in that far north held vestiges of an older people now only remembered. There were places wild rice grew, bonelike trees, and other plants that grew like hands reaching toward sky, and the cleared places of cattle. A person could go from water to water, land to land in that broken country. To keep the Hungry Mouth content while we passed it, Husk took a bag of tobacco from his pocket and fed it to the water, then he added cornmeal and bread.

AND THEN Fur Island came toward us. It was a dark island a little over two miles across, with rocks and trees. Behind it, other pieces of land floated in the distance.

It seems to me now that as we neared the island, we went into another kind of time, one that floated down through history, and like the lake we traveled, was unsounded and bottomless in places. Bush would say there were those who believed oceans from one side of earth entered oceans of the other, and perhaps the lake was like that, maybe it had a sister lake on the other side of the world—because it was said that the whales of one hemisphere sang the same songs as those of other whales far around the circle of the planet. They spoke the same language. They knew what had happened to water, to their sisters. Husk said Einstein believed time would bend and circle back to itself, maybe in the way that planets orbit. And I think he was right because I remember clear as yesterday how it felt to go there, to Fur Island, that day. As if time were nothing at all.

Whatever it was, I was traveling backward in time toward myself at the same time I journeyed forward, like the new star astronomers found that traveled in two directions at once.

I opened my handbag and took out the gift Dora-Rouge had pressed into my hand, the frog of my snooping. It was so small, so intricate and perfect, a life stopped in its living, trapped inside the ancient pitch of a tree. It was warm to the touch, and beautiful and sad at the same time. I hid it deep in my bag. Already I believed in the power of water. I believed water might leap up, open my palm, and take Dora-Rouge's gift from me. Or perhaps it was that I did not trust my own grip on things and I feared losing more of myself than had already closed behind me, like the water behind us that gave no hint of our passage. I put the amber in the only safe place I knew, inside my bag at the bottom of a closed-in darkness, and I thought, it's shining in there, casting its light.

The island we traveled toward had a history. Over the noise of the boat, Husk told me about the frogs on Fur Island, how thick they were, how people had once heard them from miles away. He said at times they sounded like drums, and that they were conceived by rain. They slept through years of drought, buried in the ground, until the time was right for their emergence, and then, on that island, gleaming in mud, frogs would come out of the darkness, bronze-eyed, golden, and eating their own skins. On rainy nights they appeared and were plentiful. They were sacred beings. One year they would again rise from the mud of the island, he said, the place they called the Navel of the World.

The names, Husk said, were like layers of time.

IT WAS A SMALL ISLAND, one of immense beauty. It had been hostage to that beauty, to its own plentitude, because it was inviting to animals and men alike. Rich, fertile, hilly in places, it was once populated with marten, otter, and beaver, a large concentration of animals in so small a place. When the water wasn't frozen, animals were stranded by their solitude on this island, where Europeans sought their skins and other wealth. This place of trade and barter was a meeting place, a crossing ground. But after all that, it became an isolated parcel of land; now Bush was the only one who was there and she lived there year-round, during both the mosquito season and the near-arctic cold of winter, two facts that by themselves said much about her stamina and persistence.

There was more to Fur Island, I would learn. In the summer of 1924, two wolf children were found there. They'd been left behind by their parents—no one knew what happened to them—and gone wild. The children were raised by a pack of wolves. From wolves they'd learned how to evade explorers and priests, even in so small a space, how to cross ice in winter, how to avoid the Hungry Mouth. When finally they were captured—it had been accomplished through the killing of the wolf pack—they had night-shining eyes, dark and astonished to see human beings, creatures vaguely familiar and shadowy, but remembered by the children in a bad light and as ruthless beings, never to be trusted. They didn't survive, that boy and girl. Dora-Rouge told me this. After being found they fell into a state of despair. The captive lives that held most humans could not hold them. They saw through the savagery of civilization. They grieved something fierce for their lost kin, the murdered wolves. Dora-Rouge remembered these two light-skinned, dark-eyed, tangle-haired children. Their wary eyes were the standard against which she measured all other wild things, including Hannah Wing, my mother, whose own fierceness and danger made the feral children seem tame by comparison.

It was on this island, too, where once a Briton declared himself king and strutted about like a foolish rooster until he was deposed by French trappers. And where a milkstone, flowing with healing mineral waters, was dynamited at the order of a bishop who wanted to spite the superstitious natives who said, and even worse, believed, that they'd been healed by those milky waters. One of his own priests had been cured of smallpox by these white, bubbling waters that came from stone, but even so, the bishop maintained that any healing in that place must have come from the devil, who lived under the land. Because of the killing of the waters, the Indians who journeyed there for healing let Christianity pass them by; they didn't want a god that made them sick and took away the remedy.

Fur Island endured all of this, and somewhere, beneath it, the healing milk still flowed, frogs remained buried and waiting, and the wild children were still remembered by the trees.

STRAIGHT AHEAD OF US a yellow shaft of sunlight cut through a rolling mist. In it, I saw the smaller island beside Fur Island. It was a broken-off raft of land populated by spiders. In sunlight, the webs looked like a craziness, slow and silver, one which was taken apart and rewoven nightly as if to capture whatever came close. It was a peat island and it would have floated here and there, except that Bush kept it tethered to Fur Island by rope. The spiders, she said, kept the insect population down. They needed that in the north. Another reason she kept it tied was that this region, known as the Triangle, had long been in dispute between Canada, the United States, and tribal nations. Bush didn't want the island of spiders to be part of the conflict between governments who had fought territorial battles over even smaller pieces of land. But most important, the two pieces of land had been one in the past, like Pangaea, a continent of puzzle pieces now separated by water. They were kindred spirits, one male and one female. Bush thought it would be too lonely for those pieces of land to drift far from one another.

From the first time I saw Bush, I knew she, like myself, understood such loneliness. She, too, had only thin, transient bonds to other people, having grown up on the outskirts of their lives. At first when I saw her, I thought she was a deer, thin and brown, smelling the direction of wind. She was standing at the edge of the island when we arrived, her dark, already graying hair down around her shoulders. She seemed rooted where she stood, at the boundary between land and water. She looked taller than she was. She was sinewy. I could see it was true that she might battle a force no one else would fight, as Dora-Rouge had told me.

She knew we were coming, even though there were no phones, not yet any citizens band radio. She had known I was moving toward her. She'd felt it, she told me later, sometime after I first saw the gap between her front teeth.

As the lake had grown shallow, Fur Island grew larger. What had been covered by water not long before was now mud. Bush stood barefoot in that dark, newly exposed clay, as if she'd just been created by one of the gods who made us out of earth, as if she'd risen up like first woman, still and awed by the creation. Around her were jagged, rough-looking rocks. Next to the harshness of these dark stones, she seemed deceptively soft. She wore a light green dress, the color of water, and I could see her thin legs through the skirt; they were tight and strong. In a slight movement, with sun reaching through clouds, the lake's reflected light and the moving shadows shimmered across her. She was, in the first moment of my seeing her, equal parts light and water. And she had the closed look people wear when they are too much alone. It seemed that I would interrupt nothing in her life. But even so, seeing her, I was witness to a kind of grace I was hard put to describe; I've seen it carried in the stillness of deer and I've felt it in the changing power of seasons. It was only a glimpse—that's all I can say with words—that there was something about her that knew itself.

The world of water, in truth, had claimed her the way it did with people, the way it would one day claim me, although nothing (on that first day) could have convinced me of this. I was afraid of water. I couldn't even swim. But still, something inside me began to wake up right then and there. It was only a felt thing. It turned over like a wheel. I sensed already that the land on Fur Island, the water, would pull a person in, steal from them, change them, that it would spit them up transformed, like Jonah from the belly of the whale.

As I stepped out of the boat, I nearly lost my balance. It was the land, too, like the water, already trying to take possession of me, to bring me closer. The mud took in my feet and ankles. When Bush offered me her hand, I took it, but I felt like an intruder, awkward and unwanted in this quiet world.

THE PATH up to her house was lined on both sides by stones that were painted white. Green light fell through the trees. On the island it was not yet early fall. That's how much difference a small angle of light could make, a few miles. It seemed moist there, as if water dripped from leaves. Large snails left shining pathways behind them. With its trees and ferns, its undergrowth, the island was dense with life and the beginnings of life.

As we neared the house, we passed by a large pile of bones. At first I thought these were more painted stones, but Bush said it was the skeleton of a sea turtle that would one day come together again, large as a room. For a living, she assembled things. She put together bones for LaRue, who sold them to museums and schools, and she put them together with devotion, as if the animal would come back down a road of life that had been broken through the felled forests. The island itself was a place of undone, unfinished things and incomplete creations. Not only were there the turtle bones and organ pipes destined for a church that was never built, but even a ship had been left there in parts. Long ago several men had tried to rebuild a new ship from parts of the old wreck, then abandoned it when it was only half-built. Parts of it were still visible behind the house, as were the ruins of an older house, a charred stone chimney.

The house was hard to see from the path, so it seemed that we walked toward a wild, uncertain destination. But then it came into view. It was made of dark gray stones and covered with vines. The Black House, some people called it, because it was so dark. But in its hiding it looked beautiful to me. The soot-colored stones that

now made up the walls had been ballast carried by early ships, discarded once the ships were weighted down with the skins and
forests they took from the island, thrown overboard like the beluga
whale in the Hungry Mouth of Water. The ships vanished and returned, leaving behind a mountain of such stones. Mortared together, the dark, round stones smelled of earth.

The doorway into the Black House was low and small. A tall
man would have to bend to pass through. But none of us was tall.
We entered upright, which was the best way to step into Bush's
world.

While the house looked heavy and dark from the outside, it was
lighter inside than other northern houses. With mosquito season
over, Bush left the windows open, so that the vines crept inside and
reached across the inner walls. Maybe they, too, were incomplete
and searching for a sister vine.

The wooden floor, built from timbers and decks of the same ship
that unloaded the ballast, had settled unevenly. *The Turin* was the
name of the ship that had been wrecked there in a terrible storm,
leaving the bodies of men to remain preserved in water, while only
the wood of the boat washed to land.

It was a thick-walled house with a rounded wooden ceiling,
domelike, made of lodgepole pines. There were no curtains at any
of the windows, and one large room served as both living area and
kitchen. A black-and-gray cookstove sat beside the low sink along
one wall, a small light above it, and a potbelly stove was near the
green table and benches. There was no bathroom, no electricity,
and no mirrors, because, as Bush said, mirrors had cost us our lives.
I would come to call her house the House of No. It was defined by
what wasn't there.

Bush cleared a small pile of bones off the table. "Sit down," she
told me. She had a soft, low voice. As she said this, she set the water
to boil. As Bush and Husk talked, I looked around. At the shelf of
books. At the view from a window. Outside was a garden with
cornstalks. The turtle bones were visible from the house. Even as
Bush and Husk talked, I could see that nothing about me escaped her
vision. I felt her attention, her eyes following me, and all the time she
served us coffee and cookies, tomato slices with onions, and butter

and Wonder bread, she looked at my hands, at how I sipped the too-hot coffee she placed before me. She saw the scars on my face, even the tattoo I had made on my own arm, the initials of Lonnie Faro, a boy who once lived up a street from me. She saw these, the marks of my life. I didn't cover them up. I didn't even lean forward to let my hair fall across my skin. And my eyes, too, were busy. I studied her as she sat across the table, her muscled arms lean and feminine. I saw that she had a largeness, not of build and stature, but of someone who, as Dora-Rouge said, had battled unseen, unnamed forces. Next to her I would always feel ungainly.

At seventeen, a girl thinks mostly of herself, but from what Bush and Husk said, I knew there were larger concerns than mine. Not only was the lake at a record low, but dead fish had been found belly-up on the south shore and a few poisoned otters were found mired in mud. "The fish are dying by the hundreds up at Lake Chin," he said. Though he hadn't wanted to burden me, I heard the concern in his voice, the silent dread, still unformed, that comes to people when their world is threatened. It was in the air, stronger than words. It had crossed the water before us in the shape of two young men.

When Husk left, I walked with him to the water, then I stood a long time at the changing edge of lake and watched his boat grow small. The water seemed moody and capable of change at any moment. I had an urge to call after him, to have him turn the faded *Raven* around and take me back.

MY BEDROOM in the small three-room house made of dark ballast was stone on three sides. "My room." I liked the sound of those words even as nervous as I felt. It was the first place that was wholly mine. The fourth wall was painted pale yellow, the color of fog on the day I arrived on the ferry. A blue woolen blanket covered my bed, and there was a small pine chest of drawers. A braided rug lay on the cool floor that was made of ship timbers. One of the vines came through the window like a dark green hand. The first thing I did was to put it out and close the uncurtained window. I did not want the world to sneak in on me. Like the missionaries, I was threatened by its life and the way it resisted human efforts to control it.

On that first day, after Bush showed me my room, she went out to her garden to check the corn and other plants. I saw her from the window. She seemed to know, without my saying so, that I needed time to look around the house. She knew, also, that I would watch her, that I would see her working, slow and patient, always with purpose. I was permitted to spy on her in a way, to know her before I had to give her any part of myself or take anything from her.

REMEMBERING, Bush once said, is like a song. It has a different voice with every singer. On these days of my remembering I see her as she was then, plain as day, bent in the garden clearing among the corn plants and sharp-edged pumpkin vines. I see, too, the altar of that first day. It was on a table in a back corner of the room. It was a shrine of sorts, for me. Bush, neither Catholic nor Protestant, was a person of the land, but she kept statues of saints and crosses along-side eagle feathers, tobacco, and photographs of loved ones. Just in case. So it looked ornate, the altar. Two red candles burned before three pictures of me as an infant.

In one photograph, I was held uncomfortably in the arms of Hannah Wing. She was not a natural mother, I could see. Wrapped tightly in a blanket, I looked at her with frightened eyes and it seemed that, even then, I pulled away from her. In another picture, Agnes, the large, bear-clad woman of her youth, held my hand. In this faded photo, I looked more like a miniature adult than a child. In the last picture, Bush gazed at me, her thin dark arms around the child I had been. I was resting on her hip, my legs about her waist. I looked nothing like the baby pictures I carried around, the ones I found in the twenty-five-cent Take Your Own Photo machine at Woolworth's where I'd worked for two months, pictures left behind by someone else.

In the photos on Bush's shelf, there were no scars, and in one, the one with Bush, I was smiling. About what, I could not have said because the smiling stopped long before my memory, as much as I had of it, began. I did not remember her, nor did I remember having been loved. I had an entangled memory, with good parts of it missing. I was returning to the watery places in order to unravel my mind and set straight what I had lost, which seemed like everything to me.

The altar frightened me. The candles and pictures made me feel as if I had died and been wrapped in a saint's shroud in a European church, nothing but bones and parchment inside yellow cloth, with candles burning to save my soul from children's Limbo. What I didn't know was how I had been loved by Bush and fallen through her hands like precious water, as Agnes put it, or how Bush had fought hard for me against the strongest of our enemies, a system, a government run by clerks and bureaucrats. I didn't know that Bush had held a mourning feast on my behalf. I didn't know that I had once been in grave danger from the woman of my emergence, Hannah Wing, who had lived with Bush in this place. Hannah, who had disfigured me.

The altar, like the mourning feast Agnes told me about, and like the songs, was something akin to sympathetic magic, designed to bring me back. Who would have thought that an altar, a holy table with two eagle feathers, tobacco, and cornmeal, a shelf in a house on an injured island might have been my protection from all the people and events that had conspired against me. Or that it had summoned me from afar like Agnes' old song for lost things, and drawn me back to the north.

There was a picture of my mother on the altar. She was still a girl, frail and with a dull-eyed staring. I was larger-boned than she was, and sturdy. As I looked, something in the picture caught my eye. I leaned closer and took the photo of Hannah in hand. Behind her, there was something or someone, a spirit, ghost, another presence who was only a shadow or blur, but distinctly real. I thought I heard a woman's voice whisper near my ear. With animal fear my hair stood up on my neck and there was an odor suddenly in the air. Almond. Sweet.

It was nothing, I told myself, at most a glare of light or a double exposure, a thumbprint, perhaps, but all the same I went quickly away from the table. The talk about the mouth of the lake had made me edgy. It was only that, I told myself, that along with the daily conversations Dora-Rouge had with her departed husband and the many stories they'd all been feeding me.

But I had truly entered a different world, a tree-shaded place where unaccountable things occurred, where frogs knew to wait beneath dark ground until conditions were right for them to emerge, where water's voice said things only the oldest of people understood.

SOMETIMES NOW, I see the island as it was then, how the vines indoors grew red that autumn and fell to the floor, and how I swept them away. Those hungry, reaching vines that wanted to turn everything back to its origins—walls, doors, a ladder-back chair, even a woman's life. They wanted to cover it all and reclaim the island for themselves.

And I remember that on my first night, Bush browned elk meat and made a broth, stirred it together with tomatoes. We ate the elk stew with wild rice, sweet corn, tea with spoons of sugar. The smells in her house were hospitable in a way she was not. It seemed the only sounds in the house were not our voices, but the sound of forks against plates, the sound of the cups as she set them on the white drainboard. I did the dishes in near silence. This would become our unspoken arrangement: she cooked, I cleaned. Now and then one of us would say something, for the sake of politeness, but it was strained. Bush asked me how it had been with Agnes and Dora-Rouge. I said, "Fine," and nothing more, and I resolved to go back to Adam's Rib with the next boat.

As evening lay down upon the house, Bush said, "It's getting dark." She went outside to put gas in the generator and it hummed and, as God had done in one day, Bush created light. The sound of the generator was nearly deafening in the silence.

When I went to bed that first night, I heard Bush pouring water, moving things into their places, and when the generator went out I lay in bed in darkness, with no mother, no light. Again, I thought, the House of No, and the darkness stared me in the eyes, a wilderness I had never known in any of the three Oklahoma counties where I'd lived, empty and alone even then. It wasn't true darkness facing me; the moon was large and bright. But it seemed the most full darkness to me, that light. I was as incomplete and unfinished as all the other things on the island. I faced the wall and tried to sleep.

I remembered so little of my life that sometimes I thought I had never really existed, that I was nothing more than emptiness covered with skin.

Now even my illusions began to drop away. I had created a past for myself and now, I knew, it was about to be dismantled, taken apart and rewoven the way spiderwebs on the floating island changed every night. Only a short time before, my life had been one thing. Now it was something altogether different. There was nothing for me to measure it by any longer. There was not even so much as a mirror in Bush's house for me to recall my image. Only my pocket mirror. So, on the first night, in the bedroom where moonlight fell on the floor, I spoke my made-up story inside myself one last time.

In it, I was born wet and shining and open-eyed in a sunny room. That's how I imagined my beginning. In the light of sun, with the radiance of dust as it floated through sunlight, the air full of it, and I was one of the chosen. The birthmark of Indians, a blue hand of God, was on my back as if to comfort me. Perhaps God himself had rocked me in his arms, and I was loved. I'd heard once in a Baptist church that God loved me so much he knew the number of hairs on a person's head. I tried to count mine, lifting one strand at a time. But I gave up on the number of hairs, and that was when I created the story I'd lived by as a child. In it, my mother was beautiful and kind and her love for me went deep. Sorry to leave me, she died in a large bed with a flowered cover and beloved people, relatives, all about her. I was the last thought on her mind. When I was a child, this mother was the one I talked to in my many sleepless nights, eyes squeezed shut, praying to her as I cried. She was the one whose voice I heard inside myself. She told me wise things. She told me I was bound for happiness. I had long comforted myself in this way, held up in the hands of this story. But now, I knew, my story had worn itself out. The women in the Triangle said Hannah was still alive. I would find her and she would be ice. That night I felt something watching me, the vines perhaps, wanting in, or something animal, come in the night. Night itself, in all its vast and infinite dark space, peered in at me, but nothing took me by the hand.

And the altar was gone the next morning. So was the presence of the child spirit that had come to stand beside Bush's bed the morning I'd arrived at Adam's Rib on the ferry.

IT WASN'T LONG before our days, even in the heat, were spent preparing for cold weather. The predicted rain did not materialize, the lake was at a record low. Not a cloud passed over. The sky was clear and mostly blue. Bush went out to her garden late at night, as well as in the earliest parts of the day. She touched her plants as if coaxing them to rise. I would watch her, standing back in the shadows of my room so she couldn't see me. I became the observer of her, the watcher of all the mystery in that place of large snails, mosses, and stones that had given milk. At times I saw her walking down to the lake. She walked slowly, as if she had all the time in the world. Sometimes she worked on the turtle. From the door and window I saw it begin to come together. So large, it was. I could hardly believe such a thing had lived in any sea. I felt sorry for it, so out of its element, and when I first learned to swim, I imagined myself as the turtle. I was slow and I saw my arms pull back the water from before me. And some nights, as I sat in a chair on the ground or watched from the window, at the misty edges of land and water, Bush became something else, something nearly invisible and silent, as if she were a kind of goddess with a beautiful song and Levi's and graying hair.

BUSH WAS a brooding type of woman. She was, most always, exactly as she appeared to be. She had no need or use for social graces. Complex and simple at the same time, she was the right woman for the island of frogs, the island of feral children and wolves, of healing milk.

I don't remember what it was about her I most disliked, but even in all the beauty, the discomfort of my being on the island with her was like a claw in my chest. It nearly hurt, her silence. Something in her, I felt, was unreachable. She carried a bit of darkness about her eyes. It wasn't the kind of darkness that grows when someone is sick, but a deeper kind, the kind a well of water holds. I didn't like her, but why should I have been different from anyone else? Surely not just because she had once loved me. And not because she was the one who knew my story, because she was in no hurry to tell me anything she knew about my life.

For a long time, I did not unpack the suitcase. I was convinced for days, then for weeks, that I would return to the mainland soon with Husk. I watched to see when our supplies were low, sending a psychic message across the lake, closing my eyes, praying to water and whatever else might reach him. Seeing him in my mind's eye.

But just before he came each time, with Archway cookies for me, Bush divulged a part of the story I'd wanted and searched for. Once in a while, as the wind came up and the leaves blew from the trees, Bush would say, "Your mother was like the wind. Sometimes she was the winter wind and she chilled our bones and snapped frozen branches off the trees." My mother, she said, was a storm looking for a place to rage. But there were times, she said, when Hannah was a warmer wind. "We were fooled then. We'd let her near and then she changed into ice and turned against us."

With Bush, I didn't feel as soft as I had on Adam's Rib. I said what I thought, as if to fill the great silence. Once, frustrated with these tales, I looked at her and said, "You're just saying that to keep me here. You just want me here to do all your work."

And she laughed.

Taking offense at her, I went to my room and slammed the door. Sheepish, I came out in time for supper.

But it was true; she said just enough to keep me there. And I had to earn each word. I helped her prepare for cold weather. I sealed the gaps around windows, brought in wood. Bush disappeared at times, taking a canoe out into the water, returning with fish. I helped where I could, in spite of my anger and frustration. Some days I worked beside her in the garden, or at the stove or sink. At times, she put the bones for LaRue in place and told me another piece of history. Once, waiting for water to boil, she told me about the two trappers everyone called Ding and Dong. Each had accused the other of trespassing his traplines, springing the other's traps and stealing the animals from the trap. The conflict grew. Finally one of them shot the other, then set out for the far north, where no one would bother searching.

She put a pin in a vertebrae. "You know who it was? Who stole from the traps?" She looked at me.

I resented the quiz. "What's your point?" I said.

"It was Wolverine; they do this."

I looked at her. "What's that? Wolverine?"

"That's what everyone wants to know." She laughed. Not a hostile laugh. An easy one.

"Is that all? You're just telling me that?"

Later, out stacking wood for the coming winter, I said, "You are too strange." I was surprised at my own honesty, but who could lie on such an island?

And she said, "Your mother was a skin that others wore. The man your mother lived with kept animals in cages and they would cry at night like humans."

I stacked the wood, washed dishes, used Pine Sol in the outhouse, and thought, always, about her few words. Sometimes they made sense. But still there were times I was determined to leave the island. I didn't like it there and I wasn't comfortable with Bush. I didn't know then that what I really wanted none of us would ever have. I wanted an unbroken line between me and the past. I wanted not to be fragments and pieces left behind by fur traders, soldiers, priests, and schools. But so many nights, when it began to get dark, Bush would go outside and fill the generator with gas and create warm light and a room full of intimacy and she would say one more thing, just enough to keep me there, just enough to tie me to her and the island as if I were staked to it like the little floating raft of land with spiders.

And so I remained.

One day I unpacked the suitcase and put my clothing in drawers. Husk came and went many times. I swept the floors that had been at sea and I began to like them, and the stones, and the still-open windows. I grew accustomed to the green reaches of the vines and the floors that creaked at night when Bush walked over them.

WHEN RAIN FINALLY CAME, it started at night. I'd carried a lamp to my room and sat on my bed until late, thinking, trying to remember Dora-Rouge's animal song. By then I had given up closing the window and one of the vine's leaves had turned red. Green dragonflies floated in on the last of warm breezes, and drifted around the room.

A light rain fell at first, but soon it grew stronger, then fell in great torrents. It had the force of a sea behind it. There was roaring thunder. The sound of water lashing down filled me with such a longing, an ache in my chest I could not yet fathom, but now know as the animal heart yearning its way into being, pulled out of a song. I was drawn to the window, magnetized. Outside, the white stones of the footpath were shining beacons. In a flash of lightning, the trunks of trees were straight and pale, and downhill the island of spiders was visible. The sky broke, pieces of earth and mud flew up against the house and the water shining on the turtle bones made the skeleton look whole and alive, a pale turtle wanting to swim in the falling sea of a wet darkness.

With the window wide open, I lived inside water. There was no separation between us. I knew in a moment what water was. It was what had been snow. It had passed through old forests, now gone. It was the sweetness of milk and corn and it had journeyed through human lives. It was blood spilled on the ground. Some of it was the blood of my ancestors.

When I slept it was deeply, finally. I slept into another light as the sound of occasional thunder jarred the floor of the house.

At the first light of morning I sat up in bed. The storm by then was dark green and there was still a rhythmic song of falling water, but a larger noise was behind the rain, a great disturbance of air. I went to the window and looked up. In the first spread of light above us was a cloud, a great cloud of flesh and feather so thick the sky itself appeared to be moving as the wings of tundra swans clattered together, as they pulled themselves south. Their voices seemed to wake the land itself, which at that moment lived only for the great, beautiful birds, the sky full and moving. I wasn't dreaming. I had no need to dream. This world I'd entered, however strange, was dream enough with its dark roots, its instinctual light and full sky. I had traveled long and hard to be there. I'd searched all my life for this older world that was lost to me, this world only my body remembered. In that moment I understood I was part of the same equation as birds and rain.

F I V E

AFTER I SAW the way storms
moved in, I began to wonder how Hannah had survived the storm
and its angry waters. I wondered at times what she, my mother, had
thought of that world with its island of spiders, its fish leaping out
of the lake, the plaintive cries of loon and wolf. What had she seen
in the low sky that rested on water and land? What had she thought
of the storms that moved in so quickly and gave themselves back to
water? I wondered, too, what the world had thought of her. Our
lives, the old people say, are witnessed by the birds, by dragonflies,
by trees and spiders. We are seen, our measure taken, not only by
the animals and spiders but even by the alive galaxy in deep space
and the windblown ice of the north that would soon descend on us.

S I X

THE PEOPLE at Adam's Rib believed everything was alive, that we were surrounded by the faces and lovings of gods. The world, as described by Dora-Rouge, was a dense soup of love, creation all around us, full and intelligent. Even the shadows light threw down had meaning, had stories and depth. They fell across the land, and they were filled with whatever had walked there, animal or man, and with the birds that flew above.

Or, as Husk put it, "One day this will be proven true. You wait and see." Even the tools and the fishhooks were alive, he maintained, and the ball-peen hammer.

At first, when Dora-Rouge and Husk said these things, I saw earth as a seed, with some great life stored inside it, waiting, the way a blood spot waits inside an egg for the next division of cells. And gradually I saw this world as that which gave birth to fish, the great natal waters parting to make way as birds left the sea and opened their wings in air.

The stones, too, were alive, the stinging nettles, the snails of Fur Island, and the tree which folded its leaves when touched by human hands. When I thought of this while walking the island, I felt its life. I remembered and loved it. I suffered for the felling of this world, for those things and people that would never return.

Not only this, but the division between humans and animals was a false one. There were times, even recent times, when they both spoke the same language, when Dora-Rouge's song was taken into account. "When humans forget to respect the bond," said Bush, "Wolverine takes away their luck in hunting. That's why LaRue never catches or takes a living thing."

I didn't ask again what a wolverine was. I'd already begun to think it was an animal with no true description. This time I just listened.

Bush was right about LaRue, the dealer in bones and hides and preserved fetuses. One day, after the rain, he knocked on the windowsill to get my attention. I went to look out. "Where's the glass?" he asked. The window was wide open.

"Go to the door," I told him. It seemed more proper.

He had come to take me on the long-ago promised fishing trip. He was tall and had to bend over to get through Bush's door. "Are you ready to go? It's still wet out. It's the best time to catch fish," he said.

"Ready? You're late." It was obvious I was perturbed. I didn't try to keep this secret. It wasn't just in my voice, either. I looked him over thoroughly. It bothered me that he'd come to my window.

"Hey, it's tomorrow, isn't it?" He shrugged, barely apologetic. Even his hat was camouflage. He didn't want the fish to see him coming.

Finally, I consented to go. Fishing was a skill I might need in this place. And I might also impress Bush with my catch.

"Just a minute," I said. "I have to tell Bush." But he followed behind me to the garden.

"I'm going fishing," I yelled at her and started to walk away, but as soon as he saw Bush, LaRue smiled and ogled her and walked straight into a branch. Bush didn't seem to notice at all. It was as if he were invisible to her. And LaRue himself wasn't the slightest bit humiliated, as I would have been.

He canoed to a little cove not far away, a quiet place with water that, unlike LaRue, looked deep. We stood awhile on the grassy shore. "Here," he said, handing me a pole. "When you get a nibble, lift up." He demonstrated how I was to jerk the pole.

"Okay," I said. I practiced a few times.

"Hey. Watch that hook."

"Sorry."

I decided to walk a distance away from him. I saw a place I thought fish would like.

"Hold still!" he whispered loudly. "Just walking they can hear your feet on ground."

"Well, I want to go in the shade."

"Shh. Don't talk. They can hear your voice."

According to LaRue, my red T-shirt, also, was too bright. "They can see you," he said. Also, they could feel our presence.

"Here, use this." He handed me another weight, instructing me how to drop it into the water and move it slightly along. "You aren't holding still enough. Oh, shit, you got a bite. Pull up! Jerk it! No, it got away."

Again I tried to find my own spot.

"Be more still."

"Then how come I'm the only one catching any," I said, and I made a big show of the one, new to my hook, trying hard not to show my excitement.

With all my noise, my visibility, my loud feet, I was the one who caught fish. And not in any of the manners, styles, or techniques he insisted I use. And not jerking them as hard as he instructed either. I felt an inner glee.

As we left, LaRue put my two northern pike on lines and pulled them, thrashing, through the water alongside the boat. "Aren't you supposed to kill them first?" I asked. I felt squeamish and sorry for the fish as they struggled to be free.

"This keeps them fresh."

I didn't like it. They wanted to live. When finally we stopped just short of the path to Bush's, he said, "Come over here," and placed them on rocks and cut the skin off them while they were still alive, not killing them, not removing their organs.

"Kill them!" I insisted.

"They're too hard to kill." He was irritated. "They don't feel anything. They don't have nervous systems. What, do you have a Bambi complex or something?"

"Then how can they feel your presence? Kill them," I insisted. He was a poor excuse for an Indian.

Inside myself, I knew different things about fish, and I hadn't even lived among other natives. I knew it from my heart. He offended the spirits of fish, I know this now, inside and out. And not long after the killing of the fish, a storm moved in suddenly, a dark cloud running in from the horizon, looming over us all at once. A wind came up, then pelting rain, half-ice, and as we headed toward the house, I felt the electric surge of lightning through my body, my hair rising up, a jolt in the spine.

"Shit! That was a close call!" LaRue said. "Hurry!"

I knew the lightning sought him out. I moved away from him. Of course, he would say it was just coincidence.

Another bolt touched down.

When we reached the house, Bush was at the door, worried about me. I could see that she did not want to invite LaRue in, but due to the storm, she had no choice.

After he left, I told her about the fish. She said there are consequences to human sins. "Some say Wolverine is a human gone wild," Bush said. "That's how it knows to hide out and escape capture. They know how to walk in the prints of other animals, especially those of men, like a shadow following them. That's how Wolverine watches to see how humans treat the animals. And you never know where Wolverine is. He could be in the bushes outside your house. You would never see him. He's a dark animal, large-jawed, with strong teeth and a terrible smell. A person must be careful what they say about the animals. They have another kind of listening. They can even hear your thoughts.

"There are proper ways of approaching animals and fish," Bush said. "Just as there are proper ways to approach a woman." She was putting together a beaver as she said this. She fed it a pinch of ground bark. "LaRue knows neither of these." She worked slowly.

I have never forgotten how LaRue left the fish on a slab of stone, without skin or flesh. They were still alive, gill slits moving. Just a reflex, LaRue said. I hated him. I was certain Wolverine had trailed LaRue's big feet, gone to meet him in a wide circle, to take away his luck and good fortune, both of which were already greatly diminished. I vowed I would never fish again. But he'd been partly right, I think now. About what the fish knew or heard.

• • •

THERE WERE TIMES when I felt strangely comforted by Bush's words, by being on the island where I could see anything and everything coming toward us from all directions across water, could smell chimney smoke from a fire I had made myself. On those days there was a kind of peace. But at other times, even on warm days, I felt a chill. At those times, even during the most ordinary moments, there was a wariness in me—I kept an eye out for Wolverine or other furtive creatures. I would occupy myself by straightening up my room and cleaning my comb and brush, looking at the amber, and at my own face in the tiny smudged mirror that I kept inside my purse. It was the only mirror in the house and sometimes I looked at myself in moonlight, in private. I noticed I had sad eyes, and made a mental note to look more cheerful. I tried to imagine what I'd look like without scars.

One day I dropped the mirror and it broke into many pieces. For a while I kept these, looking at only parts of my face at a time. Then I had no choice but to imagine myself, along with the parts and fragments of stories, as if it all was part of a great brokenness moving, trying to move, toward wholeness—a leg, an arm, a putting together, the way Bush put together the animal bones.

Finally, I gave up on the pieces of mirror. I gave up on all surfaces, even the taut skin of water. I knew what it held, what it could hold. As for people, I began to read their eyes to see what kind of souls they had. To look deeper. Bush, for example, had a soul strong as hardwood, and she was loved by the land. Nature loved her. Frenchie was a spirit sad and masked.

I began to see inside water, until one day my vision shifted and I could even see the fish on the bottom, as if I was a heron, standing in the shallows with a sharp, hungry eye.

I did fish again, after all, in the canoe with Bush, finding the fish with my eyes.

"How do you do that?" Bush wanted to know.

I was proud of my new talent. "I just look," I said.

We treated the fish well. We respected their lives and their deaths. We put them out of their pain as soon as they were caught.

I was the only one I knew of who could see inside water. No one else could do this, not even Bush. She approved of my gift. She said

I could see to the bottom of things. She was good at fishing, but I was the lucky one.

ONE NIGHT I dreamed of a woman in a white-walled cave sewing together pieces of humans, an arm to a trunk, a foot to a leg.

When I told her this, Bush said, "Wouldn't it be wonderful if we could piece together a new human, a new kind of woman and man? Yes, we should make some new ones. Start with bones, put a little meat on them, skin, and set them to breathing. We'd do it right this time. They'd be love-filled, the way we were meant to be all along."

I thought about how things on the island were all in parts like my mirror. Even the land there was broken. Perhaps that is what I went there to do, to put together all the pieces of history, of my life, and my mother's, to make something whole.

ONE NIGHT I heard music coming from the island, as if the land itself were singing. It was an eerie sound, like wind blowing through a flute. It was the first time I'd heard the organ pipes behind Bush's house. The pipes were not far from the ruins of the older house, and not far from the shed which stored the animal pelts Bush had taken from trespassers years back.

The immigrants had believed wilderness was full of demons, and that only their church and their god could drive the demons away. They feared the voices of animals singing at night. They had forgotten wild. It was gone already from their world, a world according to Dora-Rouge that, having lost wilderness, no longer had the power to create itself anew.

Bush called them the reverse people. Backward. Even now they destroyed all that could save them, the plants, the water. And Dora-Rouge said, "They were the ones who invented hell."

For us, hell was cleared forests and killed animals. But for them, hell was this world in all its plentitude. That's why they cleared space to build a church on the mainland and sent for the pipe organ, as if a church would transform this world into a place with title and gold.

At the time the organ pipes were being carried to Adam's Rib there had been a massacre. For the first time native people had declared war on the newcomers. This was the result of a misunderstanding. Only one year before, to the south, cannons and guns had been carried into the interior, and now the poor tribes, already diminished and desperate from disease and starvation, believed that a shipment of stovepipes was new weapons. The uprising that followed, created by fear, left two hundred settlers dead. When word of this carried, the bishop ordered all of the organ pipes to be hidden on an island out in the lake so no one would see them and misinterpret their meaning. The pipes were left on Fur Island amid old beaver teeth, broken pots, piles of fish bone, the bones of swans, and pieces of copper.

The men who unloaded them thought it was god who had directed them to the copper. He must have wanted them to find it, to have it, they reasoned, or he wouldn't have arranged this war against the settlers.

We sat at the window, in the last light of autumn.

"An old man on one of the islands tricked the men who were after copper," Bush said. "They came to him and asked if he knew where it could be found. 'Over there, on a far island,' said the old man. He made a map and pointed them toward the west. 'You have to cross the deepest lake,' he told them. 'If you go right away, you can miss the ice. If you wait, it will all be covered by snow. Then you will have to wait for spring thaw.'

"All night they were busy. They packed dried fish and flour. They packed lanterns and tools and at daybreak they set out on their journey, following the map that would lead them into the inland waterways and to islands.

In that way, the old man rid his people of the outsiders who dreamed of wealth, those who wanted to turn copper into gold, who built castles of ice and watched the little bit of light dance across them as they thawed and once again became water.

"Keep these tricks in mind. Someday you may need them," Bush said.

I THINK sometimes of the colors of the many worlds. The colors of the four directions. For us those colors were red, black, white, and yellow. Fur Island was the golden world, I came to think, the world of yellow light, pale copper, sun, and corn.

The corn that grew there grew in no other place. They were small plants, with tiny cobs and sweet yellow and milky-white kernels. It was the oldest corn on earth, having originated in South America centuries ago. It had been given to one of the Fat-Eaters of the north when they had navigated their way around the tip of the southern world in one of the many unacknowledged journeys Indians made before the advent of Columbus. It was the same journey, according to Dora-Rouge, that brought the frog in amber to the north. Corn and amber alike were passed down from generation to generation.

Although the Fat-Eaters, my ancestors, ate mostly meat and fat, Dora-Rouge, as a girl, became one of the keepers of the corn. The kernels were preserved in large dry leaves, the likes of which no one in the north had ever seen. Always they were watched over carefully. In the past they were stored in a cool dry hole beneath encampment tents the people used as they followed animals and fish. After the Fat-Eaters were confined by the government, the corn was hidden and protected beneath the dark floorboards of their houses, in little clay holes that were dug out in permafrost and insulated. Everyone thought there might come a day when the lives of the people would depend on corn.

One day, Dora-Rouge had given Bush a little handful of the corn mothers and said, "If anyone can grow these, it is you."

Bush worked hard for results. Even though the growing season was only ninety-four days, she grew graceful, tall plants. They grew rapidly in Fur Island's black soil. She was a slow, careful gardener, happy when she worked. Through the labor of her hands, ripening pumpkins hung from trees, tomatoes grew, staked up and tall, and tender squash spread along the ground.

Whenever I helped Bush in the garden, removing the last corn from the stalks, I walked between the rows and listened to the rustling sounds of the plants. They were extremely sweet, those little ears of corn the island yielded, as if the inner milk of the land, the healing milk the bishop had dynamited, expressed itself through the plants.

And from Bush, I also learned water. A little at a time. I learned the crossing to the mainland, the ways and distances to the other islands where we went to gather wood. Little by little I learned to paddle and steer. I learned the route well, so it wasn't long before I knew the shortest distance from the island to the hook of mainland, knew where the warm spot was and how to circle around it. I hardly noticed how I grew strong, my hands rough, my arms filled out. It happened gradually. I don't know how it is that people change, or what is required, or how it moves. I know only what it feels like to change; it's in the body, in the stomach, in the heart. They ache and then they open. I felt it then; Dora-Rouge said it happens all our lives. She said that we are cocoons who consume our own bodies and at death we fly away transformed and beautiful.

ONE SUNDAY, Bush and I filled the canoe with corn, pumpkins, and squash to deliver to the mainland. Bush pulled it out into the water, sat down in it quickly, and waited for me. She always wore a dress for canoeing. It was easier. I saw the logic of it, too, after a time. No wet pant legs. Nothing to bind. We could better form ourselves to the boat. And Bush wore her shoes on a lace over her shoulders, so in case we capsized, they would not be lost. On this Sunday, she wore the same green dress she'd worn the day I first arrived on the island. Then, I'd thought it homely, but now it seemed attractive.

Bush had learned to paddle from John Husk and some of the older men who now lived along the Hundred-Year-Old Road. It was an old style of paddling that, for some reason, white men could not duplicate. It was rare for anyone to use it at all in these days, especially a woman, no less a mixed-blood from the South. It had been used before, in a deeper past. It was a silent steering, a slow, steady stroke that pulled us easily forward. Bush found water easy. She knew its rhythm well, its movements and currents. In a canoe she could slip away, glide through and between shadows, be hidden in dim light. Water was her element, I thought. Me, I was more the element of air, light and invisible, moving from place to place.

As the canoe moved naturally, the way earth does in space, there was a certain light low across trees. I could smell and feel the change of season.

TO MY HAPPINESS, at Tinselman's store where we went for supplies, I met Tommy once again. I stood at the counter with Bush as she paid for a canned ham and a bag of flour. I could tell he liked me because he tried too hard to look at other things and he swallowed as if he were guilty, the way they do on television when Barbara Walters has their number.

And I knew I liked him, too, because when I first spotted him, all I did in the store was put my hands in my pockets and look at the cans of Pet Milk, the shelf with hooks, lines, and sinkers, all things whose names sounded something like love.

He tried to appear confident. "Let me show you around," he said.

I smiled and looked around the room as if he meant to show me the store.

"Go ahead," said Bush. She nudged me a little.

I looked at her. "You sure?"

"Just meet me back at Agnes' house." Her eyes were bright.

As we left she said, "Oh, Tommy. We've got food for you. Don't let me forget."

Tommy took me to the Hundred-Year-Old Road, where a tired-looking old woman was bent over a plot of garden, staking up pumpkins, and a man sat on the porch in an old couch.

"This is where I live," he said. "Come in."

I shook my head no. "I'll wait out here."

"Be right back." He ran inside. I watched the woman move slowly, a kerchief on her head. Her body leaned forward, pulled by gravity and weight. The houses were faded out by years of weather. A few broken windows were replaced with cardboard. I was uncomfortable there. I thought the traditionals, the old people, knew things about me. I was afraid of them, of the people who'd witnessed the near death of our world. I thought then that old wisdom and tradition did not have to pass through the human layers, the first filters of humor and business and love. But later, I found that just by walking along this road, I grew calmer.

The people along the Hundred-Year-Old Road lived at the edge of a once forest, now stump and branch. Farther in, beyond the stump forests, was a thick forest, the only thing that remained from the logging days of tough, bristling blond-headed men with large hands. What wasn't cut was saved, not by the loggers' satisfied needs, but by a war which required men. So these woods did not become matches or toothpicks or the whirling sands that blow where forests no longer stand.

When Tommy and I returned to Agnes', we sat in the truck and talked awhile. Then I said, "Do you want to come in? Just for a minute?" He got out of the truck, came to open my door. We walked up the path slowly in each other's company, the way couples do. Tommy had such dark eyes, crow wings could have been in them. Or night. That's what I kept thinking as I tried not to look at him.

The first thing Agnes said to me was, "You're filling out." She looked me up and down. And in the presence of Tommy, I turned red.

It hadn't been that long since I'd last seen Agnes and Dora-Rouge, but the first thing I noticed was that Agnes' clothes had grown too large for her. Dora-Rouge didn't look like herself either. The dentist had arrived the day before with her new teeth. They were overly white. Light caught on them like the teeth of Tony Curtis in *The Great Race*. She smiled widely at Tommy. She'd always called him a hunk of a man. She said, "The hunk is in our living room."

Wearing her new dentures, Dora-Rouge thought she looked young again. And it was a day when she felt close to Luther. So after greeting us, she just smiled radiantly as if no one else were present, just she and Luther. I wondered sometimes what the inside of her mind looked like, if it was furnished with old clothing, furniture from the past, the memory of forests and wolves and Luther's first kiss.

Husk, after greeting us, sat reading at the table. He didn't need a magnifying glass, like Agnes did. "Just what I thought," he said, absorbed in the magazine.

"What's that?" Agnes wanted to know.

"Now they're finding out that insects are intelligent."

Agnes' bones were more visible under the skin of her face. She was quiet, tired, and she'd not turned her garden yet that autumn, had already let it fall to the weeds that had been imported from France and Britain, weeds that she'd painstakingly pulled every year before, alien weeds that took over the land. She was colder, too, I could see. In addition to her open coat, she wore a heavy scarf about her neck.

Dora-Rouge said to me, later, in the privacy of her bedroom, that Agnes sometimes threw out a pan or silverware by accident and forgot where she was. Just that morning, according to Dora-Rouge, she had lost the teakettle, then found it in the bath.

Agnes herself admitted to this later that day as we drank Watkins Kool-Aid.

"It's probably just the change," Dora-Rouge said, as Agnes trimmed the older woman's whiskers. "You forget things that way."

"The way she forgets my age," Agnes said to me. "She forgets how old I am. And she's my mother, too."

"You can talk straight to me, Ag," Dora-Rouge complained. "I'm here in the flesh, you know."

I MADE many trips back to Adam's Rib before the freeze. Often I paddled alone to the mainland, sometimes taking corn for Agnes, or to visit with Dora-Rouge. At times I put lotion on her bony back. She said it reminded her of bear fat. And each time I returned, I saw Tommy. Always, I looked for him.

By then I was learning to swim, even in the cold lake, even though I was still afraid of its depths and sank like lead. When I told Bush I wanted to swim, she said, "Are you crazy?" But she, too, thought it was necessary for anyone living in the center of water the way we did.

She instructed me from shore, sitting on the black, craggy stones. "Come on in," I'd yell at her. "It's great."

"Are you crazy?" she'd say again. She hunched her shoulders and shivered. "Swim like your arms are long. Smoother. That's it."

It was hard for me to keep from sinking. I shivered.

"Pretend you're a turtle."

I gasped for air. I thought turtle. And that was the key. Suddenly I was clear, old and strong, a turtle, like the one on the island, moving through sea. My hands pushed water away. It was this I held to in my mind. I could swim. I imagined myself moving through oceans.

Then, at times, Bush was quiet. There were times she had a look on her face, nervous and edgy, and I knew she was thinking about the dams and the northern people and I knew, even then, that she would go north, travel whatever course was necessary; I knew where it would take her.

AUTUMNS were noisy events. Animals prepared for winter. The snowshoe hare lost its summer fur and went white, and the last of the birds ate what they could to prepare for flight. Chain saws cut wood. Everything turned red as fire. The inside of the world was rust, the slow fire of oxidation, as Husk called it. A patient fire that burned through metal, as with all the old ships rusting out there in the lake.

On Fur Island a person could feel and hear where the faraway and ancient began. As seasons changed, I thought I heard voices in the wind, the wind which returned there each night, the wind that lived on the island and sometimes talked to us through the organ pipes. I felt and heard the first voice of winter already singing, trying to insinuate itself into our bones. Even air seemed fire red, with its sharp chill against skin, and the leaves falling.

It was during this change of seasons that I began to see. To see that there were three women and myself, all of us on some kind of journey out from that narrowed circle of our history the way rays of light grow from the sun. Only a month earlier I knew none of these women, or even that they existed, and now our lives were bound together (in truth as they had been already) by blood and history, love and hate.

We busied ourselves with chores, Bush and I. Nights lengthened. By then I had learned to use the wedge and ax. My arms grew strong. It was a constant labor, preparing for winter. We still traveled the other islands to get wood, and the stack grew. I was surprised at how much we needed. With moss and caulk, Bush and I chinked holes around the windows. Fruits that grew on the island we dried and canned. Some of them, apricots, peaches, felt like the soft skin of Dora-Rouge. We filled jars with tomatoes. I stepped back to admire our work: the glass-contained red fruits of the island; to look at the woodpile, the golden and ash colors of bark, with rings that told

years of drought and flood. It was the first time I had ever seen my
own work before my eyes.

"WOLVERINE is a fierce mother, they say." Bush was running a
cord through the bones. While she spoke, her hands assembled the
skeleton of the small wolverine. From time to time she offered a
pinch of cornmeal and fat to the skinless, sharp-toothed jaw, feeding
its spirit. Things depended on this, on respect. The order of the
world did.

If I could watch Bush long enough, I thought, I would see the
meat and skin and fur return to the bones. I would see an animal
begin at a bony center and grow. The wolverine eyes would start to
shine. It would breathe. It would move. It would run into the shadows of brush. It would be an act of new creation. Like first woman,
first man, from clay.

People say that in the beginning was the word. But they have
forgotten the loneliness of God, the yearning for something that
shaped itself into the words, *Let there be.* Out of that loneliness,
light was conceived, water opened across a new world, and people
rose up from clay, there were dreamers of plants and deer. It was
this same desire in me, this same longing for creation, and Bush's
spare words were creation itself. I had been empty space, and now I
was finding a language, a story, to shape myself by. I had been
alone and now there were others. I was suspended there on the island of snails and mosses, snow and windstorms, and I was quiet
for days on end, but like Bush's wolverine bones, I was partaking of
sacred meal and being put back together.

By then, Bush spoke of my mother, the girl filled with ice. There
are things living in humans that bruise the sweet-bodied human
fruit, she said, things like what poisoned the hungry tribe of my ancestors. Rage and fear. Mortal wounding. She knew the wound and
how it was passed on, the infinite nature of wounding. But she had
not known before about the failures of love, the remote indifference
of a god, people only a shade away from evil, an atom away, a speck
of dust.

I drank swamp tea and listened. I took in my life. At night, as winter approached, there was the sound of the lake talking to the sky, re-

vealing some part of itself or what lay inside its blue-green light. The lake was recalling the memory of last year's ice, the jewelry lost in its waters, the fishermen who'd fallen through storms, and who lay inside it even now. It was a wet autumn and there were snails on darker rocks in the shade, and their shining paths that were journeys we couldn't know.

ONE DAY ON THE MAINLAND, Bush and I went to the home of LaRue, who so offended the fish. She stopped at the door before going in. Then she let the screen door slam. I heard the sound of animal paws scuttle away to hide. I stood just inside the door waiting for Bush to get the boxes of bones from LaRue. It was too cool in there, too dark. It was a frightening place to me, a place where muscles and flesh were boiled away from bones. Large beetles with iridescent backs were stored in small glass containers. LaRue paid Bush to assemble the bones for schools and museums. She was a woman who put things together. That was the reason for the turtle curing in sun.

They conducted business as I looked around. There were bear teeth, a pheasant with a red face. Curiosities, he called them. A stuffed bobcat with a cigar in its mouth.

After we left, I said to Bush, "This is terrible. What about selling shirts?" I looked at her. "I can help. I know how to sew."

It was true, I did, and I hated it. I amended my words. "Or I can cut and you can sew. Then you won't have to work with him."

"Except, when I put the bones together," Bush said, "I help the soul of the animal." I think she hated to sew, too. "When I put them together, I respect them," she said. "I feed them and consider their skills. I think of their intelligence. For instance, Wolverine is a thief. He stores food. He knows what men need and he takes it. He steals the flints of the people. I respect him for this. And he removes animals from traps and frees them if he is not hungry."

She leaned forward as she spoke. Whenever Bush talked about the animals, she took on their ways of moving. She became bright. I think she preferred them to people. I think she had the brilliant soul of an animal, that she lived somewhere between the human world and theirs.

Like me, Bush had trouble sleeping. Many nights I heard her pouring water, moving things into their places. She wore jeans and walked as if she had all the time in the world. She was slow that way and she liked to wander the island. One night, giving up on sleep, I went to the window. Out on the path of whitewashed stones, I saw Bush walking down to the lake.

She was haunted by what the two young men had said when they'd gone to Fur Island to tell her about the dams and river diversions. She dwelled on it. Sometimes, after a long silence, she'd say, as if we'd been talking about it, "Yes, I think I'll go up there."

Throughout autumn, she fell into their words, worrying about the people, the animals.

And there were other words. "You want to know more about your mother," Bush said on a chilly day when a new angle of slanting light above us was at the top of the trees. I waited. Like the others, she too searched for a beginning. My beginning was Hannah's beginning, one of broken lives, gone animals, trees felled and kindled. Our beginnings were intricately bound up in the history of the land. I already knew that in the nooks of America, the crannies of marble buildings, my story unfolded. This, I suppose, was the true house of my mother. The real place from which I originated was in the offices of social workers. Bush's anger was still strong about what had happened with Hannah, with me. It never diminished, that anger. The social workers were unable to do what they should have done. But what was there to fight, she said: a caseworker with an office full of abused and neglected children she'd picked up late at night, a locked file cabinet, lost papers, a hierarchy of administrators and secretaries? It was systems we ended up fighting. But it went even farther back than that, to houses of law with their unkept treaties, to the broken connections of people to the world and its many gods.

"Your mother was a door," Bush said. "Always closed. But sometimes I thought she was a window, instead, because through her I glimpsed scenes of suffering."

Even young, I understood this in a way. I understood already from what the women said that my mother was stairs with no destination. She was a burning house, feeding on the air of others. She had no more foundation, no struts, no beams. Always, a person would think she was one step away from collapsing. But she remained standing.

We lived in the dark blue house at Old Fish Hook, Agnes and I, when your mother washed up with nothing but a dirty comb and the clothes she wore on her back. She walked out of the dark, cold water. Agnes saw her first. She said, "My God, it's Harold's daughter."

We carried her to the house. I was afraid she'd stop breathing. She didn't make a sound. She was white with shock.

"She even has that smell," said Agnes.

It looked like she was born of the storm. And she was so cold. I said to her, "Let me dry your clothing." I gave her some fresh things, but she would not undress. A day or so later, Agnes went out and bought her new clothing, thinking that would help, but Hannah still wore the men's pants and large shirt.

There was something not right with her. I couldn't put my finger on it. But I told myself it was the circumstances, the cold water, the wreck, the dark clouds and waves. "Where do you think she came from?" I asked.

Agnes said there's one place she comes from for sure, the body of Loretta, because she had that smell of bitter almonds and apple seeds. I smelled it, too. And she had the same red hair and dark skin.

I felt for her; she was half Harold. Agnes' granddaughter by blood. You could tell just by looking. And so we took her in.

Her fingernails were broken, some to the quick. Maybe she'd clawed her way onto a log. Maybe that was how she escaped the water. She couldn't have survived the storm on her own. Or maybe, Agnes said, there'd been some other kind of help. A spirit or something. Me, I didn't believe those superstitious things.

One day Mrs. Illinois came by to tell me Hannah'd gone into her house and stolen her dark gray shawl. I had seen that shawl, I said to Mrs. Illinois. I remembered it.

Later, when I asked Hannah, "Where is the shawl?" she looked right at me and said she hadn't taken it. I could almost believe her, even though I'd seen her wrapped up in it. But her look of honesty made me doubt my own eyes.

*Other people, too, found her in their houses or at their clotheslines.
And she wore one thing over another, a stolen green skirt over the
large men's pants we found her inside, a brown dress on top of that.
Even when it was hot. By then, even though she denied it, I knew she
was the thief. I posted a note at Tinselman's store saying I would replace whatever she took. People signed their names and the item she'd
taken—Frenchie: cardigan sweater with blue pearl buttons; Wiley:
work shirt. I think now that clothes were the only protection she had,
the only skin between her and all the rest.*

*I watched her walking about in all that clothing, looking larger
than she was, looking like a ragpicker and an old, broken woman instead of the girl she was. Her eyes had no trust, not in anything or
anyone. They were dark and flat. No light. It was the expression the
tortured wear. Even now I study their faces. Their faces are like Hannah's face. Even now I look for a clue. The darkness beneath their
eyes. As if it would explain things people do to one another.*

*The old people said it was soul loss, an old sickness. I tried to put
their words out of my mind because no one knew the antidote for such
disease. But still I could not rid myself of their words. I started to think,
if there was soul loss, where would it go? Where would a soul wander?
How could I get it back? There must be a way, was what I thought.*

*We were afraid of her. I didn't know why, exactly. I'd always been
brave. I was never afraid of anything, not dark or ice. I'd hunted deep
forests in the dark of night and I was stranded once on an open ledge of
ice, peering down into its blue fracture, and even then I was not
afraid; I knew I'd find a way to live. But with her, even the corners of
the house were dark. They seemed to be in pain. You could feel it. You
could almost see it. There are those even now who say it was evil. They
still call it a bad spirit, a heart of ice. But I didn't want to believe
them, because once I did, I knew nothing could be trusted, not water,
not children, not even love, and I believed in the power of love. But
even that would fail us.*

*From the very beginning she didn't sleep. She paced at night. Like
she was trapped, or something was trapped in her. Not insomnia or
tossing and turning in bed, you understand. She didn't sleep at all. I'd
hear her feet. They sounded so busy. I thought she'd exhaust herself.
Many times the covers were not pulled back and the bed had not been*

touched. Other nights when I'd look in the room, she appeared to sleep, lying at peace, her breathing relaxed and regular, but the minute I walked away, her feet again creaked the floorboards.

Sometimes she sat in a corner and became still. She became a part of the wall itself, nearly invisible. The old people used to say that animals in danger from men could shrink themselves, go off into a cave or lake or beneath a stone where they would hide until the world was safe again. I think it was like that. Maybe she waited for the world to be safe. She was a body under siege, a battleground. But she herself never emerged. The others, with their many voices and ways, were larger than she was. She was no longer there.

One day the smell was so bad that I was determined to give her a bath if I had to hold her down and wash her myself. The acid odor was deep in the house by then, in the walls and floors. I'd been patient enough. I heated water on the stove. I filled the metal tub and called her over. Two more kettles of water were heating on the stove to keep her warm. I stood in the kitchen beside the tub. "You have to take a bath," I said. "Take off your clothes."

She must have sensed my determination. She cowered at first, but one by one, to my surprise, she took off the layers. I watched her from the corner of my eye while I grated soap. Fels Naptha and Lifebuoy. There were chiggers that year. I tried not to watch her, I felt so bad for her. I didn't want to be one of her abusers. I got her a cloth. I looked away. I didn't want to frighten her. I cleaned the countertop again as if it needed it. But she did not fight, not this time. She removed the pants while I wiped the table. She came down to a swimsuit, much too large. But when I saw her in her small, bare nakedness, I stopped and stared. Beneath all the layers of clothes, her skin was a garment of scars. There were burns and incisions. Like someone had written on her. The signatures of torturers, I call them now. I was overcome. I cried. She looked at me like I was a fool, my tears a sign of weakness. And farther in, I knew, there were violations and invasions of other kinds. What, I could only guess.

I held up first one of her arms, then another. I washed her back and poured water over her. She sat still. She waited for me to hurt her.

Back when the lii plants were plentiful, Dora-Rouge used to make a sleeping medicine. It was a precious, rare medicine because so many *of the plants had disappeared with the felled trees. That night I gave her some of it, thinking if she would just sleep, if only she would sleep. But even then she didn't and soon I realized that They came awake at night, those who'd hurt her. Them. Those who walked the floor in her skin.*

Some people believe the northern lights steal people and carry them up into the sky. Maybe that was where she went long ago. That's what some people said. By then that was what I hoped. I hated to think of her still in that abused body. I hoped she'd been taken up in the hands of sun.

Everyone had a name for what was wrong. Dora-Rouge said it was memory and I think she was the closest. After a time, I thought, yes, it was what could not be forgotten, the shadows of men who'd hurt Loretta, the shadows of the killers of children. What lived in her wears the skin of children. That's what I thought. It walks with us, inside those we know.

As I looked at her from scar to scar that day, I could feel the edges of her. I touched the scars on her back and I could feel the hands of the others. They had ice-cold fingers. They had hearts of ice. Just like the old people said.

Sometimes I could hear the voices that were not hers. They'd murmur at my ear. Or I'd feel the wings of something brush by me. The priest said she was a miracle in reverse. It was out of his domain, he said, when I took her there. "Whose domain is it?" I wanted to know, but he didn't answer.

Some people even thought the storm originated with her, that she'd stepped out of it just like she was passing through a cloud.

One day in a rare moment of speaking, she told me a hand lived inside her. It was fingers, fist. At night it crept out of its home, her body, and tried to molest her, to strangle her. At first I thought her words were just part of the sickness. I didn't pay them much mind. But one day I came in from shoveling snow and when I walked in the door something pushed me back. It's true. I know you must doubt this. So did I. But it nearly knocked me over and it wasn't her. She was in the far corner, her back against the wall. What struck me was powerful and large, and it was cold. It felt solid but I saw nothing. My dog was alive then, barking at what I couldn't see.

The religious people would never go near her. She tested their faith and next to her, their faith failed. She molested one of their children. This was what she'd learned, you know, and whenever she walked by a person, they felt what lived in her. They felt the world that was ruined and would never be whole again.

So we went to see Old Man on the Hundred-Year-Old Road. She still hadn't slept. I still heard the walking sounds at night, the way an animal or man might sound in a room, closed in, in a jail.

No one except me would stay in a room with her. I was the most brave. I was willing to live with her, or them, whatever it was. To help her. And Old Man, too, was not afraid.

Whenever you go to see Old Man, there is silence first. Maybe you take him cloth or tobacco or food. Then, maybe you eat. After that you say what you want. But he knew why we had come. He picked up a feather as soon as we entered. He accepted no gift. He offered no food. He went right next to her. "She is the house," is what he said. He waved the feather. "She is the meeting place."

I didn't know what he meant at first. But I saw it in time, her life going backward to where time and history and genocide gather and move like a cloud above the spilled oceans of blood. That little girl's body was the place where all this met.

"They used to call back lost or stolen souls," Old Man said. "They beckoned spirits out from an innocent body." What was needed was a ceremony, he said, the words of which were so beautiful that they called birds out of the sky, but the song itself would break the singer's life. No one still alive was strong enough to sing it. Not him, he said. Because things had so changed. Not any of the old men or women. And there was a word for what was wrong with her, he said, but no one would say it. They were afraid it would hear its name and come to them.

Still, she had such perfect fingers and toes, a delicate face. All I could think was that she was the sum total of ledger books and laws. Some of her ancestors walked out of death, out of a massacre. Some of them came from the long trail of dying, people sent from their world, and she was also the child of those starving and poisoned people on Elk Island.

"I can smell it," Old Man said. "I can see them. All of them. She is the house, the meeting place."

S E V E N

I AM THINKING of my past. There are powerful songs. Husk, who saw everything in terms of science, told me once how metal bridges were taken down, collapsed by the song of wind, a certain tone, a certain pitch of wind. If wind spoke across a bridge just right, he said, the bridge would fall. But there were songs with other strengths. People say this and it is true. According to John Husk, Bush knew a song that broke down other kinds of bridges. It had to do with the wrong beings walking down from sky or across water. Or maybe rising up from the ground. Through her words, through her singing, something was taken apart. Bush learned these songs, he said, not because she wanted to, but because she had to keep some things from being put together again. Because the beings in Hannah came from other places. She had to take out the bridges between bad spirits and people, to close bridges between those places and here. And she sang to keep the spirit bridges closed, to keep them from coming back together again. She knew the pathway, he said.

At the time I didn't know what he meant by this or what lived behind the words, but now I've seen that bridge and it wasn't so unlike the ones that were being built up north, with muddy, earth-moving water flowing beneath them, bridges that should not have been there. Animals in the path of it were killed, people's lives displaced, plants and lives gone forever to make way.

"Last night a man hurt me," your mother said one day. No one had come toward us that winter. I would have seen if they had.

"He came in here," she said. "See, my pants are all stretched out."

I looked. It was true, her pants were stretched, torn at the seam.

Another day she said, "A ghost unbuttoned my dress." It was true. Her dress was open, and she, Hannah, had a look of terror on her face.

"Did you see that man come in here? He was carrying my head." Hannah said this.

She broke the window. I saw her do it. And she said she didn't, even though I stood right there. "I saw it with my eyes," I told her.

"No, I didn't."

I almost believed her. I doubted my own mind, my eyes. It took a while before I knew she told the truth. That there was a man come in the night, a ghost. Anyway, it was the truth to her. Because of the others inside her. They were the ones who had done what she denied. They were the ones who were dangerous.

Old Man said you could sing the soul back if you knew the old song. All I could figure how to do was to sing myself into her. I thought, if all this could dwell in her, maybe I, too, could go inside. To understand them, the ones who lived in her, to coax them out, to cajole them into stillness and rest. I wanted to know where she had gone. I thought there must be a way to call lost souls back.

And so I did it. I prepared myself. I slept outdoors on the sacred ground. I sang. I fasted. And one day a part of me stepped inside the girl and looked around. I saw the hand she spoke of, heard the voices in languages neither of us knew. I could see how dangerous it was. An inescapable place with no map for it. Inside were the ruins of humans. Burned children were in there, as well as fire. It pulled me toward it, like gravity, like dust to earth and whatever it was, I had to call on all my strength to get away.

• • •

WHILE THE BIRDS MIGRATED SOUTH, noisy and swift, we prepared for the trout run. In the dimming light of fall we lifted nets in the clear water of the stream. The fish were thick. The water seemed full of them, turning crowded and wild, shining in the light of afternoon. They were thick, the flashing sides of them, the white stomachs, as if the waters themselves were thrashing. It was dark when we returned home along the white stones of the path, a storm brewing out in the other world.

One day I went to Adam's Rib to purchase some caulk and plastic to place over the windows.

"Let me see you," said Agnes. "You are getting busty. Are you gaining weight? It's about time."

But Dora-Rouge said, "It's my time to die. I need to go back home to the Fat-Eaters. You can come, Angel. Your mother is there." And then she drifted off. "There are things Bush won't tell you about your mother."

"Won't tell me?"

"Bush will never tell you about the killing of the dog. She's never talked of it yet."

This was all she said. But she was wrong about Bush. She did tell me. She told me on a day when the last rain fell, before water froze, before the clouds transformed themselves into six-sided flakes with a fleck of solar dust at each one's center.

One day she killed the dog. I heard him yelp. I ran out the door to see where he was and he lay still and bent. She kicked him. There were needles in his mouth and nose and ears, and he'd been cut, the red blood on the fur, matted, one foot cut off. He died panting, his tongue hanging out of his mouth.

It haunts me. All this time I wanted that out of my mind. I can't bear to think of it.

That's how dangerous she was. That's what I want you to know. I loved the dog. I loved you. But we were all afraid of the naked ice inside her. We didn't want to send her away because it was not her fault. At least we thought that. But it wasn't long, anyway, until she drifted away, first to the north, where she lives now, then to Oklahoma. We were grateful she was gone.

And then there was you. When she returned, she was pregnant with you. Then we needed to keep her here. We knew she would kill you. You, yourself, seemed to know what you were born to; I heard you cry one time when you were not even in the house. Agnes heard it, too, or I wouldn't have believed my own ears.

She would kill you. Husk said that was a law of probability. He also said that a glacier gives off what it can't absorb, blue light and beauty, and that you were the light given off by your mother.

ON THE ISLAND THAT YEAR, I thought if it was true that there's no true north, no still center, no steady magnetic pole, how could I believe anything I'd learned before? Even land moves. So in a swampy place where peat fires burn for years with the power of rising gas, I learned to doubt things I'd previously learned. And so, too, I began to believe things, like the stories Bush told, things I would not have listened to months before.

I would one day understand my mother. I would one day take in the fact that we were those who walked out of bullets and hunger, and even that walking was something miraculous. Even now I think of it. How the wind still sweeps us up in it. Even now there are places where currents meet and where people are turned to ice. I understood it first like this: the mouth of a river goes one way; my mother was the opposite. Things and people fell into her like into the eye of a storm, and they were destroyed. Like the black hole Husk had described to me. I understood things then in the manner of Husk's telling. Except for how I emerged from Hannah and how there are rages and wounds so large, love is swallowed by them and is itself changed, the lover taken in and destroyed.

AUTUMN MOVED BACK and made way for winter. A wind began to blow the leaves and they swirled upward and were gone. The windows creaked. Where did the wind gather its strength, I wondered. That was what I wanted to know so I could go there.

Husk brought us Agnes' old treadle sewing machine that had sat beside the cot. It had gold leaves painted and engraved on it, and a bunch of silver grapes. It was the first time I'd seen it dust-free and now I noticed it was a lovely machine, dark cherry. Bush showed me the technique for sewing ribbons, and how to finish a sleeve. We borrowed another, perfume-scented sewing machine from Frenchie. This one was electric and Bush used it only when the generator was on, doing hand hemming at other times.

I sat for hours, aching, and moved my legs rhythmically. It was a good idea at first, this shirt business. But when the first needle broke, I stood up and paced with frustration. It was just the beginning. Thread broke if the machine wasn't threaded perfectly. Once, the oil leaked onto a precious, nearly finished shirt. Sometimes the feeder wouldn't move. Then I would cuss under my breath and go outside to look at the lake. Everything that could go wrong, did. The bobbin was not wound right and I'd rip out a seam, start over. I hated to sew. But I did it over and over and soon I grew patient with it. From school, I remembered Psyche and how she had to separate a hill of grain one grain at a time. Perhaps I was separating grain.

Perhaps I was remaking myself. As with the machine, I tried to put words to things over and over, in the way Bush put together the skeletons. They would one day look like a living animal, with eyes of glass, clean fur. But for them, something was missing, always. The spirit was gone. They would never breathe. For me, it would be different. One day I would wake up and know that everything had started to change, that I was no longer empty space, that I had become full, or was growing toward it. It would start with a small, warm circle inside my stomach. It was longing. It was sadness. It was moments of joy. It was new dreams I blamed on Dora-Rouge's potion for sleeplessness. It was everything that entered through my eyes, the northern lights that were bright and gauzy clothing on night's skin of darkness. It was moose meat given by the hunters, and the fish Bush caught, and Husk with his theories.

A wind began to blow, a storm from far off. Then rain fell, a hint of winter. And on land, the air filled with ice crystals and the odor of smoke. Grasses became stiff, earth solid. My footprints in mud were iced over. There was the sound of a distant wolf.

The lake froze, moved slightly, and with the sound of broken glass, re-formed itself.

And what I pieced together was more than shirts or dresses,

sleeves and collars. From my many grandmothers, I learned how I came from a circle of courageous women and strong men who had walls pulled down straight in front of them until the circle closed, the way rabbits are hunted in a narrowing circle, but some lived, some survived this narrowing circle of life.

E I G H T

IN THE NORTH, people measured their lives by the winters and kept account of what happened in each one. As with what I called the "House of No," some winters were remembered by what wasn't there. There was the winter of no wolves, the winter of no ptarmigan, the time of no children. There were winters, too, of terrible presences, the appearance of influenza, the winter of frozen rain that covered snow in a hard shell of ice so that it broke the legs of deer and moose and left the snow red with their bleeding. This was the winter Frenchie's horse fell and froze into the ice while it was still alive, melting the ice with its warmth as it sank deeper. It was the time of shadows, they said. A woman was found inside a block of clear ice that year. And certain currents of air met near the water and turned a man to ice.

And I belonged to that winter. I was born one February inside a snow so deep it collapsed the roofs of houses. I crossed infinity to come to life through an angry, screaming woman, as if I arrived from the place where storms were created, a world where bad medicine was made from the bodies of women and men, the milk of deer, the loss of land. I arrived in the place where traders had passed with sleds of dead, frozen animals.

According to Bush, I was born in a house of snow.

It was a winter when snow fell so thick in trees it crowded out what light was left and the white men, in such darkness, believed it was a total eclipse.

Roofs collapsed under winter's weight. Trees swayed and groaned. They complained of so much heaviness that even their voices were weighed down. And all the houses, too, were covered with mounds of snow that shifted in the wind. And the midwife said she heard you crying when you were still inside your mother.

When you left forever the waters of your mother that night, that early morning, cold went so deep the trees outside your birthing place shattered from inside themselves and flew apart. The explosions of heartwood sounded like gunshots. Bark flew in all directions across the snow, hitting a window, hitting a wall. Remembering history, the people dropped and hid themselves on cold floors. Except your mother, who was not threatened by anything as simple as gunfire.

The midwife was Ruby Shawl, a small, square woman with a red headscarf, perfect hands, and a peaceful face. She presided over the passages of people into both life and death. And she was miserable when those were the same person. She hated to be at both ends of the same life. She went to the one-room house your mother shared with a trapper, a man who took in troubled young girls on the pretext of helping them. Hannah was one of his girls, but he was not there the day you were born. He had gone out to check his snares and follow his trapline to the north. For trappers, February was a busy time; furs were at their thickest.

When she cut the birth cord that connected you to your mother, Mrs. Shawl didn't say what she said to the other mothers at every birth. She didn't tell Hannah, "Say good-bye to your baby." She watched Hannah closely, as if she knew that the good-bye would be permanent, she told me later, as if she knew why.

The sky was clear for a few moments that first night and Mrs. Shawl could see by the light of snow how heavy the snow was, the trees bent under the weight of it. Looking up, she told me, she saw the roof begin to bulge inward, but she was afraid to go out and clean it off. She did not want to leave you alone with Hannah. She feared you were in danger. She felt what was to come.

She avoided sleep the first days of your life, listening to the trees creak with the weight of snow, guarding you, fearing to let dreams take her away from the dark, cold room and the fiercely awake woman who gave birth to you. She melted buckets of snow but each bucket yielded only small amounts of water. Ruby Shawl had children at home, and a husband, but she stayed on with Hannah, hoping the bitter weather would let up. She was sure help would come, but no one appeared. She could see the snow-covered road, but no one walked it.

You were a good child, and didn't fuss, she said. The firewood was mostly gone and there were only a few staples of rice and dried milk. Hannah's breasts were dry. Like her mind and heart, her body had nothing to offer. It had already abandoned you.

The snow was tireless and without end. One day the roof sagged so much that it seemed sure to collapse; mice scratched about in corners and inside walls.

After waiting for Hannah to sleep, Mrs. Shawl finally, in that terrible freeze, had no choice; she pulled on her boots, bundled herself in her coat and red scarf, salted the ice-covered steps and went silently outside to shovel snow off the roof. I can see her in my mind's eye, her round belly, her breath stopped before her face, the red clothing she always wore. The snow was so deep that she climbed it and stepped onto the roof with ease. She worked quickly. In such cold, there is always too little time.

As she returned, winded, she heard Hannah fumble at the lock. When she tried the door, it was latched from inside. "Let me in!" she called. She rattled the door, hit it. Steam from her breath froze, surrounding her in something like a halo. She went around the house and tapped the little windows. "Hannah! Open the door." The windows were frozen over with breathing and steam from within. She could see nothing through them, and she was wasting precious time in the terrible, ungodly cold. And so she had no choice but to find her way through the bitter wind to where I lived at Old Fish Hook, as it was called then. Hannah, she thought, would listen to me.

It wasn't quite a mile walk, but she had no snowshoes and now and then she fell through the snow up to her waist. There were trails the wind had made, where a shining crust had formed on the snow, and she tried to walk on these trails.

Tree limbs had broken along the way and Ruby Shawl moved several of the fallen branches from what she thought was the path. By then a cutting storm of sleet slanted down, the kind you can hear as it hits the snow. Under different conditions the sleet might have been a good sign because it meant the sky was warming; but in fact it only made the journey more treacherous. She hurried along. There was the light of winter, its sheen across the white and frozen world. It was beautiful, it always is, but there was no comfort in it; it was a beauty like Hannah's, dangerous, and it made the whole weight of winter fall at the back of Ruby Shawl.

I'd been at work, chipping ice from inside the door. I held a dark blue umbrella up against the sleet. I chipped ice with only one hand. In such cold, the sounds were sharp and brittle, hollow winter sounds. At first I didn't see Mrs. Shawl. When I looked up, I saw that Ruby's scarf had frozen to her hair. She was staggering, exhausted. Her face was burning, her lips looked pale. I went to her at once. I slipped my hand inside the older woman's bent arm, took her through the door, and sat her down in front of the stove. That kind of ice and cold steals a woman's mind and voice, so Mrs. Shawl said nothing as I heated coffee and wrapped a warm blanket around her. The umbrella sat on the floor beside her, frozen open. Outside, a chill wind roared through the trees. It rattled frozen limbs.

As soon as the midwife sipped the coffee, and took her voice back from the cold, she said, "You need to come with me, and we should hurry." She stood up, ready to go.

I slipped on my rubber boots. I put on my black coat. I was afraid for you.

Along the way a tree branch broke and crashed in front of us. Neither of us spoke. We went around the fallen branch and hurried along, half-running, both of us certain you would be hurt. I fell on a strip of glare ice along the way and bruised my thigh. The snow began to fall again. We wasted no time.

When we arrived at the trapper's house, the door was still locked. "It's Bush," I said. I hit the door with my fist. "It's Bush. Let me in."

At once, the door opened, but there were no sounds of footsteps along the wooden, settled floor. Hannah was not the one who opened it, even though no others were there to be seen. Inside, there was little warmth. There was only a thin, spare fire in the stove, and the firewood was gone. Hannah sat in a rocking chair across the room, her back to the door. "She's not my baby," she said. "My baby died at birth."

You were nowhere in sight. The firewood was gone.

I pretended to sip from a cup of cold coffee. The room was so chilled, our breaths were like ghosts speaking themselves into existence right in front of our faces.

Rocking in the chair, Hannah looked like a child. The midwife looked at me. Knowing Hannah, I was careful to sound calm. By then, I had learned how to speak with her. "Where is the baby?" I asked, surprised at how calm I sounded. I was quiet and slow, trying not to upset her, but all the while I looked for you, in the trash can, the closet, beneath the bed still spotted with birth blood.

"It's in none of those places." Hannah listened to me move across the room. She was smart. She could hear like an animal, stronger and better than other people, more like a lynx or wolf.

The midwife was crying. "It's my fault," she cried. "I knew better than to leave her." It crossed her mind, she said later, that a child born to such a woman might have been better off dying.

"Keep it away from me. It's not mine," said Hannah, meaning you, the baby. She held a lock of her red hair. The rest of it was beside the bed, a pile of fire cut through by scissors.

An empty black kettle sat on the stove smoking over a dwindling flame. I took it off the fire and looked inside. I was afraid that I would find you there.

But you were not in the kettle. You weren't in the oven, either. And you weren't smothered beneath a pillow. I went outside, glancing back at windows that were frozen over with all the breathings. There were no tracks outside. Nothing human could survive such cold, I was certain, but I began walking a circle, an ever-widening spiral across snow and ice, and there were no tracks to follow and you didn't cry out. You didn't even kick or wave your arms.

Maybe you were resigned to fate, to a birth delivered to ice. I found you tucked into the branches of a birch tree. You were still and blue and a thin layer of snow had fallen over your head and naked stomach, the

kind Indians call pollen snow because it meant more was coming, that
winter would continue. You were alert, alive, but silent and cold as ice.
I put you beneath my shirt, next to the warmth of my body, and you
searched for a breast. You searched out warmth. You wanted to live.
You were tiny, you were cold, and you wanted to live.

N I N E

IN WINTER, when living stood
still, it was easy to forget that seeds lived in the ground, dark and
preparing for spring. There was a fresh smell to winter, clean and
moist, and snow drifted over the turtle bones and whirled around us.
The other seasons might have been only imagined by need or desire,
because when winter occupies the land, it makes its camp everywhere. You cannot step through its territory without knowing that
what has fallen over the land has a stronger will than ours, and that
tragedy is sometimes held in both its hands.

That winter was no different. Joppa Ryan, Tommy's cousin at
Old Fish Hook, was killed in a freak accident when the jack he was
using to change a flat tire slipped on the ice and hit him. Then
Frenchie's visiting daughter, Helene, a woman I'd never met,
walked off drunk one night across the lake and disappeared. Her
footprints in a new layer of snow led to the Hungry Mouth, but no
one was courageous enough to go retrieve her body. None of us
wanted to risk being swallowed by the lake. It made me sad to think
of her, but the healing outpouring of tears comes slowly in winter,
if at all. Like everything else, like water stopped in the rivers, tears
wait for spring. Grief is forced to a halt. Frenchie, held in this grip
of winter, did not cry. She went pale and quiet beneath the rouge.
By then, I'd forgiven her for asking about my face.

Several times, Dora-Rouge said she should have been the one who died. She grew even more insistent about going home to die.

But if tears and human lives were stopped, the wolves were not. Their cries of raw nerve made up for the lack of human mourning. "Look," Bush said one day.

I went to the window where she stood and looked out.

"They do this every winter. They know the skins of their ancestors are stored in there."

A few of the wolves, not quite a whole pack, circled the shed that contained the furs and traps. They looked at the wood as if they could see or smell the trapping gear through the walls. It made them restless, their breathing visible as they paced. If we understood their language, their cries might tell us all that had happened on the island.

There were many voices of winter, not just the wolves and crows. There was the wind against out sheltering walls, the wind that sang across swirling snow. Never silent, the ice of the lake pushed against itself and cried out. It broke and healed, groaned and gave off green light. From a spot at the window I would think of all the things lost in Lake Grand—jewelry, wedding rings thrown in by hurt and estranged people, boats, fishermen from the storms, and now Helene.

Even silence was loud on Fur Island. There were soundless walkings. The quiet flying of owls. The absent voices of flown-south birds.

Sometimes, as we sewed, and the trees creaked or the gales of wind howled around us, Bush took a straight pin from beneath her teeth and in a quiet voice she spoke of my mother. Firelight moved across her face. "You see how powerless we are against the wind." As if to confirm something while cold crept under the door, Bush took a piece of cloth, got up, and filled the gap beneath it. She didn't have to tell me more to say, "Hannah was like that." By then I knew what she meant. Indifferent elements, and cold. She meant that a person can't blame the wind for how it blows and Hannah was like that. She wanted me to know that what possessed my mother was a force as real as wind, as strong as ice, as common as winter.

Occasionally we had the noise of a visitor. Now and then, Husk drove his enormous truck over the ice with groceries and heating oil and cans of gas for the generator and always with wood, our utmost necessity. He brought Archway cookies for me. At these times, after he stamped the snow from his feet, there would be talking and laughing. And Tommy came over, sometimes at the urging of Agnes. She worried about me. It wasn't good for me, she said, to be isolated on the island, not with Bush and her long, brooding silences. Tommy always brought deer or moose meat and we smiled stupidly at each other as we sat at the table or walked through the snow on our hand-crafted snowshoes. Sometimes I went back with him to the mainland.

But for the most part, Bush and I were quiet for hours—sometimes it seemed like days—at a stretch. It was a full and caring silence, and in it we were all that existed, the dark gray stones of the house moving through howling, boundless space, the planet traveling around a weakened sun, the windblown ice glaring up at sun's diminished power. In those days even the wolves seemed remote and far away. Darkness came early and nights were long. At times I put my sewing down, stationed myself at one of the windows, and stared out at the stark white land where rabbits were burrowed beneath heavy trees.

The tracks of animals wrote stories I couldn't yet decipher, being new to this place. There were places on snow where a set of tracks vanished in mid-path, next to a snow-embossed fan of wings, a rabbit or mouse lifted up in the claws of a hungry god.

Soon I barely remembered the vines that crept inside the windows, or that this world was capable of heat and growing corn, green moss.

THROUGH THE WINDOW one January afternoon, like something glimpsed from the corner of my eye, I caught sight of a dark shape being shadowed by smaller ones. I squinted into the glare. It was a solitary cow moose, thin-legged, with winter fur. She was dark and great, stranded on slick ice, unable to move without falling, while the wolves walked toward her with their heads down, their muzzles frozen. They spoke to one another from inside themselves and slowly they circled her.

She was defenseless on ice. She would fall. She was old and alone. She had no calf, no mate, no protection. The wolves had selected wisely.

I heard the stranded moose cry out. I turned away and put my hands over my ears.

It was an ancient ritual of hunger, but the laws of winter were a justice foreign to my nature. At times I could not bear this world. At times I was sorry I'd gone there. Bush said winter was like a wound healing because of the way everything closes in, grows over itself. But winter was too large for me.

That night I swallowed the potion Dora-Rouge had prescribed for my sleeplessness. In the dark, chilled room, I undressed and slid into bed, covering my face with blankets, feeling the safety and warmth of my own breath. But I could not block out the helpless vision of the moose.

Bush, too, looked out the window some days. By now the wind was blowing snow under the door and knocking at the window. It sounded like someone wanting to come inside. As she stood there I smelled and sensed that there were things Bush did not say. What wasn't spoken was as cold as what was said. Ice heart. That was Hannah.

But I had my secrets, too. For a long time I kept to myself a missing part of my own story. In the early part of my search for kin, I'd found a sister in South Dakota, my blood sister, Henriet, younger than me. I never told anyone how I'd stolen the money to find someone to track her down, had walked into a neighboring house one night and taken the money off a nightstand while the people slept. It wasn't really like stealing, I thought. It was dire necessity. Fifty dollars was what I paid a man to find her, and I had slept with him, too. No one could ever prove who'd stolen the money, though everyone suspected me. I'd had such hope when first I found my sister. It was like finding my true name. That's how it felt. I hitched rides across the plains to get there. Finally, I found my way with a truck driver, delivering cattle to a feedlot in a silver truck that smelled of the animals, was weighted with them.

Henriet wasn't related to Agnes. She had a different father, so I told myself it was all right to keep her secret. But the truth was, I didn't speak about her because her existence both horrified me and filled me with despair. She was lovely and quiet, but she was a girl who cut herself, cut her own skin, every chance she had. Her eyes were innocent and trusting, but her skin was full of scars. She cut herself with scissors and razor blades, as if she could not feel pain. Perhaps it was more than just wounds. Perhaps it was a language. She spoke through blades, translated her life through knives. I took a bracelet to her, but when I saw its sharp edges I pretended I'd gone empty-handed and gave her instead some of the cash I'd stolen. She never spoke. We just looked at each other. We sat and smoked one cigarette after another. Only she put hers out by pinching the end with her fingers. She could not be hurt. That's what she wanted to show. Not by anything outside her, that is, not anymore.

AT NIGHT, as the wind blew against the Black House, I lay in bed and thought of Hannah. Some cold nights I felt myself close, come together in the way ice grew across water, at the edges first, then suddenly, all at once, in the same way Bush said winter fills in the world, like a scar. At first the ice could be broken easily, then only with an ax, then it could not be broken at all. It locked in whatever was there—boat, fisherman, floating wood, all stopped in place. A cold firmament, beautiful and frightening, solid and alive. I could hear it, the tribe of water speaking.

Winter was such a place of shifting boundaries that I remembered, heard, and felt things that had not been there before. I began to understand Dora-Rouge's memory, especially on nights when I heard the sound of drumming inside the lake. It came from the frozen water. I believed what the old people said, that fish were a kind of people, like the wolves, and that they wanted to live as much as we did, those of us who had been born to a destiny of death and survived, passing through like small fish through a hole in a net.

During the long dark nights, I remembered or dreamed of the animals taken, marten, beaver, wolverine. I saw their skinless corpses. I heard their cries and felt their pain. I saw their shadows cross snow, ice, and cloud. We Indian people had always lived from them and in some way we were kin, even now. Behind my eyelids were the high loads of furs on freighter canoes going down a river, and thin, tall men in dark clothing walked toward me. There were women who looked like me and carried pictures of Mary and Jesus. They wore mirrors as if they were gold, on their belts, around their necks, pinned to dresses. The light caught on them and threw a glare on me, my face in every one. The people wore rags by then. There was nothing to warm them. Then the mixed-bloods turned against the others the way dogs will turn against their own ancestors, the wolves, in order to eat, to live. Loretta was sold into sickness and prostitution, and those things followed Hannah into dark, dark places.

IN THE SHORT HOURS of daylight we were busy. Now Bush and I made skirts. Our time was spent gathering cloth. The table was covered with patterns made of newspapers, folded fabric, and ribbons on spools.

Time vanished when we were frozen inside. As we pieced together cloth, it snowed. Wind opened the door of the shed and banged it closed again. Together we went outside and as the wind inhaled there was a moment of silence in which we heard the sound of the northern lights. "Listen," Bush said, and I heard the shimmering of ice crystals, charged by solar storms.

One below-zero night, as streams of light moved through the sky, and the solar winds were strong enough to blow snow, I dreamed that the wolves of the island, torn out of their deaths, were stirring about and holding counsel and looking for their human children. Another night I dreamed a plant. I drew the plant on paper and the next time I went across ice and cold to the mainland, I took the drawing to Dora-Rouge. "Oh, I know that one," she said, when she saw it. "That one grows up above us." She looked at me thoughtfully, as if it weren't at all unusual that I had dreamed such a plant.

Those dreams of mine, if that's what they were, lived inside the land. Maybe dreams are earth's visions, I thought, earth's expressions that pass through us. Although sometimes, to make myself seem larger than I was, I liked to think I had visions.

"There were always plant dreamers," Dora-Rouge said, picking a thread off my sweater.

In bed at night there were times I could see in the dark. My fingers grew longer, more sensitive. My eyes saw new and other things. My ears heard everything that moved beyond the walls. I could see with my skin, touch with my eyes.

ON THE MAINLAND when I visited, while Agnes pared potatoes, Husk told me and Tommy the news—that in a magazine he'd read he learned how we are made from stars. He said maybe visions, dreams, or memories existed because time, as Einstein thought, was not a straight line. He said it explained why I saw things, like the ancestors glittering with mirrors and carrying iron kettles. I lived in more than one time, in more than one way, all at once. "That explains Dora-Rouge, too," he said. "How she talks with Luther."

Yes, I thought. I understood. I saw yesterday and sometimes it looked the same as tomorrow. That's why Bush was dreaming her way north in the short hours of daylight, dreaming the way a bird studies the stars and waits for spring, for a certain moment, agreed upon, when all the birds would fly away. That's why the words of the two men from the north had created a need in her, I think now, a feeling that she should go there, up to the far land of the Fat-Eaters. It was that time in our history when the past became the present. There was the death of Raymond Yellow Thunder, the old Lakota man who was tortured and killed in a VFW lodge in Nebraska by God-fearing, God-loving men and their wives. There was the formation of the American Indian Movement. Red women and men all coming to new life. But Bush's determination rested on other things as well. She was a woman of heart, of land. She and the world were all of a piece. She would not permit any more worlds to be gone or taken. The dams would not be built. It was simple, her feeling. "The river cannot be moved," she said out loud one day, as she looked at maps of the north.

Because roadblocks would again be put up in the spring, she decided to travel there by canoe. Since my mother was thought to be up there at a town called Ohete, or New Hardy, I would go along.

FOR HOURS, when she wasn't sewing or reconstructing a badger for LaRue, Bush bent over maps. Then she squinted out the window as if she, too, had once been snow-blinded, or could see in the darkness around us the labyrinth of waterways that went all the way north. She called her plan "our secret." She spoke about which ways the currents ran and wondered aloud where side currents were likely to be. She sat close to the heat of the fire and plotted first one route, then checked it against another, working us through a maze, gauging distance, time, and space with the precision of a mathematician. This was no simple operation we were undertaking, I could see.

Sometimes I called her Marco Polo as she kept a list, writing down what we would need to take with us that next spring when thaw came rushing over the land. We would need an ax, she said, a little saw, and cooking pans that fit one into another. We would carry a small amount of dry wood in the canoes and take Sterno to cook on, in case it rained, and in case the wood along our way was also wet. We would have to find our way around obstacles, maybe the floating logjams of foresters, possibly dangerous rapids. According to "our secret," we would leave early in the year, because that was when the fish would still be hungry and food plentiful. But it also meant we would encounter swarms of mosquitoes and blackflies. If we waited until later, she said, who could predict if the dam would already be built or not?

It seemed to me that the weight of our journey increased tenfold each day. From inside the house made of dark gray ballast, I felt us sinking, the way a weighted boat drops down water, falling to the bottom, resting there like the Skidoos and bodies and skinned animals in the Hungry Mouth of Water.

It was my fear all along that we would be lost and that there would be no way to get our bearings. And from everything Bush said, from all the maps with their different topographies, I knew we were going, however much she planned, into strange waters, a geography that was whimsical at times, frightening at others.

Obsessed with the faded squares of paper that represented land, she tried to unravel all earth's secrets. I saw that she searched for something not yet charted. Besides, like a compass in this northern place of underground iron, the maps were not reliable.

Outside our windows, the icicles looked like teeth, as if we lived in the open mouth of winter. There were white passages of animals, and the drifting, changing boundaries of winter.

ONE DAY Bush looked up at me where I stood before the blue-gray light of the window. "Look at this," she said. She sat at the green table, a map in front of her, a cup of tea beside it. "These are almost all connecting."

It was true. The waters were linked together like a string of beads connected by a single thread. The rivers and streams all looked wide enough, according to her, to be passable by canoe. It was a replica of an ancient map. Bush turned the blue map over and examined it for a date. There was none. "This had to be made sometime between 1660 and 1720."

I stared at her. "How can you tell?"

"Because those years there were no northern lights. There are stories about it. It tells how the people were deserted by the lights from the sky. At the same time the lights abandoned the people, the tribes came down with the breathing illness, the spotted disease, and were invaded by French fur traders."

I looked at her. I didn't understand the connection. Maybe it was the spell of winter that had come over her, I thought.

"Don't you see? There would have been more thaw without the protection of the solar dust. See the difference in the amount of water?"

She opened another map to show me the discrepancy. I studied it as if I understood, but the only thing I knew for certain was that Bush could put together things far and beyond shirt patterns and the bones of animals and the stories of lost children. With my own eyes I saw that none of the maps were the same; they were only as accurate as the minds of their makers and those had been men possessed with the spoils of this land, men who believed California was an island. Bush said those years also showed up in the rings of trees.

I was intrigued by the fact that history could be told by looking at paper. I'd wondered before what it was about the maps that occupied Bush's time, and now I, too, became interested. I could see it myself. Just as I saw sleds with frozen animals. A deeper map. At times I would pore over them beside her, the lantern lighting the table in front of us. They were incredible topographies, the territories and tricks and lies of history. But of course they were not true, they were not the people or animal lives or the clay of land, the water, the carnage. They didn't tell those parts of the story. What I liked was that land refused to be shaped by the makers of maps. Land had its own will. The cartographers thought if they mapped it, everything would remain the same, but it didn't, and I respected it for that. Change was the one thing not accounted for. On the other hand, it gave me no confidence in the safety of our journey that we were venturing into such a vast unknown terrain that might mislead us, a terrain that had destroyed other human missions and desires. It was a defiant land. It had been loved, and even admired, by the government's surveyors, for its mischief and trickiness and for the way it made it difficult for them to claim title. Its wildness, its stubborn passion to remain outside their sense of order made them want it even more.

Another day, after one of Bush's long silences, she laughed out loud at the ignorance of Europeans. Out of the blue, she said, "Beavers. None of them ever considered how beavers change the land." She was right. Beavers were the true makers of land. It was through their dams that the geographies had been laid, meadows created, through their creation that young trees grew, that deer came, and moose. All things had once depended on them. And on these maps, we could read back to how land told the story of the beaver people. It brought back the words of Dora-Rouge. One day she told me that earth has more than one dimension. The one we see is only the first layer.

WHEN BUSH WASN'T WORKING or inside looking at maps, she dressed up in warm clothing and went out alone to fish. She would go to the hole in the ice, the one cut with an auger, drop in a weighted lure or decoy, and wait. Closer to the mainland, others had set up their icehouses. I remained in the house. I failed to see the pleasure in sitting on ice in a little shack that maybe had a radio inside, a heater, maybe even an old chair sitting on the lake, and a rattle reel on the wall. Or carrying home fish stiff enough to use as sled runners, which some people did.

When she'd come in, it was usually with a frozen walleye or a poutfish. But I remained indoors or, occasionally, I took off on snowshoes from island to island, watching animals and studying their tracks, and when I walked from land to land, or cut wood, or daydreamed at the window, it was always with a head full of knowledge or stories I'd gained from Husk or Bush. Out walking one night, with the full moon in the indigo sky, I thought how the people once believed that birds migrated to the moon for winter. Perhaps out of memory or longing. They thought the moon was an egg and a mother bird, large and white in the sky, and that they were going back to their origins. Agnes had said, "While some people see a man's face on the moon, we see the shadowy gray outlines of birds." And it did look as if they were there, stopped in flight before moon's round face.

And when the birds arrived, it was said, they told pitiful stories about us poor, wingless fools who had no choice but to stay behind and freeze. They were sorry for us. And they were happy, always, to return in spring, to see which of us had lived and which of us had not survived the winter.

WHENEVER BUSH TALKED about my mother, I could feel a tall shadow walk toward us. I felt its presence in the room with us, while beyond our walls, as we talked or sewed, the ice outside talked with the wind, gambling about which of them would one day get the better of us.

One day after Bush spoke of Hannah, it came to me that I was all Hannah had. Not in the way of love. Not to care about. But I was what she could use to barter a place in the world. I was what, when she carried me, other people smiled upon, people who might have feared or hated her before. I was her money. I was her fare. She had needed me for this, if for nothing else. And for this reason I was of use to her.

That day I caught Bush staring at my face. I looked down, embarrassed, but she said only, "Some people see scars and it is wounding they remember. To me they are proof of the fact that there is healing."

And one day, as I sat close to him in the truck, Tommy touched my face and said, "Tell me about the scars."

I looked at him. I thought how I'd asked Bush about my scars. I thought of the last time I'd seen myself in the little piece of mirror in my bedroom. I thought how scars were proof of healing. "What scars?" I said.

IN THE SHORT HOURS of daylight the world sparkled like precious stones. One day in late January, when the ice was deepest, and the owls had already begun their mating songs, I wrapped myself in a coat and scarf and went outside to get wood. It was a cold so fierce it hurt to breathe. My breath froze, nearly solid, in air before my face. My nostrils turned to ice. My lungs closed up. It was too cold to snow, but not yet cold enough to stop all human machines, and while I was there with my arms full of wood, there was the brittle noise of Tommy's old rusted Dodge crossing the lake, along with a sharp cracking of ice. Holding the wood, I watched him arrive and I forgot the cold.

He wore one of my shirts that day beneath his coat and vest, the shirt with the bright green ribbons, and he carried a white-wrapped package of moose meat. While I stood, he parked, jumped down out of the truck, and opened the door of the house for me. While I unloaded the wood, he went back to the woodpile and picked up another armful, breathing a hello, smiling at me on his way. That's still what we did, smile at each other. The worst thing about love is its passionate foolishness.

Inside, Bush put on a pot of rice while we stood before the heat of the stove, warming ourselves, self-conscious, still smiling.

Then, after we ate, Bush urged Tommy, "Have more rice." He complied. He worked hard and needed food.

The night before, Bush had called out in her sleep, and now she looked tired and drawn, so she retreated to her room, to rest, she said, leaving us alone to talk about small things.

"What have you been doing?" he asked me. His hair was still mussed from the cap. I smoothed it. He grabbed my hand. He kissed it. More smiling.

"I made ten new shirts." I showed them to him, all fresh and stiff on hangers. He admired them. I had to admit, they did look beautiful, all fresh new cloth, red and blue ribbons. "I'll take them all," he said.

"You wish."

"How's Bush?"

This was what we'd say. Then I would ask about his many grandparents. But always beneath the words was something warmer, a happiness at being together. Under the surface of our skins, our words, even young, we were already a woman and a man together.

Tommy was different from the boys I'd known before. They were interested in cars, rock-and-roll music, ball games, and girls; they were children. He was a provider already. He hunted and fished, both with painstaking compassion and respect for the animals, the way it was supposed to be done. Already I loved him, though I didn't know what he'd think of me if he knew about my life.

Before long, I knocked on the door of Bush's room. "I'm going to Agnes'. Do you want anything from the store?"

She just said, "No." She didn't even think about the question. She sounded sleepy.

I laced my boots and grabbed the shirts to take to Tinselman's. I liked the freedom of being able to leave without permission. As we were leaving, Bush opened the door and rushed outside without even a coat across her shoulders. "Angel! Tommy!" she called out. "Wait. I just thought of something." She was breathless from the cold air and her hair was tangled. "Stop at LaRue's, would you, and see if he'll send back the old map. He'll know which one I mean. Just tell him the oldest one."

"Okay. I'll see you tomorrow," I said. I slid over to sit close to Tommy. I put the shirts neatly in the seat by the window. Then we drove off across the blue-gray lake. I looked over at Tommy, then out the window, smiling as we crossed over the slow fish that were beneath us, the waiting weeds.

"What?" he said in that way men do when they want to know if a woman cares for them, sorry they can't read her mind. There was a crunching sound as tires drove over the snow.

"Nothing. I'm just thinking."

I had money coming from Tinselman, so after I left the new shirts, I stocked up on flour and some instant coffee. I bought two bottles of Coca-Cola for Bush. She liked Coke but would never buy it for herself. It was still sold there in the machines where the bottle has to be slid outward along a maze, into a slot, and then pulled straight up. And I bought her some Jasmin soap, a new item, and Pet Milk. I was careful not to buy more than I could carry in my pack. I wanted to walk back and I didn't like to pull a sled. It gave me a shoulder ache.

THAT NIGHT, I stayed with Agnes and Dora-Rouge. From the window I could see there was a circle around the moon; another snow coming in. Such snow-light in February, like the month I was born, with the light behind a grayness.

In the cot that night, I dreamed of islands with moss-covered ruins. The dreams rose up in such a way that I began to believe such places existed. Dreaming, according to Dora-Rouge, was how decisions were made in older times. That's what she said that morning when, like a young child, I climbed into bed with her. As tough as I'd once thought myself, I was making up for all the mothers I never had, resting my head on a pillowcase covered with blue flowers, pulling the cover up to my neck. Both of us lay on our backs, warm and comfortable. "I dreamed of stones," I told her. I looked at the water stains on the ceiling while we talked. Dreams, she said to me, were how animals were tracked and hunted, how human lives were carried out in other times, other places.

As uncomfortable as it was, I had missed my little cot in the living room and the smell of Agnes' bad coffee and dust. Agnes still slept in the bedroom with John Husk, even though she said he snored something fierce and then said it was her. This made me smile. I believed it was her all along.

"You're getting hips," Agnes said at breakfast, looking at my body.

I laughed. "Yeah. Great, huh?"

"How come Bush never comes over anymore?"

I sipped Agnes' terrible coffee and lied. "She's busy sewing. She sews all the time. She doesn't want to work for LaRue any longer." It wasn't completely a lie. I didn't tell her that Bush sat in front of maps and pondered a way up to the territory of the Fat-Eaters. She would think Bush was crazy. I had doubts, too.

Agnes shook her head. "It's too hard on her eyes to sew that much."

I had thought this as well, that it strained her eyes to sew and to put the tiny bones together into animals and then, after all that work was done, to squint at the lines on maps. She never gave her eyes a rest. But her vision was sharp and accurate. She could see a snowshoe hare against a background of snow. Like Agnes and me, it was Bush's back that ached from sleeping on poor mattresses and cots. From bending over work. We were a sisterhood of bad backs.

I DREADED going to LaRue's. Bush had just dreamed that he'd purchased two mummies, a mother and a child, the child curled up between the mother's bent knees. And Agnes said it was true. She had seen them arrive in two glass-and-wood containers. She, like Bush, knew that the bones and dry flesh of the dead belong in no human dwelling.

I knocked on his door and was relieved that there was no answer, that I would not have to go inside. Through the door, I could smell the furs and bones and formaldehyde, could see in my mind's eye the world's largest beetle; it had a deep-green back. I left a note for LaRue, sliding it under the door.

As I walked back on Poison Road, Tommy drove up beside me and stopped. "Hey." He opened the door. "Need a lift?"

I jumped up into the truck and rode with him back to Agnes' house.

"You want me to drive you home?"

Home. It was such a certain word, so sure of itself, so final. But I liked it. "No. I'll walk."

"It's no trouble," he said.

But I insisted on taking off on foot across the lake. "I need to walk," I assured him. I cherished my times with him, but for now I wanted to walk and think about my dreams, and whether or not Bush was truly crazy. To my surprise, I was getting used to silence, I found it rich and necessary. Tommy and I would have our time. I knew this. I was patient. "I need to, Tommy. I need to think," I said. Besides, I knew his grandfather needed him that day. Agnes had told me the man was having trouble seeing.

As I walked across the frozen lake, I went past a few people who were ice-fishing. Some played radios. I heard the music as I passed, each radio telling something about the person who was fishing. The Beatles. Tammy Wynette. The Polka Kings. I waved as I walked past. That's how it was there. You met someone on the road, you'd wave. You pass them on water, in a boat, you lift a finger. On ice, you nod and smile. They all knew me by now, most of them. It was not a large village.

IT WAS A LONG WALK to Fur Island. As I crossed the lake and heard its voice, I thought of Husk's words, that the world was alive, as the people there said. The lake was alive. I was sure of it. Not only when it was large-hipped and moving, but even when it was white, contracted, and solid. The Perdition River flowing beneath moving ice was alive. So was the ice itself. And even the winter that sang itself into our bones. The air shimmered around me like the moment before a lightning strike, intricate ice crystals falling from a cloud.

I thought of seeing the northern lights, and that Husk had told me once that there are shining plankton who join together and make a spiral of light in the ocean, that there are many other things in nature that twist around that way, the Milky Way, the double helix of humans. The northern lights were part of this, I was sure.

By the time I returned to Fur Island, the light had already faded. I was warm from exertion, but the moment I entered the house I felt a chill. Bush sat at the green table in the dark. Beside her, a pitcher of water was crusted with ice, and the fire had gone out. She had been crying. She didn't seem to notice I was there.

"Bush?" I said this tentatively. I lit a lantern.

"The beavers," was what she said, as if that explained her blue lips, the house it would take hours to reheat.

It was the beavers. I understood. I did. I understood in one word: the beavers were nearly gone, our lives nearly extinguished along with theirs, our world transformed by those who could never have dreamed this continent in all its mystery, in all its life and beauty. It would never recover itself.

I understood, too, that winter could lodge itself into a person's bones so deep they would forget they were human.

I busied myself. I put wood on the fire. I wrapped a blanket around Bush's shoulders. As soon as the stove was hot, I heated a can of soup and made her eat. Then I warmed water in the turkey roaster and placed her feet in it. Taking control, I said, "Tomorrow we're going to visit Dora-Rouge and tell her what you're up to. John Husk will be glad to drive us back."

THAT NIGHT I kept my door wide open. I said it was to let in warmth from the main room, but I really wanted to be sure Bush was all right. I woke a few times and checked on her. She slept soundly. With her hair on the pillow she looked vulnerable and soft, her eyes closed peacefully.

The next morning, I put extra wood in the stove, then closed the flue partway to keep it burning slow and steady while we were gone.

"I don't know," Bush said. "I don't think we should tell them about this."

"We're going to. This is crazy." I sounded forceful and more certain than I was, but just as we prepared to leave, LaRue arrived with the ancient map. He smelled of men's cologne and wore a new, starched shirt. His hair was combed back into a ponytail at the back. He was handsome, I had to admit, in the Tom Jones kind of way, but I knew all the reasons Bush did not want him. His dark house was frightening and smelled of things that should have been buried or thrown into mud or water or the air from which they came. His walls were covered with shelves that held preserved animals. He had bowls of glass eyes that stared out as if taking the measure of all people. He wasn't careful with fish—he offended them—and I was sure that was what had jeopardized our lives that day on the lake, even though I had paddled with him through the storm begging forgiveness of the water people, the fish people. He didn't care enough for life.

I looked at Rue. He was too eager for her love. His eyes practically bulged out, despite the way she kept him at a cold distance. But it wasn't really Bush he wanted, it was a woman, any woman. It was his loneliness he wanted relieved. I eyed him some more, looking for good things, redeeming qualities. She would never give in to him, I could see that. At the same time I thought maybe he had potential, maybe I could get through to him. Bush's solitude made her, in my opinion, a little crazy. Of course, his presence made her even crazier. As he took the map out of a tube, I thought of all the older men on the mainland, and how none of them could have kept up with the likes of her. Maybe I'd make him my project.

"What sign are you?" I asked him impulsively. "No, don't tell me. Let me guess. Scorpio."

"How did you know?" he said.

When he touched the map, the corners turned to dust. He was making a sacrifice to get close to Bush. This, I thought, was optimistic. It was the way men behaved in old stories. They went on a mission, a quest, performed a task, overcame an obstacle. Brought back Golden Fleece. He had probably come right over the Hungry Mouth and survived.

He unrolled the map carefully for her. I stood behind them and looked. The map was truly beautiful. It was undated but very old. The yellowed paper had disintegrated at the edges. It was the most ornate map I'd ever seen. It was painted in a Greek blue that still had, in places, a bit of brightness to it. Cherubs were at the edges, blowing air. There were water monsters, including a horned serpent with a tail. The serpent, or dragon, had once been yellow, maybe even gold. Waving lines with arrows recorded the directions of currents. Mudflats were depicted by paintings of sinking things; in the far-right corner, the hand of a drowning person reached out from the mud. At the top, part of a boat was going down, a boat with Indian people chained together as slaves for the far continent.

"Just look at that," he said. He held a magnifying glass. He leaned closer, then sat back and let Bush peer through the curved round lens. He was happy just to be in her presence and had a satisfied look on his face, as if he were about to eat a fulfilling meal.

Bush said, "I dreamed you bought two mummies."

"What? How did you know? I want to start a museum someday. They were a good trade."

I thought quickly. "Do you want some coffee?" I asked them.

"Well," she said, "I dreamed them, LaRue. I heard them say they want to go back to clay." She sounded businesslike, the way she did around LaRue.

"No," he said, looking at her, surprised.

"I heard them." She said this louder, as if it would make a difference to him.

I heated the water, my back to them. LaRue took advantage of my absence. Certain I was out of earshot, I heard him say, "But why not? You might even like me."

He was ruining my plans for him.

I heard her chair scrape the floor. "That's it, LaRue. I don't work for you any longer! I quit. Now." She tried to sound calm. She got up and began to pack bones back into the clean white boxes, even bones she'd already put together.

Before more damage could be done, I poured the water quickly and hurried back with coffee that, like LaRue, wasn't warm or strong enough.

Bush pretended, for my sake, that nothing had happened, but her face was red. She sat back down.

"Here's the coffee," I said. It barely had an odor.

After only a moment, she got up again and bustled around the room. She took apart the wolverine bones, put them in a white box, and put them on the table for LaRue.

I thought quickly. I decided to go back with LaRue and the bones. I said I had errands.

Bush was relieved not to be forced to tell our secret to Agnes and Dora-Rouge.

"I'll be back tonight," I said. I wouldn't leave Bush alone again. "I promised Agnes I'd help paper some shelves."

Bush, still mad, raised an eyebrow. "Agnes? Paper shelves?"

I thought of Agnes and her messiness. It was a poor excuse. "Well, really I want to see Tommy. You know."

She had doubts, I could see that, but there was no reason for her to keep me there and she did know Tommy and I were sweet on each other.

I felt guilty, and sneaky. I was doing the unthinkable. I was going to manipulate her life. I was going to manipulate LaRue, the only man there in her age range. Whether she liked him or not, her world was too secluded. Sometimes, accustomed to her aloneness, she'd speak as she cooked. She'd say, "Kettle. Onion." When she brought in sweet-smelling wood, she spoke it by name, "Spruce. Birch." And at times her eyes would get a faraway look to them. I wondered how it must have been before I was there, when she was alone in cold, deep solitude, in winter darkness.

As I went out the door with LaRue, I called over my shoulder, "I'll see you tonight."

Almost as soon as we were on the lake, I looked square at LaRue and said, "You will never get her like that. Or any other woman either."

"What?" His eyes opened wide. He skidded sideways on ice as he looked at me, then straightened out the wheel. He said nothing. Silence by then was familiar to me, so I didn't mind. I let it be for a while. Then I said, "Your approach is all wrong. Turn on your car lights."

He stared straight ahead, and when he finally spoke, he looked at me and said, "You know what? Your problem is you think you know everything."

"Well, what about your problems?" I emphasized the plural. "If I were her I wouldn't want you either. Hey. Watch where you're going."

We lapsed again into silence. He swallowed, I noticed, and his face was somewhat flushed. After a while, I said, "I have some suggestions. Do you want me to tell you?"

"What? No." As if offended.

But I went on anyway. "No woman would want a man who kept mummies. Those things have got to go, LaRue."

T E N

IT WAS TOWARD SPRING that Bush gathered up the maps to go to the mainland. By then she had our course fixed in her mind and she was easier about things. "Come on," she said impatiently.

I followed. The ice of the lake, while still frozen, was beginning to thaw and it was slushy as we walked over it.

All around us, spring was a wonderful quickening, a smell of newness in the air, a brightening of light. Trees, freed up, were being moved by the wind. They creaked as the wind spoke through them, telling winter to hurry away, singing back the sun, the green new shoots of living things. At the roots of dry brown grasses were new soft beginnings. The tips of gray rocks were emerging from snow. Everywhere was a sound of water dripping, running, surfacing.

Spring was a statement of faith, trust that all would be well, that light would return. The faithful earth was swept with the religion of the season. Opening. Rising. Muddy, soft, and renewed. I believed spring entered not only our dreams but those of the moose and wolves. Soon we would all be about, back to our lives.

DORA-ROUGE and Agnes were glad to see Bush. They'd worried about her and now they greeted her with warmth and love. But she was too occupied with the journey to be civil. Almost as soon as we stepped inside the door, before my boots were even off, before she removed her coat, Bush announced, "I've thought it over. I'm going. No matter what you say." She was ready for an argument. She sounded unlike herself.

"Where are you going?" asked Dora-Rouge.

"You're getting kind of busty," Agnes said to me.

I pretended not to hear. But I'd seen myself in their new mirror and yes, I was changing.

"I'm going up to the headwaters and bay." She was abrupt, as if they would try to change her mind.

"Take off your coat, dear," said Dora-Rouge.

"Maybe you didn't hear me." With an edge of stubbornness. It wasn't so much that she thought they would argue her out of it; it was because when thaw comes, everything moves more quickly, even words.

"Where did you say you are going?" said Dora-Rouge.

"To the Fat-Eaters."

Dora-Rouge lit up, hearing about our plans. "How wonderful." To me, she said, "I was born up there, you know," as if I'd forgotten about the First World in the divided waters and lands of the farther north, her stories of the Fat-Eaters, who lived three human territories to the north of us and who were our ancestors. "It's where I want to go so I can die in peace."

"We're going to take you with us, Dora," said Bush. Her voice was soft again.

I hadn't heard about this part of the plan. My mouth dropped open. Against my will, I said, "What?"

Agnes looked dismayed. If Dora-Rouge went, it was to her death. So far Agnes had kept her mother alive by not going home. Not only that, but if Dora-Rouge was going to her final resting place, Agnes had no choice but to go along or seem uncaring.

Dora-Rouge could not hide her excitement. "Really? You're taking me?" She said this with wonder, but after she heard our plan, her spirits fell, as if for the first time she grasped reality. "But I'd just be a burden to you. It would be such a hardship to take me along."

"Traveling there, Grandmother, everything is a burden."

At least Bush was honest. She could have denied it.

She turned then to Agnes. "We will take you, too. I know you wouldn't want her to go without you. And she wouldn't go without you. But it will be hard work. We will have to walk over several portages and distances on land."

Bush had plotted out the easiest route with the least number of places, portages, to cross on foot. Still in her coat, she unfolded two maps before them. "We'll be traveling out of the way at times, but in a roundabout way that will make it easier in the long run."

"Take your coat off. Make yourself at home," Dora-Rouge said. "How have you been?"

"I'm going to do it," Agnes said, even though a furrow formed between her brows. "I can handle it."

I knew she'd go whether she wanted to or not. This journey seemed unfair to Agnes. Sitting next to her mother, she leaned forward to look at the maps. Two gray-haired women at the kitchen table, water steaming on the stove. "No, I'm sure I can make it."

I didn't know then what all was involved. I knew only what Bush had told me. Dora-Rouge would have to be carried. "No problem," I'd said, when Bush told me this. I'd calculated Dora-Rouge's weight to be not much over seventy pounds. I was strong and even though my back was bent from bad beds, it was not hurt from lifting, so what was Dora-Rouge to carry, I thought, such a light weight. I didn't yet know the heaviness of canoes and all the rest that we would carry, lift, and drag.

"I was always good at rapids," Agnes said. She spoke the truth. I had heard about her safe traveling through rapids and white-capped waves. She was something of a legend. Tommy told me that the old people had seen her go down small falls and sit erect and guide the canoe safely to its destination in situations where other people would only cower or cover their heads and toss it all to fate.

"But there is a way," Dora-Rouge said, "where we can stay in the water most of the time. I remember it. It was how they brought the whale down. It was the route they used to carry all the furs away from their bodies."

These, the furs of my sleep.

Bush looked at Dora-Rouge for some time. Dora-Rouge's way

was not the path she had planned, I was certain. Doubt was a shadow on Bush's face and I could see the thoughts that crossed her mind, hear the words her tight lips wanted to say. She didn't want to disagree with Dora-Rouge, but I saw that she thought the older woman might be wrong.

I looked at Bush's face, trying to read her expression. Her eyes were like the small, round pictures of Mary and Jesus, or the little mirrors we'd so desired, mirrors our lives had fallen into, our faces had died inside. In her eyes, too, I could almost see the carrying of Dora-Rouge across land, through mud, over stones, inclines, and drops. It was as if it were inside me already, the future, alongside a memory of place, people, and even hardship. And in my mind's eye, I saw the freighter canoes with scores of men and tall mounds of skins taken from the naked backs of beaver and marten and fox, the open-eyed, childlike animals that lived in the Hungry Mouth.

Husk had told me once about planaria, that when fed pieces of their ancestors, they would remember tasks the gone ones had known. It was a cell-deep memory, he said. Maybe that was why I saw and thought what I did. Maybe places and people are like this, too, with a sad homing, a remembering of what has gone before us.

"Yes," Dora-Rouge said, confirming her own words. "It was called the Million-Dollar Trail. We used to travel it. It was an old waterway. It offered hides and skins to the Europeans who never dreamed this land, who had no eyes for it. But I remember it."

I, too, saw the watery paths. I'd dreamed them, lakes clear as glass, lakes that were black water and rocked against land, sure as tributaries of my own blood.

Agnes said, "Mother, you are not that old."

"Yes. Yes, I am." She looked directly at Agnes. "This time I really am."

Dora-Rouge had already told me that there were plants up north that made useful medicines. She longed to find them. I could see her mind already clicking. We'd collect seeds, roots, beginnings.

Bush squinted at the map, as if losing her focus would yield to her eyes Dora-Rouge's open way. She softened. "Where is it? I've looked for it." She placed her elbows on it. "I've looked and looked and I just can't see it."

Dora-Rouge placed her hand on Bush's arm. "These maps are not our inventions. Maps are only masks over the face of God. There are other ways around the world."

AS WINTER CONTINUED to slip away around us, I watched small islands of ice move down the river. At first I felt excitement about our journey. We were going. Four women, each of us with a mission. I was going to meet my mother, who lived near the Fat-Eaters. Bush was going to see what was happening to the water, to see if what the two men had said was true, to help the people. Dora-Rouge was going, first, after plants that were helpful to the people, and then to die in her ancestral homeland. It was Agnes whose task was going to be the hardest. She was going to deliver her mother to that place and grieve. Agnes began to sadden from that day on, even to the point of agreeing with everything her mother said. Even when Dora-Rouge was clearly wrong, Agnes kept silent. This worried Dora-Rouge. "Are you all right, Ag?" she'd ask. Husk, too. He tried to comfort her. He said death was only matter turning into light or energy, that we were atoms, anyway, from distant stars, and that we'd once been stones and ferns and even cotton. But I, too, was selfish. I wanted to keep Dora-Rouge.

One day, as it rained lightly, Frenchie arrived at dinnertime, her neatly arranged charcoal hair misted with the rain. She wore a long blue chiffon scarf around the neck of her jacket; it matched her eye shadow precisely and it trailed like a river down her chest. And she pushed an office chair, the kind on four wheels, with a seat that swiveled. It was gray. "This was poor Helene's. She brought it home with her. Dora-Rouge, I think you can use it."

Frenchie's eyes were swollen. She'd been crying for days. Thaw had come and now she was miserably sad. She wanted nothing more, she said, than just to see Helene's face and touch her hand one more time. All she could see inside her mind was Helene curled up and settled at the bottom of water with the whalebones, the Ski-doos, and old trucks. And Helene was such a vulnerable vision floating in those maternal waters of Lake Grand, like an infant waiting to be born instead of a woman who'd just gone into death.

THAT NIGHT, LaRue came by on the pretext of bringing us some fish, but he was coming to see Bush. I knew he'd seen us walking to the mainland. He was out that morning, returning from his trapline. I'd seen his steps. I recognized his footprints by now. It was one of the talents of the north that I gained.

"How was the trapping?" Husk asked him.

"They were all empty. No good. It's the wrong time of year, I suppose." He eyed Bush.

Agnes said, "But surely they are hungry after winter. And moving about."

"Maybe they are hunted out." Husk shook his head. "That has happened before." I could see that Husk remembered the time he'd been forced to trap and hunt the last of dwindling populations.

"Hey, where'd you get the chair?"

Dora-Rouge said, "From Frenchie." She was learning to push herself in the chair, using a crutch with a rubber tip as an oar.

"I didn't even know you typed."

"Real funny, LaRue," I said. I caught the scent of LaRue's cologne. It was no wonder he had such bad luck snaring anything, animal or female. It was his smell. He might as well have carried a radio. But I didn't tell him. I wanted his luck with animals to be bad. As I looked at him, I wondered why I had made it my work to bring together Bush and Rue, two people so unlike, LaRue believing animals felt no pain and Bush, like the traditional people, knowing the world was alive and that all creatures were God. I had wanted, before now, to tell LaRue about pain and animals, but I knew he would never believe a girl. I would have to wait for science to back me up, watching the magazines for hard evidence. I'd learned this from Husk. And I knew LaRue believed in things like science and printed words. But Husk said some things were so obvious the scientists couldn't even see them.

"Guess what?" Dora-Rouge said to LaRue. "We're going north!"

He stared at her, then at Bush. "What? Is that what that map business was all about?"

When Rue heard the full details of our travel plan, he looked at us and shook his head as if we were victims of a dreadful malady.

"Hey! It's spring. What else can I say?" And he laughed, certain we wouldn't go, certain that we joked.

"Thanks for the encouragement," Bush said. She sounded cold. But he was right in a way. Spring was a season of madness. The warming air and thawing water brought people to a kind of hysteria that could not be helped. After winter's numbness and isolation, people were suddenly possessed by a great restless longing. I felt it, too, and it was beyond describing. It caused men to rush across ice in pursuit of something they themselves could not quite see or track, and to fall through the dark fissures growing in ice as it separated from itself. Women moved out of their homes, headed for another man or town or country. Younger men, powerless against it, shot themselves. And as we sat there at Agnes' table with LaRue, Frenchie sat on the cot and continued to cry. Later, after Rue left, she hit herself in her own heart with a grief that had built all winter.

John Husk gave her some brandy.

She drank it, leaving her lipstick on the rim of the glass.

WE STAYED over that night. Early the next morning I put a kettle of water on the stove. The stove wasn't quite hot enough. I poked in the coals and blew air on them, saw the orange fire flare up. I clanged the lid back on.

About LaRue. I thought, even as distasteful as his comments had been, he was still the only prospect for Bush. I dropped hints to her. I boiled water. I said, "He's kind of good-looking, don't you think?" It was part of my plan to make him seem desirable.

She was surveying one of Husk's fishnets for rips, a ball of twine and a large, curved needle in her lap. "Not really."

"I think he has potential. He's kind of cute."

"No, he's a lost cause." She said it cut-and-dry, without a thought. She put twine through the large hole in the needle.

Suddenly she looked at me. "Why are you so interested in him? Is there anything going on?

"What? Between us? No. Not me," I said quickly.

• • • •

THE FOLLOWING DAY, there was a memorial for Helene at Frenchie's house. It was a small house and crowded with people. There were even some I had never seen. They'd all been closed inside most of the winter and looked thin and pale. I was late. I'd been talking with Dora-Rouge, who decided not to attend. It was too much trouble for her, she said. She was resting for our trip.

As soon as I walked in the door, I was handed a plate and sent to the table to fill it. The table was heaped high with food—breads, rice, stews. I wasn't hungry, but I ate. Death meant eating, as if food would protect us from our own. There was plenty of food that year, as if to celebrate, even at a funeral, that hunger had not again taken up residence with us.

Frenchie wore a black chiffon scarf on her head, tied under her chin. She ate absentmindedly, looking up with her great sad eyes at nothing, taking a sip of wine, then one of coffee. She said this was how she liked to drink, to come down and up at the same time.

Tommy was there with the people of the Hundred-Year-Old Road. They cried. They had lived so long and seen so many of the younger generations gone, but even at that they had been unable to convince later generations to follow the paths of the older ways. The secrets of their longevity were to shun the ways of the white world and remember to live each day with reverence for all that was around them.

Other people cried, too, in that way my people had, and still have, of weeping out loud, without self-consciousness or apology or embarrassment. I'd never met Helene and my own eyes remained dry in spite of how their crying touched me. I took the dishes to the sink and rinsed them. I carried coffee around the room and filled cups and then stood looking out the kitchen window as steam rose from the sun-covered land.

The gathering was meant to dignify the loss. Helene would not be buried. Instead, Frenchie wanted to bury her favorite things. That day, the men had heated the ground with a torch and placed hot rocks on it. It was hard work, but finally there was a long, narrow grave, deep and wet. What was buried in Helene's place, inside an old wooden grub box, was a ring of silver, a pair of Cree shoes someone had once given her, a piece of red earth she had believed could heal varicose veins, a marten fur, and a hair comb made of old tortoiseshell. A picture of a young man she had once loved went into the box, along with an unopened bottle of Tweed cologne, and a pocketknife that served as both a sharp blade and a beer-can opener. The grub box with Helene's things was placed inside a small blue canoe and it was buried, with Helene's favorite doll, blond-headed, and wearing a red scarf, the doll sitting behind the grub box, as if to paddle. It was lowered into the thawed ground, and clods of dirt were thrown in on top. But what touched me most was that they buried with her a song that was not ever to be sung again. Her song. I tried not to learn it as we stood around the wooden box. Frenchie sang it in a dry voice, stopping a few times, her throat choked up, and then beginning again. The mist of the ground floated behind her as she wiped her eyes on her sleeve. The others bent their heads even more.

I would never forget that song, buried or not. I thought, this is the way to keep the song in our memory. By making it forbidden. By burying it. It haunted me. I hear it still, the song of a woman I never met.

TOMMY WENT WITH ME back to Agnes' house. He carried the black cast-iron kettle that contained stew. Above us, I could feel the life returning to the trees. Tommy said, "Think of how many people have carried this kettle."

I did. I thought of it. It was iron that had probably been mined from our own earth. Suddenly I saw how old it was, this kettle. It had witnessed the killing of my people. It had been fired by trees no longer there, and forged in the presence of women talking at night. Now Frenchie's tears were a part of it, too, and God only knew what other sorrows. Agnes once said it had contained a soup of rocks, twigs, and moss. Food for lean times.

It had other uses, too. It had bathed my grandfather, Harold, when he was an infant. It held a river. It was alive. I thought I'd heard sounds from it one night. Now I told Tommy and he nodded like he knew just what I meant. I think he was proud of me for hearing such things.

Outside, too, I heard singing in the distance. And I could still hear, in my own ears, the song we were supposed to bury and forget.

I looked in on Dora-Rouge. She slept like a child. I pulled her door silently closed. "Why don't I fix us some coffee?" I said.

I measured out twice the amount of coffee grounds that Agnes would use. I stood in front of the stove, suddenly silent. Tommy stood behind me and took me in his arms and held me. I felt the warmth of the stove on my stomach and thighs, felt his warmth along my back. I bent my neck and he kissed it and I realized I was crying, that my face was covered with tears I hadn't known were there, and he turned me around slowly and wiped them away, and tenderly he smoothed my hair. I felt his rough wool shirt against my cheek. We hated death and feared it, at least I did, but its presence, as it always does, made us desperate for love, the shining part of life, and to make love, to enter creation. I believe it happens this way to ensure that life will go on, that our people would continue.

Love is a beginning, a secret warmth that grows, something that comes alive; inside skin a soul turns over and opens its eyes. Love, I realize now, is a third person come to stand between the loving two.

From the next room Dora-Rouge said, "I can hear the grass growing."

I looked at the kettle on the counter. The sunlight came inside it and filled it. It was a new angle of light, springtime, one I'd never before seen in this place.

WHEN THE LAKE was mostly thawed, when there were only a few islands of ice floating in the water, I decided to paddle to the Hungry Mouth. Near it I felt an undertow, a pull, as if something wrapped itself around me. I thought I saw hands, human hands, pale white and thin, and the face of the beluga and the red scarf of a snowmobiler. I sang Helene's song as if to leave it there.

OVERNIGHT, all at once, it seemed, the world became green. In one day the snow was gone, the dark earth visible. Because of the sudden thaw, I could believe a god, any god, created water in one day, animals in another. In still another, trees were set to bud, then opened. There was a change in light. Ice moved and floated. It hit itself. Then parts of it broke away. There was a loosening, winter breaking in half, then in smaller and smaller pieces, all the way down to atoms and particles. The world was filled with sound. It was a wonderful din, the many voices of spring, the running of water, the ice breaking up, the wind and stars telling birds the way home so that they could fly even while asleep, return, and take count of us wingless people.

Even the island of the spiders came unmoored and began to float away, and Bush sent for Husk to tow it back to its place at Fur Island.

In this way winter struck its camp.

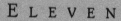

ELEVEN

"THE SKINS of the dead are traveling toward us," said Dora-Rouge.

I was having trouble lighting a fire in the cookstove. I blew on the smoking embers, then looked over my shoulder at her, sure I'd hear a prophecy or a vision from the other world. Instead I heard Bush's squeaky-wheeled red cart rattling toward us on the road.

I went to the window. Against the soft, new green of springtime, Bush looked small. She wore her fishing vest and her hair was loose. She pulled the wooden wagon behind her. It was piled high with a mound of animal skins, and it looked as if a large animal tracked her, smelling her steps, and creeping forward. Mud swallows flew up from the road as she walked. I could tell by the way the wagon moved that the thick, gold-tinged furs of wolves and dark beaver hides made for a heavy load. From the window I waved at Bush, but she didn't see me. She looked straight ahead.

The men had smoothed the road the previous day, raking rocks and filling in potholes, but a brief night rain had returned the road to its uneven, washboard state. Now the stubborn puddles reflected blue sky. Bush went around them. Once or twice, she had to turn around and use both hands to tug the wagon along.

She parted with the skins unwillingly, I knew. They meant something to her, more than just the symbol of her fight with the trappers. They were what was left of a past. Grasses and moose meat lived in the pelts of the wolves, water and trees in the skins of beavers. But she no longer worked for Rue; the nearly assembled turtle bones and shells sat in pieces outside her dark stone house like ancient things cast out of a changing sea. In order to buy provisions for our journey, Bush was forced to sell the furs that rattled behind her on the road.

It was the day before our journey. All of us were busy with preparations. I went back to the stove. The fire didn't take. I held another stick match to the kindling. This time it caught and the little fire roared in that smaller way fires have of sounding like their large relations who sweep through forests and consume everything in their path—trees, burrows, and nests.

Before long, Bush and the red-painted cart squeaked back down the road. This time the cart was loaded with sacks of oats, Carnation powdered milk, dried meat, three pairs of olive green lace-up rubber boots, and what was left of the beaver pelts, which Bush planned to take along to trade at outposts and stations along the northern waterways. In the north, some things were more valuable than money, and these were prime pelts, old, but thick and dense.

"It's damned inconvenient, if you ask me," Agnes mumbled as soon as Bush was inside the door. For the last few days, Agnes had wandered around the house nervous and distracted, unable to remember what she was doing. Now she'd forgotten why she had come into the living room.

Bush carried an armload of supplies through the door. "Give me a hand, Angel." She ignored Agnes' complaint.

I lifted the furs onto the cot. They smelled of cedar and were slightly dusty.

Agnes, I think, was angry about her mother's planned death. She was angrier still that she had no choice but to go along on the difficult death journey. But her anger, I figured, had a root of sadness. I followed her back to the little laundry room off the kitchen. I chatted with her, trying to distract her. "Do you think the weather's going to stay warm?" I asked.

She glared at me.

"What would happen if we had trouble up there?"

"What are you?" she said. "The FBI?"

I backed out and went into the kitchen. I pretended I was busy, but I kept an eye on Agnes. She wore a sour look and ran clothing through the wringer. When she came to Dora-Rouge's white blouse, she ran it through as if Dora-Rouge were still in it and she was punishing her, but her eyes were moist.

Dora-Rouge was every bit as stubborn as her daughter. It had long been her dream to return to the land of the Fat-Eaters to die and she wasn't going to let any child of hers keep her from doing one more thing in her life. She was beyond that now. "You don't have to go," she told Agnes.

It didn't escape anyone's notice that by now Dora-Rouge was the only one who believed wholeheartedly that we would complete the journey. Even Bush now realized the magnitude of our respon-sibility. She wore a stern, tight-lipped look. It didn't help, either, that all the men thought we were crazy, and even worse, they said so. Justin LaBlanc spared no words when he said to Bush, "The strongest men wouldn't do such a stupid thing as that. And with old Dora, too, carrying her and all." But in spite of everything a quickness filled the house as we packed. Agnes cleaned out her drawers and tucked her large underpants into a backpack. I rolled my jeans to make them more compact.

I picked up a rubber boot. "What are these?" They had lace-up supports at the ankles.

"They're for us. Here, hand me one." Bush sat down on the cot next to the furs. She pulled off a shoe and tried on the boot. "Yes, I think they'll fit." She stood up and tested it. "My old ones don't have enough support." She didn't mention that they were nearly ruined from her run through the thickets and that she'd placed them on the woodstove to warm. "Now, that's what I call a boot."

"How attractive," I said.

The boots were all the same size, 7. A little tight for me. It was all they'd gotten in. That's why they were on sale, the price marked on them with red pen: $4.98.

When I'd arrived there such a short time ago, I cared only about what I looked like. My eyes had been lined in dark blue and I showed only the good side of my face. I never gave much thought to what things were like inside me or how I felt. I had never cared what was practical, either. I'd walked to school, through snow, in white plastic shoes, my red-painted toes squeezed up tight inside them. And now I was going to wear army boots, tall ones at that.

I wondered if we'd reach our destination, the four of us. *Destination.* I liked that word, with its hint of fate. I believed in destiny as much as I believed everything was a sign. It had been a sign to get Agnes' letter with the folded dollar bills. It was a sign when a woodpecker tapped at a dead tree. Sometimes a person smiled at me a certain way and I knew we'd be friends or that our fates would, in some way, overlap. Once, I'd dreamed German words. *Achtung. Halt.* The next day two boys from Munich in dirty jeans showed up at the A&W and I went off with them to Frontier Days in Cheyenne, Wyoming. I was sure it was meant to be, that my dream was a sign. I was always looking for signs. I even called the two boys Stop and Look. But as I packed for our journey, I wondered about this particular destiny, if it was really ours. Maybe there were others to be pursued. Maybe destiny was a limitless, open road. Something dark and doubting weighed me down. I tried to talk those doubts away. Angel, I said to myself, you are being silly, Angel, you are this, you are that. As I went through my clothing, fresh from the line, I had feelings of dread and joy, hope and futility all linked together at once, as when people's destinies twine around each other like roots or vines. I had it in my stomach, that feeling of doubting, wondering if it really mattered if we stayed or went. Maybe we would head toward our destinies all the same without this trip, the four of us. And though my grandmothers accepted me without misgivings, slow as I was in their ways, and as fast as I was in others, I had cold feet. Bush trusted I could do the work, could paddle and lift, could hunt if I had to. But I was not so sure. What did matter to me was how much I wanted to find my mother, Hannah Wing, whose red hair was braided and twined together with my own, at least in color. I wanted to know the truth about her, whatever it was.

We worked all that day, chatting busily about what to take and what to leave until our supplies and equipment filled up the small living room. To my annoyance, Agnes worried about everything. She fidgeted and fussed over whether we had enough toilet paper, whether we should take the gray wheels from the office chair we now used to wheel Dora-Rouge about. "Just in case she needs them," Agnes said, but Dora-Rouge said, "Honey, don't worry so much about me. There's not a smooth piece of land between here and where we're going, anyway." But that only gave Agnes something else to worry about.

I helped to pack all Dora-Rouge's things into boxes to send to the people she was leaving behind. It was a sad chore, but I closed and labeled cardboard boxes of silverware, old moccasins, and carnival glass platters wrapped in newsprint. I folded an unused nightie and a bottle of wine from 1947 in a box for Frenchie and then I went to the bathroom to wipe my eyes. I'd packed herbs and seeds, including a few kernels of corn, for the old people on the Hundred-Year-Old Road.

When we were quiet, there was a weighty, downpouring silence which took up far more room than words and tents. At these moments, Dora-Rouge pushed her chair around the room with the canoe paddle, drifting as if she were already on water. She glided to the window and looked out in one last attempt to memorize the land, the fresh green light of the trees, and all the things she would never see again, even the broken-down, rusted old cars she'd complained about so often. Her eyes grew soft, reminding us all that this was an unhappy occasion.

Dora-Rouge felt guilty about depriving the others of her death. They saw it as a hardship of the heart, she knew, but the old land was calling her, and she had an unflagging loyalty to the land and to her own heart, and she had to obey. But once she said to me, as I put a paperweight in a brown bag, "I don't dare come back. They'd hate me for putting them through all this. Give that weight to Justin, will you?"

Afraid of the silence, I asked Bush again how many days she thought it would take. I already knew the answer. Bush played along with it, though. She closed her eyes, trying to calculate the distance by dark fathoms, and as if I had never asked the question before, said, "Thirteen. I'm sure of it."

"That's pretty optimistic, if you ask me," said Agnes. She handed me another roll of toilet paper. "Put that in the top of the bag." She'd already added odds and ends, lotion, an extra knife. "Put this in, too." She gave me a container of Morton's salt. "We might get dehydrated."

And Bush replied, "In a lake?" She stood there with her hands on her hips, a woman's gesture that to this day needs no words.

THE SOUND OF VOICES and fiddle music floated down the road toward us as we walked toward Frenchie's going-away party. Agnes hummed to herself in the manner that said she was in her own private world, which was often those days, as she tried to drown out the sound of our watery plans and the death talk of Dora-Rouge. I walked beside her in silence, my own mind still occupied with thoughts of fate and destiny. Tied in her secretary chair, Dora-Rouge looked like a scrawny hostage as Bush pushed her up the road. John Husk walked slightly ahead of us.

"He's the alpha male of the pack," Dora-Rouge joked. "Just look at him." He wore a starched white shirt, freshly ironed. Above us, bats flickered through the night sky.

Every once in a while, Agnes stopped humming and added some last thing to the list of what we should take. "We might need aspirin," she would say, and, "Don't let me forget the witch hazel."

Frenchie had done her best to blow up some balloons, but they were halfhearted little affairs. They were tacked to the door next to the "Bon Voyage" sign, and they were as wrinkled and rosy as Frenchie herself.

Inside her house was another world. Suddenly we were among the smell of perfumes, the bright blue vases and colored waters, the noise and flickering of the television that was always on and never in proper adjustment.

Dora-Rouge lit up with more than just the fluttering light of the televison. "Just look at this room!" The others parted like the Red Sea to let her pass.

It was going to be an occasion, I could see that. Frenchie would call it a "festive occasion" if she hadn't been so sad from the loss of her daughter. Still, she tried her best. Red carnations and baby's breath had come in from the florist by Tinselman's ferry. I'd for-gotten such things as greenhouse flowers. This was a measure of the distance between the Oklahoma I grew in and the north, and I was like one of those flowers, a forced bloom in unnatural condi-tions.

Dora-Rouge was transfixed. "I'm so glad I can still see!" With these words, everyone saw the room through her eyes. It was grand, full of people, everything scrubbed clean and shining. Even the walls were washed and, to Dora-Rouge's amazement, the windows had no streaks. Frenchie laid down her fiddle to hug Dora-Rouge. She was shoeless in her Sunday dress with the large red peonies. She hugged us tightly, one at a time. When she bent over Dora-Rouge, Frenchie's wonderful and sagging breasts bulged out a little above the low-cut flowered dress, and I smelled the rose water she had splashed on her skin.

Frenchie went back to fiddle playing, but only in B-flat—and she laughed. Her face, like Dora-Rouge's, looked full and bright, this time without the use of false color. While she played, Justin LaBlanc himself sat near her, the transforming power of love incar-nate, a bottle of Dr Pepper in his hand. He smiled and tapped an unpolished brown shoe on the floor, and when she wasn't playing and he wasn't eating, they held hands like young lovers. Justin looked slightly embarrassed around the other men, but it was them or Frenchie and, as he said, he'd had enough of them with their talk about fish and poker and bait. "And Frenchie's a good-looking woman. She's still got nice legs for a woman her age."

"When did all this happen?" I asked.

Dora-Rouge said, "The night the mirror broke."

Two young men, with their paper bags of liquor, had closed themselves into the bedroom. One woman asked Frenchie if she shouldn't kick them out. "Not tonight," Frenchie said, but every-one could already hear their slurred voices and smell the whiskey. Mingled with the fragrance of soup, bread, and perfume, it was a powerful kind of smell, an intoxicating poison that passed through the overheated house and made it seem damp as a swamp.

A few children from town ran through the house. Their parents tried in vain to silence them. Frenchie looked at the three boys and one girl with both a wistful amusement and a worry that they might break an Avon bottle or glass figurine.

A large tureen of wild rice and ham soup sat at the center of the table.

I followed Frenchie into the kitchen. "Can I help?"

She bustled about, getting silverware out of the drawer. "Oh, sure, honey. Put these soup spoons out for me, will you?"

The table was nearly ready. People were already lining up. Near some cloth napkins were bowls of warm water. "What's this? Soup?" Justin asked. He was first in line. Everyone stood behind him.

Frenchie peered out from the kitchen. "What's what?"

He pointed at the bowls.

"For washing your hands." She went back to the kitchen and didn't see how the people looked at each other. Even though they wanted to, no one smirked or laughed. "Finger bowls," they would say later, and they'd say Frenchie is just that way, it's how she always was.

When Justin opened a bottle of red wine, the two men from the back bedroom appeared as if by magic, their own bottle stashed away on the closet floor amid unmatched shoes and a few bright, low-cut dresses that had slipped off the scrawny shoulders of hangers. One of the two men was round and light-skinned. He wore a cast on his hand and wrist. He smiled at me in a way that was embarrassing. The other was dark and bone-thin, a red bandanna tied around his forehead, just above his eyes. They filled their plates and glasses and went back into the bedroom.

By the time Tommy arrived with four of the quiet people from the Hundred-Year-Old Road, the house was filled with a happy mood and the sound of forks on Melmac. My cheeks felt hot. I had sipped some of the wine when no one was looking. Others, plates balanced on their laps, could not stand up to greet or touch hands with the Hundred-Year-Old Road people, who all entered wearing solemn looks, reminding us of the importance and seriousness of the gathering and of our journey. At first no one but me seemed to notice, and it made me mighty nervous to see their faces, as if they thought we'd bit off more than we could chew. Or that we were all four going to our deaths. I had that feeling right away, and then, one by one, the others grew quiet until even the bright room itself dulled.

Wiley was dark and small. He was the one with the young wife, Chiquita, and she stood beside him, all of twenty-four, her hair pulled straight back. Wiley wore a thin cotton shirt with a sleeveless tee beneath it, his pants high. He remained standing and waited for the room to grow quiet, then he said a prayer for Dora-Rouge's safe departure. In spite of the new serious mood of the room, a few people smiled throughout the prayer, and looked at each other, especially Frenchie and Justin. I smiled at Tommy, hoping our lack of solemnity would not undermine our fortune with the Great Spirit as we traveled to the far place of my mother.

The Hundred-Year-Old Road people had intended to stay only awhile, but before long they, too, were carried into the merriment. What with the cut flowers and the fiddle, and the rare, noisy children, the happiness was contagious, in spite of the impending loss of Dora-Rouge. "It's the way I always wanted to go out," she said. After a while, even Wiley smiled and said, "Well, I might as well make a night of it," and he poured himself a glass of Coca-Cola, and in the house of perfumes and powders, bottles and tins, it seemed for once that everyone was prosperous, and we had joy, at least half a night's worth.

I watched Chiquita, wishing I knew her better. In spite of her hair, and her attempts to behave in a traditional manner—she really did try—she seemed younger than me, more protected than the girls I had known. Chiquita was impressed, for instance, with the perfumes on Frenchie's table and didn't try to hide it. "You have Avon!" she said. She opened a red bottle and smelled it. "I love Persian Wood."

"Why don't you keep it, dear?" With her hands, Frenchie pushed back any argument Chiquita might have had.

All night Chiquita held the bottle she was given, as if someone would steal it from her, or it would slip through her fingers if she let her guard down. I made a mental note that when we returned from the Fat-Eaters, I would give her some girl things. She was deprived, living with Wiley.

Then I turned my attention to Tommy. He ladled soup into a

flowered bowl and brought it to me. We stood together, afraid of our love and the words it might utter, so we said nothing. Only now did I think of how we would be apart. Now I was dreading to go.

Across the room, John Husk was well pressed and shining clean. Close to him, Chiquita passed the bottle of perfume beneath Wiley's nose. He wrinkled up his face. "You don't like it?" she asked. "He doesn't like it," she said to no one in particular, like a girl who'd taken up talking to air because she lived in the presence of the hard-of-hearing.

LaRue watched Bush from across the room like a predator who had just spotted a helpless lamb. He was dressed in the fashion of the day, pointed-toe shoes and tight pants, his hair loose at his shoulders and a pair of sunglasses hanging out of his shirt pocket. At least it wasn't a leisure suit, I thought. I gave him a stern look, but he didn't notice me at all; he had eyes only for Bush, who didn't cast a single look at him. She was preoccupied with listening to Mrs. Illinois. Her face, in deep worry as she listened and nodded, made me think about our journey, tomorrow's undertaking. Tommy took my hand, still quiet, and I leaned against him, feeling the strong warmth of his body.

About nine o'clock, people's attention again turned to us. Between sips of cola and wine, the men were full of advice for our journey. It was partly that we were women who were about to venture into the deep world of broken waters, and partly that the men believed we were touched with a craziness and it was their duty to set us straight. They must have thought we were giddy with confidence and not with wine. That's why they wanted to remind us of all the dangers ahead. They wanted us to know that we were journeying into a watery place most men would not want to endure, and that the dangers were real.

"This time of year is bad for bears," one man said to me.

"I know that," I said. I blushed to hear my haughty voice. It sounded like adolescent disdain. But my shortness was wasted on him.

From every corner the advice continued. "You have to mark your trails," one man said, and Wiley added, "Break twigs in case you have to find your way back. It's easy to get lost up there." It would have gone on all night except for the fact that Mrs. Illinois silenced them. "Hush," she said quietly. "You're worrying the girl. They have Dora-Rouge. They'll find the way."

The room quieted, but now that our trip was mentioned, Bush unfolded one of the maps beneath the light of a lamp and asked a few questions of the men she knew had journeyed into the far north by canoe. She went to the table and pushed dishes and cups aside and they all gathered in the light of a pink flowered lamp. Which currents were useful, she wanted to know, and which places had falls and steep portages to avoid.

"Why don't you let me do your face sometime?" Frenchie asked Chiquita, ignoring the concerns of the men, ignoring, too, the people bent over the map at the table. She had her priorities. Chiquita, so excited and deprived at the same time, smelled her perfumed wrist.

Only a few of Bush's questions were answered, and even those answers did not sound too certain. What had seemed so far away even a day before now stared us in the face. I no longer wanted to go. I knew this clearly, as well as I knew the love lines and life lines of my own palm. I had a bad feeling about it. Bush had hatched this plan in winter, under the crazy hand of cold and dark. I hated to admit LaRue might have been right. I had never been completely sure about Bush's sanity. Now the panic rose in my chest. But I knew I would go. I was dead clear about it. And I would utter no word of dissent, not even when the men said a thirteen-day journey was next to impossible. The furs were sold, the canoes were already on *The Raven,* and we were packed. This was a fate I accepted. But even so, Frenchie's house felt suddenly chilly. I told myself this was what it felt like for a bride, getting the jitters before her wedding. It was last-minute nerves.

Mrs. Illinois pulled up a chair beside Dora-Rouge. She called her by her old name. "Ena," she said. "Ena, do you remember that medicine on Sleeper Island, those tiny plants with round leaves? Could you bring me some?" But as soon as she spoke she remembered Dora-Rouge would not return. Too late, she clapped her hand over her mouth.

"It's all right." Dora-Rouge answered with grace and strength.

"I'll send them back with Agnes." She was going to say something else, but the clock on the wall called out ten o'clock and, relieved, she said instead, "Let's see the news."

It was a troubling time, with difficult news. The war in Vietnam would soon be over, but the deaths, to everyone's shock and dismay, were still carried across oceans and land by the invisible waves and particles of air. On a closer front, the American Indian Movement was gaining momentum in the cities. We'd heard a little about the goings-on in Wounded Knee, but we were hungry for more information. We wanted to see and hear more from the young men with braids. They sounded strong as warriors to us. Many of the people in the room admired them, even the older ones, and some had already taken to letting their hair grow and wearing it, once again, in growing-out braids.

If the American Indian Movement got little attention on television, the dams and diversions of rivers to the north were even more absent. They were a well-kept secret, passed along only by word-of-mouth. We would have known nothing about them if not for the young men who canoed from place to place, telling people what had happened.

The news disturbed Justin. As if he could bear it no longer, he exploded in red-faced anger. "Those young men act just like Reds!" Communists, he meant. That's what he called AIM members. Everyone turned away from the gray light of the screen and stared at him. He didn't seem to notice. His eyes were watching the screen. But Frenchie, too, stared at him. "What?" she said, as if she hadn't understood. "What?"

"They're Reds." He repeated this in an angry voice, still looking at the screen, oblivious to the openmouthed stares around him.

"Why, Justin LaBlanc. How can you say such a thing?" Frenchie didn't wait for his answer. "They're right! You can see with your own eyes what's happening." Her face turned pale and she began to tremble. She stood up awkwardly. "I can't believe you feel that way!" She walked quickly to the room where the two men drank among the doilies and talcum dust and mirrors. Her high-heeled shoes clicked behind her. "Get out," I heard her say. "Get out of here now!" She slammed the door behind them and they stood before us, red-eyed and sheepish, all of us staring at them as if they held a clue as to what was going on.

We watched the rest of the news in uncomfortable silence, pretending Justin hadn't spoken, but soon after that, a few people drifted out of the house toward their homes. They held Dora-Rouge tightly a long time before they left, and they cried. With both hands, Mrs. Illinois held a hanky to her face and sobbed into it.

After a while, Bush took a glass of water in to Frenchie. She was gone awhile and when she came back out I asked, "What did she say?"

"She's crying." And more quietly, so no one else would hear, "She's drinking their whiskey." The two men were empty-handed and unsteady, still standing.

But just then Frenchie flew out of the room like a storm. "Get out of my house!" she said to Justin. Her face was red and puffy. Justin went over to her and touched her shoulders with both of his hands. He bent down just enough to look squarely into her eyes and, as if he were talking to a child, he said, "I was wrong, baby, it's just the old U.S. Army in me talking. Ever since being in the service I hear the voices of the sergeants, and they even speak right out of my mouth. Like how you hear your mother. The thing is, it's their words, not mine."

Husk and LaRue looked at Justin LaBlanc as if he were crazy. Then they exchanged a glance between them. LaRue shook his head as if to say, "He's got it bad, and an old man, too."

To prove how sorry he was, Justin ate one of Frenchie's cookies, the ones he had hated before. She was still red-faced. She sat down at the end of the table.

Frenchie had been right, all of us agreed. Luckily, Justin, using the army sergeants as an excuse, had saved face in their eyes. If anything, they respected him more for admitting he was wrong, because they'd all been mad at him, too, they had just kept their own mouths shut.

By the time we were ready to leave for the night, Frenchie was pacified. Just a moment after we stepped out the door, she said, "Wait. I have something for you."

She went inside. When she returned she placed, in Dora-

Rouge's lap, two of the precious bags of wild rice she was storing for relatives. They were contained in flowered pillowcase cotton and tied with pink ribbon.

ON THE WAY HOME, Agnes walked beside me, carrying away some of the wilting hothouse carnations. Light clouds drifted across the full moon. She looked up. "Do you think it's a good idea to leave during the full moon?" By now everyone was accustomed to her anxiety and no one answered.

Husk pushed Dora-Rouge and her wheeled secretary chair over the bumpy road, the rice heavy in her lap. Even though he hadn't had a single drink, the secretary chair Frenchie had sent on the ferry from her daughter's place would speed up now and then, with a will of its own.

"You're damaging my kidneys," Dora-Rouge said in a shaky voice. "Slow down."

Husk obeyed for a few moments, but before long, distracted, he would speed up the pace again.

"I mean it! Slow down." Her voice rattled. She put out a tiny foot as if to stop the chair. A darker cloud moved over the moon.

"I'm so sorry." Husk's white shirt shone through the darkness and with his black pants it looked like there were no man's legs beneath it. I watched the floating shirt and the soft, white hair of Dora-Rouge move through the darkness of night. The smell of Frenchie's perfumes was still in our clothing. Dora-Rouge bumped along the narrow road. The lights of houses fell across the deep spring grasses and a soft breeze moved them like waves of water. It was a beautiful night, the grasses bending, and Husk in his luminous shirt. Agnes hummed, her voice deep and soft, this time not just to drown out the voices of others, because we were quiet. It was one of the songs strong enough to need no words.

ON THAT LAST NIGHT, whenever I closed my eyes to sleep, I had visions of our traveling. In the darkness I saw the two canoes like thin lights moving through water, or silk-fine cocoons, the bodies brilliant inside them, waiting to grow wings. Sun played across the shimmering skin of water. Floating, I looked down from above and had no sense of what world was there except that it was alive, immense, and it took us in. For great distances ahead of me was the shining water. But a kind of sorrow stood by the bed. I pulled the sheets to my neck as if I could keep it from me. Maybe something I didn't know was dreaming me. Somehow I knew I would lose a part of myself on this journey, as if, when we cast off into water, I would step outside my skin. It was a kind of dying. And I was afraid. Before then I'd feared that night and sleep could swallow me, that I would drown inside darkness, but now my fears grew to contain lakes and rivers and things with teeth.

I pulled back the covers. Barefoot, I went to the kitchen after Dora-Rouge's bitter sleeping potion, but before I reached the bathroom, there was a soft knock at the door. I tiptoed over. "Who is it?" I whispered, leaning against the door. But I knew who it was. I opened the door. Tommy stood on the porch. A light wind moved the trees outside. "I want to be with you," he said.

I buried my face in his chest and let him in. We lay down together in silence on the cot. We were close enough that I could feel his heart beating. We stroked each other's hair. He caressed me with infinite tenderness, touching my face lightly. His arms were dark and strong against the white sheets. Our bodies made an agreement with one another, that one day they would be lovers. Soon, on the crowded little cot, I slept, my head against his shoulder, with none of Dora-Rouge's potion in my stomach.

WHEN I OPENED my eyes Agnes smiled simply and said, "Did you remember to pack the rice?"

I nodded.

She must have watched us sleep for a while before she woke us, looking at our bare arms casual in the square light from the kitchen, our hands half-open in that sleeping kind of faith bodies have that they are safe, a trust lost in daylight.

For a moment Agnes busied herself folding blankets, then she turned away and went to the kitchen so that we could get up without embarrassment.

Through the window the first morning light was a line of red.

Beside the cot, Tommy's boots sat in an angle of yellow kitchen light. They looked comforting in a domestic kind of way.

The bacon smelled good and it was already cooked. Bush sat at the table. She studied the maps in a last, almost desperate, effort to understand the territory.

"You can never be sure," Dora-Rouge teased. "But we're already lost."

There were last-minute details. Agnes put an extra shine on the stove, arranged the wilting carnations, and dusted a shelf that she usually overlooked. For Tommy, Husk cracked three extra eggs on the side of the black iron skillet. They sizzled in the grease.

No one said a word about Tommy's presence. It was a natural thing. I was the only one nervous about it, not that we'd done anything but sleep. And how unlike me that was. I thought how different my own people were from the ones I'd lived with in Oklahoma. Here, sleeping with a man wasn't an offense. True sin had nothing to do with love; it consisted of crimes against nature and life. But it might have been that they all wanted me to love Tommy so I would never leave. Whichever it was, I liked it.

IT WAS A MORNING full of fire smoke. As we loaded our supplies into the rusting truck, I hung back a little. Whenever I looked at Bush, we shared a gaze of common concern. We were caretakers on this trip. Most of the work was up to us, and neither of us knew for sure how we'd get Dora-Rouge across all that space. God only knew how many portages. Dora-Rouge, of course, insisted there would be few. There would be roadblocks, we were sure, as the police tried to keep all but the local Indians out of the Two-Town area. That's what the Fat-Eaters' territory was called on maps. And for all we knew, the waterways might also be closed off by the time we reached the Fat-Eaters. Then we'd have to turn back. Or worse yet, they might shoot at us.

Dora-Rouge said, looking at me, as if reading my mind, "We'll find a way." She was composed and seemed larger than usual, with calm eyes.

Agnes rummaged through the packs at the last minute. She stretched tall to reach one that had already been loaded into the truck bed. Awkwardly she unzipped pockets, searching inside, still anxious that she'd forgotten something. She looked weary. When the truck was finally all packed, she returned to the house to look things over one last time. Leaving, she could not bear to close the door behind her. She left it open.

Bush boosted her up into the truck. Then, after Bush was in, Tommy put Dora-Rouge on Bush's lap. Dora-Rouge glared at Husk, still mad at him from the night before. "This better be easy on my kidneys."

"I'll drive slow," he said.

Bush said didn't the air smell good.

After Tommy and I climbed into the rusted truck bed, we were off. I turned and looked back at the house one last time. The torn screen had been sewn a few days ago by Agnes, a last jagged touch, with blue thread. The red chair sat beside the door. The door itself watched like an open eye, waiting to see us return to simple fires and sleepings. Inside were the closed cupboards and cleaned-out drawers, the for-once empty kettles.

We rattled down the road as morning rolled across the lake, its first sunlight a red fire on the windows of buildings we passed.

A FEW CARLOADS OF PEOPLE waited to see Dora-Rouge off. I was surprised to see them. Frenchie stood and wiped at her eyes with a perfumed handkerchief embroidered in yellow silk, Justin at her side. The two young men had slept by the lake all night, and now, with dried grass in their hair, they looked surprised that the party-goers were present.

From behind the sound of tackle boxes I heard water lapping at the land and the clanking of fishermen loading up their boats for the day. Tommy and I unloaded the gear and carried it, bit by bit, to the rocking boat. It was going to be a tight fit. A loon spoke a solitary word. Suddenly everything was ready, and then it was a tearful good-bye as John Husk started the motor and *The Raven* began to cut its way across the lake. Agnes hollered something at Bush. Bush leaned forward to hear her, but Agnes' words were whipped away by cold wind as soon as they left her mouth.

"Did you get the mosquito net?" Agnes asked. I nodded.

OUR FIRST PORTAGE, the first real step of our journey, was long, steep, and rocky. The men helped us over this first stretch of land. Tommy slipped the food pack onto my back. It was an enormous weight, more than I had imagined. I thought this didn't bode well. Day one and I was already overloaded. It wasn't just food, but pots and pans as well, even a stove. He patted it as if that would make it lighter. "How's that?"

"Okay," I lied. I started up the rocky path. My ankles felt as if they would break under the weight, and it was difficult to breathe. I stumbled. Once, Bush came up behind me, loaded like a pack burro, and I complained to her. "This is killing my ankles." But then I looked at her and wanted to laugh. She carried a pack of clothes, tents, and a tarp, all on her back, with paddles and seat cushions in her hands.

"The boots," she said. "You need them." She put down her bag and rummaged through it until she found them and sat them on the trail. "Put these on." She leaned backward, bent to an almost sitting position, and struggled into her pack again.

With Bush's help, still nearly falling, I worked myself out from under my own pack and sat it on the ground. I took off my shoes and pulled the army-colored rubber boots onto my feet. They didn't feel much better, but at least they had laced-up ankle support.

Bush picked up the seat cushions and paddles.

"Wait a minute," I said. I couldn't lift my pack onto my own back.

She put down the paddles and cushions to help me.

Then I loaded up, trying to stand beneath the weight. I handed her the paddles.

"We need a choreographer," Bush said. But I didn't smile. Not even a hint of a smile. Already I was exhausted and we'd have to lug the heavy furs, too, next portage, without Husk and Tommy. Not to mention carrying Dora-Rouge. Discouraged already on our first day, I followed Bush up the hilly portage and half-slid down the other side. It was treacherous, with loose stones and muddy, slippery places, a hint of what was to come.

I wasn't the only one with doubts. Once, on that first day's trip, we realized Agnes had not kept up with us. Bush back-tracked and found her sitting on a stone, breathing heavily. Her hair was damp with sweat. When I saw her I felt a sinking sensation. I didn't hold out much hope for this trip. I was sorry Bush had ever told Dora-Rouge about this idea. We wouldn't reach our destination for two weeks, longer if the men at Frenchie's party were correct.

For day one, I had a bad attitude. I fell into step beside Bush, wondering aloud why we couldn't find a way to break through all the highways, rails, and airways that were closed to protesters, and why Dora-Rouge couldn't wait a little longer to die. I'd thought all along that if we remained, Dora-Rouge might live longer, that it was a way of keeping her. "I don't want her to die, anyway. Besides, why can't we just drive there? Why does everything always have to be so hard with you?" I said this, though I knew why we couldn't just drive. It wasn't just that we would never have reached our destination, but that there were herbs to gather, places Dora-Rouge wanted, needed, to visit.

Just then Tommy came up behind us and I tried to look like all the work was a breeze. He carried Dora-Rouge as if she were a bag of feathers. She was bright with excitement. It was the land of the voyageurs and she said she could almost hear the French songs coming out of the ground. "Can't you hear them?" she asked. She said the older, Indian songs were just behind them. Tommy carried her past us, his boots noisy on the gravel. She looked back at us and gave the sign for okay, joining her thumb and index finger together as if she were doing all the work herself and it was nothing. But even Dora-Rouge didn't cheer me. Nor was the green beauty of the land any consolation.

Even so, underneath it all, something beckoned, more than my mother, more than healing plants or dams. For Bush, water was the summoning thing. For me, it was something I had yet to understand, but it compelled me.

By the time we reached the place where land ended and new water began, John Husk was walking beside Agnes, carrying some of the furs. I could see he refrained from voicing his concerns. Tommy, with his muscular legs, had passed three effortless times to my one, the last time carrying the new camouflage canoe with his head inside it, as if it weighed nothing. Paul Bunyan, I thought, smiling at him.

Then, too soon, we were at the water, ready to strike off on our own. "You might need this," Husk said, offering Bush the handle of a pistol. "The ammo is in the waterproof case." He pointed it out. The red case sat on top of the food pack.

Bush took the gun without a word. Her hopes, like mine, were sinking, and everything added to the weight we had to carry—the gun, even the heavy hopes—and then suddenly it was solemn, it was the time I'd dreaded. We were leaving. Husk looked tired. He kissed Agnes. A long kiss, caressing her back. He held Dora-Rouge in his arms a long while. He called her "my mother," and he stumbled when he turned away with tears in his eyes.

Dora-Rouge looked at Husk and Tommy and at all the things and places she'd never see again. This world was a beautiful place, filled with life. Even the air was a soup of love and pollen and stars; that's what she'd always said, and then she settled down into the canoe as if she had always lived there.

As we paddled away, both Dora-Rouge and I looked back every few yards and waved to the two men standing at the water. Each time we looked, John and Tommy grew smaller and farther away. Then, one time, I turned back and they were no longer there. Where they had stood a moment before was just emptiness. I waved anyway, feeling a sinking in my stomach and chest. Above us, the ravens called out.

Agnes and Bush were in the larger canoe, both paddling, although it was only a halfhearted attempt on Agnes' part. Dora-Rouge, the furs, and I were in the other.

Soon Bush pulled up alongside our camouflage canoe. "The waters are swollen. That's to our advantage." She softened when she looked at Dora-Rouge, who was curved into the canoe, seeming at peace, with the furs about her. "How are you doing, Dora?"

"Never better," she said, the light reflecting on her glasses. "Just look." All around us was the green of opened spring, the new leaves reflected by water, the gleam of sky beneath the canoes.

WE PADDLED long and hard that day. Sometimes I fell into the rhythm of it. Then, it seemed effortless. But the rest of the time, I hid behind my sunglasses and windblown red hair, and cried. And when we portaged, even with the new boots, I cried when I walked, from the weight, from the ache in my ankles, from my belief that this trip was a pipe dream. I cried when I lifted Dora-Rouge, and when I sat still. On top of all that, I, who had never admitted to being lonely, had a terrible first touch of loneliness seeing John and Tommy vanish, and it all was made even worse knowing Dora-Rouge would soon be gone from my life forever. If anyone noticed I cried, she kept silent about it.

The shadows lengthened into late afternoon and we were settled into a rhythm when it dawned on Agnes what she had forgotten. She sat bolt upright. "Oh no! My coat!" Her hand flew to her throat. "I forgot my coat!"

Bush and I stared at her.

Agnes' eyes filled with tears.

"It isn't too far yet," Dora-Rouge said. "We should go back for it."

We stopped paddling, the two canoes side by side. With the late sun reflecting off its surface, the water rocked us, the trees behind us, all around us. I knew if we turned around, we would have to cross the long portage again by ourselves, and we would have to say another good-bye to John and Tommy. As it was, I could think of nothing but sleep.

For a long time Agnes considered this. "No," she said. "It would take at least another day to get back to Adam's Rib on the lake. Look how long it took them to tow us." She seemed unconvinced, though. I think she hoped we'd ignore her words and insist on returning, but she said, "I'll just have to do without it."

Dora-Rouge meant it when she said again, "We should go back."

And Agnes meant it when she said, "No," and waved us on.

EARLY EVENING we stopped to set up camp. I was exhausted beyond anything I had ever known. With a clattering of poles the tents went up, and Bush and I unrolled the sleeping bags. It was only around six o'clock, and there was a beautiful, rosy light to the sky, but I fell immediately into a deep sleep, leaving Bush and Agnes to cook, clean up, and put the food pack on a rope high up between trees, far away from bears. I didn't even smell the chicken of that first night's feast. I slept on a rock that would have been unbearably miserable at any other time in my life.

The next morning I woke with aching muscles and blisters on my feet that had gone unnoticed the day before. I ate the leftover fried chicken hungrily while Dora-Rouge stared at the sky with its soft clouds.

Once under way on that second day, we made good time, and in the warm sunlight of late morning, the pain in my arms dropped away.

The current was with us most of the day, and so was the wind.

All around us were the wide shining spaces of my dreams. Sometimes it seemed as if we were the first people who'd passed here. Near one island, we paddled through strands of spider silk, the paths and creations of other lives reaching out from themselves, drifting sheer behind us, and stuck to our clothing and boats as if we were carrying away the threads of what we were leaving, or unraveling some fabric of the past.

There were only two portages the second day. Both were short and both were on Bush's map. Along one of them were unfolding ferns, horsetail, and deep, cool shade, a beloved darkness of the earth. Turtles out in the lake had pulled themselves up on rocks and logs, and the sunlight glistened on their shells. Beneath sky, the water was blue.

At midday we stopped at the first island to rest and eat lunch. "The vichyssoise is highly overrated," Dora-Rouge said, drinking powdered, reconstituted soup.

At this place, Bush cast out a line and caught three shining fish. Northern pike. Not wanting to build a fire just yet, she wrapped them in plastic and placed them in water to keep cool. We ate them that night, laying them on evergreen boughs to let the grease drip off, according to Dora-Rouge's recipe and direction.

DORA-ROUGE, the woman going home, was going backward in her memory as well, in that way a single life travels a closed circle. As she floated in water, she thought about the time when the Indian agents came to take her away to school.

She was twelve, she said, lithe as a snake.

I was a tomboy. Always scrambling up the trees. I caught the most bottom fish of all, you know, and I was just a girl. My nickname was Walleye. "Hey, Walleye," the boys would say. I was just tiny.

The agents from the school caught me, but I managed to escape from their big, pale hands, the way a fish would; I slipped out.

They scared me to death. Their eyes were so blue, I thought they were evil spirits. They were tall, too, more than any men I'd ever seen. I escaped. I ran. I felt the thickets grabbing at my skirt.

Once, when I looked back, I fell over a rock. I knew my leg was broken, I heard it break. But as bad as it hurt, that's how bad my fear was, too. I crawled home, crying. I cried all the way. The skin of my palms and elbows was all broken open by the time I got back.

Ek, my mother, set the leg and she made a splint of willow bark.

The next year, when they came again to round up children for school, I was slower. They caught me. I held to my little sister tight and wouldn't let go. The men hit us to get us apart. It was so sad. When they carried me away my little sister held out her arms, her nose bleeding, her eyes streaming tears. "Ena," she said, "Ena, don't leave me. Somebody please help us, please!"

I can hear her and see her. She wore a brown dress, a dress that had been mine. She held her arms out to me. It still breaks my heart to remember. It was just a few years later when little sister, taken to another school, walked into the snow, lay down on it, and froze to death. I wouldn't have even known except some boys came by the school and told me. I went home. Thirty-two miles, too, and it was winter. I wore seal boots I'd stolen from a teacher. Some stolen sunglasses, too. Because of snow blindness. Oh, it was a terrible walk. That long night I slept in a cave of ice. I knew about winter spirits that prey on the souls of young girls, but I was too tired to fear them. I heard when you freeze to death, you get sleepy first. You see things. I saw my mother stirring a kettle. She looked so beautiful. We were always happy. We had such love. I shook my head to keep awake. But I saw my father walk right out of winter with frozen meat the way he always did, a lynx on his back. Like he just stepped out of a blizzard. He looked like he was made of snow. I dreamed of my brother. He used to swing me up in his arms. "Ena," he would say, "I hope you grow up ugly, so no man will want you. Then you have to stay here with us. We get to keep you."

By the time I got home, my fingers were frostbitten. But it was a small pain next to that memory of having seen my sister cry and call out my name, begging the righteous men to let me go.

DORA-ROUGE LOOKED at her hands as if she was seeing them young, new in all this history. They were full of memory—the soft touch of her sister; the father who'd taught her to drive a team of dogs along their trapline, their faces nearly covered with cloth and fur to keep them warm. Through her I could see into the past. I saw the deep past, even before the time of Dora-Rouge.

In the past, I'd heard, it was a woman who saw the first white men arrive in a boat. They were floating toward her. Before she'd seen the wind-filled sails of the graceful boat of death, she thought it was a floating island and that it carried strange and beautiful beings instead of the tormented world that was its true cargo. No one could have guessed its presence would change everything until she and her people would want to lie down on ice, like Dora-Rouge's little sister, and die. The woman who saw the island coming toward her didn't know beloved children would be mutilated, women cut open and torn, that strong, brave men would die, and that even their gods would be massacred. She didn't know of horses, the long-necked ones, that would stand in one place in the winter and freeze like statues and still be there next spring, aloof and majestic and blue, with frozen manes and ice crystals shimmering in the air all around them.

AS WE TRAVELED, we entered time and began to trouble it, to pester it apart or into some kind of change. On the short nights we sat by firelight and looked at the moon's long face on water. Dora-Rouge would lie on the beaver blankets and tell us what place we would pass on the next day. She'd look at the stars in the shortening night and say, "the Meeting Place," or "God Island." True to her word, the next day we reached those places.

God Island, according to Bush's maps, was now named Smith's Island. It had been an old settlement. We paddled toward it in silence, slowing ourselves as we neared land, drifting toward it. There was a sense of mystery about it. A few tall, moss-covered stone walls remained half-standing at one end of the large island, like a crumbled fortress. A sense of richness dwelled on this island, as if it were inhabited by people to this day unseen but present all the same.

A very tall man had gone there in search of copper mines, Dora-Rouge told us. He was part of a tribe from the east, but had become lost, and instead of the copper, he found this island inhabited by small women and only a few short men. Instead of continuing his search for the island of red silver, he remained. Eventually he took several wives, women who bore taller children, all of them beautiful and copper brown. Whenever strangers came, they thought the people were so beautiful and straight they looked like gods.

"God Island," said Dora-Rouge. "It's an appropriate name. The people there feared no evil and wanted not," she said. "Look, it still has the trees."

It was true, there were ancient trees in the center that looked as if they belonged in a southern swamp. They were something like cypress.

Even from a distance the island had a feeling of intimacy. It was open and inviting. I thought maybe that was why the tall man had stayed. Or perhaps it was the word "God" that was inviting to me, a word I thought I knew too much about. The one who had tortured Job, who had Abraham lift the ax to his son, who, disguised as a whale, had swallowed Jonah.

I know now that the name does not refer to any deity, but means simply to call out and pray, to summon. To use words and sing, to speak. And call out that island did. I heard the sound of this strong land. It was so lovely that, skeptical or not, I wanted to stay there for the night.

"No. We should move on," Bush said, even though the island seemed to plead with us to remain. "All the campsites are taken."

When I looked back, I agreed with her. Something lived there, something I didn't understand, but would always remember by feel, and when I felt it, I would call it God and that was how I came later to understand that God was everything beneath my feet, everything surrounded by water; it was in the air, and there was no such thing as empty space.

Now, looking back, I understand how easily we lost track of things. The time we'd been teasing apart, unraveled. And now it began to unravel us as we entered a kind of timelessness. Wednesday was the last day we called by name, and truly, we no longer needed time. We were lost from it, and lost in this way, I came alive. It was as if I'd slept for years, and was now awake. The others felt it, too. Cell by cell, all of us were taken in by water and by land, swallowed a little at a time. What we'd thought of as our lives and being on earth was gone, and now the world was made up of pathways of its own invention. We were only one of the many dreams of earth. And I knew we were just a small dream.

But there was a place inside the human that spoke with land, that entered dreaming, in the way that people in the north found direction in their dreams. They dreamed charts of land and currents of water. They dreamed where food animals lived. These dreams they called hunger maps and when they followed those maps, they found their prey. It was the language animals and humans had in common. People found their cures in the same way.

"No one understands this anymore. Once they dreamed lynx and beaver," Agnes said. "It used to be that you could even strike a bargain with the weather."

For my own part in this dreaming, as soon as I left time, when Thursday and Friday slipped away, plants began to cross my restless sleep in abundance. A tendril reached through darkness, a first sharp leaf came up from the rich ground of my sleeping, opened upward from the place in my body that knew absolute truth. It wasn't a seed that had been planted there, not a cultivated growing, but a wild one, one that had been there all along, waiting. I saw vines creeping forward. Inside the thin lid of an eye, petals opened, and there was pollen at the center of each flower. Field, forest, swamp. I knew how they breathed at night, and that they were linked to us in that breath. It was the oldest bond of survival. I was devoted to woods the wind walked through, to mosses and lichens. Somewhere in my past, I had lost the knowing of this opening light of life, the taking up of minerals from dark ground, the magnitude of thickets and brush. Now I found it once again. Sleep changed me. I remembered things I'd forgotten, how a hundred years ago, leaves reached toward sunlight, plants bent into currents of water. Something persistent nudged me and it had morning rain on its leaves.

Maybe the roots of dreaming are in the soil of dailiness, or in the heart, or in another place without words, but when they come together and grow, they are like the seeds of hydrogen and the seeds of oxygen that together create ocean, lake, and ice. In this way, the plants and I joined each other. They entangled me in their stems and vines and it was a beautiful entanglement.

"I KNEW there'd be another plant dreamer in my family someday," Dora-Rouge said. Her mother, Ek, had been an herb woman. I got it from blood, she said. I came by it legitimately.

"Can you draw them?" she asked.

We searched the packs for a pencil. But we had forgotten a pencil, along with all the other things we'd left behind: combs, pencils, paper, keys.

Bush lit a match, blew it out, and handed it to me. "Here. Try this."

I laughed. If the world came to an end, I wanted to be with Bush. She could make do with anything. "What a good idea," I said. I appreciated her. Bush could find water in a desert, food on an iceberg. She knew the way around troubles. These waters were the only things that muddled her.

She tore open a brown bag, flattened it out, and laid it before me, almost reverent, a map awaiting creation.

I drew carefully, but after a while, the smudges vanished into the paper, so I merely began to remember the plants inside myself and describe them to Dora-Rouge. "This one is the color of sage," I would say, closing my eyes, seeing it. "It opens like a circle. It grows between rocks."

"That's an akitsi plant," said Dora-Rouge. "It's good for headaches."

SOME MORNINGS as we packed our things, set out across water, the world was the color of copper, a flood of sun arrived from the east, and a thick mist rose up from black earth. Other mornings, heating water over the fire, we'd see the world covered with fog, and the birdsongs sounded forlorn and far away. There were days when we traveled as many as thirty miles. Others we traveled no more than ten. There were times when I resented the work, and days I worked so hard even Agnes' liniment and aspirin would not relax my aching shoulders and I would crave ice, even a single chip of it, cold and shining. On other days I felt a deep contentment as I poled inside shallow currents or glided across a new wide lake.

We were in the hands of nature. In these places things turned about and were other than what they seemed. In silence, I pulled through the water and saw how a river appeared through rolling fog and emptied into the lake. One day, a full-tailed fox moved inside the shadows of trees, then stepped into a cloud. New senses came to me. I was equal to the other animals, hearing as they heard, moving as they moved, seeing as they saw.

ONE NIGHT we stayed on an island close to the decaying, moss-covered pieces of a boat. Its remains looked like the ribs of a large animal. In the morning, sun was a dim light reaching down through the branches of trees. Pollen floated across the dark water and gathered, yellow and life-giving, along the place where water met land.

ONE DAY we came to a long swamp that neither Bush nor Dora-Rouge could identify. Agnes looked at us with her arms across her chest. Bush furrowed her brow and looked around as if a clue to our location could be fathomed by the shapes of trees or the sounds of birds. She took out her maps and looked at the lay of the land, trying to decipher any familiar shape. Dora-Rouge rested her scrawny back against a bedroll. "Well, we've passed God Island and the ribs of that boat. We must be at . . ." But just then, before she finished speaking, Bush once more unfolded the map and held it open, and as she did, the creases split, the map came apart, and parts of it fell from her hands.

Dora-Rouge laughed. "Throw it away."

But even after that, useless as it was, there were many evenings Bush would look at a piece of the map, hold it up in the light and stare.

I never understood why she placed so much faith in paper when she trusted nothing else about the world that had created those maps. She wanted to know where she was at any given time, as if not knowing would change everything, would say there was such a thing as being lost. Whenever frogs in the swamp ahead of us began to sing, she fretted. "There's no swamp on any of the maps, not here, anyway," she'd say. Or when we crossed a stream, "I wonder if this is Willow Creek."

From the west, soft clouds floated over. We set up camp. I placed stones in a circle and built a fire, then walked across the rocky island and entered the cold water. For a while I floated and dog-paddled and looked at the land on which we were camped. There was smoke from our campfire. It was a place of mosses, lichens, and calm water. From the water I saw Agnes off by herself, singing, walking toward a group of trees.

I was swimming stronger than ever. The water was cold and it was sharp against my skin, as if it had blades or edges. But I swam.

My arms were lean and newly muscled. I moved through water easily. Then, refreshed, I dried myself, pulled on my jeans and sweater, and went about the job of gathering more wood. We had worked out our routines by now. We had our roles. Wood gathering was one of mine. And fire building. Bush and I set up tents, unrolled sleeping bags. Agnes cooked.

Soon we had boiling water and black coffee, and I saw Bush walk toward us with two large fish on a stringer.

I teased her. She was a dreamer of walleyes, I told her.

Agnes looked at Bush, looked at the two fish, and said, "Where's yours and Angel's?"

ONE EVENING it seemed cooler. The air had a different feel, rarefied, clean, and thin. Wolves in the distance were singing and their voices made a sound that seemed to lie upon the land, like a cloud covering the world from one edge of the horizon to the other. We sat around the fire and listened, the light on our faces, our eyes soft. Agnes warmed her hands over the flames.

There was a shorter time of darkness every night, but how beautiful the brief nights, with the stars and the wolves.

THE NEXT DAY, as if we'd become too complacent, a dark cloud of mosquitoes rose up from swamps and marshes. It was late for them, Bush said. Up to now, we'd just been lucky. She reached to the bottom of the clothing pack and took out four white cloth hats and shook them until the brims opened. I laughed but I was grateful she'd brought them. "Where in the world did you get those?" I asked. They looked vaguely like safari hats. Bush was too busy searching among the clothing for veils to answer me.

Within a few moments we looked like brides on safari. The insects landed on the netting, attracted by our warm breath. Already the droning of them made me anxious. I was grateful Bush had remembered the nets. We had to cover our hands, as well. The high noise of the mosquitoes, as they came near me, tightened my stomach. I waved them away, but more of them seemed to slip around behind any movement I made.

"Don't bother to fight them," Dora-Rouge said. "It only wastes your energy." Then she said, "I don't know what I had in mind. We should have been drinking swamp tea."

Yes, I remembered the tea. People in the north had used it for centuries as tonic, as repellent.

"We forgot it," Agnes said, but she did not say that Bush, in her zeal to keep our packs light, had probably left it out.

Bush set to work making a larger fire, a smudge, and we put green wood on it, grass, and leaves until smoke was all around us.

"We need to get the tea leaves," said Dora-Rouge, coughing.

My eyes watered.

But even if we found swamp tea that day, it had to build up; it would be a few days before enough tea was in our blood to keep the insects away. In the meantime, the insects tortured me the most, flying toward me with an electric sound, finding the places I'd neglected to cover: the hole in my jeans, the gap between neck and shirt collar. Pant-leg openings. "It's because you eat too much sugar," Agnes said.

Later, I heard stories, accounts of caribou and men killed by mosquitoes, almost bloodless or drowned as they submerged themselves to get away from the tiny swarming insects.

At darkness, when the mosquitoes abated for a time, Bush went out to gather stalks and leaves of the tea. She was careful in the canoe as she paddled toward the swampy regions where both mosquitoes and swamp tea grew, taking with her a light that would, unfortunately, also wake many of the insects prematurely.

I saw her move across the lake, the water silver and heavy as mercury.

Mosquitoes are one of the oldest forms of life. They were already there when the first people lit their fires of smoke. That's what Dora-Rouge said. Their ancestors heard the songs of my ancestors, she said, and they were there when the French passed through the broken land singing love songs and ballads of sorrow. They were there when the fur traders paddled swiftly through rivers, up and down, searching for furs and for the dark men who would offer them for trade. The mosquitoes remembered all the letting of blood. They remembered the animals sinking down into earth.

Sometimes I thought I could hear these things myself, the lonely, sad songs coming through trees and up from the banks of their destruction. Always, behind those songs, I heard our own deep-pitched songs that were the songs of land speaking through its keepers. Sometimes, too, I heard the old ones in the songs of wolves. It made me think we were undoing the routes of explorers, taking apart the advance of commerce, narrowing down and distilling the truth out of history.

We were still and let smoke curl around our bodies. The next day I resorted, finally, to wearing mud in order to protect my too-sweet skin, and to draw the sting from the bites. In what we thought of as evening, the mosquitoes and swarms of black flies were a shadow, a dark cloud, clinging to the tents. I was ashamed to be so afraid of them, more afraid of them than of bears or wolves, or even wolverines. But one evening we looked at each other, our veils covered with alive, dark mosquitoes, mud on our faces, gloves on our hands, and I started laughing. It was contagious, the laughter. Agnes said, "It's not funny," but even she laughed.

ON OUR JOURNEY, Bush opened like the lilies that flowered on some of the islands, at first tentative and delicate and finally with resolve. It was as if she had needed this place and all the water, to sing in, room to hold out her hands. Water and sky were windows she peered through to something beyond this world. Or perhaps they were mirrors in which she saw herself, her skin, her hands, her thighs, all brand-new. She was as uncontained as she had previously been contained by skin, house, island, and water. Now it seemed there were no borders. In shadows and in deep woods, she vanished, or she danced a slow dance, or she talked to the land. Some nights I sat beside the fire and saw her against the deepening sky, walking toward us, or sitting on a rock, or moving into the woods, stealthy as an animal. Time dropped away from her. Her eyes softened. She might have been thinking of the things she had been dealt in her life: the betrayals, the unhealable wounds made by Hannah, the loss of me, the solitudes she had needed and thrived on.

At times, too, I heard Agnes singing, talking the old language, mumbling inside a tent.

Agnes remembered the bear more strongly now and, even without her coat, she talked with it. Dora-Rouge sang low songs that sounded like wind. She read things in the moving of waters; she saw what couldn't be seen by us as the land and soundless mists passed by.

As for me, I was awake in time that was measured from before axes, before traps, flint, and carpenter's nails. It was this gap in time we entered, and it was a place between worlds. I was under the spell of wilderness, close to what no one had ever been able to call by name. Everything merged and united. There were no sharp distinctions left between darkness and light. Water and air became the same thing, as did water and land in the marshy broth of creation. Inside the clear water we passed over, rocks looked only a few inches away. Birds swam across lakes. It was all one thing. The canoes were our bodies, our skin. We passed through green leaves, wild rice, and rushes. In small lakes, dense with lily pads, tiny frogs leaped from leaves into the water as we passed.

Sometimes I felt there were eyes around us, peering through trees and fog. Maybe it was the eyes of land and creatures regarding us, taking our measure. And listening to the night, I knew there was another horizon, beyond the one we could see. And all of it was storied land, land where deities walked, where people traveled, desiring to be one with infinite space.

We were full and powerful, wearing the face of the world, floating in silence. Dora-Rouge said, "Yes, I believe we've always been lost," as we traveled through thick-grown rushes, marsh, and water so shallow our paddles touched bottom.

The four of us became like one animal. We heard inside each other in a tribal way. I understood this at once and was easy with it. With my grandmothers, there was no such thing as loneliness. Before, my life had been without all its ears, eyes, without all its knowings. Now we, the four of us, all had the same eyes, and when Dora-Rouge pointed a bony finger and said, "This way," we instinctively followed that crooked finger.

I never felt lost. I felt newly found, opening, like the tiny eggs we found in a pond one day, fertile and transparent. I bent over them. The life was already moving inside them, like an eye or heartbeat. One day we passed alongside cliff walls that bore red, ancient drawings of moose and bear. These were said to have been painted not by humans, but by spirits.

ONE DAY IT RAINED, but we passed through this day, too, as if nothing had changed, not the tree trunks black with water, not the shining rocks, not even the low clouds curling through land, winding between the wet, dripping branches of trees. It seemed there was no difference between the water below us and the water above.

There was lake after lake, island after island, and then, one day, we traveled down a calm river in silence. It was a lush day. Pollen blew through the air and landed on water like yellow snow. Smiling, I looked back at Bush and Agnes behind us. "Dora-Rouge," I said. "It is so beautiful."

At river's end, where water emptied into a lake, we came to gray walls of stone that held other paintings, red and black. These were of moose and wolverine. "Look," I said. I stopped paddling. A rain cloud passed over, and it was our good fortune that a light mist fell because when the rock wall became wet, we could see that the wolverine had wings. Invisible in the dry air, those wings waited for water to expose them. A white bird, too, was now visible. "What people," I wondered aloud, "had such vision?"

"Your people," said Dora-Rouge. "Mine."

Beneath the surface of the water were more paintings, just visible.

"The water must have risen," said Dora-Rouge.

It was true. Our paddles touched the tops of trees. On the land many trees were half-submerged. They stood in water, still rooted, looking like bushes growing along the surface of water. We still had a part day's travel left in our arms, but we decided to set up camp high on this island that was partly drowned and worth examining.

I undressed quickly. I wanted to swim through these waters by the wall of drawings.

"Be careful," said Agnes.

Entering water, I lost my breath. The water was colder than before. And it was clear. Through water, the flooded land looked perfectly normal, except that grasses swayed with the currents and not with the wind. A trail was still visible between the drowning trees.

I made my way to the painted walls and dived, eyes open. Never had I seen water like this, so clear and deep. I thought of Bush, standing before water one day, saying, "Two parts hydrogen, one part oxygen," in her dreamy way. When I was inside water, I understood how these simple elements married and became a third thing.

Fish were painted at the lowest depth of the stone walls. Just above them were several red deer, standing as if startled by a twig breaking in the underwater forest. They were prepared to run off the stone and through water. I forgot to breathe, swimming as if once again, as before birth, I had a gill slit. In that moment, I remembered being fish. I remembered being oxygen and hydrogen, bird and wolverine. It was all there. I felt it in my heart. But I could never think what to call it after that. I only knew that I and my many mothers had been lost in sky, water, and the galaxy, as we rested on a planet so small it was invisible to the turning of other worlds.

As I left water, I smelled rabbit cooking. Agnes was cheerful with the promise of fresh meat. I stood near the fire and squeezed out my wet hair. "Where'd you get the rabbit?"

Bush was using some of her own hair to tie a fly. "I pretended I wasn't hunting," she said. "Watch it, Angel. You're getting me wet."

"Come on, tell me. How'd you get it?" But I knew how. I'd seen her set a snare once, with twine, twig, and a single nail.

"There was a place like this in Oklahoma." She looked around. "With rock paintings of bear. No one knew about them. They were in a forest." She pulled some of the hair through a loop. "My uncle lived in those woods. Once he saw thirty bear walking through the forest together. He said they were growling and roaring and breaking trees as they went. He was scared to death. He tried to find a place to hide where they couldn't get him. He thought of a tree. But bears climb trees. He knew of a cave, too, but any place he could think of, bears could reach. But they were so powerful in their walking that they forgot all about men."

"That's hard to believe," Agnes said.

"I know. That's why I'm sure my uncle didn't make it up."

Agnes brushed some ashes off my leg. "I wish I had my coat."

Dora-Rouge divulged Bush's hunting trick to me. "She caught it with a snare. All she needed was fishline and a stick."

Bush put the fly aside. It looked exactly like a mosquito.

"I hope that's not a decoy," I said.

THAT NIGHT Agnes went to bed early. The rest of us stayed up late, talking. As we stirred dried apricots into hot water, we heard Agnes in the tent. All the talk of bears sent her to seek the one she had known. Now she was trying to talk with it, trying to summon the bear that had been her ally since she was twelve.

Without the coat, Agnes seemed to be without skin, and the little bit of flesh she still had looked loose enough to step out of, to leave behind. She slept longer every day. She felt penned in, she said, by the boat, the sleeping bag and tent, even by her skin. She was tired. I told myself it was nothing; it was due to the absence of her coat. Now she tried to summon the bear in new ways, singing bear songs, doing a hidden dance she called bear walking, talking to the bear with her eyes closed tight and reverent.

Watching her, worried about her, I started to think: What if something happened to one of us? There was no one to help us. We were alone.

Dora-Rouge seemed to be thinking the same thing, pursing her lips, watching Agnes, even shielding her eyes from the sun when she looked at her, to see her better. "Maybe it's nerves," Dora-Rouge said, as if I'd spoken my worries out loud.

"The Europeans called this world dangerous," she said. And I thought I understood: they had trapped themselves inside their own destruction of it, the oldest kind of snare, older than twine and twigs. Their legacy, I began to understand, had been the removal of spirit from everything, from animals, trees, fishhooks, and hammers, all things the Indians had as allies. They'd forgotten how to live. Before, everything lived together well—lynx and women, trappers and beaver. Now most of us had inarticulate souls, silent spirits, and despairing hearts.

"When hunters of the past killed an animal," Dora-Rouge said, "they blinded it. They did not want it to see what things they did to its body. They tied the feet of killed birds together so their spirits could not follow them home. They cut the paws off bear so their souls would not chase them." But now, she told me, the men were haunted by something else, by something inside themselves they'd tried, but failed, to forget.

"That's why animals and people stopped talking to each other."

But sometimes on this journey I thought I heard the voices of the world, of what was all around us—the stones, the waters flowing toward their ends, the osprey with its claws in fish, even the minnows and spawn. I heard trees with their roots holding ground.

"Once we could ask them to do something for us, to find our way home, to take away pain," said Dora-Rouge. "And they would help us. I believe this knowledge was given on the tenth day of creation," she said. And those that didn't know it were unfinished creations, cursed to be eternal children on this earth, lacking in the wisdom that understands life, even the diatoms precious and strange.

Creation, according to Dora-Rouge, was an ongoing thing. On the eighth day of creation, Dora-Rouge had told me, human beings were given their place with the earth. "By then some of the humans must have drifted away, across the newly formed waters, toward even newer land," she said. "Or maybe they just had poor memories, but there must have been some reason those people thought there were only six days of creation and one of rest, that they thought it ended there. Then, on the ninth day was the creation of stories, and these had many uses." They taught a thing or two about doing work, about kindness and love. She told me there were even stories to show a way out of unhappiness. Another day was devoted to snails and slugs, night crawlers and silverfish, roaches. Then there was the creation of singing and songs. "If those drifting ones would have stayed behind, they might even have learned the antidote for war," she said. "But they heard only as far as the creation of war on the sixth day. Thieves were created on that same day, too."

With tenderness I looked at Dora-Rouge, her white hair, her face with light coming from it. Never, I thought, was life so good, were women more wonderful.

At times I saw something shining in the depths of Bush, something I thought I could reach inside and touch, take out, turn over in my hand, and love. She was the closest thing I had to a mother. And if she was the closest thing to a mother, Dora-Rouge, who insisted she was born new every day, was the closest thing to God. And I was partly made in the old woman's image, right down to the owl-beak nose and dark, curved brows, and when she spoke the days of creation, I believed in them.

LATE ONE DAY as I built a fire, I saw Bush out in the smooth water. Like a dark-headed otter, she surfaced for a few moments, only to slip down the cold surface and disappear. I watched for her to surface again. She was at home in water, an element given shape by what contained it. She was water. Agnes once told me there were rumors how the men she'd slept with believed they swam across her.

That night, I rubbed oil into Agnes' back. She lay beside the fire, holding a cloth to her chest, the oil shining on her dark, naked back. When she fell asleep in the warmth, Dora-Rouge covered her with the skins and it looked as if a large animal breathed there. Dora-Rouge sat all night awake beside her, now and then tossing old cedar into the fire, releasing its smoke and odor.

ANOTHER EVENING, when we'd fallen into a steady stroking rhythm, our canoe drifted into a shaft of red sunlight. That evening, Dora-Rouge led us to some other rock paintings of moon and lynx. The paintings themselves, she remembered, were on steep cliff walls. When we found them it was still light and they were reflected on water, the lynx gazing down at itself, looking at its twin as if they had just met for the first time. It looked as if it could step away from stone, enter water, its own reflection, and come alive, the way spirit meets matter. Something about the paintings, done so long ago, tugged at the edge of me; at the older mind still at work in me.

Agnes leaned forward, reached into the water, and tried to lift the moon from the surface. When she touched it, it broke; the lynx wavered on water.

THAT SAME NIGHT, when the sun was a long path across water, we saw a canoe move toward us, traveling in the path of light. Inside the canoe sat a white man and woman. Between the man and woman was a white dog. We watched them approach. As they neared us, a heron rose up from the edge of water.

"Look," said Dora-Rouge, "they've made love. They are shining."

I barely heard her. Instead, I waved and hollered. "Hey!" I had nearly forgotten there were other people in the world. I came quickly out of lost time, silent space. Now all I wanted was a tube of lipstick. "Over here!" I put my fingers to my mouth and whistled. I would have stood up if the boat had allowed it. The two waved back.

Their canoe was overloaded to within only inches of water. It looked like any movement would sink them. They looked so foolish, I nearly laughed. But for the first time, I saw our own little flotilla through the eyes of others and we looked as much like fools as they did, four Indian women, one old and birdlike, having to be carried about while she gave out commands and directions she had made up from somewhere inside her old, brittle bones.

The dog stood up and barked. The canoe tilted dangerously, threatening to overturn. "Sit, Tyler!" the woman yelled.

Agnes took in the sight of the blond hair, white eyebrows, and pink skin of the two people and was silent.

The young couple, Bob and Jean, had been flown in and dropped off a few days earlier. The man, although an experienced canoer, a frequent journeyer here, thought perhaps they were lost. I didn't yet realize that the faces of land and water had been changed up above us, nor did I know what such change meant. I thought him merely inexperienced.

As he pulled up to us, smiling, he asked, "What's the name of this island?" He pointed to it. The woman lifted her paddle to her lap and waited. "We must be lost," he said.

Dora-Rouge knew he wouldn't understand her usual answer, about how we'd always been lost. She had sense enough not to say it.

The dog, a white shepherd, wagged its tail and panted. "Tyler. Sit!"

It was late and it had been a good full day's traveling, so Dora-Rouge invited the couple to remain with us that evening. "The company would be good for us," Dora-Rouge said, after observing my excitement.

"YOU CAN'T GET AROUND the Se Nay River anymore through the old way," the man told Dora-Rouge as we sat beside the fire. "You have to take another route."

"Why not?" She looked at him with keen interest.

"We saw it ourselves from the plane. It was socked in. The Big Arm River has been diverted into it from above. They had to drop us to the west so we could get another passage, and even that one is probably no longer passable. It was nearly all mud then; by now every bit of it must be."

Dora-Rouge turned this over in her mind as we sat together by the fire, the white shepherd with its head on my lap. I scratched its ears. "How bad is the river?" she asked.

"You wouldn't want to travel down the river." He brushed himself off. "It's too rapid."

"Luther," Dora-Rouge said, calling on him. The man looked at her with a strange expression. But Luther said nothing. Maybe he was silent because of the couple. They looked startled and exchanged a glance with each other. They looked around the campsite to see if we had another person with us.

Agnes, I noticed, was behaving in a strange manner. Finally, she got me alone, walking out of the bushes back toward the fire. "There's something wrong with them," she said. And later, when I was washing a pot in the lake, scrubbing it with sand, she whispered as loud as possible, "They are cannibals, those two."

Once, that evening, she even said to them, "You're cannibals, aren't you?"

The man and woman smiled and ignored her. They remained polite as she stared at their faces with apprehension. They pretended not to notice. It was, after all, a known fact that people went crazy in these broken, water-split lands.

"There's a bog fire up ahead," the man said to Bush.

"How far is it?"

"You can see a trace of the smoke from here." He pointed. We all looked. We saw only a blue glow in the sky, the gases burning off.

Dora-Rouge smiled at the couple. "And what are you doing here?"

"We're going to live in the wilderness." The woman's skin was the color of shells, surprisingly pale, as if she'd been protected from light all her life, worn nothing but black.

"How wonderful," said Dora-Rouge, her dark eyes happy. "I'm going home to die."

The young woman grew silent. I could read on her face how she thought it was bad enough that one of us was crazy; now there was also the presence of death.

That night, Bush cooked wild rice and fried bread and we shared a feast. The young couple got the short end of the stick, I thought, when it came to food; they had fresh oranges and after I ate one, I stared at the rest until they offered me another. I had no pride left. I would have stolen them if I'd had to. They were beautiful, full globes, sweet and filled with juice.

While I ate them, Agnes leaned toward me and whispered fierce words close to my ear, "Don't eat it. Don't eat their food."

I hoped they wouldn't hear her, but they did, and they looked at each other often. Agnes, just as often, looked afraid, leaned close, and hissed, "I mean it."

The young woman looked around, nervous, as if plotting an escape, and later, when we'd all gone to bed, the couple got into a fight. Above the snoring of Agnes from the next tent over, I overheard, "Those women are crazy."

"She's just old," the man said. "They're okay. Just let it be." He wanted to remain, if for nothing else, I thought, so he could tell about these women and me, the dark girl with scars and long red hair, and how we floated in outmoded canoes, carrying furs and Dora-Rouge.

But the woman kept crying and then she became angry and said, "They are plumb crazy. If you don't leave now, I'm going home."

It wasn't long before I heard the sound of tent stakes, the rattling of metal, the sound of cloth zipping. By morning the young couple, their dog, and their oranges were gone.

"What could have happened?" Bush said, looking at where their tent had been. She looked disappointed. Agnes looked relieved. As I pushed the boat into the water and stepped inside it, I gave her a dirty look.

Then I settled into the space that, by now, seemed created just for me and Dora-Rouge.

After we'd gotten out a ways into the water, Dora-Rouge turned and looked at me. She said, "Those women are plumb crazy," and laughed.

YEARS BEFORE, it was said, cannibals appeared this way, from out of the path of water, rowing in from the horizon just the way Bob and Jean had done.

Once, it was said, a man and a woman floated up from the depths of water in a boat made of human skin. They appeared on a path of light, came over the horizon. It was an old, old story. They wanted to devour humans. The woman gave birth to twins that were war and starvation. They had a white wolf with them.

Wolverine, they say, was the one who saved them. He sprang the human woman from the trap and he made two skin bags of the murderous infants called hunger and war, and filled them with berries and meat and offered this to the humans.

IT WASN'T LONG after meeting the young couple, after wishing for lipstick, that I felt once again strange and wild, as if we hadn't crossed paths with other people at all, as if we were the only ones who moved through this world. Agnes returned to talking the bear language, Dora-Rouge to saying "Go around this bend," and Bush once again retreated into her own world, inexhaustible and animal.

Out of the four of us, I was the most stable. I had my two feet, if not on the ground, close to it.

FROM THERE we traveled northeast. Ahead of us, just as the young man had said, was the peat fire burning in the bog. Bush shaded her eyes from the sun and looked at the gray smoke and waves of heat that rose. It had burned for over a year, the gases from underneath fueling the flame.

From somewhere behind the smoke and heat came the hypnotic sound of frogs, rhythmic as a heartbeat from the swampiness of beginnings. Ravens flew up, calling out as if they were the voice of smoke. The fire itself seemed to be alive, a red-and-black animal that grew, sparked out of the richness and rot of underground, out of ancient plants and insects that had fallen there. Moths flew toward it.

The smell of smoke burned our nostrils and eyes. We tried to make a wide circle around it, passing through a shallow swamp with tall dark reeds and a breeze that made a shushing sound as it bent grasses. I stepped out of the canoe into the mud and pulled Dora-Rouge along through liquid earth. As I dragged her, Dora-Rouge looked me in the eye and asked point-blank, "Do you think Agnes is sick?"

"Watch out for the branches," I said. I waded through the silty water. The mud pulled at my boots.

A branch nearly hit her. She ducked. "Do you?"

The same thought had crossed my mind more than a few times. I cast a glance toward Agnes. She looked pale. "I think she's just tired."

I didn't notice when Agnes had first begun to look sick, but now, she looked drained of energy. Her ankles were swollen. In one place on her leg the skin was cracked and fluid seeped from it as if she were waterlogged. But she hadn't complained at all.

Bush, too, had been watching Agnes, and when we came to dry land, she said, "Let's stay here for a day and rest." She'd already pulled her boat to land, not caring if there was any argument from the rest of us. We weren't far now, Bush was certain, from North House, a point that indicated we were returning to humans; we were not far from our destination. "We're already way past due, another day wouldn't mean much."

I went to gather wood for the fire. Luckily, there'd been a hot, clear sun. Wood was plentiful there and ready to burn. Agnes followed me. "I'll help you," she said. She breathed heavily.

"That's okay, Grandmother. I can do it."

But Agnes still followed. I walked slowly so she could keep up, and when we walked into a stand of trees, she said to me, "Listen." She fumbled for the right words. "Listen, if something happens to me, I want you to let me lie out for the wolves and birds; would you?"

I studied her face, but said nothing.

Agnes didn't look back at me. "That's what I want."

"Okay." I broke off a dead branch, bent down, suddenly awkward, and picked up several pieces of wood. I handed two of them to Agnes, then picked up some more and laid them across my own arms, smelling the sharp, resin-sweet odor of trees, and we went back to the camp.

"What did she say back there?" Dora-Rouge asked, when Agnes was out of hearing distance.

I put down the wood.

"I saw her talking to you." Dora-Rouge looked concerned.

I struck a match. "Nothing," I said. I changed the subject. "I think I'll wash some clothes. Do you want a clean dress?" We would be meeting people at North House. I wanted a clean shirt.

But I paid close attention to Agnes after that and avoided Dora-Rouge's sharp questioning eyes.

That night, Dora-Rouge hardly slept at all. Strengthened by mother love, she sat by the fire beside a sleeping Agnes. She leaned toward her daughter and covered her with beaver skins. Agnes didn't wake when the older woman touched her.

Inside my sleep that same night, a rust-colored root grew in a circle around itself, forming new bulbs and connected tubers, splitting and multiplying. A first green shoot moved toward light. I saw it clear as daylight.

"Redroot. I believe that must be redroot," Dora-Rouge said the next morning, when I described it. "I can't be sure. But if you dreamed it, it's what we need." She squinted at Agnes. "Wolfsbane, too."

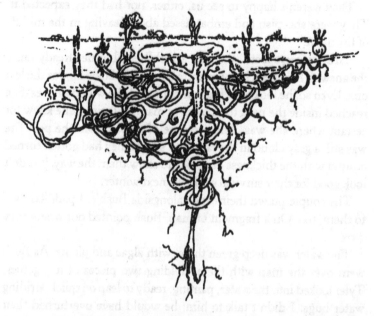

LATER, as I knelt above the pan of warm water, I thought of the ancestors who showed Dora-Rouge the directions for travel. My life, before Adam's Rib, had been limited in ways I hadn't even known. I'd never have thought there might be people who found their ways by dreaming. What was real in those land-broken waters, real even to me, were things others might call the superstitions of primitive people. How could it be, I wondered, that all people who came from their own earth, who lived there for tens of thousands of years, could talk with spirits, could hear land speak, and animals? Northern hunters were brilliant hunters. Even now they dream the location of their prey and find it. Could they all have been wrong? I didn't think so.

The old world dawning new in me was something like the way a human eye righted what was upside down, turned over an image and saw true.

IT WAS only a short time later that we once again came across the pale woman and man. Agnes looked at them with foreboding. "They're following me," she said.

They weren't happy to see us, either, nor had they expected it. They were sheepish and embarrassed about leaving in the middle of the night.

"Are you guys lost?" the man asked Bush, but he already knew the answer; he'd been in these parts before. He knew he was the lost one. Even so, he looked at Bush in hope that she would say yes. She reached inside the pack for a piece of map. This time, she knew for certain where she was. The presence of smoke from the peat fire was still a gray cloud in the far south sky. If they had gotten turned around with the thickness of smoke to show them the way, it didn't look good for their survival skills the next winter.

The couple pulled their canoe alongside Bush's. I paddled over to them, too. On a fragment of map, Bush pointed out where they were.

The water was deep green there, with algae and plants. As Bush went over the map with them, holding two pieces of it together, Tyler looked into the water, panting, ready to leap on quick-striding water bugs. I didn't talk to him; he would have overturned their canoe.

"We must have gone in a circle." Without hesitating, he said, "Thanks," turned the canoe around, and started away.

"Wait," Dora-Rouge called after him. "Do you have a pencil?"

He reached into his shirt pocket. His pen was hooked to a credit card. Bush tried not to smile.

"Thank you." Dora-Rouge took the pen and handed it to me. "Do you have any paper?" she asked him.

He looked at his companion. She was thin-lipped. She shook her head no. She was anxious to leave, and probably happy we didn't ask why they'd pulled up stakes in the middle of the night, but I could see that she was simply too exhausted to dig around for paper. By then, Bush had handed me another paper bag.

Dora-Rouge said, "Just a minute." She held up one scrawny finger to the man. "Go ahead. Draw the plant," she told me.

While I sketched it, the man paddled away from us, eased back, only to pull away again, as if he thought he could vanish when we were off guard. When I was done, I said, "This is it," and handed the brown paper to Dora-Rouge.

"Have you seen this plant growing anywhere?" Dora-Rouge held out the drawing to him. "It used to be up here." The light of the water reflected on her skin.

"Tyler, be still!"

The man studied the drawing. "Yes," he said, and in this, at least, he seemed knowledgeable. "Yes, I'm sure of it. It wasn't this year, but for the past two years I saw it growing. It was on the far side of North House last year. Close to the Flower Islands. Here, give me the pen." He made a map for us. It showed a place with numerous tiny islands scattered through the water.

"I know where those are," said Dora-Rouge.

Two large twin pieces of land he diagrammed, writing beneath them "Flower Islands." Then, quickly, as if to make up for lost time, the couple said good-bye and paddled south. We watched them depart. The pale dog with blue eyes looked back at us. The blond hair of the woman looked white in sunlight.

"Agnes needs this plant," said Dora-Rouge to Bush. "We'll have to go up there."

I could see that the little string of islands was far away, would take us out of our way, but not, I hoped, by far.

As we neared the Se Nay River, our plans to bypass it had to be given up because some of the waters leading to it were now only mud and our canoes could not pass through it. We'd have to risk the river even if it was all rapids. The river itself was now the force of two rivers, the Big Arm River having been diverted into the Se Nay. This added distance to our journey.

As we neared the Se Nay River, the land began to change. It was rocky and darker. We felt the breeze from the river. First, it was soft, but that was only its deceptive voice, whispering. As we neared the river, it strengthened into a cold, stiff wind, and even that was a lying breath. In truth, the river was a deafening roar and was virtually impassable. As we reached it, I saw how it rushed down, overfull, and was held in check, in some places, only by rock walls and steep cliffs. The water of two rivers, forced into one, was deeper and wider than it should have been, hitting the walls far up the sides and spreading out wherever it could in other places, taking down trees.

"This can't be the Se Nay," Bush said. She shook her head. In places, the muddy brown bank was washed away. She looked pale. I was panicked.

Bush worried about the details, trying to understand how this river had been affected, how much the land and waters might be changed. It was a puzzle. If they'd diverted the Big Arm River, as the man said, it would mean that certain waters ahead of us might be closed, others flooded. Bush tried to see the large picture, but it seemed impossible. She checked the pieces of maps that were, by now, committed to her memory, as if there were something she might have missed. She tried to figure out the lay of the land, to predict what we'd find. We'd already seen some of the flooding, mudflats where other rivers had failed to empty into their destinations.

The Se Nay yelled out in a voice so loud, nothing could be heard above it. "It's angry," said Dora-Rouge. I leaned toward her to hear. "The rivers are angry. Both of them." That was why it was a strong roar, she said, so loud it sounded like earth breaking open and raging.

"Come with me, Angel," said Bush, already walking toward the Se Nay. The wind whipped up off the water. It swept Bush's hair from her shoulders. Her sweater blew tight against her as she tried to walk along the edge of the water, hoping we could find a way to travel some of it on foot. I hoped, too, that around a bend or over a rock, we would find a calmer river. But the stone walls that held the fierce river were high, much of the ground impossible to pass on foot, let alone carrying a boat and a frail old woman. Everything was slippery with moss and spray. We turned and walked back.

"We can't do it," said Bush. "It's like this all the way down." She looked worried. "We can't travel it." She shook her head. Her words were nearly drowned out by the noise.

Dora-Rouge nodded at Bush, her own white hair blown back from her face. "Yes," the nod meant. Reading Bush's face. Yes, we could do it. We would travel it. The old woman knew this. We would have to risk the water. The only other thing was to turn back.

Who could say what might have happened to the world behind us? It could be a closed place by now, what with the building of dams, the waters dry in places we had canoed through. Not only that, but if we turned, we'd have to go against currents.

Standing against the wind, Bush and I looked at each other. Should we turn back? we both wondered. We could overrule Dora-Rouge. Our faces were hopeless, our eyes contained a question. But neither of us knew the answer to this. There was no longer a thing such as "should." Everything had changed. We'd gone too far to turn back. Not too far in distance alone, but too far inside ourselves. No longer were we the women who left Adam's Rib. And as for me, the girl I had once been could never have paddled through rain as if it were not falling and camped in wet mosses. Those women would never have sung ancient songs at night so assuredly, or spoken to spirits that walked through forests and gave us their permission to enter. That girl would never have known how spirits hung above the water like fog, would never have heard stories in the land we passed over, or given herself up to a trail that went any map's wrong way.

Now our arms were strong and we were articulate in the languages of land, water, animal, even in the harder languages of one another. I'd entered waters and swamps, been changed by them. I'd dreamed medicines, some that could be found in this world no longer, like the one for arthritis, and I remembered the plentiful days of ongoing creation.

It was for all these things that Dora-Rouge was going to talk to the churning river, the white and muddy foam of it, the hydrogen and oxygen of it, and convince it to let us pass safely. All this she did while we watched.

It would have been a lie if any of us had said we weren't afraid, and it would have been a lie, too, if we'd said we believed completely in Dora-Rouge as she sat on the bank of the river and spoke. We could only see her lips move. We heard nothing she said. But after a while she nodded at us. "It will let us go," she said loudly, and that was the final word. Before we placed the canoes into the fierce, charging dark water, Dora-Rouge said a prayer, opened her hand, and tossed tobacco into it. Her eyes were closed, a high-pitched song coming from deep inside her. I could barely hear her for the sound of water. I only saw her sing as her voice was taken away from her by the windy river. But I could see she was loud and strong. When the tobacco disappeared into the water, I was without faith, but I did what Dora-Rouge said.

My canoe went into the water first, and from the moment it was there the current tried to swallow it. My arms shook as I held it, the spray hitting at my face as I watched Bush lift Dora-Rouge and, knee-deep in water, carry the old woman toward the rocking canoe. I was soaked to the skin already and shivering and the strong current pushed against my legs even where it was shallow. It took all my strength to stand there. I held the canoe while Bush lowered Dora-Rouge inside it. The cold spray of water blowing against us was muddy and violent. And then Bush held the other canoe while Agnes climbed inside. Agnes was pale with terror, her legs wide apart in the water. She eyed the churning of water about the rocks. Even where it was deep, it looked rocky. And she was the one who was fearless in rivers. Unsteadily, she sat down, holding her shirt tight at the neck, as if it would keep the cold water from seeping to her skin, but she, like the rest of us, was already wet and her hair had come down around her face and neck.

And then Bush knelt inside the canoe like she was praying. I watched as she tried to paddle, but suddenly, Bush's canoe was gone and before I knew it, we were behind her, dropping down. I screamed out, though no one could hear me. Even Dora-Rouge looked afraid, and she was the one who'd been certain we would make it through, the one who'd worked out a deal, whatever it was, with water. Her eyes squeezed shut. She dropped down deeper into the canoe. There was the sound of a rock hitting against the underside. My heart beat with fear. I'm dead, I thought. If we didn't make it, we'd surely drown. We hit eddies and whirling currents that tried to turn us sideways. All the time, the cold water pelted us, wetting our hair, chilling our skin. I tried to paddle, and my arms hurt, but it was no use. For a moment I'd catch a current just right and then the canoe would shift, would seem to enter air, turn, then drop. The water carried debris in it. I was afraid of being hit by one of the long trees with still-green leaves. There was no hope of stopping or slowing. These two rivers had probably never liked each other in the first place, I thought. We were held in the hands of fighting water. We were at its mercy. Then I remembered John Husk telling me to catch the current and ride it like an animal, and finally, I gave up, giving in to gravity and to the motion of it, allowing my hips to move with it, not against it. Like riding a horse, he'd said.

I tried to watch the willows and branches that grabbed at us. For brief seconds the water would be slack, then treacherous again as we sped past hills and groves of trees, moving through shadows and blinding flashes of sunlight, all of it so fast we couldn't see how birds flew up along the river edges, could only see everything else that was falling with us down the cold, muddy waters. In places, it narrowed and snaked off in new directions. But we passed through, passing places where the riverbanks had collapsed and the torn roots of trees reached out of a loamy smell, as if to keep us from going north where winter lived. We passed burned woods, traveled through darkness and mud and silt, and finally we were taken to the end of the rapids, and something godly brought us through. Maybe it was the words of Dora-Rouge, after all, that saved us, words both Bush and I would later wish we'd heard and remembered. Or maybe it was blind luck, pure and simple. But whatever it was, the four of us, drenched and breathing hard, climbed out of the water and lay down cold and exhausted on firm ground. Even Dora-Rouge worked up the strength to pull herself along by her hands. After a while, Dora-Rouge, wet, her muscles strained, said, "Those women are crazy," and began to laugh. She had tricked something, all right. She was sure of it, even if she wouldn't tell us what it was. Maybe it wasn't water she'd bartered with, after all, but she'd struck up one hell of a deal with something, Bush said. What she'd traded in exchange, she wouldn't say, but this much was clear: something godly was bringing us through.

TWELVE

THE ORIGINAL PEOPLE AT North House, the first ones, kept their dead on Bone Island during hard winters, carrying or pulling them there by sled to await the first thaw, when they could be buried. Then came the Europeans, who left the bodies of their horses who did not survive the cold. Soon, too, they took the bones of their pigs to that place. The pigs had carried diseases that wiped out tribes of people, and all those dead were left on the island, too. In the spring of 1913, three British men arrived. They rowed to Bone Island and found seething white maggots more than a foot thick consuming all the newly thawed flesh. There were so many dead that they called it the Island of Maggots. After that it became the place where the ill were sent during contagions. No one except the dying would go there or even take their boats or canoes close by. Later, lime was poured over all the bodies so they would decompose, leaving behind only a few sharp teeth and a finger bone or two. A song of wailing came from there. People maintained it was only the wind.

Now we passed Bone Island on our way to North House. We didn't stop, but I thought I could hear the tragic crying of wind, weeping for what had happened there.

• • •

DESPITE THE FACT that it was summer, North House, a one-time fur post, the place where we could stock up on goods and rest, looked wet and cold and dark. It appeared to be made up of one large building with a black roof. As we pulled the canoes to land, a swarm of dogs ran down to the edge of water to greet us, wagging their tails in gestures of friendship. Following behind them were three dark-eyed children who stared at us as if they'd never before seen women. I held some gum out to them. They took it and put it in their mouths, but continued to stare at us. Then, from behind them, a big-boned German woman, still drying her hands on a towel, came down to see what the commotion was all about. She was a large woman with reddish-blond hair, not her natural color.

"Shoo!" she yelled at the dogs, shaking her towel in their faces. Despite the fact that she commanded a kind of order and obedience from humans, the dogs ignored her and continued to snarl and bark, one of them with his head up, howling like a wolf, another yapping like one of those poodle-mix lapdogs of city women.

The woman, Gita, smiled at us. She had a soft look that tried to belie the fact that she was clearly in charge here. Immediately she tucked the towel in her belt and set to work, helping us ground the canoes, leaning down, large-armed and heavy, her hair in an un-kempt bun, her eyebrows each a single, thin-penciled line.

"Come with me." She said this with something like authority. "I'll get you a cold drink."

She watched as Bush lifted Dora-Rouge. "She doesn't walk? Wait a moment." She turned to the kids. "Go get Ivan's chair!" She waved the kids away with another shake of the towel. In her hands anything became a tool for getting things done. "Hurry up, now." The dark-eyed children ran off. She lifted our packs up onto gray rocks and we waited.

Soon the children returned, pushing the chair, and the woman, Gita, helped Dora-Rouge into the chair as if she had once been a nurse, using one foot to put down the footrest at the same time that she turned and set Dora-Rouge down like a bag of rice or flour. "It's my husband's chair," she said. Then, as if we might think her unkind, "He doesn't need it right now."

Loaded with a pack, she took us first into a part of the building that was something like a bunkhouse. Except for a few small windows, it was long and dark inside. The windows were cut low to the ground to allow sun to warm the floor. The entire building contained the smell of men, and a few of them stood about looking at us as if they'd seen no one except this German woman for the longest time. Most of them seemed European, though there were a few men with tribal blood. They were easy to spot; they were softer, their bodies more relaxed. They had different walks, different eyes from the others.

"Men, out!" said Gita.

The men were clearly accustomed to following her orders, and, obedient as children, they left.

"Go get the rest of their packs," she yelled after two of them. "Bring them up here."

"Drinks are on the house for women," she said. "I get lonely here with just the men. But only drinks." She was a practical businesswoman; she didn't want us to think we'd get a free bill of fare. "The food you must purchase."

As much as we wanted to clean up, we headed straight for the dining hall. I stared long and hard at the pastries and sweets, as if I'd never seen them before.

"Go ahead," Bush said. "Pick one."

"Wait a minute," said Agnes. To Bush she said, "Did you bring any money?"

"Yes. I have some left from the skins. It's enough."

Agnes smiled. "Go ahead, Angel, take your pick." And then Agnes picked two, which was a relief to me. Her appetite, at least, was good.

Shortly after we went back to the bunkhouse, Gita brought over trays of sausages and fresh, hot, buttered bread. I was hungry and the food was wonderful, but even more than that, I was tired. We all were. Dora-Rouge had already dozed off. Fatigue moved across my muscles and bones. I was relieved we would be able to rest there a few days.

• • •

THE NEXT MORNING, after we ate breakfast, Gita turned toward Bush and me with a suspicious look. She eyed us sharply. "Are you here after the Spanish silver?"

"Silver?" Bush looked at her like she was crazy. I thought it was a joke and broke out in a large smile. Bush said, "What silver?"

"You haven't heard?" Gita sat up straight and looked from one to the other of us to see if we were lying. Our faces didn't betray us, but she said, "Yes. Everybody has heard this." She pointed outside. "It's what most of these men are looking for."

"No, we haven't heard of it," Bush said.

I looked out one of the windows as if I might see a Spanish galleon turned on its side by the trading post. Instead, all I could see were the mixed-blood men sitting back watching the white men make holes in the ground.

"So you really haven't heard about the silver." It was more of a comment than a question. In a while, she changed the subject. "The men don't talk much, you know, not even to each other." I'm afraid we weren't much company either. We had become used to silence and to the sounds of nature. There was something jarring about being there. The pulse of human activity was too quick for us. We would need time to adjust to places of noise, business, order, and rules.

The trappers were easy enough to make out; they had deeper features than the silver chasers, an eye of solitude. The silver-hunters were all of a kind, it seemed. They alternated between dreaminess and high anxiety. Even with strained muscles they would go outside each morning and dig a new hole. In the evening, they were still at work, dusty and fatigued. Some concentrated on depth, others moved from place to place, making shallow holes, searching, but all of them worked as if riches would escape them.

Some of the darker men worried that the forest would become only piles of gravel, and that the waters would be dredged and ruined. These Indian men were quiet when the others, more unruly and tense, were around. They were also thoughtful. They brought Dora-Rouge tobacco, sweet grass, and a few yards of nice cloth that some of them had bought for their women at home. This was the custom. Then they sat and talked with her. They were kind to me, acknowledging my presence, and they were interested in Bush and Agnes, but it was Dora-Rouge they wanted to know about. She spoke the same language they did, only a different dialect, and everyone, especially Dora-Rouge, found this comforting. It made her feel how near we were to our destination.

As for the silver, one night, some time ago, a man who was digging a grave had found several Spanish coins near North House. Word of the discovery had spread quickly and men poured into North House to lay claim to the riches. In the mysterious way a rumor travels, the story grew larger all the time, so now some believed that veins of silver and gold ran through the granite and limestone. Even if the coins had not been enough to summon the needy men, their imaginations would have urged them on. They were like men with buck fever, men who would think another man, a dog, even a motorcycle, was a deer. They were possessed. Each believed he was the one fated to find the money, that it was his destiny. This made friendship impossible between them; no one could be trusted when so much was at stake. There was a theory, too, just started, that galleons had gone down in the lakes of the region, that the Spanish had found a passage from the sea into this place of divided waters and land.

The men, digging earth, had lucky charms that would lead them to coins and other shining things. They had prayers, even though they were not, under normal circumstances, praying men. One fellow wore his mother's picture in a silver locket. Every few hours, he rubbed the shining back of it and prayed for his dear mother to guide him to the silver. Another used a rabbit's foot that he carried always in his left hand. One watched for signs from God in patterns of weather.

And two young men, a set of twins, used a Ouija board, which said yes to most all of their questions. "Is there silver on the left side of Peat Hill?" they asked. Yes. "Is there silver near the propane tanks?" This time it didn't move, even though they sat for an hour, at least, with their fingers lightly touching the beige plastic heart, and trembling. They thought surely this was a sign and dug near the propane tanks until one of the tanks rolled down into the hole and hit a building and exploded, starting a fire that was now only a black, scorched place behind the barracks.

"We hope they never find any silver," said Gita. "Though God knows it would be good for business."

Some of the men slept in the fort. Others pitched a tent or lean-to on the site they had a hunch about and wanted to claim, afraid someone would take over the place if they left.

Gita's husband was more subdued than she was. It was easy to see how they made a good marriage. He barely spoke at all and she was seldom quiet. "What's your name?" he asked us, then said, "Oh, Agnes Iron? You've got a package here. We expected you a week or two ago."

Weeks, I thought. We'd only been gone weeks. Bush and I looked at each other, aware again of time and commerce and men digging their ways to hell, thinking it was heaven. It seemed like we'd been gone for years.

Agnes knew at once Husk had mailed her coat. It was a heavy package wrapped in taped-together brown paper bags. Agnes beamed. She was delirious with joy. Husk had sent along a note that she didn't share with us, but she chuckled when she read it and color returned to her cheeks. For Dora-Rouge, Husk sent some canned salmon. Bush got a new lure. There was an astrology book and chocolate bar for me, along with a letter from Tommy, saying that he was considering traveling to the Fat-Eaters to meet us. He had met a man, a rabble-rouser from a southern tribe, who thought he knew how to enter the territory via back roads and water channels, even if all the other entries were blocked off.

Bush bought a newspaper at the post store, but there was nothing in it about Wounded Knee. And there was no word about the dam project we were headed toward. "How can that be?" she wondered aloud, but it was no surprise to her that these things were covered up.

I felt free and light during our stay there, our stopover from swamps and portages. It was good to walk without carrying anything, no backpack, no food, no old woman. It was good to have a few nights' decent sleep, to be inside walls. I took a walk with Agnes and her coat, and hid a smile as she pretended not to be looking around the ground for silver, but I could see her eyes looking this way and that for anything the men might have overlooked, anything shining.

"What would you do if you had money?" she asked me.

"I don't know. I'd have to think about it."

At North House we slept in beds, real beds, the luxury of which was beyond imagining, even with bumpy mattresses and used-up blankets, even with the smell of working men's skin and clothing. While we were there, the men slept on the other side of the room, and Gita put up a curtain between us. None of them, she assured us, dared look in the direction of the curtain, as if Gita herself would jump out and chide them. In the mornings I could hear them pull on their pants and zip them. Worse even than hearing them, I could feel how much each one wanted to be the one to strike a claim. It was a tension, a kind of feverish energy that, once started, could not be stopped. It was like one of the rules of physics Husk would tell about, an object set in motion. To make it worse, the shoveling began at the crack of dawn, or what seemed like dawn, not that the hour was easy to discern with nights so brief. But whatever the time was, their noise began during the precious hours of my sleep.

Behind the main building, Gita had a little garden that she'd nurtured. It contained future turnips and big-leafed potential squash. She loved the plants. One morning when one of the miners began shoveling there, she ran out the door and yelled at him. "Stop that this minute! There is no silver! No coins. Nothing. *Nichts.*"

AS SOON AS the young men spread the word that four Indian women had come out of the water, native people from nearby came to see us for themselves, bringing food and shirts and other items we might need or want. One young woman offered earrings to me. They were long and silver. "But not Spanish silver," the young woman said. She wanted no misunderstandings. She stayed to talk a long time beneath the trees, and played a tape of Barry Sadler, "You tell me no war, no war, no war again my friend." "The Eve of Destruction."

It turned out that some of the visitors had known about Dora-

Rouge, and one woman who came to visit, as old as Dora-Rouge, said she was related to the Hundred-Year-Old Road people. Her name was Jere and she was born at Adam's Rib. She missed it and wanted to know what the Hungry Mouth of Water had eaten in the years since her presence there. "Two Skidoos! Really?" She put her hand over her mouth. "Were the people still in them?"

Jere and Dora-Rouge talked all the next day. From what little I understood of the language, they talked about the time when every-thing was still alive. That's what they remembered and missed. It was what all the old people longed for again, the time when people could merge with a cloud and help it rain, could become trees, one with bark, root, and leaf. People were more silent in those days. They listened. They heard. After they talked, the two old women cast long, brooding looks about the post and at the men who broke open the ground. The next day, Gita brought raisins, almonds, and dates, and joined us in our talking, eating, and tea drinking.

And then, too soon, we made preparations to leave. I hated to go, as if we were leaving people we had known longer than a few days.

ON THE MORNING we left, the Indian women came to say "Good-bye, sister," and we promised them we would be back. They reminded us that water levels had changed and our directions might become confused.

"Precious metal," Bush said as we paddled north once again, as if the diggers were a mystery to her. "What do you think they really want? What does silver mean to them?"

Agnes said she thought it meant the world was ending.

In a history book I once read, Cortés was quoted as saying, "We white men have a disease of the heart, and the only thing that can cure it is gold." With those words, with that disease, came the end of many worlds. So Agnes could very well have been right: precious metals signaled an ending.

WITH THE COAT BACK in her possession, Agnes rallied some-what. She still seemed slightly confused, but overall she seemed happier. She sat erect in the canoe and looked once again like a bear. Behind her, Bush paddled and steered through fine, long grasses and lakes, and once again we traveled, some evenings to the sound of wolves, some days with the warm sun on our backs. Once again we dropped down into the rhythm of it, forgetting our lives in the other world. For me it was as if there had been no years in school learning numbers, no fights, no families who wouldn't keep me. Gone were the times my hands were tied down so I wouldn't hurt myself. None of it mattered now, not the lives on Adam's Rib or Fur Island, not even the future. What mattered, simply and powerfully, was knowing the current of water and living in the body where land spoke what a woman must do to survive.

We slipped back into a deep wildness, into beauty and eeriness where spirits still walked on land, and animals still spoke with humans, toward a place where wolves and their ancestors remembered the smell of Dora-Rouge and her ancestors from years before.

WE CAME TO THE Place of Sleepers. It was on the edge of a mainland where there had been no electric light since 1920. At that time, inventor Nikola Tesla had sent a surge of energy all the way from Colorado Springs across the continent. With no way to measure or sell it, this light would have been free and available to everyone, but this, of course, was not permitted. The Sleepers, as the people who lived there were called, refused to pay for what could have been free, refused light on principal alone. All light, even oil-light, or that generated by gas, was abolished. They chose, instead, to live by natural cycles. It was a small act of resistance, but the people were healthier for it. In the long darkness of winter they slept like bears, waking only now and then to stretch, eat, make love, and fall asleep again.

The Place of Sleepers was partially submerged. Only the tops of a few hills, once tall, were dry. Again, I was surprised that the water was clear. I'd always thought floodwaters should be murky and dark. Peering down as we passed through, there were trees, and even a few buildings that hadn't fallen or floated away. A flag on top of a pole still waved, as if the currents of water were merely a gentle wind.

Dora-Rouge was distraught that this place was so nearly under water. Below it, not long ago, one of the first dams had been built, flooding the Place of Sleepers and other islands to the south. One woman, we heard later, had refused to leave. It was said her bones still floated inside her little kitchen, alongside dish towels and a tablecloth and a measuring cup.

This was just the beginning of what we were to encounter. With more than one dam being built, much land was now submerged. An entire river to the north had been flooded and drowned. Other places, once filled with water, were dry. Farther on, there were larger vistas and missing islands. Dora-Rouge said the mouths of rivers had stopped spilling their stories to the bays and seas beyond them. New waters had come to drown the old. Other rivers had dwindled to mudflats. Dora-Rouge cried to see it, and it was after that when Agnes complained of a headache and developed a fever. Bush boiled willow bark to make tea for her, but Agnes was not cured by it. Nor was she helped by Husk's letter and her coat. Dora-Rouge looked at her and said, "If only we had some wolfsbane or redroot, I think it would help. We should be at the Islands of Flowers soon."

EARLY THE NEXT DAY I saw what looked like snow. It was a long while before I realized that what I saw were petals floating on water. We had reached the flower islands, two large parcels of rich land. It was said about these islands that the wind had carried flower seeds inside a tornado above water and dropped them down upon the dark earth. So many blossoms had piled up on the land that I could see their color even from a distance, and as we drew near I saw another bog fire burning behind the islands, so that the sky appeared deep gray. As we approached the land, petals blew into our canoes from the trees. Small, delicate flowers fell on us. What a tender place, one where spring seemed again, newly present. I removed a petal from Dora-Rouge's hair.

"We're very close to Ahani, the old land," Dora-Rouge said to me. She looked in the direction of the north. "Maybe only another two days. But Agnes is very sick and we must get her the herbs. Her blood's not right. I can see it with my eyes."

I nodded. I'd noticed myself how bad Agnes looked. Agnes was exceedingly cold, even with her coat and the beaver skins placed around her. She remained chilled and exhausted in a way that was alarming. She was chalky-skinned and clammy.

Dora-Rouge tried to calculate the distance where the redroot grew. It was decided at first that the rest of us would wait on this island of flowers while Bush went for the plants. I would remain at the campsite caring for the two older women. This was the logical thing. Next to Dora-Rouge, Bush was the best navigator, and she was strong. But then, Dora-Rouge reconsidered the plan "Angel, you are the one who dreamed the plant. I think you should go. Maybe the plant will call to you. Maybe it would be easier for you to find."

Bush argued against my going. "It's too far for her to go alone."

This was true. I had only followed along on this journey. I hadn't once guessed where we were. I preferred it that way. But like a woman, I said, "It's okay. I'll go for the plants." Besides, since surviving the Se Nay, I thought I could live through anything, that something or someone was on my side. I felt almost immortal.

BUSH PACKED FOOD in a small bag for me to take along, and before I knew it, I was leaving the place of flowers on my own, paddling, according to the cannibal's map, toward the medicines. I was to dig redroot at night. That was the best time to collect it. Then I would go to another place where Luther had told Dora-Rouge the wolfsbane grew. As I left, I glanced at Agnes and thought how small she looked.

Alone, the canoe was easier to navigate. The smoke that rose behind the flowered islands would be a helpful guide. The piece of map Bush insisted I take with me was in my pocket alongside the man's drawing, both wrapped in plastic in case it rained or I capsized. The islands the man had mapped out were over a half-day away and to the west. I'd be traveling against currents some of the time.

I fell into the rhythm of the paddle, the water. The boat moved as if with its own life now that I was alone. I glided through a reedy passageway, a channel shown on the man's map. I tried not to think how, in such channels, it would be easy to get lost. It turned out to be an entrance to a lake with calm waters. There was a new face to the land and the water looked like glass. I became deeply silent, taken in by it, as I pulled the boat through what looked like blue sky. A wonderful silence set into my solitary journey. Even though I needed to move quickly and was worried about Agnes, I felt peaceful. A loon called now and then. A hawk floated above me, whistling. Even with the mission at hand, I felt newly created in a fresh, clear world, as if seeing for the very first time.

When I reached the first island I combed the ground, every bit of it. I was certain it was the right place because the man had mentioned cast-off whiskey bottles. I searched for the redroot with all my soul, but it was not there. Nor, as it turned out, was the map accurate. I wondered now why we had believed the lost man Agnes had feared.

By then the sun had curved around the sky to the other side of heaven. The day had deepened into a rare gray-blue. Soon, clouds formed and moved with frightening speed across the circle of sky, carrying the possibility of a storm. I wondered if I should make a camp, but I worried about Agnes and had a feeling that told me to go farther, around the little circle of islands.

And so I followed this instinct, as Dora-Rouge would have done, and at the next landing there were more green and amber bottles, a large pile, and it was there that I found the red-rooted tubers. According to Dora-Rouge's directions, I was to dig them at night. I waited until what I thought was deepest night, the ideal time for picking roots. When it felt right, I carefully moved earth aside and dug out some of the roots, thanking them. I put the plants in the bag, then went on into the strange green light of short nights, my paddle at times soundless. I loved the water and traveling alone. I sat back and closed my eyes a moment, drifting, and when I jerked awake, I realized some time must have passed. How long, I couldn't say. It was as if someone had put a spell on me, to make me sleep. There was rainwater in the canoe and I was cold and damp. I was unsure of where the water had taken me. How could I have slept through a rain, I wondered, angry at myself.

The next plants, the wolfsbane flowers, had to be cut in early morning and so I traveled on quickly, through the yellow light of what I hoped was dawn. The new yellow cast of the sky made all the plants look as if light shone out of them, and they made odd shadows, clear and sharp.

With more ease I found the wolfsbane. I cut the blooms and put them in paper in order to dry, then turned to hurry back, still confused about day and night, wondering how long I'd been gone.

AS I RETURNED to the island bright with flowers, I saw something floating and blue, far out on the shining water. It was a few moments before the small raft of blue flowers, all in a mound, took shape in my eyes. Even though they were far away, I thought I saw butterflies, and I thought, too, that I could smell the blooms, a sweet, intoxicating perfume.

Bush had been watching for my return. As soon as she saw me, she came to help pull the canoe to ground. I sat down to get my wet socks off. "What's that out there?" I asked, pointing toward the flowers on the lake. I pulled off a shoe.

She said nothing. I looked at her more closely. She had swollen eyes as if she'd been crying. Dora-Rouge, too, sitting on the ground, was silent. "What's going on?" I wanted to know. I felt a panic in my chest.

All of us looked at the blossom-laden canoe afloat in clear water.

"It's Agnes," Bush finally said.

"Agnes?" And then I noticed that the blue-gray coat was across Dora-Rouge's lap. I looked at the canoe of flowers and understood immediately that Agnes was dead. She was what floated. But still I stared at Bush in disbelief. "What? That can't be," I said. "I have the plants." I opened the small bags, desperate and in a hurry. Shaking. Some of the roots fell to the ground. "Here they are. Here."

Bush put her hand on my arm.

I pulled away. "But they're right here!" I bent over and picked up the plants I'd dropped. I held them in my open palm as if offering them. As if begging for time to reverse.

"It was supposed to be me." Dora-Rouge started to cry. She held a dirty hanky to her eyes.

BUSH, out of habit, unloaded the canoe. Seeing that I hadn't touched the bag of food, she heated soup and gave it to me in a cup.

I drank it quickly. I was thirsty and drank long and deep from the water jar, too, and then fell asleep on the ground, my eyes still crying. At some time while I slept, Bush covered me with Agnes' coat. Once I woke up crying because I saw Agnes and the bear walking together in the yellow sky. I thought the flowered boat floating in water couldn't have been real and that I was only dreaming, and I heard Agnes singing along Poison Road, the way she did, coming back from water. The bear walked beside her, blue and nearly beautiful as it had been when Agnes was a girl.

I had been gone nearly three days, Bush told me later, though it was hard to tell with the days lengthening and the cloudy storm that passed over.

Above the canoe were butterflies, large and white. I begged God to let Agnes rise. I willed it, certain God would feel my pain, strong as it was, and would listen, would let Agnes step out of the boat, floating like the moths and butterflies just above the water, and come toward us.

"We'll have someone come for her," Bush said quietly. "We're not far now." She folded some clothing and packed it inside a bag.

It seemed wrong that there was nothing to do. There were no officials to report to, no one to tell of the death. All we had was the small body of Agnes, whose last desires were, as she had told me, to be eaten by birds and wolves.

"I'll remain," Dora-Rouge insisted. "I want to stay with Agnes."

"No, Grandmother. We can't leave you." Bush lifted her.

"No! Leave me here," Dora-Rouge insisted. "I'm staying." She began to wail about having to go away from the flower-laden boat that held her daughter. "Agnes. Ahi!" Speaking the old language.

"I'm so sorry, Grandmother." I wept.

Dora-Rouge struggled against Bush as she picked her up.

"God damn it!" Dora-Rouge hit at her with her frail fists, crying. "I can't even walk away from you. I can't even escape. I have to stay!" she said, but we lowered her into the boat, cradled on top of the coat and the beaver furs. She covered her eyes with her small crooked hands, held them over her face.

The smoke shifted to the south, and as we left, all three of us in one canoe, I looked back at the flowers adrift on the lake.

AFTER THAT, it seemed to me we merely drifted, that there was only an appearance that everything moved, only an illusion that we traveled, that light and shadows shifted about us.

We talked only about things that needed doing. "Hand me the pot," Bush would say. Or, "Is there enough firewood?"

Death had tricked us. Dora-Rouge's life would be unbearable after Agnes' death. And she blamed herself. It was only later that I learned how she believed Agnes' death was part of the deal she'd made with water.

A chilly drizzle fell. For part of one day we didn't travel in it, but finally, since the tent was damp, our clothing soaked, and the rain showed no sign of letting up, we decided we might as well move on. Soon it became a cold, downpouring rain.

I wondered, later, if they'd told me that Agnes had died not long after I left just to protect my heart. I'd taken too long to return. Maybe they'd changed time around to spare my feelings. I could never know, but the flowers looked fresh. They might have put her out on the water that very day. Or perhaps it was the odor of decay that had made them cover her with sweetness and cast her adrift. Whatever it was, the vision of the boat of blue flowers, floating between blue sky and water, would live in my eyes forever.

FINALLY, we came to the last island, the last portage. On the trail were plentiful moose tracks. "This is a good sign," said Bush. We followed the tracks. But when we came to the crest of the portage, we were shocked to see that there was no lake. Where water had once been was now only a vast region of mudflats. For much distance, all we could see was mire, some of it still wet enough to reflect light as it stretched about us.

Suddenly Bush cried out, "A moose!"

I looked, but could see nothing.

Bush pointed. "Right there. Look."

The moose, with its antlers, looked at first like a branched tree. It was sinking into the mire. It wasn't far from us and it was desperate, trying to escape. We were close enough to see both fear and fire in its eyes. Trapped in earth hunger, the great maws and teeth of land that swallow all things, it bent its forelegs and tried to pull itself out.

Bush could not bear it. She rummaged through the pack, looking for rope, her hands shaking, but soon she realized it was a poor, weak gesture on her part. The rope was tethered to the canoe with flowers. The rope would have seemed a tiny thing, anyway. The moose was large, gravity even larger.

We thought of every way to save it—branches, logs—but we could find nothing that worked and the moose shook its head, hunched its muscles in an attempt to climb from the liquid earth, and then rested, becoming a great and deep stillness, trying once more to keep its head out of the mud. "Swim!" I said beneath my breath, my eyes closed, "swim!"—but it was with the same futility of my prayer for Agnes to come out of the flowers and walk toward me. The moose cried out with a woman-sounding cry and, finally, it was embraced and held by a hungry earth with no compassion for it. Bush held my hand; I buried my face against her, arms tight around her, and wept. For the moose and for Agnes.

When I last saw the moose, its eyes were focused inside its life, in the last spark of being. I would remember this, its head back as if to breathe one last, precious, sustaining breath of air. Then, when I opened my eyes, it was gone. "I hate God," I said, wishing the mysteries of creation, the fire of stars were a nature separate from that of death.

"It isn't God that did this," said Dora-Rouge.

THE MUDFLATS were vast. They were what had been lake before the diversion of a great east-flowing river to the west of them. The ground stank of decay and rotting fish and vegetation. We could not get across the mud; we had no choice but to turn back and go in another exhausting direction. Knowing we were near had kept us going, but now we felt hopeless. Now, too, there was nothing left to eat but a few oats and rice, and we were uncertain how much longer it would take to reach Two-Town, our destination. The world had changed as we traveled, and in such a short time. For all we knew, the next corner we rounded would be just as unpassable as this, just as ruined.

THIRTEEN

▼

A LARGE SKY OPENED ABOVE us, bright and wide. After all the travails of our journey, our landing should have been a momentous event. We'd crossed time and space to be there, had lost Agnes and our other moorings, had seen the order of the world reversed. Now we were nothing more than survivors no one knew or cared about, in a place that smelled of rain that wasn't there, a place where light and mud, the first elements of creation, seemed to be turned against themselves. For what had we done this? For two women to die? For me to find a mother who had only injured me in the past? For Bush's ideas about justice, and her rage over how governments treated their earthbound people? Now the absence of Agnes was a felt thing and we'd endured hardship to be in that place where mud and silt wanted nothing more than a misplaced foot so it could swallow us the way it had swallowed the moose. We'd been beguiled.

I gathered Dora-Rouge up in my arms and carried her to a soft place in the grass which Bush had covered with the furs. As I carried her, I smelled the tender odor of old skin and felt her hair against my shoulder. It was whiter than before, her skin sun-darkened and lined more deeply.

· · ·

THE TWO-TOWN POST, only ten minutes from where we landed, was the meeting place for the towns on either side of it. In it was the only telephone for public use, the makeshift infirmary where a visiting doctor examined the sick once a week, and where the schoolteacher was flown in to teach the few remaining young people to read and tally numbers. Mail was delivered and picked up there, news exchanged. It was where boys, home from boarding schools for Christmas, flirted with girls, and where men winked at women in winter scarves, and where old women condemned them all for such behavior, even though they remembered their own youths. Under ordinary circumstances it would have been filled with people who gathered there to shoot the breeze. But these were not ordinary times. The townspeople were all gathered elsewhere to talk about the continued building of dams. And despite the abundance of dry goods and packaged foods, the store felt empty and unpleasant. Maybe it was what had happened there, long ago, when early owners starved a band of people and locked them outside in the cold of a miserable and hungry winter.

The dark building sat beside a few thin-looking conifer trees. It was nothing like the store at Adam's Rib, or even the dank, wet interior of North House. The town store, Two-Town Post, had thick, bulletproof walls. At the Two-Town post, a person could purchase live bait, cloth, shotguns and gun oil, traps, and Campbell's soup. There was a sturdy scale for weighing hardware, and in a glass counter were knives of all sorts, those for skinning, bone-cutting, and Swiss Army knives with corkscrews and bottle openers. But now the building was partly empty. It smelled musty and of tobacco, all kinds and shapes of it—snuff, Bull Durham, cigarettes. Flat, brown bottles of whiskey, the kind that fit in a man's back pocket, stood undusted on shelves. Red cases of ammunition looked as if they'd been there for years. But this was deceiving because both ammunition and whiskey had a high turnover in this territory.

Just then, from behind the store, we heard the noise of a chain saw. We followed its ripping sound, past the chained, barking dogs that, like all the tethered dogs in the north, tested the limits of their chains. The owner-through-inheritance, Mr. Orensen, was outside between two sawhorses, a jumble of cut wood beside him, and sawdust in the air like an autumn tempest.

He caught sight of us out of the corner of his eye. Slowly, he straightened up. He was tall and angular, with enormous hands, larger than I'd ever seen before, larger even than Tommy's. He wiped sawdust off his glasses with a handkerchief. In no hurry, he brushed the shoulders of his red shirt, then walked toward Bush and me. The chain saw idled behind him. He didn't expect this interruption to take long. "What can I help you with?" He walked with us to the door, brushing the yellow dust off his sleeve.

It took Bush a while to speak. If it were up to me, I would not have found the words. "We've come up from the south," she said, her voice faltering. "By canoe. We lost our mother back there. We need someone to go after her body." Bush hesitated. "We couldn't carry her."

He said, "Just a minute," and went outside to turn off the saw. This was going to take time.

The silence was startling.

While Bush spoke with him, I walked about the post, absent-mindedly looking at the skinning knives, trying to dull my own guilt. I was the cause of this trip to begin with, I knew. It was my search for home, and for Hannah. Worse, I'd failed Agnes, falling asleep as I traveled away from the islands of blue flowers to find the medicines, losing track of time. Tears came to my eyes.

He spoke into the phone. "Orensen here." To Bush he said, covering the mouthpiece, "There's a volunteer search-and-rescue team. They'll probably use the mail plane and a canoe. You have to pay for the plane, though."

She nodded.

It wasn't long before the sirens sounded, and then there was a silence that could break hearts and Orensen's clear blue eyes watched us as if he recognized our parts in the death and judged us.

He was, in truth, suspicious of everyone, and even more so of us. Women seldom traveled alone through there; this made him doubly sure we were lying. It was in his eyes. He, like the other non-Indians, was worried that a new protest had been scheduled to begin, "Where you from?" he wanted to know, his eyes piercing mine.

"Adam's Rib," I said, as if the place was just around the corner.

Bush looked about the building at the empty old chairs and benches. She was uneasy with the silence. She knew people from there and how they talked. They were worse than Italians, worse even than the women at Adam's Rib. She wondered out loud where everyone had gone.

A meeting had been called. That was why the store held no people. There were fears it would be like Wounded Knee. Already too many other Indians had arrived and they were stirring up trouble, and the white people thought they were all dangerous. There weren't as many as at James Bay, but there were enough to clash with the government, the police, and BEEVCO, the corporation that was building the dams. One judge had ruled already in favor of the native people; another had overturned that decision, sharpening the conflict.

WHEN WE RETURNED to Dora-Rouge, she was crying. Like a queen on her throne of bear coat and beaver fur, she sat, as if to belie the fact that her face was swollen, her eyes red. The death of Agnes remained with her. It always would. For all of us. It came in waves the way rings of water circle out from a dropped stone. Or aftershocks. When she saw us, she said, "This is all my fault."

Bush argued. "It's not. I'm the one who came up with this foolish trip."

"You? What about me? It's my mother we're looking for."

Dora-Rouge was resolute. She looked from me to Bush, then away as she said, "Yes, that's all true, but I'm the one who made the deal with water."

"What deal?" We both stared at her.

She crossed her arms over her chest. She didn't answer. Instead, she changed the subject and told us she couldn't count on Luther anymore. He was slow in responding to her. Even when he was young, she said, he couldn't handle tears, and he'd always eased himself away from conflict. "He told me, he said, 'You made a bad deal back there, Ena.' I won't be joining him, after all, that's what he's mad at."

"What deal?" Bush asked again.

LATE THAT AFTERNOON, the search team, a plane and two canoes, returned. The men said that as near as they could tell, the wind had blown the canoe to land. The body was nowhere in sight. They'd even tried to drag the waters and found nothing.

"So," said Dora-Rouge, as if something she'd known all along had been confirmed. But later, when Dora-Rouge was out of earshot, I heard the men say that they had found the canoe. Pieces of its frame had been gnawed by teeth, probably by wolf or bear, they weren't sure. "I don't want it on my shoulders to tell the old lady," said one. Even the rope was chewed, he told Orensen, maybe by a porcupine that liked the salt or maybe it was Wolverine who knew how to pull the boat in from water strewn with petals.

I was relieved when I heard this. It was what Agnes had wanted, to be eaten by wolves and birds, to have her hair woven into bird's nests in spring, along with twigs, fishline, downy breast feathers, and moltings. After that, on the chance that she had been eaten by wolves, I called every wolf I saw Grandmother.

"Where's the meeting?" Bush wanted to know. The place was still empty.

Orenson, with his white eyebrows and intense blue eyes, said, "Why do you want to know about it?" He moved a box from the shelf.

Sharp-creased Levi's sat on a shelf in the only sunny window of Two-Town Post. The side where light hit them was faded. It was the identifying mark of Orensen's store. It also said a world about him. He left them there because he was used to each thing in its place, including people, and that was where the jeans had always been, even before there was a window, and that was where they were going to be, no matter what.

The next day, we went again to Two-Town Post. Dora-Rouge said, "Leave me here with the things. See if you can get a chair for me while you're at the post. I need some dignity." Her voice was weary, but she was in command. She was anxious for us to leave. She said she needed silence to think. "And send Husk a letter. Tell him what has happened."

A board near the door of the post had notices and ads with rooms to rent, some in exchange for labor. While Bush wrote Husk and

purchased supplies, I looked through the ads. There were places
that offered meals, but most renters in these places were men who
didn't like to do for themselves. I took down a few house numbers,
both at the place of the Fat-Eaters and the next town over, in Holy
String Town. Then I saw the sign "Public Showers" hanging on the
wall. "Bush, look. They have showers."

"They're free," the man said. "I'll rent you some towels if you
want. They're fifty cents each."

Bush pulled some crumpled bills from her pocket and gave him a
dollar. He handed her two skimpy white towels. "Only one's working. That one." He pointed. "The second one's plugged up."

I TURNED THE KNOB and stood in the falling water, eyes closed.
Behind my closed eyes, I saw the canoes, the fine spiderwebs, the
lily pads, the swamps, and bog fires. I saw the boat of flowers, tethered, a sight which would long haunt me with its beauty and its
pain.

The hot water was a heavenly thing. It was the many hands of
touching gods. It had traveled rivers. It had been to places we'd
been. It came down like manna.

"Hey, save some for me." Bush knocked. "The heater's not that
big."

While we changed places, my hair wet and still tangled, the
smell of hamburgers from a back room of the post pulled me toward it like a magnet. This was Angel Iron, as I now called myself,
in heaven.

CLEAN AND FRESH, we left the post, both of us drinking Coca-
Cola from iced green bottles and carrying another along for Dora-
Rouge.

Now that I was clean, I wanted a bed and sheets. "Shouldn't we
look for a room?" I asked Bush. "I've written down some ad-
dresses." I was anxious to get settled in somewhere and to sleep in a
real bed. I dreaded one more night of camping.

"No, we'd only have to move all our things right away. I'm too
tired. We'll camp by the water tonight and get a room tomorrow."

"What about the wheelchair for Dora-Rouge?"

"Tomorrow."

I scrambled to keep up with Bush.

When we reached her, Dora-Rouge sat, leaning back on the furs. "You two look like a hundred dollars." She raised herself up. "Is that Coke for me? Did you bring an opener?"

We looked at each other. "Sorry," I said.

Dora-Rouge looked at the chilled Coke. "I used to be able to open bottles with my teeth."

"That's probably why you have new ones," Bush said.

HOLY STRING TOWN had earned its name because the houses and buildings were laid out along a single road like rosary beads on a string. The first priest there had hoped and prayed to convert every household and tenant who had tumbled in along the string. In some cases it had worked, but there were people who, although they lived in houses, still listened to other gods. There were people the priests and Episcopalian clergymen thought too sinful to change, but they'd rushed to the challenge anyway, and failed. These were the people who had entered the white world like breech births, whose feet had stepped into it first, long enough to wear wool socks and laced-up oxfords, whose legs were covered with gabardine or denim. They wore belts around their waists and their chests might have been covered with striped shirts or blouses, but that was as far as the birthing went. Their souls and minds stayed inside the older world, floating in natal waters, and they still heard the heartbeat of the Mother Earth and received her ancient sustenance. The priests and preachers had given up on these people. Partway inside both worlds, they were sometimes in neither, and they still spoke with spirits, and feared them.

But now the priests had other things to think about. Holy String Town had been overrun by machines that traveled up and down the String, as it was called. Dump trucks and front-loaders rumbled along, and new roads were being cut into the already wounded forests. The trees, mostly conifer, were being cut. On top of it, ever since the flooding of the place had been planned, there was a stepped-up effort to strip the land's resources. Drilling rigs were allowed past the roadblocks that were meant to keep local natives in and other Indians out. The land was being drilled to see what else could be taken, looted, and mined before the waters covered this little length of earth. And at night, the workers drank and fought. Prostitutes only needed to curl a finger at them, or lift a brow, and the men would follow. This was fresh ground for the tired priests and vicars. For them, at least, it had possibility.

For us, it seemed, there was little possible. The next morning, Bush and I once again left Dora-Rouge at the camp and went to look at two of the places with rooms to let. Our budget was small for now, and our choices were limited. The first room we looked at was dark and sat beside a scrap heap. It smelled of unwashed skin.

"We don't rent to women," the proprietor said, as if we'd want to stay there under any conditions.

We walked toward the Fat-Eaters. There, at the next house on our list, an enormous light-skinned woman came to the door, red lipstick full on her lips, the kind that leaves prints on coffee cups. Like Frenchie's. The best thing going for this place was that it was not in String Town, which was too dingy and noisy for our tastes.

"Is the room large enough for three?" Bush asked as I looked around. There was a flower box under the outside window, with plastic geraniums.

"It's just one room, honey. Twin beds," she said to Bush. Mrs. Lampier was her name. "But you could put a cot in it."

I was afraid she'd say that.

She led us to the room, a cigarette in her hand, smoke flowing behind her toward us. "I have an extra cot," she said. Inside, the walls were pink and a small chandelier hung from the living room ceiling. It looked out of place in the old, square, and nearly dilapidated house, like a new, shiny diamond on the hand of a worn-out woman.

The walls of our room were as pink as Mrs. Lampier's skin, and there were prints of *Pinkie* and *The Blue Boy* framed on the wall, and a chest of drawers. We would share the kitchen with her, and she had a little propane stove and a generator. "The electric goes out at eight sharp," she said. "The generator uses too much gas, you know. Up here, gas is expensive." She smiled at us. "What are you doing here, anyway?"

"Looking for our relatives," Bush said.

"The room'll take three people easy." She smiled at me. "Your relatives? Well, there's not that many people here to make them hard to find." She had a sweet but gruff voice, from smoking. She looked close at my face, then at Bush, who looked wrinkled and dry. "I'll go get the cot."

"It's okay. No hurry."

"Who's your relatives?" She put her cigarette in the toilet. At least we'd have a bathroom. Unlike the House of No on Fur Island.

Bush didn't seem to hear her. She asked, "Say, do you know where I can get a wheelchair?"

"What do you want with a chair?"

"Our grandmother can't walk."

"Well, will the front stoop be too hard for her?" Mrs. Lampier lit another cigarette with the silver lighter she kept in her pocket.

"No, she's light as a feather. Angel, here, can lift her."

"There's a clinic down on Potelee Road." She pointed the way. "You have to turn left on Atchuk Street to get there."

I could tell she wanted to know about our relatives, but she decided to wait until later and said nothing more about it.

Bush gave her twelve dollars as a deposit. She put the money inside the pocket of her housedress.

As WE WALKED AWAY, I said, "But Bush, I want a bed!" I was emphatic. "Not a cot." We headed toward the building on Potelee. "A real bed that doesn't fold in half. I'm only eighteen and my back aches like an old man's." It was true. I was stiff every morning.

"It's only temporary."

"Well, I don't hear you volunteering for the cot."

The closed-down clinic was housed in a small, unpainted building. It had been closed for over a year, no employees to be found except for a doctor no one would visit unless in desperation. The people had given up on western medicine anyway, and what with a drunken doctor, they either died, went to a medicine man, or traveled to the city.

"I wonder where our landlady has been all this time?" I said. "She must still think it's open."

What Bush and I didn't yet understand was that in the world of the two towns, everything a person needed was hard to come by. What they wanted was rarer still.

"Check with Father Bly at the rectory," said a neighbor of the clinic who came to check us out. "He usually keeps a few."

The rectory, easy to find, was almost as stark as the clinic, except that it was painted white, and the windows were trimmed in blue. The door knocker was shaped like a fish. Bush lifted it and knocked. But no one answered. The shades were drawn. The church itself was locked. We stood in front of it and looked around. While Holy String Town was a long thin line, a single road, the town of the Fat-Eaters was laid out like a cross along two roads, with smaller, more narrow roads between.

Bush looked at me. "Wait a minute. What about the other church? I remember Dora-Rouge telling me the town had a cathedral of miracles."

I shrugged. "I don't know. I never heard that. It must have been before my time."

As we walked down from the church, Bush stopped a man on the street. Although he was young, his chest was caved in. We asked him about the cathedral.

"It's near the fire station." He gestured toward the place where the fire truck was parked. "But I can tell you, it doesn't work. I went there myself and I've only gotten worse." He coughed, as if to emphasize the failure of miracles. Bush thanked him and we walked at a quick pace toward the fire station.

The little church, if it could be called that, was small and brown, another temporary building. It was little more, on the outside, than an abandoned house. A person would be hard put to believe any miracles had ever taken place there, except that in the healing room were three wheelchairs, several leg braces, crutches, and quickly sawed casts that had been thrown down beside the altar. And just inside the door was an opening in the floor, filled with sacred earth that any woman or man, whether religious or not, could touch, could let pass through their fingers back to the ground, and carry with it their ills and cares and dyings.

Bush bent and touched it and closed her eyes. Then she went to the altar and looked over the three wheelchairs as if she were shopping. The one she chose was wicker. It had been painted white, though it was peeling in places. A name, Mother Jordan, was written on its back in fancy red letters. A soft blue cushion, dingy at the edges, was in the seat, still indented, as if Mother Jordan had just that day stepped out of it and walked away, back to her life, past the fire truck and ambulance, and past the scraggly four trees at the bottom of the road. Bush turned the chair around and pushed it toward the door.

"You're just going to steal it?" I stared at her.

"God won't mind. Anyway, it's not really stealing. I'm borrowing it, is all."

I could see there was no point arguing with her.

"Besides, what good is it doing in here?"

But I wasn't so sure. Bush was acting like a stranger, willing to steal some poor person's wheelchair. I hoped this wouldn't bring us bad luck. "What if Mother Jordan comes back for her chair? How do you know the miracle is permanent?" I asked.

Bush brushed aside my questions. "People always care too much about the dead. For the living, Angel, sometimes you just have to take it."

I followed her out of the little church. The only thing we pushed was my guilt and fear of being arrested. We went over the hill, along the trees, and down to the water. I had to admit that the big white wicker chair, with its weavings and circles, looked lovely in that world. It was almost as good as a new chair, maybe better, except that it squeaked and was difficult to push. But when Dora-Rouge sat in it, she said the best part of the chair was that it creaked. "People will hear me coming." She smiled. It was a chair Frenchie would have loved.

We pushed Dora-Rouge first to the post. She wanted a hot dog. "It looks just like it always did," she said, looking around. She looked at the tobacco and knives and dusty books. We bought a Coke for her, and there was a can opener on the wall. It was the second time she smiled that day. Then we went past the only fire hydrant, up the slight hill, and along the bumpy street and plank sidewalks, all the heavy furs in Dora-Rouge's lap, the blue bear fur slung halfway over the back of her elegant chair, and then we went to Mrs. Lampier's.

The third time Dora-Rouge smiled was when the three of us stood before the self-glued mirror tiles in Lampier's pink room, *Pinkie* and *The Blue Boy* reflecting from the wall behind us like anemic guardian angels. "We're a sight!" she said. "At least they won't mistake us for whores." She laughed, showing her pink, babylike gums. She laughed so hard tears formed in her eyes. Bush said, "My God, we do look horrible." I joined in, too, laughing at how life was precious and dangerous and absurd all at once.

Jean Lampier rolled in the little black-and-white, ticking-striped cot, folded in its metal frame like a trapped animal, and smiled as if she guessed our joke.

When she left, I said, "We should get our things." Used to living in a city, I didn't think it wise to leave our packs at the edge of water.

"No," said Bush. "We've been carrying them all this time. I don't want to do it one minute more. I'll get someone to fetch them."

Before long, she found two boys from the town and offered to pay them if they'd carry the packs and canoe to Mrs. Lampier's. But when the younger kids returned, they were empty-handed. "Jon robbed you," they said. "He stole your things."

Bush paid them anyway. Then she went striding down to the shore, swinging her arms, looking for the teenager named Jon, and to see what, if anything, he'd left behind. I followed behind her, and behind me, the boys, who thought this was much fun, were swinging their arms just like Bush.

When we reached the site, the canoe was gone. So was the food pack and the tent and sleeping bags. All we had left were a few clothes. Fortunately, we'd carried the beaver pelts in Dora-Rouge's lap.

"I'm going to find that kid." Bush stood, her hands on her hips, looking at the empty place where they'd been, as if the canoe, the packs, the life jackets would all float up from beneath the water or out from under the jutting gray rocks.

FOURTEEN

IT WAS A RAW AND SCARRED place, a land that had learned to survive, even to thrive, on harshness. At first it seemed barren to me, the trees so thin and spindly, the soil impoverished, but soon I felt a sympathy with this ragtag world of seemingly desolate outlying places and villages. It was a place of rocks and mosses. Water ran all across the earth's surfaces in every way it could, in rivulets and bogs, ponds and streams, all of it on its way to a river where it would roar away to another America or to empty into a bay. I understood this water to be the source, the origin of all the land. I saw the land in its fullness, even the trees that had been twisted by wind and dwarfed in poor soil. Everything had become strengthened by desperate and hungry needs, and by the tracts of running water. Like me, it was native land and it had survived.

And in time it would be angry land. It would try to put an end to the plans for dams and drowned rivers. An ice jam at the Riel River would break loose and rage over the ground, tearing out dams and bridges, the construction all broken by the blue, cold roaring of ice no one was able to control. Then would come a flood of unplanned proportions that would suddenly rise up as high as the steering wheels of their machines. The Indian people would be happy with the damage, with the fact that water would do what it wanted and in its own way. What water didn't accomplish, they would.

FIFTEEN

THE PEOPLE THERE were called the Fat-Eaters, although the original name for themselves had been the Beautiful Ones. Their territory now was the settlement built around a little hill where the church sat, painted white with dark blue trim. Most of the people at the territory's outermost edges had been resettled after having lost their own lands to the hydroelectric project, lands they'd lived on since before European time was invented. They were despondent. In some cases, they had to be held back from killing themselves. These were Dora-Rouge's people, and mine. This was why Dora-Rouge's return to her land was not what she'd hoped or imagined. It was nothing like the place she remembered. She looked around. She said nothing. She didn't need to. The despair was visible on her face. Her eyes constantly searched for something familiar that was not there. I fell into a gloomy stillness, watching her. Dora-Rouge had gone home to die in a place that existed in her mind as one thing; in reality it was something altogether different. The animals were no longer there, nor were the people or clans, the landmarks, not even the enormous sturgeon they'd called giants; and not the water they once swam in. Most of the trees had become nothing more than large mounds of sawdust.

The few familiar things that remained, Dora-Rouge touched

with tenderness: the gnarled trees the loggers thought not worth their trouble and had left behind, the stones, the swamp plants. And it did mean something to her to be where her ancestors had walked, no matter what the land had been turned into.

The resettled people lived in little, fast-made shacks, with candy and Coca-Cola machines every so often between them, and in Quonset huts left behind from the military who had recently used this native land as a bombing range. The better places were inhabited by men who'd come looking for oil, and a few loggers who were after the last of the trees.

The people were in pain, and even if Dora-Rouge had known the people of this last generation or two, she would never have recognized their puffy faces and empty eyes, their unkempt, hollow, appearance. It was murder of the soul that was taking place there. Murder with no consequences to the killers. If anything, they were rewarded. Dora-Rouge saw it and grieved.

One day, Dora-Rouge, in the white wheelchair, said to a young woman, "What has happened here?" The girl looked at the old woman with contempt and quickly moved away.

The young children drank alcohol and sniffed glue and paint. They staggered about and lay down on the streets. Some of them had children of their own, infants who were left untouched, untended by their child-parents. Sometimes they were given beer when they cried. It was the only medicine left for all that pain. Even the healing plants had been destroyed. Those without alcohol were even worse off, and the people wept without end, and tried to cut and burn their own bodies. The older people tied their hands with ropes and held them tight hoping the desire to die would pass. It was a smothering blanket laid down on them. The devastation and ruin that had fallen over the land fell over the people, too. Most were too broken to fight the building of the dams, the moving of waters, and that perhaps had been the intention all along. But I could see Dora-Rouge thinking, wondering: how do conquered people get back their lives? She and others knew the protest against the dams and river diversions was their only hope. Those who protested were the ones who could still believe they might survive as a people.

The pain in Dora-Rouge's joints worsened from having to see this. Her color was poor, but something or someone had guided her there, she said, and it had drawn me along the full route with her. How else could she have known the way, so twisted and odd as it was?

WE'D BEEN THERE about a week when one afternoon Bush went to a settlement meeting up at the blue-trimmed church. While she was gone, I pushed Dora-Rouge to the post to buy some Hostess chocolate cupcakes, the ones we both craved. An old man, sitting beside the gun cabinet, watched Dora-Rouge as she sat in Mother Jordan's chair. He frowned and studied her face, looked away and back. Finally, he said, "Say, weren't you the woman with the corn?" He was dark and slight. Beside him sat a shaggy dog with yellow-tinged fur. The man wore a sweater that read "Eddie Bauer." I thought that was his name but he introduced himself as Tulik. He had been a tribal judge.

"Yes, that was me." Dora-Rouge said it in a distant way, in the same past tense he had used, so that it sounded as if it were no longer her but someone else. I suppose, truth be known, she was not the same woman who kept the kernels of corn that came from the place where people had spirits akin to hers. By now, "akin" meant wounded; no one wished for such kinship. Dora-Rouge tried to turn the wheelchair toward him, but her small crippled hands only succeeded in rocking it. A half-eaten chocolate cupcake in hand, I went over and turned the chair for her and moved her toward the small, barrel-chested man. I drank some soda. His skin was dark, his face bones fine and delicate, and he had happy eyes.

"I remember you," he said. He wore baggy pants and had short hair. "You are Ek's girl."

She smiled at him despite the sadness in her eyes. "Yes, I'm that one."

"Well, I'm her cousin." He pulled his chair closer to Dora-Rouge. He said a few words in the old language and then they sat in silence, looking straight ahead, as if behind them, or to either side, the world was too painful to see or remember. I felt as if they were speaking with their minds, communicating in a full silence that excluded me. Maybe it was the silence of change witnessed, something too full for words.

He squinted at her as if he, like all the other old men I'd met, had been snow-blinded in the past, and he opened a brown bag of food, took out a sandwich made of Spam and white bread, and handed half of it to Dora-Rouge without speaking. Without speaking, she took it. She loved Spam, and for just a moment I think she forgot there were no happy young people in that place, none at all.

I left them alone. I went outside and walked on the planks that were laid down across the swampy land. I wasn't sure if it had been a mired bog before the damming, or if it had been a lake. A board-walk made of old wood floated on mud. It was moist and swollen, and algae grew in the spots where it was rotting. I walked along in the direction of water, to the west. Once, I slipped on the moist wood, and just caught myself from falling into the mud. The dark ground pulled at my foot. It tried to take me in the way it had swallowed that pitiful moose, a slow but firmly held tugging. My shoe was gone and I could see there was no use going after it, so I walked on without it.

A part of me remembered this world, as did all of Dora-Rouge; it seemed to embody us. We were shaped out of this land by the hands of gods. Or maybe it was that we embodied the land. And in some way I could not yet comprehend, it also embodied my mother, both of them stripped and torn.

We'd heard about Hannah from various sources. Word traveled quickly in small towns, even where there were two towns for gossip to visit, hang its hat, and drink coffee. Mrs. Lampier, when learning why I'd come, said nothing, but her eyes betrayed her thoughts. Other people, too, on hearing that I was one of Hannah's daughters, would say a few words in the older language and then be silent. This made me all the more anxious to find her.

When I finally reached the lake, the water was dark. At first, I wanted to wash my muddy leg, but it was quiet and no one else was there, so I hid behind a rock and some trees at the edge of the lake and removed my clothing. In spite of water's hungry desire and its cold temperature, I entered the near-black lake and immersed myself. My skin tightened. Such a cold baptism; it took my breath

away. It was colder than any water I'd entered before. I didn't count
the seconds that would pass before I was in danger of dying from
exposure. Hypothermia was commonplace in these waters, I knew,
but I had stepped out of my rational mind along with my sweater
and jeans, as if it were just another article of clothing. In the cold
water, my feet hurt. I hoped the water would cleanse all the pasts,
remove griefs. Inside it, naked and alone, I held my breath past my
own limit. I saw my body as from a distance; it was an unwavering
flame in the dark room of water, a wick of warmth holding fire in a
cold chill, holding light in the vast, immense darkness. I floated in
what wanted freedom, in what white men wanted changed.

I saw my arms, strong from the paddling, my legs, naked and
thin, and my face with the hair flowing back with the current. I
thought how Dora-Rouge had told me once about Eho, the old
woman keeper of the animals. She had been sent down to the
mother of water to bargain for all life, nearly swimming to her
death. She was the woman who fell in love with a whale in the heart
of water and did not want to return to the human worlds. She knew
and could command water. She drifted to where the world was
composed long ago in dark creation. Because of her, the animals
and other lives were spared, but in the end, Eho could not remain
in water or with the whale of her loving. Soon, back on land, she
died. Now men and women were to be the caretakers of the animals, that was what the Great Spirit said, according to Dora-
Rouge.

When I came up gasping for breath, I saw Dora-Rouge and
Tulik walking down the little planked incline to the shore. Tulik
with his funny walk, with his dog beside him, was pushing Dora-
Rouge in the white chair. A redheaded woman with dark skin
walked beside them. It was my mother. I knew it at once. I fell into
a cold stillness made worse by the water's temperature. Quickly, I
jumped out of water, and without drying off, dressed, shivering,
my fingers blue.

"What do you think you're doing!" scolded Dora-Rouge when
she saw me. "It's too cold for that. Look at the water. It's even
black." She waved her thin arm and shook her fist at me. "And
showing off your bare fanny, too!"

IT WAS ON A SUNDAY when Hannah came to see us, when I surfaced to see them walking toward me. Someone had sent word to
her at the settlement of Hardy that her great-grandmother and her
daughter had been at the Two-Town Post and wanted to see her.
Bush was at one of the settlement meetings and it was a good thing,
we all knew, for Bush was still vulnerable, still caught in the between of good-and-evil forces that were Hannah. Whatever she'd
fought in Hannah was still waiting to wage the same war, break the
tie, and settle old debts. Dora-Rouge and I both could see in a
glance that Hannah still resided in a dangerous world, or maybe it
was that a dangerous world lived inside her.

"Let's go to my home. It's more private," Tulik said. We all
walked together past the store and on to his cabin.

Dora-Rouge continued to scold me. "Where's your shoe?"

I pretended not to be cold. "I lost it," I said, but while we
walked, I searched Hannah's face for signs of myself. Hannah was
heavily made up and she didn't like to be looked at. Now and then
she turned her eyes toward a place where nothing was, but she
never once looked at me with those eyes outlined in black. I didn't
know what I'd expected to feel, seeing my mother for the first time,
maybe happiness or anger. At best a kind of peace, something that
might order my life and explain me to myself. Like Bush traveling
north, I wanted a map, something fixed, a road in. I wanted to see
what was between this woman and me, a landmark, a bond. I had
imagined this meeting so many times, but none of them was like
this. Any path between us had long since been closed. She was, as
Bush said, a wall, a place to go with no foundation.

Tulik's house was named Lynx House, from the days before
houses were numbered. It was surrounded by a fence made of whalebone, and as soon as we went indoors, a woman with protruding
teeth and glasses—Auntie was her name—and a young boy looked at
us, saw that this was not a social call, and went out the door. Tulik
himself went to the far corner of the room and sat near an old wooden
radio, mending his fishing nets. He pretended he was not listening.
They were small, close quarters, and anything but private.

Hannah was quiet for a long while, and in that waiting, as I

looked at the floor, I realized that she feared me more than I had
ever feared her.

Finally, she said, "I never hit you." Only that.

I looked at her for a long time. I was no longer numb from the
water, but I still felt cold. I saw her. For her, I was the accuser, the
sign of her guilt. I wore the wounds of Hannah on my face. They
were evidence of what had happened.

Still, she had come to see me.

"I never laid a hand on you," she said to me. "I think you ought
to know that."

I could only look at her, and what I saw was more ruined than the
land. My hopes for this reunion were gone.

Dora-Rouge said, "What's that? I hear a baby crying. Do you
hear it? It sounds like it's just over in the trees."

Hannah glanced again in my direction. "You look fat," she said,
which later made us all laugh because I was much too thin; I had
lost all my extra weight, and then some, carrying canoes and supplies and Dora-Rouge. My face was even raw-angled and masculine in its leanness.

"Can't you hear that?" Dora-Rouge said again.

"Maybe it's a cat," Tulik said. He, too, went outside.

What Hannah said, that she'd never hit me, was almost true. She
hadn't laid a hand on me. She had used weapons against me, I
learned later—hot wire, her teeth. Once she'd even burned me with
fire. And it was only later that I felt a rage uncoiling inside me at
her words, but even that was a rage built on sadness and loss. It was
not the rage of a directed hatred, not the cleansing fire of heat, not a
sharpened-to-a-point rage, not even a seeking-justice rage. It was a
futile anger that had no practical use in the world, and so I had no
choice but to contain it; it had nowhere to go.

The others kept their eyes averted, as if my heart would break
under their gaze, but I felt their pity. And I knew by then how
badly I'd been hurt by her. I could see that there was no love inside
her, nothing that could love me, nothing that could ever have
loved. She tapped her finger impatiently on the table a moment,
looked as if about to speak, then stood up and went out the door.

"Wait," I called out. I tried to follow. I wanted more than that. "Wait," I said, but she continued walking, and finally I stopped.

As she left, the mail plane flew over. It shook the walls. Mr. Tulik, as was his daily custom, went to greet it. Hannah, seeing him follow behind her, began to walk faster, as if he, too, were chasing her. I watched her vanish. She looked back again at Tulik, then ran down the road to get away and soon she simply slipped out of view.

I went inside, weeping, and when Bush returned, she came to me and said, "I'm so sorry, Angel. But I hope you believe me; it's not her fault."

"But I came all this way."

"I know," said Bush. She took me on her lap like the mother I never had.

ALTHOUGH I TRIED AGAIN to contact Hannah, I didn't see her again until two weeks later, when she was dying. By then, we'd been forced out of the room at Mrs. Lampier's. The policemen had come by with an order to evict us. Too many people, it read, were inhabiting too small a space. The fire department wouldn't permit us to remain. But we knew it was because Bush had been going to the meetings and had fierce opinions about the dams, and she'd been speaking out.

We made an attempt at finding a new place, one we could afford. But nothing was available. No one would rent to us. So, with nowhere else to go, Tulik insisted we move into his house, the house surrounded with the whalebone fence, the pieces of which looked like teeth though they were ribs. "Ena, you're practically family, anyway," he said. He called her by her real name.

Even so, Tulik had little room. Or what we called room, anyway. We could help keep up the house, he told us, though no one could ever keep up with him. He had mighty energy and he needed little rest. Worse, he was more orderly, even in a small, crowded place, than Dora-Rouge had ever dreamed of being. The only person he allowed to be messy was the dog, Mika, who left fur in her wake. Mika was the offspring of two of his favored onetime sled dogs.

Indoors it was dark. It was a house where, in summers, outside light came in through cracks in the walls, and in winter, the light from inside fell out across snow and ice, looking like fracture lines in the earth where inner light and fire were opening, breaking out. Like Pangaea.

The house itself was brown wood, stained from the weather, and some of the wood was beginning to rot. It had once, long ago, been painted white.

A small globe of the world sat in one of the windows. Tulik used it when he read the news, which he did daily, and when earthquakes occurred, he looked always at the other side of the world to determine where aftershocks might strike. Always there was balance, he said.

He was a tribal judge, one of the elders. Despite the fact that he'd gone snow-blind once while out with his dog team, and still squinted in bright light, he was a good hunter. With Tulik, it seemed as if the world had conferred something special on him. People recognized it and valued him.

He lived with his daughter, Auntie. She was called that not because she was an aunt, which she was, but because the word sounded comforting and so like the language of her mother, like some other gentle words from the north. So it was a name, not just a title.

The young people all called Tulik Grandfather, and all of us in the household called his grandson just by the name Grandson. I didn't even know his Christian name, Calvin, until years later, in court.

As neat and orderly as Tulik was, that was how sloppy his daughter, Auntie, was. She balanced him out, she said, like aftershocks around the globe from a recent quake. Then she laughed. Auntie, one of the few people at the Fat-Eaters who wore glasses, had been a star trapper. She was a wide-boned, rugged woman who laughed often and deeply, told off-color stories and sang. She wore tight jeans and she was taller than most. She was a woman who lost things, left her keys in the car, left her glasses in places she could never see. She was trying to quit smoking the first day I met her, and when we moved in she was working on a dark blue quilt in order to occupy her hands. I remember her, always, as I saw her that first time. She sat in a little slant of light from a lantern, a light that fell across her face and touched the edge of her glasses. And she wore a red cotton sweater.

Bush and Auntie hit it off like old friends. They were change-minded in the same fierce ways, but they had different ideas about how it should come about and they argued incessantly until their voices were little more than background noise. They were both so idealistic that they seemed younger than they were, and neither of them was tolerant of injustice of any kind. The two of them balanced each other as well, not in the realms of order and chaos, as with Tulik, but like day and night, summer and winter, two parts of the same thing. Bush was quiet in her ways, while Auntie was loud and often mistaken for aggressive. She would rise to any occasion as long as there was conflict; the rest she left alone. And she carried her medicine with her always. Not in the kind of bag made out of the tail of a beaver—those were considered improper and offensive to the animals—but she carried her help in soft white doeskin. And in both women, no matter how they tried to hide it, there was a softness that shone through. Together, I thought, as I listened to them talking outside at night, they formed the one woman I wanted to be someday, with a large portion of Dora-Rouge added to the recipe like flour or leavening, the thing that held it all together.

Another woman lived there but only from time to time, a tiny woman named Luce. She came from a reservation down South. She had come to be with her family; they were protesting the diversion of the rivers, which ultimately would affect their own waters down below. Luce, proud of her intellect and her ability to read, looked at the weekly papers through a magnifying glass. She, on reading what was happening in the world, would always say, "It's time we stop this." And, "This must end."

"NO MORE COTS," I declared to Bush, on moving into Tulik's house. I looked him, too, in the eye with courage and said my back hurt.

"Okay. No problem," Tulik said. He smiled what I came to call his no-problem smile. "We'll fix up the sleeping platform." It was a wide shelf, the thing people with large families and frequent guests used to house others who traveled from place to place fish-

ing or hunting. Entire families slept together on them, the many
children tossing and turning, and parents snoring. Seeing it, I was
sorry I'd spoken. By contrast, a cot now looked like a room at the
Hilton. Plus, a cot would have been too small for Grandson and
the cousins who visited now and then, curling up beside me, and
stealing my blankets. I felt shunned, relegated to the world of
sleeping children, and was sorry that I'd ever complained. But I
kept silent about this. I had pride, but I began to sleep with Agnes'
coat over me.

AT FIRST I hated having no privacy in Tulik's crowded space, but
then I learned that privacy, like beauty, was skin-deep. Also, I
claimed a corner of Tulik's for my own in daylight hours, a fraction
of the little room on the side of his house where the cabinet radio
stood with no electricity to fire it. I placed my amber there, in the
corner the room slanted toward, a pillow to sit on, my hairbrush
and pencils. I wrote my dreams there. Sleeping with the blue fur
coat, I had many.

I grew accustomed to our closeness. And to our silences. We had
ourselves more strongly than I'd ever had in any private room.
There were never invasions into thought or dream. The others
knew the secret of dwelling inside their bodies, remaining there.
They knew the secret peace of silence. And I grew to love Tulik. We
were close, he and I. When I woke in the intimate space of morning, Tulik was already awake. At the break of day I heard his movement, his footsteps on the floor, the sound of the door opening and
closing, the morning smell of smoke. After he went outside, when
the door closed, I'd get up and pull on my jeans and go join him
outdoors, my hair still tangled. Together we were quiet as we prepared for the day, him praying, me being silent, looking toward the
marshes to the east. Then, when we were done, I'd go back inside,
splash water on my face, wake Dora-Rouge and give her a warm
washrag to clean herself. She had begun to fail since losing Agnes.
Daily, as I combed her hair, she seemed weaker.

One morning outside, Tulik looked across the land and said to
me, "You know, Angel, here a person is only strong when they feel
the land. Until then a person is not a human being."

I looked at him, not certain of what he meant. But it occupied me, this thought, and soon I saw that Tulik was right. On this land, a person had to live by feeling. There was no other choice. Dreaming, too, could be counted on; the best hunters still found their prey by dreaming the maps to the dark eyes of deer. There was a deep intelligence in this, and I, too, was feeling the rhythm of it inside myself. My heart and the beat of the land, the land I should have come from, were becoming the same thing.

One day while I was out, Tulik returned from the mail plane with a letter from John Husk. It was addressed to Agnes. Dora-Rouge told me to open it. It was written neatly. It said:

> Dear One,
> LaRue bought The Raven for $125 and I'm using the money to come see you. I hear there's a way to get there. We're worried here because we haven't heard from you. How is your mother? Did Angel find Hannah? We had a strange ice storm, and so close to summer, too. The fish are still dying. I'm worried about you. Should be there about the 5th.
> Love everlasting.

So Husk had not received the letter telling of Agnes' death, after all. Now it was too late to get word to him. We were certain the mail was being intercepted. I looked forward to his visit both with happiness, because I'd missed him, and with apprehension for the grief he would discover, finding Agnes gone.

"The fifth?" said Dora-Rouge. "That's coming up soon."

S I X T E E N

WHAT DO YOU THINK?"
Bush spread the beaver furs on the platform and looked at Tulik.
Tulik's assessment of things went beyond his skills as a judge. His
appraisal of people was most always on the mark; he could size up a
man's drunkenness in a glance, could determine when a child
would be born by the way a woman walked, and whether it would
be a boy or a girl. He knew the best time to plant a cold-weather
garden, and he knew the winters of furs. Except for that of Wolverine, that is, because he, like everyone else, couldn't remember seeing one, just a hint, a wide head in the shadows of trees.

The furs were heavy and rich, even I could see that. Tulik laid a
hand on the thick fur on top. "This one, one like this, would bring
fifty dollars."

"You're kidding." Bush looked at him to see if he smiled. This
was an extremely high price for the time. It was 1973, and the top
cost of a beaver fur was thirty dollars, even with inflation.

But Tulik knew these things because he'd had a hand in them for
so long and he had an eye accustomed to weighing and measuring.
Beaver furs he knew the best. "It's a heavy fur. This one was taken
in the winter of 1948."

"How do you know?" I asked him.

"It was the year when winter was early. It fell in August. Beaver

were few that year," he said. Exporters had intercepted several
traplines the year before and taken all the furs, leaving the native
trappers no choice but to overtrap in order to trade for food and
supplies at the post.

"You see these longer hairs? And the thickness?"

I leaned forward and looked, touched the dark pelt.

"A skin this size then was equal to that of two lynx." He looked
at the fur beneath it. "This one is 1936, the time when a nearby village grew so hungry and cold they set out for a hunt carrying only
rotted meat and sinew to eat. It was all they had."

Starvation, even now, was not to be spoken except in English or
French, as if saying it would bring the skinny ghost of hunger back
to the people who feared it. So all Tulik could say was that the
hunters had vanished. They had gone far north to the place where
beaver built dams of stone, to that spare place where the wolves became so hungry they were forced to eat beaver and sharpen their
teeth on rocks. That was the year the dead remained frozen outdoors until late spring, standing, blue and thin and solid, gazing
out at where hunger had come from.

IN THE OLD DAYS, according to Tulik, the world was created by
Beaver. "Yes," he said. "There were no other creatures but them.
They were the ones." This was when trees were still in sky reaching
down with their roots, looking for a place to take hold. It was when
the world was still covered by water. At that time, ice lay down on
half of every year. They were the ones. Beaver took down trees from
the sky; they brought up pebbles and clay from somewhere beneath the vast waters. They broke the ice that had shaped itself over
the water. They swam through it and they made some land. With
pebbles and clay. When trees were still in the sky. They laid sticks
down across the water. It was like a trail the new creatures and nations and people to come would walk across. In those days the faces
of spirits lived on the water and windblown snow. There were no
other creatures, none, except beaver who rose out from the darkness beneath waters, out of the lodges and dens and burrows of the
world, places the rest of us have never seen, places at the center of

earth. The only light was what came from inside the stars, from inside the yellow of trees. There was just freezing and thawing until Beaver took down some of the trees from sky, leaving nothing behind but teeth marks and wood chips. Beaver brought up clay and mud from the deep. Beaver created a pool, then a bog, then living earth. When Beaver shaped the humans, who were strangers to the rest of creation, they made a pact with them. They gave their word. They would help each other, they said. Beaver offered fish and waterfowl and animals. The people, in turn, would take care of the world and speak with the gods and all creation. Back then, the people could hear the beaver singing. Back then they still sang out loud. A song haunting and sweet. Back when there were no lights except in the eyes of animals. This is true. It's what Tulik said. Like the voices of children coming out of water, so beautiful.

WE LIVED THERE by natural light. Each morning, with the cracks of light coming through the walls of the cabin, we all sat together and drank coffee and ate greasy bread with margarine and sugar on it, a diet which agreed with me. At this time we related our dreams to one another, seriously at some times, and with laughter at others, as when Dora-Rouge dreamed she was a lounge singer. But whatever the dream, the faces of Tulik's family were open faces, the eyes tender in a way I had not known before, even at Adam's Rib.

ONE MORNING, just after the arrival of Husk's letter, I dreamed my mother was dead and that there had been a storm of ice pellets violently crashing to earth.

"What did the place look like where she lay?" Tulik wanted to know.

"It was a small room." I tried to see it again. "Snowshoes hung on the wall above her bed."

He fingered his thin mustache.

"The floor sloped," I told him.

Tulik said, "You better pack your things. You will have to go to her."

I looked at him for a long time, at his short, thick eyelashes, his narrow bones. Then I got up from the table and went to my corner of the room and packed a few things.

Bush stood up as if to help me, but both Tulik and Dora-Rouge shook their heads. "She should go alone," Dora-Rouge said.

Bush looked embarrassed.

Tulik pushed back his chair and got up from the table. "I'll see if I can get a drop-off with the mail carrier." As he walked out the door, he looked back once at Bush. She had doubts about me going to the place where Hannah lived. But things had changed. My need for protection was gone. If the dream was right, Hannah was harmless now. Bush was, after all, from another land, from the south, from another people. Maybe she didn't understand this, I thought. The land here might love her, but it did not tell her the things it told the rest of us. It kept secrets from her. It excluded her. At times she even seemed lost.

Bush watched Tulik walk away.

"We're in luck," Tulik said when he returned. He was cheerful. He had offered the mail carrier's son and assistant twenty-six dollars, nearly all he had, to take me to Hardy. "Mikky will take you. But you have to go today," he said. "Hurry, get your things." He took the money from behind the coal bin. It would cover a little more than gas.

I bustled around. "I'll pay you back. I promise."

But he only laughed in that deep way of his, soft at the same time his manliness would never be in doubt, even at his age. Even in his Eddie Bauer "fashion plate" sweater with blue snowflakes on it, the sleeves were pushed up to reveal his muscular brown arms. "Is that all you're taking?" he said.

But I had already learned how little to carry, how little I needed. Now how little I wanted.

And when the young man, Mikky, came to take me to the plane, I carried only one small plastic bag of things.

As we walked to the plane, we chatted idly about the weather. Alongside Tulik, Bush followed behind us, trying to stay out of the way. Then, before I knew it, I climbed up into the little two-seater, strapped myself in, waved good-bye to Bush and Tulik, and the plane rattled across the land, over small houses, waters, the broken forests of trees. There was smoke in the air above spare, tired-looking settlements.

We stopped once to pick up mail from a village, and then flew again over waters, canvas tents, shabby villages, and shabbier towns. Once we saw wolves curled up in balls beside the blood-wet rib cage of a deer. Mikky, the mailman's son with rosy cheeks, flew lower to show me. "See? Right there." He pointed.

"I see them!" I said, excited.

Finally, the wheels touched down near the remote and quiet Hardy. Mikky let me off at the point where the road to Hannah's ended. He took out a piece of paper that looked official, scrawled a map for me to walk by, and left me standing at the edge of the dirt road that he'd used as a runway.

I watched the plane leave, the grasses and bushes whipped by its wind. Then it was all quiet. I felt abandoned. I tried to get my bearings. There was no sun, no way of determining which way was which, but I set out to walk the four miles, following the map. I thought of Tulik's words about strength, and as I walked I felt the land, the way a human being might feel it.

There was an overpowering silence, not even the sound of a bird. Nettles grew between trees, and it seemed the land had overgrown the human worlds that had wandered through. They'd left their marks, however; I passed a rusted bulldozer, a burned-out area, and a place of cut trees where a road had once been planned, started, and then forsaken. Beyond that, away from the trees, was the place where military planes had used Indian land for a bombing range, for target practice.

Woodsmoke came, blue-gray, from a little cluster of buildings that were partway down a small hill. My heart skipped, thinking it was Hannah's. But according to Mikky's map, I turned off before reaching those buildings. Wind carried the smoke, passed by me, and then vanished. A dog barked in the distance.

And then I came to my mother's house. Behind it was a clothesline with a few squares of cloth hanging from the wire, no wind to make them move.

It was a shabby house, unpainted, with tar paper over some of the walls. The door of her house had no lock. Where a lock had been was broken wood, as if the door had been jimmied. I stepped on the wooden box that served as a step, not knowing if I should knock or go inside. I was afraid now that I was at Hannah's, but before I could turn around, a young man opened the door, and for a moment we stood looking at each other. He didn't blink. "I heard you coming," he said. He'd expected me, though he was not prepared for what I looked like. "You look like her." I nodded. "I heard that one of Hannah's children was back." It wasn't the scars he looked at, I knew, it was the resemblance to Hannah, which I myself found frightening.

He was dark and very thin, with a large chest and legs too long for his short body. He wore a flannel shirt and a dark gray sweater, as if it were autumn, and he opened the door wider, for me to enter.

I went inside.

Another man sat beside the window, reading the weekly news, a little paper of only eight or ten pages. He nodded at me, then followed my gaze to where Hannah slept, pale and drawn up, the way a child might sleep. Above her were the snowshoes of my dream. "It won't be long now," he said.

I nodded.

He folded the paper and got up to leave. He put on a red hunter's jacket. He took my hand in his a moment. "We were waiting for you. We'll go now." At the door he turned and said, "You'll need some food. I'll bring you some. And milk, of course."

Again, I nodded. But after he left, I wondered if they were too easy about it, if we could get help to save Hannah.

The house of Hannah had an old, familiar smell to it—of lard, which thickened the air; of strong tea; and of something else I couldn't name, but that my body remembered. I wondered if it was the sweet smell of what Agnes had called cyanide.

It felt cold. I buttoned my jacket while I looked around. It was a one-room house and, like in my dream, the floor had settled lower on one side than on the other. The bed, too, was lower on one side than on the other, and Hannah was held in it as if contained in a hollow. If she moved, it looked as if she might fall.

I watched her sleep for a few moments. The blanket, pulled up over much of her face, rose and fell with her breathing. I was nervous. I didn't know what to do. "Hannah?" I said. I sat down at a slant on the chair beside her bed. I felt dizzy. She said nothing. I pulled back the cover and looked at her. There was a wide, blood-stained bandage tied around her middle. One of her hands was curled against her cheek. "Mother?" I said. Still, she did not stir.

Shortly, the man came back with coffee, a thermos of stew, some biscuits, and powdered milk. He put the milk on the table. I watched him, how he moved, catlike and strong. "Thank you," I said. He ladled stew into a brown plastic cup and handed it to me. "Venison." He sat down at the table across from me while I ate, but just for company. I ate in silence. When I finished eating, he left, and I heard his boots loud on the wooden box outside the door, and then I was alone with my mother and her demons, if such things existed, and I guess by then I had come to believe they did.

THERE WAS a curtained partition dividing the room. On the walls, true to my dream, hung rope, chains, snowshoes, and pans. Darkness itself seemed to hang there by a nail. The cupboards were nearly bare, and there was no water, except what was in a jug. The floors were damp and smelled moldy from the weather, but the house was clean. Clothes hung neatly on nails. And there was an oil stove.

On the kitchen side, three old brown plastic dishes were in a cabinet. In another were salt and a few slices of dry Wonder bread. Hannah's house, like her body, even from my beginning, had the same little or nothing to offer.

Her lips were dry, her teeth had what looked like dried blood on them, and her breath was foul. She tried to say something, but she didn't see me, I was sure. I soaked a rag in water and held it to her lips. "What is it?" I asked, looking at her face that was so like mine.

She looked old and young at the same time. She had white roots to her hair. I thought of Bush saying of my mother that it was not her fault. I wanted to have compassion, but even now I felt the pain of betrayal, abandonment: she was leaving so soon after I'd found her. I didn't understand that Hannah had died long ago. I looked long and hard at her, trying to memorize her face with my eyes that knew how to turn things upright again.

I looked around for anything that could be of use in caring for her. My eyes also saw, hanging in the corner between walls, fish-nets and decoys. Two jackets hung near the door. Beside a bag of sugar, an empty whiskey bottle sat on the table.

There were no herbs or poultices for her, no salves or unguents, no laying on of any hands that would save her, not even a ceremony. I could see this by the set of her eyes. The presence of death was outside the door. Perhaps it had walked along the same trail I had. But I wasn't afraid of death, I decided. I went over and opened the door for it. I wasn't afraid of Hannah, either, and for this I was glad.

From the open door, a soft breeze entered the room. The cloth partition moved with it. From outside, I heard the sound of a lid on a trash can, and then there were smaller sounds, like someone talk-ing. That's when I heard the sound, a cry, that came from behind the waving cloth partition. I thought perhaps it was death speaking. I walked over and pulled the cloth aside.

There, in a wooden box, was a baby girl, about seven months of age. I stood looking at her. She was a thin child, and when I knelt over her, she grasped at my hand as if I might leave. Like me, she was red-haired and I laughed when I saw this. I have a sister, I thought, I have a sister! Already this baby was desperate. Already she had a will to live. She began to suck on my finger.

This explained why the man had brought the milk.

I picked her up. Carrying the child, I set to work. I cleaned the whiskey bottle and mixed water and the powdered milk inside it. It wasn't the best thing for an infant, but it was all I could do. I chewed some of the meat stew and put it in a spoon and fed her. She was hungry and she was a distraction from Hannah's death and my feelings of the loss of something vague, something I'd never quite possessed. But still, all the while I cared for her, I could see death and Hannah raging against each other in a fierce battle; Hannah wanted to die and had already submitted to it, but more than one of those who dwelled inside her feared it. What prowled in her, preyed on her from within, had a strong will. So it became a war between death and those whose desire to survive had been stronger than all of them; what inhabited her had no resignation to anything.

THAT EVENING, as Hannah's life ebbed, two women came to see me.

"You look like her," one of them said. She was soft-voiced and tall. She opened a package. "Here, feed her this." She pointed to my mother. It was marrow butter. For them more than for Hannah, I put some on the tip of a spoon and tried to get her to eat it. I knew she wouldn't take it, but the women, I thought, wanted to be helpful.

The tall woman said, "She wants to die. She needs strength for it." The tall woman stood by Hannah and pulled her hair back behind her ear. It was a comforting gesture. "Hannah," she said.

They'd brought fat and tea for the baby. "We've been worried about the baby," the shorter woman said.

"It's her baby?" I asked.

She looked at me. "She took it with her to see you. We thought you knew."

I remembered the day Hannah showed up at Two-Town. Dora-Rouge had heard a baby crying out in the trees.

"The man is dead," the woman told me. "The one that stabbed her. They already took him away."

I wanted to know what had happened. I listened with great care as the tall woman said, "The beginning of all this is that too many animals are gone." She said this as if I would understand. I didn't, not yet. But, I thought once again how all of us kept searching for beginnings.

"That's what started all this. Otto went to Mill Town to work. He and Hannah needed food and gas. It's always so hard here." She stopped talking while a military plane passed overhead, rattling the window and the cups on the shelves. "The planes are one of the reasons the animals are gone. Some of them died of fear. Some drowned, too."

I nodded. I'd heard what happened there, the caribou running across the flats as the water surged toward them, knocking them over, flooding their world, their migration routes gone now, under water.

I pieced together the story as well as I could. Otto, the trapper, had neither wired money to Hannah nor returned. Months passed. Finally, Hannah took up with another man. She always found a man to feed her and keep her in wine. But this man wasn't like the others. His name was Eron, and his grandparents raised him in the bush. "They stayed to the old ways, you know, they knew things, they believed things. Eron was their chosen one. He was a strong hunter. The people loved him," she said. She sat on the chair with her feet tucked under it:

"When he came back from school, that's when his troubles started. At school they told him everything he had learned was wrong, and with these two knowings, that's when he got lost. He was lost ever since then.

"After he moved in with Hannah, he began to fear her. He said to us one day, 'She carried a basket from the water. In it, clear as day, there was a dead child.' He said she carried a dead child in it."

The woman got up from the story, as if it made her nervous, and tried once again to feed Hannah some marrow. "She won't eat. It's been like this for more than a day now.

"Eron said it always felt like someone else was in the room. Sometimes more than one. Hannah's house was cold as a winter wind, he said. One night he felt something touch him. 'She's a spirit,' he told his brother. 'She's not a real woman at all.' His brother didn't think much of it at the time.

"One night, he said he dreamed a woman with long white hair, white as the snow, wearing white robes, her face white, too, with red, bloody hands. She stood at the foot of the slanting bed, her hands bloody with what she'd done.

"There were people all along who thought Hannah should have been sent away. Maybe even killed. People believed she was a danger to others. One of her children ate glass and chewed razor blades. We knew what had happened to you, your face, how, like a dog, she bit your face with her teeth. It was worse for you, maybe because you looked like her. She hated you for that, for coming from her body, being part of her."

I stared at the woman. She spoke casually. She thought I had already heard what she was telling me, but I hadn't. The chill in the room entered my spine, rose up my neck. My heart beat quickly. I tried to keep my composure, but all I could think was, it's true, my mother was a cannibal, a cold thing that hated life. But I said, surprising myself with how calm I sounded, "Did you call the police? About the stabbing."

"No. She said it was her time to die," the woman explained, as if I understood, but I didn't, I didn't know that by tribal law they were required to permit a person to leave life at their own time, in their own way.

I also didn't know that whenever the authorities were summoned to these remote areas, they charged the tribal people a fine, which they pocketed just for responding, and even at that help was rarely forthcoming; it was costly and even risky to call for assistance. An ambulance could not have passed through the way I had walked to find Hannah's. The helicopter pilot demanded cash up front. So did the hospital over in Keeneytown, showing no mercy for the people who lived in small shacks in this place that looked from afar like a cigarette burn on the face of the world. Even if Hannah had wanted to live, there would not have been help from the outside. If she'd wanted to live, they could have called a medicine man or woman, but now all the medicine people but one had gone to the dam north of Two-Town, and the one who remained behind did not work with cases such as these. He was an apprentice, and he was not strong enough to handle demons or restless beings or ice spirits that had gone to live inside a damaged woman.

"Eron stabbed himself," she said. "Before he died, his cousins arrived. He told them that she herself had begged him to kill her. Hannah dreamed of frozen bodies. 'Kill me then,' she told him. 'It's the only way.' "

"IT HAPPENED ONCE BEFORE, not so long ago," Dora-Rouge would tell me later, after we'd returned. "Just before this skin of time, that there was a woman in the grip of ice. It held her in its blue fingers. It froze her heart."

It was 1936, the starvation year. The woman lived in a house of snow, frozen in, starving, until finally she ate the flesh of those family members who had already died of cold and hunger. Human flesh was the only plentiful thing that winter. Most would sooner starve, but this woman and ice, just as in old stories, became lovers. She rolled naked in snowdrifts like a woman gone mad. A normal person, a human being, could not have survived it. That's how they knew what she was.

One day two hunters, brothers, found her cabin at the end of a path. The cabin was surrounded by snow clouds in the deep, dark blue of winter. When the two men went inside, they found her naked and laughing. She was alone, so they lit her lanterns, and in the dim light, they watched her. She smiled at them, but they were not fooled. Even in the 1930s, these things happened. Just like in older stories. This woman had slept with winter. She had eaten human flesh. Her heart loved ice. The two men took pity on her. It was not her fault that she had become winter's mistress. The youngest one said, "Let's cook her some hot soup."

While the older man built a strong fire, the other went outside and cut a dark red piece of frozen meat off the deer they'd been carrying, then placed it to cook on the fire. While the meat cooked, they studied the woman. She watched them, too, with a cold eye. She hated deer meat. That was a bad sign already. All she wanted to swallow was the flesh of the two men. That night, she hid a knife beside her and waited for them to fall asleep. She could see how tired they were after days of hunting in the cold. After they ate, she knew they would become drowsy and helpless with sleep. But the younger one saw her sneaking up on him with the knife in her hand. He let her get close. He coaxed her, edging her closer to him. "Give it to me," he said. "Give me the knife."

Now that she was found out, she began to cry. "I'm a spirit," she said. But there was another voice, a small human voice left inside her. It was this little voice, almost gone, that said to the men, "You have to kill me. There's no other way."

"It could be winter fever," the older man said, but even while he talked, she or the spirit picked up the knife and ran to stab the younger brother. Just in time, the younger brother moved aside. Instead of his heart, she cut his arm. But she was strong, he noticed. She was stronger than a human woman and when she grabbed him, the young

man couldn't fend her off by himself, even though he was a strong-muscled man. His brother helped and in the struggle, they killed her. They knew by then that she was no human, so after she died, they poured boiling-hot water into her open mouth and her wounds in order to melt her frozen heart.

A week went by, and then the men were arrested by the police. They pleaded guilty. The white jury was horrified by what they'd done. They'd killed the woman in such a terrible way. They were especially frightened by what the young men said and how they told the story with honest faces. But the domain of gods and spirits and demons was larger than that of humans, even now, and the men were satisfied, even to be locked up, knowing they had returned the world to a kind of balance: they had made the world right for their people, for seasons and thaws.

It was so others could live that they did this, and I've thought about it for years. Wars are fought for far less than this.

I HEATED WATER and washed my mother's face and hands. One of the hands, now so thin and vulnerable, was crooked; it had been broken and had healed wrong. Her skin was chilly, her eyes sunken.

"Why are you following me?" Hannah said. But it wasn't me she asked—it was air, perhaps a ghost—so I said nothing.

Outside, the breeze strengthened and I felt it enter the house and take some of Hannah's life with it. It seemed that Hannah and the persons or spirits or demons who followed her about were gathering together in a truce; they were becoming silent now.

I sat thinking of what had happened to my face, what sharp teeth had done to my life. And there was the baby in the corner, in the wooden box, a new life that had formed in this place where some hundred-year-old history was breaking itself apart and trying to re-form.

Perhaps there was balance in the world, after all, I thought. Maybe it just needed time.

DEATH STOOD IN Hannah's eyes, small and forlorn. It didn't look triumphant. Hannah was still alive, but barely. Her eyes were already set, her breathing rougher. Even death didn't want her, I could see. Maybe it, too, feared her.

I sat beside her, the still unnamed child on my lap, and whispered again the word "Mother." It was a word I'd never said. It hung, suspended in air. Like a child, I said, "Mama?" Then, like a child, I said, "Mama. Don't leave me," and through the window I saw the moving shadows of wind blow the few clothes on the line outside.

She looked small and vulnerable as she might have been once, back when she was a girl, before she was tortured into this poor shape before me.

Outside, someone passed near the window. I saw a shadow. I was crying, and I was afraid. But also I feared that what lived inside her, whether history, as Bush had said, or spirits the priest believed possessed her, would fill the room. I was afraid that when she left her body, whatever possessed her would open its claws and seize another body, and so at the very last, when the death rattle in her throat sounded like a gourd with seeds inside it, shaking, I took the baby outside and placed her on the ground, safe in her wooden box. I knew by intuition that it was a bad thing for an infant to be in the presence of death, even a kinder death than this one. I wanted nothing to enter the innocent, open-eyed gaze of this child. None of the soul stealers were going to sing this one away or fill her body with emptiness and pain.

As death grew to fit my mother, to fill her, it was like a seed of something that opened and grew inside her, as if it had known the territory for a long time, plotting its way through flesh and bone, waiting for the moment of its unfolding. Its eyes opened inside Hannah's, then it inhabited the arms, the hands that clutched at air, then, finally, its stopped heart stilled hers. At last, there was only one thing and she was filled with it.

What possessed her was now gone. It was now ordinary as air in a room, no more than dust, and with quiet footsteps. Perhaps what stole inside a person disguised itself, themselves, as everyday things, daylight, ordinary words and common rooms. Now she was humble, her body without its person. No wings to spread. Nothing.

It was death, finally, that allowed me to know my mother, her body, the house of lament and sacrifice that it was. I was no longer a girl. I was a woman, full and alive. After that, I made up my mind to love in whatever ways I could. I would find it in myself to love the woman who had given life to me, the woman a priest had called a miracle in reverse, the one who had opened her legs to men and participated in the same life-creating act as God. Yes, she tried to kill me, swallow me, consume me back into her own body, the way fire burns itself away, uses itself as fuel. But even if she hated me, there had been a moment of something akin to love, back at the creation. Her desperation and loneliness was my beginning. Hannah had been my poison, my life, my sweetness and pain, my beauty and homeliness. And when she died, I knew that I had survived in the best of ways for I was filled with grief and compassion.

BUSH WOULD COME SOON, I knew. The women summoned her on the citizens band. I was uneasy about being in the house with the body, so I looked at Hannah one more time, at the skin of my skin, the face that had given shape to mine, and then I covered her, took the baby, and walked with her to the place where there'd been a cluster of houses around a general store. I was anxious to leave Hardy. Now there were the living to think about. In another day or so, Husk would arrive, and I wanted to go back to Holy String Town to meet him.

I went toward the town, past the closed-down school which was housed in just a Quonset hut. The playground was littered with paper and bottles and cans. A breeze moved the tire-seat swings. Hardy was a little town, of sorts. The store itself had once been a post, but now it sold packaged food, fish bait and tackle, and beer, powdered milk, canned goods, and boxes of cereal. Nothing was fresh; there was not even an apple. Just Jell-O and Levi's and hard-toed boots.

The baby liked to be walked. She slept while I walked and she cried when I stopped, so I carried her until Bush arrived. In places the land was dried and white-edged, like the alkali flats in Oklahoma. Oil drums sat outside little buildings. Everything looked temporary. Nothing was planned to be permanent, but had become so by accident.

When Bush finally arrived, I met her at the road. With the baby. "My sister," I said, smiling.

Bush was solemn.

"Hannah's already gone," I told her. "Before we go in, let's go to the store and make arrangements for a burial."

"So that's the baby Dora-Rouge heard crying," Bush said. "We should learn to believe her. She's never been wrong."

In spite of the occasion, she fussed over the baby as we walked.

When we asked the storekeeper about burying Hannah, he told us a man, Saul Talese, had a backhoe. "He lives right up at the turn-off," he said, pointing out the way.

We went to Talese's place. Bush offered him her last fur; Talese saw the value of it. Without bartering, he went over to Hannah's and began without delay to dig a hole in the clearing beside the house where Hannah had lived and died.

WHEN WE RETURNED to Hannah, the room, with its smell of tea and fat, was still and quiet. I unbuttoned the green cotton blouse my mother wore, and we began to prepare her body for the burial no one else would attend. I looked for the first time at my mother's body, her arms so like mine, her bones familiar. She was covered with scars. I remembered Bush's story about the bathing of Hannah as a child, and my heart broke for her. I leaned over her and unbuttoned her skirt. Hannah was thin, her body already stiffening, her bones jutting out, her pelvis like an empty bowl. She still had on her worn-down boots. She had been lying in bed with them all along and I hadn't known it. They were the in thing for those years, pink go-go boots with a fake concho button and a fringe. I removed the boots. Inside them, her feet were bare, her toenails painted red, and chipped. And there were burn scars on the tops of her feet.

Bush wanted her arms to shelter Hannah, she said. "She looks so vulnerable now. And you can see how she was tortured." I knew Bush had loved her. "Sometimes, when Hannah was a girl," said Bush, "she would talk about the stars and I'd forget all the things she'd done and my fears about what she would do one day." Bush cried.

Together we bathed Hannah with soapy hot water, more comforting to us than to the dead. There was little cloth and we needed it for wrapping her body, and for the baby, so we first laid Hannah out on newspaper. How appropriate it was to place her on words of war, obituaries, stories of carnage and misery, and true stories that had been changed to lies. It seemed like the right bed for her. Some of the words stuck to her body, dark ink, but we did not wash them off; it was a suitable skin. Then Bush took down the cloth curtain partition and we wrapped my mother inside it. She wound the sheet around that, rolling Hannah from side to side as if she were merely a bolt the fabric had been wrapped around.

THE TWO WOMEN who had visited made fish-and-lard soup and brought it to the house. The tall one looked out the window at the machine. "They didn't use to bury them in the ground in the old days," she said. "They were aboveground then. It seems like we've got everything all mixed up."

They said that when Hannah died they had smelled a wolverine pass by. "There are even wolverine tracks all around Hannah's house," the tall one said.

"Where?" I said, going down the step.

I went out to look, and it was true.

Some people say Wolverine had things mixed up, too. At times it was said he was a human returned to his animal shape. At other times, he was animal inhabiting a strange, two-legged body, wearing human skin. Whichever he was, Wolverine had come to despise humans and they didn't feel so good about him either. But he knew them, and he knew everything about them. That's how he knew to steal the flints and other things of value to human beings and to spoil the things they needed to live by. I wondered if he was the one who stole my mother.

The people there needed the snowshoes and coats. There was little of nothing for us to take away, although when I opened one of Hannah's drawers I found the piece of amber I had carried, the frog inside it. I hadn't even missed it. She'd stolen it, taken something else away from me. And she had broken into it, tried to chip the frog out. It must have terrified her, such suspension. I think she wanted to get to the heart of stilled life, to what was held captive in the yellow blood of a tree.

As we left, I knew I was leaving something behind me, perhaps forever, and as we walked away from the house of Hannah, death closed the door, darkened the windows like smoke. The nails of the house, driven through the walls, would rust, the slow fire of oxidation would take place, and finally all of it would fall. No one would ever live near Hannah's dwelling place. They feared her still, all of them. In eight years it would be under water, the forests rotting beneath the muddy waters, the store and school floating up to the surface in pieces like rafts, the rusted machines at the bottom, unnatural and strange, and the animal bones floating, white, in the dark, cold waters, like ghosts or souls in the hereafter.

ON OUR WAY BACK, curious, I asked Bush, "Where'd you get the money for the plane?" I knew Tulik had none left. Mikky had made a special trip for her, for which she'd paid a hundred dollars.

Bush told me that at Two-Town Post she'd laid two of the prime beaver furs on the counter and asked Mr. Orensen what he'd give for them. She imitated him, telling me, "Well, they don't look like much. The hairs are uneven." He showed her what he meant, but she gave him the hard, gritty, angular look I knew so well, her eyes not wavering one bit.

"I'd say they're worth about, oh, thirty, in trade," he offered.

Bush knew traders. She wasn't fooled. "You know that's the best way for the hairs to be. So I'll take what you offered, that much for each one. That and more besides. I'll take three of those cured hams over there. And two pairs of Levi's."

When the deal was finished, she'd bargained for needles, thread, cloth for Auntie's and Luce's quilts, "and part of the money to get to Hardy, too," she told me. "And Levi's. One in size 26–30, one 29–31." She laughed about how his face changed expression. He could see that she wasn't a novice. He took the jeans from the shelf and placed them in a bag. He was so surprised, he didn't even haggle. Like Dora-Rouge, Bush drove a tough bargain.

BY THE TIME we returned to Tulik's, I'd named the baby, my sister, "Aurora." I gave her to Dora-Rouge to hold. Beaming, she said, "New skin, straight from mystery. I'm glad I made that deal with water, after all."

"What deal?" Bush said.

It was only then that we learned about Dora-Rouge's bargain with water. She had told it that if it gave us safe passage down the Se Nay River, she'd give up her so desired death to fight for it. She'd pledged her soul. "But I didn't know what I was in for."

I thought, so that was why Dora-Rouge blamed herself for Agnes' death. She thought there might have been a part of the agreement she had not understood, loopholes in the legality of the arrangement.

We heard the low howl of a wolf, so low it could have been mistaken for the wind. It lay down across the wet earth. Tulik's dog answered, remembering the wolf blood that still lived inside it, no matter how it had been bred out, no matter how people wanted to make of the animals something they weren't, as they'd tried to do with the people, as they were doing with the land. And so the events that followed were tribal cries, the old wailing come to new terms.

And then we heard the train from a long ways off. It was how sound traveled there, where sometimes a sound from miles away seemed close at hand, and at other times a person in the same room sounded far away, distant and remote. Its sound drowned out the voices of wolves.

S E V E N T E E N

THE FAT-EATERS BELIEVED
the ancestors returned in the new bodies of children, so for several
weeks Tulik, Auntie, and the woman named Luce studied Aurora's
features to see who she might be.

They pondered her, but there was great disagreement. "Look.
That birthmark at her hairline is just like Ek's," said Auntie.

"No, Ek's was on the other side of her forehead."

Tulik said, "Ek was her own grandfather. Remember?"

"But her expression is just like that of Ek's. Isn't that so, Dora-
Rouge?" Auntie tried for support. "Doesn't she look like your
mother?"

"Leave me out of it," said Dora-Rouge. "I love her whoever
she is."

But the arguments over Aurora continued. Luce, who wore a
calico dress, favored Auntie's opinion. "She's just like Ek. Look
how she keeps crawling toward Ek's book. See? She's doing it now."

This was the first time I'd heard of Ek's book. "What book?" I
asked.

"Yes, I have her book. But it's yours. It's for you women."

The book's pages were made of thin birch bark cooked into a
stew of salt and ash, then flattened and dried. In it were diagrams of
plants. Arrows pointed to parts of them that were useful for heal-

ing, a root, a leaf. Also there were symbols for sun and moon which depicted the best times of day to gather the plants.

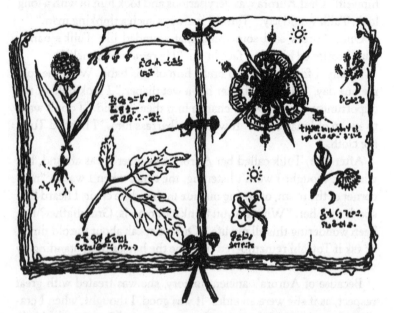

IT WAS TRUE that Aurora went often to this book written in another alphabet. She would put out her hand, reaching toward it, the little table where it rested, chattering in innocent baby talk, speaking the before-language words.

Personally, I didn't like the notion of returned souls. I believed in newness, in the freedom of a beginning outside the past, outside history. Maybe it was because I had fallen into my own life so late or because I had grown up in the white world and only come home so recently.

But out of plain stubbornness, Tulik began to call Aurora "my grandfather," and he named her privately after his mother's father; Totsohi, which meant Storm. Totsohi was a man revered for his intelligence, generosity, and kindness. He had been a keeper of peace.

While it was true Aurora had peaceful, knowing eyes, like those of an older person, I complained, "That's a big order to fill when she doesn't even know how to walk yet." But they all turned a deaf ear to me.

Sometimes when Aurora's eyes sharpened or looked especially wise, Tulik would say, with pride, "See? There he is. It's Totsohi himself!" Or if Aurora was very serious and took him in with a long look, Tulik would say, "Totsohi is always such a thinking man."

Once Aurora said something that sounded like Tulik's name. This heartened him. His face lit up. "He remembers me!"

Finally, I found a way to break him of this habit. When he told me one day, "My grandfather has a wet diaper," I took hold of the opportunity. "You'd better change him then," I said. "I don't want to see an old man naked. It would embarrass him." I handed Tulik the cloth.

After that, Tulik called her Aurora whenever I was around, but when he thought I wasn't listening, the times when I was in "my" corner of the room, or sitting outside in the white chair, I heard him speak with her. "What do you think a human is, Grandfather? I've been wondering this all my life." Or he'd speak about the old times, or ask if Totsohi remembered the time the horses froze standing by water. "I still can't get it out of my mind," he said.

Because of Aurora's ancient history, she was treated with great respect, as if she were an elder. It was good, I thought, when I cradled her and looked down into her small, round face. It would help her grow into a strong woman. She would be what I was not. She would know her world and not be severed from it. Whoever she was, it was a kind of beginning, I reasoned, because all the parts of her were new and fat and laughing.

Tulik tied the old man Totsohi's flint, what Totsohi had called a living stone, around her neck. That was how Aurora, my baby sister, became the man who had dreamed sickness and foretold the measles, who had warned the people that these diseases would kill them. She became the man who knew the songs of the water and beaver. And maybe she was part Ek, too.

I HAD A FEELING all along that Husk would not come, but I hoped I was wrong. On the night before he was to arrive I prepared for his arrival. I put pictures on the wall. He liked that, Husk did. Tulik cleaned the floors. I washed the small windows until they were invisible and streakless. Then, on the morning of the fifth, I put the bedding out on the whalebone fence to air, picked wild-flowers and arranged them in jelly glasses to spruce up Tulik's house. Everything was bright. I was excited that John Husk was coming and that Tommy, I hoped, might come with him. I still thought of Tommy daily, and sometimes at night I pretended we were together in each other's arms.

On the morning of the fifth, Dora-Rouge and I went to the String Town depot, a little wooden building with coal still sitting in a bin outside the door. But noon arrived and no train appeared. The day wore on. No Husk or Tommy arrived. My heart fell.

"What do you think?" Dora-Rouge said, frowning. "It's not like John. He always does what he says."

"But maybe it's not him. No trains at all have come in, just that empty one." It sat, its cars empty with waiting.

Soon we learned that a security force was being sent in. By now, we knew what that meant. It meant there were plans under way to begin blasting and construction once again. The only people who were able to pass through were what Bush called the soldier police, already prepared for our resistance. A roadblock was in effect. No one could travel Highway 17. And no one could come by train. The trains were carrying only freight and emptiness to be filled, and they were guarded carefully against human travel.

I cried, "I hate this place."

"Shh. It's all right, Angel."

Later that same day a light rain fell on the bedclothes laid over the whalebones, but I was too depressed to care.

That night I could not sleep. I held Dora-Rouge's sleeping po-tion in my hand wondering if I should swallow it. I'd preserved and guarded what was left of the concoction. I looked daily at the amount left in the brown glass bottle, afraid to use it, saving it for when my insomnia might worsen, afraid it would evaporate or I would drop it, afraid it would lose its strength. It seemed selfish of me to use it; the plant that went into it, like the one for headache, was beneath water now. Dora-Rouge had sent several people searching for it, but it was nowhere to be found and this added to

Dora-Rouge's heavy grief that one more sacred thing was missing from the world.

I lay there listening to the rain, smelling it. I was lonely. In a house filled with the snores and breathing of others, I was all alone.

We learned later that Husk and Tommy, reaching the roadblock, were turned back. They tried to take to the waterways in order to reach us, but were intercepted.

During the few times I slept, when a few hours of darkness went through my thoughts, I entered a world of green, a tangled-together nest of growing things. At times now it was an autumn world I saw, with white seedpods and silver filaments flying into warm air, desperate and urgent, seeking a resting place, a place to grow. There were burrs carried to new places in the fur of wolves and other animals, seeds dispersed by birds. At times I'd see the ancient lichens awake on rocks, and green mosses, soft as clouds.

When Dora-Rouge told Tulik about the plants that grew in my sleep, he said, "Dreams rest in the earth." By that he meant that we did not create them with our minds. One day, after I'd drawn a plant, he said, "I know where that one is. Come on." With great energy, he prepared to find it, rain or shine. We went searching for other plants, too, me wearing my rubber boots, trying to keep up with him. We tramped across land and swamp. As we walked through mosses, Tulik pointed out landmarks. We searched for the little elk lichens that grow at the edges where light and shadow meet. We canoed through marshes and waded in mud.

Some of the plants we would cut. Others had to be pulled by the roots, but only if there were enough left to survive. Each had its own requirements. We were careful, timid even, touching a plant lightly, speaking with it, Tulik singing, because each plant had its own song.

"I feel stupid, talking to plants," I said to Tulik one day.

"What's wrong with feeling stupid? Entire countries are run by stupid men. But," he said, "soon you won't feel that way."

Some plants we tied with string and hung from the dark ceiling of Tulik's house. Some we let dry for several days. Later we'd boil a plant or powder it and mix it with fat into a paste, with Tulik stirring the dark, bitter liquids until the house smelled dank with the mustiness of remedies. Some plants were from marshes, others from meadows. All were our sisters.

I sampled all the remedies and teas, sometimes drinking the bitterness of wormwood or maybe a cup of bluestem, to see what its effects were, all the time telling the plant, "Thank you," because you have to speak with the plants even if it feels foolish. There was the mikka plant that took down the heat of inflammation, and scilla, a tea that would open the body for childbirth. I tried the salves, ate the soapy-tasting mixtures. I began to learn them and soon, as Tulik had said, I no longer felt embarrassed.

"Sing over this," Tulik said one day, handing me a leaf.

"But I only know a death song." All I remembered was Helene's song and I was forbidden to sing it. I couldn't remember Dora-Rouge's animal-calling song, though I recalled the sound of it.

If all of Tulik's remedies failed to help an ailing person, if all his roots and songs and teas were ineffective, Tulik sent for a woman from the east. She came when there was nothing to be done but to sing into the patient, to place new songs inside their body, songs that would replace illness with a song of mending. The woman's name was Geneva and she seemed to shine with a kind of inner light. I thought of her as something like the sun, appearing from the direction of dawn, walking toward us from the eastern morning light. Geneva had a graceful walk and quiet ways, and even though I thought of her as an old woman, I realize looking back that she wasn't much over forty.

Geneva traveled with a girl a few years younger than I was. I didn't know the girl's real name, but we called her Jo. On the first day Geneva came with this young apprentice. Jo and I became fast friends. We were rare, younger women who lived with older people and learned from them, but even if we hadn't had that common bond, I would have loved Jo. In some ways, she was like a wizened old lady. In others, she was light and young. When she walked it was with an air of floating; she was quiet with an inner happiness. She specialized in treating bronchitis, yet she was still young enough and modern enough to say things like "That's cool."

Jo wore jeans and a single long braid fell down her left shoulder. She was skinny and tall and looked like a no-nonsense woman one

LINDA HOGAN

minute, but in the next she could be a girl again, laughing, her voice almost like the sound of glass or bells.

I looked forward to the appearance of Jo even though she only came when someone was in pain or sick.

One day an old man at the settlement had something like a stroke and could not get up out of bed. I'd gone to the square little house with Tulik and the two women. The man was tired-looking, and his head was turned to the side; his eyes were open, but he couldn't move. He was covered by a white sheet, his arms on top of it. When Geneva and Jo arrived, they stood on either side of him and sang. When the two women opened their mouths to sing in the small, tan-painted room, the sounds that came out were like nothing I'd heard before.

I was greedy to learn the songs. "Teach me," I said. "I want to know that song." And we would walk through the grasses laughing and singing, me sounding terrible, barely even able to keep time. Jo hardly noticed that I had no gift or talent, barely even a voice.

In those days, we were still a tribe. Each of us had one part of the work of living. Each of us had one set of the many eyes, the many breaths, the many comings and goings of the people. Everyone had a gift, each person a specialty of one kind or another, whether it was hunting, or decocting the plants, or reading the ground for signs of hares. All of us together formed something like a single organism. We needed and helped one another. Auntie was good at setting bones, even fractures where bone broke through skin. I was a plant dreamer, even though I barely understood what that meant. Tulik knew the land and where to gather herbs, mosses, and spices. He knew the value of things. Dora-Rouge knew the mixtures, the amounts and proportions of things.

Bush, too, had another gift, among her many, though I'd been led into thinking her skills were only those of fishing, hunting, and making financial deals with shopkeepers. I might never have known Bush's other gift except for the day I was at the stove putting pieces of cut meat into a kettle of hot lard. Outside, a terrible noise, a dynamite blast, broke through the land. I jumped, turned suddenly, a careless movement, and the kettle of boiling grease tipped over. My arm was burned badly, seared. I could tell at once that it was a terrible burn. I cried out. I smelled my own flesh cooking and it made me sick. Aurora yelled, too, as if to match my screaming. Without wanting to, without knowing it, my legs ran out the door and down the slope to the ice-cold water. Tulik followed behind me, unable to keep up, calling, "Angel!"

I ran from the fire until winded. I fell into the water, lay down inside its coolness.

Auntie had followed behind Tulik, and as Tulik reached me, he shouted at her, "Get Bush. Hurry!" He yelled in the old language so I wouldn't hear him. But I understood him. He said, "It's a bad burn. Very bad."

Auntie turned and ran toward the meetinghouse.

At the water, he leaned over me. Tulik was so tender. He couldn't bear for me to feel pain. His eyes were filled with tears.

By the time Auntie returned with Bush I had stopped screaming and become silent and still.

Then it was Bush who bent over me, breathless from running, her face near mine. She lifted my arm from the water and looked at it. And when she put her hand over the heat, I screamed, "No! Don't touch it!" By then I was shivering from the cold.

But she said, "It's okay. It's going to be all right." As cold as it was, she lay down beside me.

"It's bad, isn't it?" I asked, remembering the smell of my own flesh burning. I felt strangely disconnected from my body, from the pain I knew was there. Then I felt sick and started to cough.

Bush took hold of my arm, held her head over the burn. "Hold still."

I saw her hand become very red. She spoke to the burn, spoke with it, and said, "Burn, go away. Coolness enter." With closed eyes, she said, "Heat, leave this skin." She said this in many ways, as if trying to get the language right.

To my surprise the pain began to dim. The heat of it began to cool.

I'd burned my thigh as well, but didn't notice it until later. Some of the hot grease had splattered into my right shoe.

By evening, the pain had lessened enough that I could rest and sleep. Tulik looked in Ek's book to see what to use for fever. "Three-leaf," he said. He went out the door, returning a few hours later with muddy boots, a sweat-stained shirt, and the little plants that looked something like clover.

I slept that night on the bed where Tulik usually lay, behind the dark curtain, on a fur, soft and comforting. The bed smelled of Tulik, of fresh wood and sunlight. I slept.

By then Tulik had sent for salve from Geneva. The salve arrived later that night. It had been carried by runners. They'd sent the message from town to town, then returned the jar of salve in the same way, each one passing it to another as in a relay.

I had a slight fever. Bush said she thought it was from the burn itself.

Later I lay there thinking of the words Bush had used to talk fire away. I'd never heard of such a thing before. Every new thing I learned about her raised her in my esteem. Bush was still coming together in my mind.

Later I learned that there are those who can stop bleeding just by talking to it. It seemed too simple. I wondered if I could talk loneliness away, or scars. Maybe it was how Dora-Rouge had talked with the water or how Agnes had spoken with, and learned from, the bear.

AURORA WAS THE CHILD of many parents. We shared in her care. At night, in my wakings, I tended to her. Sometimes when she cried out with a dream, Bush picked her up and carried her about until she slept again. Or Tulik would stand beside her and speak with her, calling her "my grandfather," and saying such things as, "Although this world is painful, be glad you are here with those who love you." Auntie, of course, slept much too soundly to hear the child, or at least that's what she said.

Sometimes now, even as the summer diminished, there was a kind of twilight. On those nights when I was awake in the soft shadows of night, I would look at the face of Grandson, then slip outside, into the intimidating beauty of the land. I'd walk down close to water and look across at an island in the lake. This island meant much to me because of the stories told about it and my ancestors who went there and what befell them.

It was the island where Ammah, one of the creators of life, lived. On Ammah's little island were shining things, things that grew. Ammah was the one light that remained in the shadowy history that had nearly obliterated our world. Ammah fed all life and was its protector. On the little island were seeds, grains and grasses, nests and eggs. Some of the nests were nests made with the translucent, blue-edged wings of dragonflies, and these, I was told, shone with moonlight. The silky down of plants was stirred up in every passing breeze. Ammah was the protector of spring eggs, caretaker of the abandoned nests of winter, of the unborn, of promise.

One of the trees on Ammah's Island had been toppled under the five-hundred-pound weight of an eagle nest and even from a distance I could see its roots sticking up like thin fingers from the ground, reaching toward the moon. There, also, some trees were new, infant trees rising out of those that had decayed and fallen.

The seeds of corn lived there. An old man, long before Totsohi, had left the seeds from the journey south in a clay jar for Ammah to watch over. It was from the same corn Dora-Rouge possessed.

Ammah's Island was a place of hope and beauty, and no one was permitted to walk there. Never could we put a foot down on it. No person could trample hope, could violate the future. But at times, some days, I sat in a canoe and daydreamed out across the water at the place Ammah protected, and I liked to see the island on my sleepless nights and mornings. I was told Ammah was a silent god and rarely spoke. The reason for this was that all things—birdsongs, the moon, even my own life—grow from rich and splendid silence.

E I G H T E E N

WHILE WE WERE AT the Fat-Eaters, the ideas of Thomas Edison reached through narrow wires and voltages and watts and kilowatts into the virgin territory of the north. Electricity came. At Holy String Town and at the Fat-Eaters, electric wires ran, weblike, to all the little houses and huts sitting askew on the world. At Tulik's a single wire came in through the wall, traveled across the room, and ended in the white globe of a lightbulb that dangled from the ceiling.

Soon after the journeymen and electricians left, the electricity, hooked up for the first time, followed its path from the dammed water and entered Tulik's house. In a split second, the world changed. Even the migratory animals, who flew or swam by light, grew confused.

On the first evening of light, I followed Tulik and his dog, Mika, outside. There were new shadows. All across the land that had been created by Beaver and by the slow dance of glaciers centuries before, streetlights cast a pale circle on the ground.

Everyone was outside calling to one another, saying, "Look. It's on." They chatted and laughed. It was brighter than the weak, yellow glowings of lamps kindled by generators, sharper than the blue-circled flames of gaslight. And compared to oil-lights and lanterns of the past, it was harsh and overly bright.

"It looks lonely, doesn't it?" Tulik said.

I wouldn't have thought those words myself, but he was right. There was a loneliness to it. "You'd think the opposite would be true," I said.

From outside, we could see the light inside small, spare windows of houses.

Under our feet, the moist ground gave a little. The outer lights, not yet really needed, were carried by poles that had been cemented by workers from warmer climates into unsolid ground. At places, the top layer of permafrost had thawed and the poles already slanted. It made the place look uncomfortable, temporary, and chaotic. To the west was a stand of spindly trees. With the touch of light that fell across their pale trunks, they looked naked and unreal.

The people at Holy String Town were the ones who had wanted electricity. Few people at the Fat-Eaters wanted light or power, not that kind anyway, but once seen, it could easily have become a need or desire.

With the coming of this light, dark windowless corners inside human dwellings now showed a need for cleaning or paint. Floors fell open to scrutiny. Men and women scrubbed places that had always before been in shadow. Standing before mirrors, people looked at themselves as if for the first time, and were disappointed at the lines of age, the marks and scars they'd never noticed or seen clearly before. I, too, saw myself in the light, my scars speaking again their language of wounds. But it seemed the most impressive to those who had not long ago used caribou fat or fish oil to fuel their lamps.

Little did anyone know that this light would connect them with the world, and in what ways.

Before this, I had given little thought to light. Now I thought about it, and of all the things that glow in the dark and have power: fireflies, lightning, eels. Once I saw ball lightning, mysterious and strange, lay itself over the backs of cattle standing beside a road. And there was the blue of swamp fire we'd seen burning in the sky, back when Agnes was still alive, miles distant along our way to the north.

I thought of how the speed of light travels, light from the sun, even the light on the face of the radio. I had never before thought of the radio as a miraculous invention, that a crystal from earth pulled voices out of air and distance, but now that Tulik had electricity, I listened to the radio and was forced to consider also the speed of certain kinds of darkness, because it was darkness that traveled toward us. It was a darkness of words and ideas, wants and desires. This darkness came in the guise of laws made up by lawless men and people who were, as they explained, and believed, only doing their jobs. Part of the fast-moving darkness was the desire of those who wanted to conquer the land, the water, the rivers that kept running away from them. It was their desire to guide the waters, narrow them down into the thin black electrical wires that traversed the world. They wanted to control water, the rise and fall of it, the direction of its ancient life. They wanted its power.

LATER, I thought back to Tulik's words about loneliness. By then, I knew what loneliness was. It was larger than the way I missed Tommy. It was the enormous river now gone. It was drowned willows and alders. It was the three dead lynx caught in a reservoir, ten thousand drowned caribou. It was the river traveling out of its raging, swift power and life into such humdrum places as kitchens with stoves and refrigerators. The river became lamps. False gods said, "Let there be light," and there was alchemy in reverse. What was precious became base metal, defiled and dangerous elements. And yet we would use it. We would believe we needed it. We would turn buttons on and off, flip switches.

One smart village of Crees to the east of us rejected electricity. They wanted to keep bodies and souls whole, they said. Some of the Inuits said if they had electricity then they'd have indoor toilets and then the warm buildings would thaw the frozen world, the ground of permafrost, and everything would fall into it. They saw, ahead of time, what would happen, that their children would weaken and lose heart, that the people would find no reason to live.

Tulik believed them. So did I. Like the sleepers on that beautiful island in the lakes, we preferred darkness.

The one consolation for Tulik was that he could, at last, hear the old radio that he kept so well polished, the blond radio with card-board under one of its black, uneven, feet. The first thing he did was to climb on a chair, reach up to the outlet, and connect the radio that was, next to Mika, and Ek's book, his most prized possession.

"Be careful!" Auntie called. The chair rocked dangerously. Auntie went over and held it, looking up at Tulik.

When he turned it on, we heard only a little music behind the static, but Tulik smiled and said, "It sounds pretty good. Don't you think?"

The dog turned its ears forward like the one in the old Victrola ad. Tulik scratched his ear. "What do you think, eh, Mika?"

Luce, sitting under the light reading, said, "Did you know ostriches dance and shake for no apparent reason? Just because they love life and have zest?"

A RADIO PROGRAM called "Indian Time" came on daily at noon. It kept us up with Indian country news, and it wasn't long before relatives, friends, and even a few strangers came to Tulik's house at lunchtime in order to hear what was being said. And so what if it was lunchtime and they happened to be in the neighborhood and were offered food as well? It turned out to be an expensive radio, as many of the people sat close together, eating and listening. Sometimes they made comments. When Bush was present, she stood quietly beside Dora-Rouge or leaned against the wall, her arms over her chest, as if she was in a hurry and no longer rested in chairs.

After that, Tulik's little house was never quiet, not that it had been before, what with Grandson dashing around, and with Luce saying, "We'll not tolerate that a moment longer," and, "Let's put an end to this now!" as she read papers and magazines. Now the house was always filled with people and talk and music. Even those who kept to the old ways and refused electricity weren't too proud to come and listen to Tulik's radio, the tinny-sounding words broken at times by static. And now, more than ever, the house was full of talk and smoke and the smell of bacon and potatoes frying, and I wanted to go back to Adam's Rib worse than ever.

Then, one morning, Dora-Rouge asked, "Where's Bush? Have you seen her?"

Because of the visitors, I'd hardly noticed Bush's absence. In the presence of neighbors and relatives, Bush had vanished. For how many days or nights, I couldn't say.

I went up to the church where meetings were taking place. By now there were attorneys offering advice and information. I asked around if anyone had seen Bush. It was busy as a beehive there. Bush had last been seen at the post, one woman told me. But when I went there, Mr. Orensen said he thought she was at the church.

Finally, searching the area all around, moving in a circle the way she'd found me after my birth, I found her sitting alone in the trees. She'd set up a little lean-to and had a fire going and a few pots and pans, her shirt and a pair of panties hanging on a tree limb to dry. She was reading a report on what the dams would do to the land.

"Oh, hi," I said casually, as if I'd just wandered by. "So this is where you are."

She looked up with a faint do-not-disturb smile.

I looked around. "So where'd you get the washing machine?"

"It's just temporary," she told me.

But I knew why she'd moved there. It was next to impossible just to get a little quiet at Tulik's. There were even conversations going on in the outhouse. As much as I had liked to go to town, I now welcomed the rare day when the others were gone and I could stay home alone, or almost alone.

One day it was just me and Grandson at the house. Everyone had gone to the store in the closest town.

When I told her I wanted to stay home, Auntie asked me, "What's wrong? Are you sick?"

"No." I didn't tell her that I couldn't stand to listen to one more conversation. "I just feel like staying."

I asked Tulik and the others to bring two magazines back for me.

Luce, with her magnifying glass, said, "Okay. I'll pick some out for you."

I knew she'd pick out the ones she wanted to read, but I said, "Okay. That's fine." I was just anxious to get them all out of the house.

As soon as they left, I felt relieved. I watched Auntie in her red dress and Tulik and the others walking away from the house.

However, I wasn't exactly alone. Grandson, who by now had grown attached to me, remained with me that day, but I pretended he was absent and when they were all gone, I tuned in some music and danced. At times I longed so much for the world of teenagers. The young people at Two-Town, like those at Adam's Rib, had either left home to work, been sent away to school, or were in pain from the anguish disease that rapid change still carried into our lives. I wanted a friend. Even an enemy would do. I wished Jo lived closer. I wanted my old life back. And I wanted a Big Mac. And, while I was in the mode of self-pity, I wanted my own room.

With Tulik and the others gone, I could listen to music as loud as I wanted. The Iron Butterfly. Mick Jagger. I turned up the radio that day and felt it rattle the floor. Mika went outside and hid in the shadow of an old upended canoe. And I danced, thinking of how Luce had read me an article about how adolescent ostriches dance and shake for no reason at all, just because they have life and zest. I, too, danced about the little rooms just for the sake of being young, just because I had bodily energy.

That day as I stood at the sink and washed dishes, I sang and shook my hips, the music turned up loud so I could hear it over the clatter of plates and forks. I danced around the room, putting a green glass plate in the cupboard. Grandson bopped around the house behind me, in what I hoped was a poor imitation, his pants low on his little frame, his hair uncombed, as always, his smooth brown stomach showing. Little spots of news and an occasional song by Tammy Wynette came between the rock music. There were commercials for saws and Jeeps. Once there was even a proposal of marriage from Tony to Loretta. I wondered if they were the same Tony and Loretta who'd written their names on the rocks we'd passed on our journey. Their courtship, in the absence of one my own, interested me. It must be a sign, I thought, to hear about them more than once.

But if I relished, reveled in, this music and dancing, there were other kinds of dancing as well. Sometimes my heart skipped a beat, with a kind of Indian hope. Sometimes when I dried dishes with one of Tulik's threadbare rags, a feeling came over me, as if a shining old person inside my body was happy that once again the people were coming together, insisting on justice, happy that anybody could still sing and dance. That old person had seen our lives in tatters before, and saw it again now in the light of hope. And that old person, also, wanted to dance. But that day, with Grandson following me, I folded back the two little rugs and hoped and prayed the old ones liked rock-and-roll, because I wasn't yet so good at the bent-knee dancing of the old women. I was shy when it came to Indian dancing. Sometimes, at gatherings, the women would be in a line and dip and I'd see their gray hair as they moved together, their worn bodies, and I'd stand with them feeling off-rhythm and timid. When it came to Sly and the Family Stone, though, I was good, I could move, and even my aching muscles loosened up.

IN TOWN, Auntie had bought a hot plate and, on a table beneath the light, she hooked it up with an extension cord. "What should I cook?" she said to Tulik that night.

"How about some chicken."

And so she fried two chickens in an iron pan on the hot plate and we all sat around the table biting into the fried chicken. Tulik said, "I liked it better the other way. Besides, what if we forget about the life of fire?"

THE WEATHER had been unusually warm. Because of this, the newly cut road turned into deep ruts of mud that tires sank into, and the flimsy quarters built for the workmen began to settle in various ways. One day in two different places, two buildings dropped, sagged down, and vanished into sinkholes. Electric poles leaned so far down that in one place the power had to be turned off for fear the electricity would reach out along the wet surface of the ground.

We would have been delighted with the failure of the modern world if it hadn't been for the disappearance of Ammah's Island on the same day. Ammah's, where birds nested and hope roosted, simply vanished into the water. No one could account for what happened to it. But from the distance of that day, we heard the sound of rumbling machines and the rocks and trees breaking at another new site of construction.

IN THE NIGHT, while badgers, porcupines, and skunks roamed outside my many wakings, I could hear the human breathing, soft and calm, of the people inside our walls. The middle of night had been a kind of twilight; now it was bright with electricity, and the shadows of the room lay unmoving on the floor like the blue squares of cloth in Auntie's quilt. I looked through these soft shadows at Grandson, lying asleep, all wrapped up in the bear coat he'd stolen from me. At first I'd tried to take it back, even on warm nights, because at night I was afraid and felt the need to be protected from anything that might have been awake when I was asleep. But Grandson breathed sweetly and I lay awake, uncovered, listening to the floor settling, the turning over of Dora-Rouge, the occasional snore of Auntie. Only the dog knew I was awake and she would look at me and sigh, put her head near me to be caressed. Whenever a dog outside or a wolf would sing, she would lift her face to the ceiling, look at the black wire and single bulb, and call back, softer. Auntie and Tulik and Grandson slept through it, but her wild blood gave me a chill. I understood how it felt to be part one thing and part another, to be alone and away from your pack, to have a soul that wandered. I thought of Bush, how it must have been for her all these years in the north without friends, without a soul mate, sister, brother, lover. I suppose I thought all this because I, too, felt alone.

In my sleeplessness on most mornings, I heard the summer geese. Their voices fell down through the sky. But one morning, from behind the racket of the geese, I heard people coming in from the camps singing hunting songs, thanking the animals. "We love the deer," one song would say. And, "They love us, too." The people talked loudly. They drummed as they arrived. I knew they carried food, fresh meat, duck, and fish. I felt joyful. But this time, from behind their songs, from behind the geese, we already could hear the distant rumbling of machines as the bulldozers worked up above us at Child River.

That year, there would be no fishing camp because the fish were

contaminated from the damming of water and mercury had been
released from the stones and rotting vegetation. Then a surge of
water flooded the once-fertile plains. Because of the early thaw and
new roads that crossed the migration routes of animals, spring
camp the next year would not be fruitful, and people were already
worried about food. The waterfowl that lived in the water and ate
from its bottom were also becoming sick. Many of them were list-
less and thirsty before they finally died. If development continued,
there would be no drinking water left. The world there was large,
had always been large, and the people were small and reverent, but
with machines, earth could be reduced to the smallest of elements.

The house smelled of wet paint on the day the hunters returned.
Tulik had sanded down Dora-Rouge's wood-and-wicker chair the
day before, then enameled it white. He painted over the name
"Mother Jordan," but it still showed through, in need of another
coat. Auntie had made Dora-Rouge a new red cushion stuffed with
old nylons her sister in Montreal had sent to the rural women for
stuffing dolls and other toys.

By the time the hunters reached our place, they found Tulik,
who was every bit as orderly as Dora-Rouge, polishing the floor.
Rags under his feet, he scuffed about the linoleum.

Others had heard that the hunting party was just in from the
bush, and all arrived to see them and to listen to "Indian Time"
news. They teased Tulik about his cleanliness. "Don't clean just for
us," joked one of the relatives who came by.

Tulik stepped off his rags, leaving half the floor undone.

Bush, having heard the commotion of the hunters, came in from
the trees. Auntie had just finished wringing out the newly washed
clothes. Now she and Bush, with no extra chairs, were both standing, leaning against the wall. One woman looked at them and said,
"They are holding it up to keep it from falling in."

The hunters were good-natured and liked to tease. They called
me Red, and each time it was said, the women would laugh.

"Red Power," said old Luce, raising her fist, bringing more
laughter.

"Look!" said one woman, still rosy from the long walk they had
made that morning. She had long hair. "There is that salmon skin."

She took down the salmon-skin coat and examined the tiny stitches no water could pass through. It was from the northwest coast. Their work was held in deep regard.

ONE DAY, while I was tearing cloth with my teeth, making diapers, Tulik held out his hand to silence me. "Listen," he said. He turned up the radio. "There's going to be a big meeting. Listen. The officials are going to be there."

I folded a diaper. "I'm going," I said, with a voice full of determination, so no one would dispute me. I hadn't wanted to be involved in these things, but it was too hard for me to watch all that was being changed. I wanted to fight back, for the water, the people, the animals.

And Dora-Rouge, who owed something to water, said, "You can count me in, too. Angel can push me to the meeting. I'll carry the baby." Her eyes looked clear. I didn't know if she was looking forward to the fight or if she was compelled by her bargain with water.

Tulik smiled at her, his eyes lingering on hers. He liked me and he liked Bush, too, but he and Dora-Rouge had a special kind of kinship; they came from the same place, the same people, the same grief, and the same stories. He was a kind man, tender and masculine with still-powerful arms in spite of his smallness. He went over and touched Dora-Rouge lightly on the shoulder. I think he was proud of her. He thought she was singularly strong, and she was, but he knew nothing about her debt to water, and how she had no choice but to repay it.

Auntie said, "Did you know that the men building these dams didn't even know that water ran north?" Then she turned and left. With only two radios in town, we depended on word-of-mouth to pass information along. She went around to tell other people about the meeting. Also, she'd heard a road was being built across the spawning grounds of whitefish. She needed to check out the rumor before the evening's meeting.

By that evening, nearly everyone, except those still in the bush, knew about both the meeting and the whitefish.

Luce, who couldn't hear well and was becoming deafer by the day, looked up from reading one of the magazines she'd picked out for me. "It says here if two percent of all people in a town meditate, it will change the whole town." She was quiet a moment. She looked at our faces. "Say, what's going on here?"

"Let me see that," said Tulik, loud and close to her ear.

As I went outside to hang the wet clothes over the whalebone fence, I saw her reluctantly hand Tulik the magazine. It was late afternoon. It was warm and the humidity was high that day. I knew the clothes wouldn't dry before the meeting.

Early that evening—it was a Thursday—I heated water on the stove, tested it on my skin, then filled a basin with warm water and placed naked, slippery Aurora inside it. She laughed and splashed the water with her hands. By then the hunters and their families had gone over to Holy String Town and then to the post to buy provisions for their next journey out. Some planned to be at the meeting. This wasn't just us, gathering to talk about injustice. The BEEVCO bosses were going to be present to tell us their plans.

Luce, reading another magazine, looked at me above the magnifying glass and said, "Babies can swim. Did you know that?"

"Really?" I washed Aurora's hair and poured a cup of water over it.

"Look." Luce held the magazine up. It showed pictures of babies swimming. They were smiling.

"Aurora would like that. Wouldn't you?"

Aurora laughed.

When I finished washing and dressing the sweet-smelling Aurora I put her down firmly on Dora-Rouge's lap and Dora-Rouge wrapped her bony arms about her and said something I didn't understand. Then we set out for the white church that was snug above the sprawling village, the church so clean and neat that the rest of the town looked dark gray in contrast. But of course, the Anglicans had believed this was the domicile of God, who wouldn't stoop to the level of humans; it needed to look better than where mere humans lived.

We went past the clothing hanging over the fence. Auntie's red dress, the one that looked like a flag, was draped over the whale rib bones beside Tulik's Eddie Bauer sweater, Grandson's little jeans, and a pair of Levi's with the sun-faded square of light in the thigh.

With difficulty, I pushed the chair up the hill. It hadn't taken long for me to lose my arm strength. But the chair no longer squeaked. It looked gleaming and beautiful and it smelled of fresh paint.

The dark road had just been paved and oiled, even though no one had wanted the asphalt. Everyone knew the heat of sun on the dark pavement would melt the permafrost, and before long the road, another "improvement," would cave in. But for now it smelled of tar and oil, and the wheels of cars and Dora-Rouge's chair threw up little pieces of blackened gravel along the way. Dora-Rouge leaned over and looked at her tires. "It's a mess," she said. "And after all your work, Tulik."

"Don't worry." Tulik smiled. "I can fix anything."

His words offered such wonderful security and they were true, as self-building as they sounded, stripping life of fear and worry. I believed him, this man whose eye was more precise than the scale at the trading post, this man who could measure the weight of green rice in a glance, and even knew what its weight would be when processed. Even Agnes would not have fretted or worried if she'd heard those words. But I could see that Bush and Auntie, in matching dark moods, thought there were things Tulik could not fix. They looked at each other but said nothing.

In Auntie's large brown hand was the piece of paper she'd readied for a petition, which already had about twenty signatures on it. She carried it carefully, as reverently as if it were the Magna Carta, the words of a life, a people's freedom, and all of us would agree that it was. Auntie had spent the day going about the two towns and the outlying villages to tell people about the meeting and to get the signatures of those unable to attend. Now she just hoped many others were coming. To give her courage to speak, a bag of medicines in white doeskin rested in the front pocket of Auntie's jeans. She fished her hand inside the dark pocket now and then, to feel the small beaded bag against her warmth, as if it would vanish if she didn't touch it, or she would lose her strength and convictions. Her fingers believed in the bag, that something inside it would show a way to keep the dam from being con-structed, to turn water back to where water wanted and needed to be. But she was nervous. Already they'd changed the direction of one river. She knew that they would not give up easily and without a fight.

THERE WERE AT LEAST forty people, a large crowd, in the church when we arrived. The room was alive with gossip and chatter, complaints and the smell of coffee. Bush was already there, listening intently to a young white man from New York. She nodded her head at him, uncomfortable with the attention his voice and words required of her, uncomfortable that she couldn't turn away, look at anyone else, greet them. He was fervent, his face flushed with an inner fire, the kind I recognize now as an intensity that didn't always have our needs at heart, but it was a good fire to have; it was contagious and it motivated people. "Sign in," he told us. He pushed a paper toward Auntie. She looked at it, then at him. She didn't sign it. She lighted a cigarette. "Here, hold this for a minute," Auntie said. She put her bag on Dora-Rouge's lap, next to Aurora, and walked over to Bush.

The room was already smoky, buzzing.

I went over to talk to Mrs. Lampier. Aurora's eyes followed me.

I saw the young man approach Tulik. "Let me show you their plans," he said. "Here are the proposed sites for the dam." He pointed at the map on the wall. Tulik stepped closer to it. Some areas were outlined in blue, other sections were covered with blue stripes that looked as if they could have been the shadows of trees across winter whiteness. The map showed the dried riverbed above us where water had once flowed, where they had diverted the Child River into a bay. Now they wanted to move the Salt River. To do so, they had to create a new riverbed. Then they would narrow the river into the new bed a bit at a time, move it to where, finally, they could control it. The magnitude of their proposed changes was almost beyond imagining.

It was warm. I removed my sweater and handed it to Dora-Rouge to hold. Auntie circulated the petition and a pen. I watched her. With each person she approached, she would offer a touch of her hand, would explain patiently what it was that she wanted them to sign. A faded square of light was on the thigh of her jeans, on

Bush's, too, I noticed, as if that faded place marked a sisterhood. In a way, it did.

The hydroelectric proposal was so unbelievable in its conception that everyone thought it must surely have been exaggerated. The people from near Child River hadn't believed, at first, what the two young men had told them, but they woke one morning to the sound of machines in the distance. They were now worried about what other construction might be in the works. No one trusted the government and corporation officials. And why should they? They were clearly in cahoots and would go to unethical lengths to get what they wanted. And when the officials and attorneys spoke, their language didn't hold a thought for the life of water, or a regard for the land that sustained people from the beginning of time. They didn't remember the sacred treaties between humans and animals. Our words were powerless beside their figures, their measurements, and ledgers. For the builders it was easy and clear-cut. They saw it only on the flat, two-dimensional world of paper.

As I sat thinking about the million-dollar dreams of officials, governments, and businesses, thinking about the lengths to which they would go, my mind drifted off to water, to wetness itself, and how I'd wanted so often to hold my breath and remain inside the water that springs from earth and rains down from the sky. Perhaps it would tell me, speak to me, show me a way around these troubles. Water, I knew, had its own needs, its own speaking and desires. No one had asked the water what it wanted. Except Dora-Rouge, that is, who'd spoken with it directly.

As the oldest man there, and as a judge, Tulik was the person the dam-building, water-changing men seemed to address. The contractor and project boss, a tall, lanky white man, shook hands with him, but said, as if to excuse himself, "We were hired to do this." He said this as if he were certain the project would go through, and as if we would understand that he had no choice; this was his job. He wanted us to understand, or perhaps, forgive. He did seem sorry, I thought, but his words made clear that if the corporation and government had their ways, the Indian people had no say on this matter, no power to reverse what had already been decided by men with other ways, men in other rooms and houses of law, men with other skins.

Auntie stood up to speak. "We've been here for thousands of years." Her hands shook with anger. "We don't want your dams." She sounded calmer than she looked and I was proud of her. She sounded just good! But after she spoke her strong words, the man called us remnants of the past and said that he wanted to bring us into the twentieth century. My stomach turned at his words, a sick feeling inside me. He, like the others, believed that we were ignorant. It hadn't occurred to those men that Tulik knew every plant and its use, knew the tracks of every animal, and was a specialist in justice and peace. Or that Mr. Dinn, a neighbor of Tulik's, was a knife maker and a weather predictor. Luce was an intellectual, more well-read than they were or even their wives. Auntie a snow-shoe maker, a trapper. To the white men who were new here, we were people who had no history, who lived surrounded by what they saw as nothingness. Their history had been emptied of us, and along with us, of truth.

Auntie picked up the petition and handed it to him. "This is all of us. Our names. We don't want your electricity. We got along fine without it." Then she went over to the lightbulb and pulled the string, shutting off the light. The room faded into dark blue shadows with little squares of outdoor light coming in the windows. The wooden chairs that were set up in the church, even those that held people, suddenly looked lonely, standing at sad, strange angles, the floor dusty and gray. The people were silent for a few moments.

Soon a buzzing anger filled the room wall-to-wall. "That's right," said our former landlady, Mrs. Lampier. She was large and smoking and going to be argumentative. She put the case with her cigarettes and lighter on Dora-Rouge's lap and stood up to speak. She said, "We want to choose the way we live. I came here because I wanted this life. I don't want strangers coming in here and telling us what is going to happen to us."

The man folded the petition and put it in his pocket. Auntie's name was at the top of the list. "There aren't enough names on your petition." He looked at it, tallying. He was sharp; he didn't miss an opportunity. "That's another reason why we need to build the dams. More people than just you need this power. You are just a small portion of the people who will benefit."

Auntie, angrier now, placed her bag on Dora-Rouge's lap.

"What do I look like, a shelf?" Dora-Rouge said.

I don't think anyone else heard her, and I tried not to grin in the midst of such serious business.

Auntie said to the man, "You've already built a road across the spawning grounds of the whitefish. They'll die from that road. You did it without our permission." What she didn't say, and what none of us knew yet, was that there were young men outside who, by Auntie's ordain, were taking apart the road, shovelful by shovelful, opening the way for the fish to journey toward the future.

And almost as soon as she spoke, as if she'd conjured them, the group of young Indian men, finished with their work, came into the meeting. They stood in the back of the church. They listened quietly. They smelled of earth. What they were thinking could be read on their faces: they would die to save this land. There were many with that look, Dora-Rouge among them, and Auntie. Me, I was still unfamiliar with history and law. I wondered if maybe my own people weren't being too headstrong. Wouldn't it be better to have new schools and a clinic and jobs? Those things, I learned later, had always been promised, seldom delivered.

When Tulik spoke, he said, "What could be better than what we now have? We have food. We have animals. We grow our own gardens. We have everything. For us, this is better than what you offer."

"You can't keep that petition," Auntie said to the man. He pretended not to hear her.

Aurora slept quietly in Dora-Rouge's warm lap next to Auntie's bag, my sweater, Bush's jacket, Mrs. Lampier's cigarettes, and a tablet with Cree writing on it from a man who thought that if he wrote in English or French, the officials would read it. Hearing Tulik speak, Aurora began to make a fuss and Tulik lifted her from Dora-Rouge's arms. As always when he held her, she became quiet. But I could see right away that this lost him points in the white men's book. Tenderness was not a quality of strength to them. It was unmanly, an act they considered soft and unworthy. From that moment on they seemed not to consider Tulik to be a leader of his people. After that, they addressed all the men at the same time. They barely heard when Auntie, who really was the person in charge, said, "Never. Never will we let you do this."

Even if the white men didn't pay attention to Auntie, the young Indian men did. They loved her.

Walking home that night, I looked toward the direction of Ammah's Island. I thought about the land. These men would do anything to take it, change it, and make it fit their wants and dreams. A golf course would break apart the holy ground, a hunting lodge for those few monied men to come for trophies. Above all, they were certain they would win in this game of their creation. And we, the people there, were certain we would do anything to keep the land alive. These were two things that made for a dangerous situation, things that had made the room, though wood, seem to be constructed of thin glass, breakable with any quick movement, any sharp sound.

On our way home that gray night, the outdoor lights, not yet needed, were glowing from the slanting wooden poles. I knew darkness had its beauty and was, in every respect, less costly.

In the silence of Tulik's house that night, while I listened to the others breathe, I wished Tesla were alive, the man Husk had told me about as he read through a book of the inventor's patents. I'd seen a photo of Tesla in one of Husk's magazines. The man sat writing in a large room, lightning flying all around him in the background. When Tesla held lightning in his palm, the sound of thunder broke from a false sky. Without wires, Tesla could send power over the world, turn night into day, remove our fears and silences, turn them away with dawn. According to John Husk, Tesla could collapse a building with nothing more than vibration and resonance, could split earth, destroy the Brooklyn Bridge. He knew turbines and force fields and generators. He knew how to do all this at no cost. No one would profit from that kind of power. No one would steal. Tesla had known a force, a cosmic and earthbound power, a stunning light.

A FEW NIGHTS LATER, one of the BEEVCO bosses arrived to negotiate with the leaders at Two-Town Post. I looked around the room, at the people who had lived there for so long, people with knowledge and with roots deeper than time. To the builders of dams we were dark outsiders whose lives had no relevance to them. They ignored our existence until we resisted their dams, or interrupted their economy, or spoiled their sport. We'd already seen the results of the orange-capped hunters who had no need for meat.

Auntie yelled at them. "So you can fish for sport! For this! And your golf courses! And electric wires. We won't do it!" Bush, behind Auntie, put her finger in Auntie's belt loop and pulled her back into the chair. "Pipe down," she said, quietly and with a glint in her eye, admiration for Auntie's fire, because Auntie said what others kept quiet.

Reversing the truth, they would call us terrorists. If there was evil in the world, this was it, I thought. Reversal. Some of us, less strong than Auntie, thought we should sign the papers, sell the land, accept compensation. I understood this, too, because everything was in short supply there. And some thought so because they believed the government would do what it wanted, anyway. It was inevitable, they said. Maybe they were right.

"Why don't you do something about your daughter," one man said to Tulik that night.

Then it was Bush, an outsider, who stood and spoke, "Why are only white laws followed? This will kill the world. What is the law if not the earth's?" This from Bush, the woman I'd always thought so silent. She had a voice, one certain and insistent, true and clear. I was proud of her.

A FEW NIGHTS LATER, in the dark house filled with breathing and dreams, a night when deep sleep came over me, I floated downward like an animal in mud, held in darkness by something I couldn't escape. Out of the silence of that sinking, Mika began to bark and run toward the door. There was noise, and then an unnatural light flooded Tulik's house, a light harsh and white, and the sounds of machines seemed to crash through the very walls. Mika was at the door, barking fiercely.

I jumped to my feet, my heart pounding. "Tulik!" I shouted. "Something's wrong!" I felt the pulse in my temples. Auntie, too, flew out of her bed, threw on her robe. In the hard, white light, her shadow was thrown back onto the wall like a large, winged bird, her hair wild, the yellow bathrobe the wings she pulled together.

Outside Tulik's house were a bulldozer, two trucks, a backhoe, and a number of men. The little house was surrounded by workers and lights so bright that an unreal glare cast ominous double shadows along the walls.

Grandson's face was white and pale. He cried and rubbed his eyes. Aurora screamed.

Auntie threw the door wide open. She couldn't see the workers for the light. "What are you doing!" she yelled at them. Her voice was rough. "Get out of here!"

They stood protected behind the assault and shield of light. Auntie, as she squinted, waved her hand impatiently, as if it had the force to push them back toward town, back into the south, back as far as they would go, even into their own distant past. But she looked vulnerable, hair out of place, the robe wrinkled, one side of the hem still turned up.

"Shit," she said, closing the door. "It's like being poached." She lighted a cigarette and pulled the curtains over the windows.

Tulik remained calm. He combed his hair slowly, carefully, and washed his face. He was a smart and dignified man. He knew that they would not tolerate human weakness; he'd observed what his care for Aurora had cost him at the meeting because with Tulik nothing went unnoticed. He had seen how they felt, to them even sleep was weakness, a human failing. Then, slowly, he went to the door and stood a moment as the light spilled in across the floor like a flood. He didn't squint. Then he walked toward them.

"Don't go, Grandpa!" said Grandson.

But he went toward the idling machines. The smell of exhaust filled the house.

They were afraid of Auntie, I thought. I looked at her, vulnerable from sleep, the rumpled yellow robe wrapped around her.

Outside that one door, I understood, were all the cut-down trees and torn-apart land. Starvation and invasions were there, in the shape of yellow machines. The men were shielded inside their machines' metal armor, certain nothing could touch them, not in any part of themselves, certain that this was progress. They would tear the land apart and break down our lives. It would be done. It would be finished and over. It takes so little, so remarkably little to put an end to a life, even to a people.

Aurora cried in terror. The air sparked with a volatile tension—the loud machines, the unreal light, the fear and anger that welled up in us in waves so strong it made me sick; I felt the beginning of hate. This was the worst thing, I knew later, learning to hate. I thought I had hated before, families, social workers, people who had hurt me, even my own possessed and damaging mother, but this was another kind of hatred, one that would lay itself down inside me a bit at a time throughout my life, like a poison with no antidote. Some of us would hit and cut ourselves, rage, or swallow their bottled spirits, be fed only bitterness from the dark bowl of history. And I hated what those men could do to us, what they would do, what they did. In their light full with the moving specks of dust, we would all be changed forever.

I held Mika back. She snarled and strained toward them, barking, her teeth exposed.

I could just make out the men, hazy as ghosts. They had pulled a wild card and were going to play it all the way through. They knew that if they waited long enough, we would resist. We knew if we fought back, we'd be destroyed. Nothing had changed since the Frenchman, Radisson, passed through and wrote in his journal that there was no one to stop them from taking what they wanted from this land. "We were caesars," he wrote, "with no one to answer to."

We were the no one.

From the south, someone ran toward us. "Tulik!" It was Bush. She came into the house, looking over her shoulder at the machines and light. "Jesus," she said. "What's going on here?"

She had come to tell us that they were digging, that there were other machines up at the Two Thieves River. The workers labored quickly and through the night to get as much work done as they could before we could find a way to stop them. They had already chained and felled some of the older trees and moved the rock outcroppings with blasts and a bulldozer. And later they would not stop even when ordered by law. What could anyone do? they reasoned. What would happen to them even if they broke the law? A contempt-of-court citation? A small fine? They could afford that. The work would continue. They believed they would win.

At Tulik's house, these men were only a small part of a work shift, the part intended to keep us off their backs over at Two Thieves. "This must be a ploy," Bush said, catching her breath. They knew we wouldn't leave the house with them there, their threatening presence.

"Two Thieves is the place where the pelicans nest," said Luce, as she washed her face with a wet cloth, and then peered out the window into the light.

Auntie put coffee grounds in the percolator. Agitated, she moved quickly, going to the shelf of folded diapers, grabbing several, and with shaking hands put them into a plastic bag. "Angel, you and Aurora are going fishing today. Get ready."

"Fishing?" I watched her toss a bottle into the bag. "What are you talking about?"

She took some food and formula from the kitchen and set them on the table. "Here, Angel. Put these in the bag."

"Fishing?" I was confused. I moved slowly. "Why fishing?"

"Do what I say!" Auntie yelled. She lit another cigarette. Her hands were shaking.

Bush said, "Angel, she's right. Get dressed and leave."

I did as I was told. I thought there must be a secret message in this. That's how it was said, as if I would know by instinct what was meant. All I knew was that they wanted me out of the house. It was only later that I understood: these men were capable of anything. Aurora and I were the future, and above all we were to be protected, sheltered. Grandson, too, but he was from there and he would remain there; he needed to learn and see. This was his past; it was his future.

Auntie threw things into the bag—safety pins, tissues, food, anything she could get her hands on.

The bag was too heavy. I said, "Auntie, I can't." I looked to Bush for help.

Without speaking another word, Auntie unpacked some of the things, her hands still shaking, setting the items down as quick and hard as the way she'd picked them up.

I didn't want to go. I was afraid of them, that they'd open fire on me or burn down the house. But Auntie was right; it was safer for me to leave.

Auntie opened the door and yelled out to them, "She has a baby. Let her go." And then I was outside, standing in the combined light of morning and the machines. The house was surrounded. A few of the workers revved their engines to intimidate me, and me just a skinny girl with two bad teeth carrying her baby sister. That's how large their fear was. The pale blue smoke of exhaust was all around the house.

I remember thinking this: if we'd done such a thing to them, we'd be arrested and hauled away. But I was too afraid to be angry now.

One of the workers was young. He stood beside one of the machines. He seemed afraid of what I might do. His eyes were afraid, that is. His mouth was set tight and firm. He moved to stand in my way.

"Let me pass," I said. I could see his throat, young and bony like that of an adolescent. He swallowed. He wasn't going to move. My heart was beating fast, in my chest, my arms, my neck, everything heartbeat and fear. Aurora, sensing my fear, began to fuss, but then she, too, looked at the boy and became silent, alert, as if she remembered this from some earlier time.

"Don't let her go!" someone called out. The way sound carried, I couldn't tell which man yelled but soon he walked forward until he, too, stood in the false light of the machines. "Don't let her get behind us. She might have a gun."

"I don't," I said. "Look." I laid Aurora down on the ground, beside a tree stump, and emptied my pockets and the contents of the bag, turning it over, spilling everything on the ground to show them—the diaper pins, a bottle, baby food, a jar of bait, a few diapers, a soda, and a bag of potato chips that Auntie had packed in case I became hungry.

"Throw me that," the young boy said. The bottle of pop, he

meant. Maybe he thought it was a Molotov cocktail. "It's only a soda," I said. But he opened it and began to drink it, looking at me. This disturbed me nearly as much as their lights, their intrusion, though I never knew why until later, when I understood that he was one of those who thought it all belonged to him.

"Check out the baby," he said to another young man.

It all happened so quickly, in less time than it takes to tell it. Auntie, still standing at the door, screamed at the men as they felt the baby for hidden weapons. She was alarmed, afraid for me. She saw them going through my things. Quickly, she ran out. I didn't see what happened, exactly. I saw only that he pushed her and she, still in her robe, pushed him back. Leaving the bag, its contents on the ground, I stood up, grabbed Aurora, and ran with all my might toward the thin woods. I worried now only about Aurora. As much as I wanted to help Auntie, I needed even more to protect the baby. I stopped once and thought to run back, but Tulik was suddenly at my side, saying, "Go on, Angel," in a calm voice but with such authority that I would never have defied him. He startled me. I hadn't seen him coming. He'd seemed to pass invisibly through air, he seemed to be floating.

Some of the men watched me hurry away. I felt their eyes as I tried to hold the baby in my arms, my gray shirt falling off my shoulder, exposing my bra strap, and me with my arms too full to do anything about it except to hurry away knowing I was watched.

Later I wondered how these men, young though they were, did not have a vision large enough to see a life beyond their jobs, beyond orders, beyond the company that would ultimately leave them broke, without benefits, and guilty of the sin of land killing. Their eyes were not strong enough, their hearts not brave enough, their spirits not inside them. They had no courage. That's all I could figure. Maybe, like us, they had only fear. But unlike us they were afraid of what no money, no home, no job might mean.

I would wonder for years—I still wonder—what elements, what events would allow men to go against their inner voices, to go against even the cellular will of the body to live and to protect life, land, even their own children and their future. They were men who would reverse the world, change the direction of rivers, stop the cycle of life until everything was as backward as lies.

Tulik would say that such men could not see all the way to the end of their actions. They were shortsighted. They had no vision. They had no future within them, no past. That morning, afraid and confused, I walked toward the house now and then, just to see if it was still there. I tried to remain invisible, peering between the white-trunked trees. I stumbled over stones and stumps, and then, finally, I went to the edge of water and sat, Aurora on my lap.

Life had changed so suddenly. It had changed in a split second of time, in a single evening, with only as much as a poorly considered word.

As I sat at the water's edge, I thought of dwelling places, of the Oklahoma house I'd lived in that seemed it would fall over even though in truth it was straight and solid. I thought of my time on Fur Island, of the world at the Fat-Eaters that was thawing beneath buildings, its waters passing madly through other men's illusions and false visions.

That night I was fearful as I returned to the house, not knowing what I'd find. Already I saw that their dozers had driven over the whalebone fence. No one had bothered to take in the clothes. All our clothes that had been draped over it to dry were on the ground. The entire thing lay in heaps, a great skeleton of a gone thing, still covered with pieces of skin and fur: the red dress of Auntie, the jeans. It had fallen, Dora-Rouge said, with a sound like piano keys. But the work crew and their show of power were gone.

Inside, Dora-Rouge was red-eyed. She'd been crying. Auntie was smoking a cigarette. Tulik was at the window, distracted. Bush was typing with fury. The keys were hard to push down; I could see it took effort, but she was going to tell the world what happened. She was going to mail the story and photographs she'd been taking with a camera Charles had given her.

While Bush typed, Luce said, "No way can they get away with this," and in spite of myself, I smiled.

That day, Tulik had called the local police for our protection and peace, but the police never arrived.

I was upset when he told me this. The anger inside me grew a new stem and I was reckless with it. I put Aurora on Auntie's lap and before they could stop me, I went outside, jumped up into the red truck, turned the key that was in the ignition, and drove straight to town.

I walked quickly into the station—that's how young I was; I still believed in justice—and I said to the officer in charge, "They tried to run down Tulik's house." Only after I spoke did I look at him. He had thick, dark hair and glasses.

"Slow down." He sounded as if he had not heard about this, but his face reflected neither surprise nor curiosity. "Now, tell me what happened."

"Tulik's house," I said louder, in case he was hard-of-hearing. "The bulldozers ran down his fence. They tried to intimidate us."

He eyed me keenly. "You're not from around here, are you? What is your name?"

I had just taken my mother's last name. "Angel," I told him. "Angel Wing."

"Your real name," he said. He didn't sound menacing, but I felt angry. "That's it," I said hotly.

"Do you have any identification? Driver's license?" I patted my pockets as if, miraculously, I could produce them from emptiness, but I had nothing with me. My little bag was still at Adam's Rib, sitting on the floor by the cot. I'd had no reason or need to prove my identity before now.

He wrote down my name, then came around behind the counter. "All right, Miss Wing. Come with me."

"With you? Where?"

"Do you have any money on you?" He took my arm. "Be peaceful, now."

I held back. "What are you doing? Are you arresting me? What can you arrest me for? I didn't do anything." I was defiant at first, though something inside warned, be quiet. But my mouth said, "What about those men at Tulik's? They're the ones trespassing. They're the ones breaking the law."

"Do you have cash?"

I shook my head. "No. But I didn't do anything either." Then I was quiet. I went with him.

The officer led me to the drunk tank, a small room with a concrete floor.

Driving without a license. Driving a possibly stolen car. Driving an unregistered car—thanks to Auntie. Disorderly conduct.

"I have to impound the truck," he said.

I looked at him. He had sweat stains on his shirt, as if he had reason to fear me, instead of the other way around. He knew every car in this place. He had to know it was Auntie and Tulik's. I thought, he will do what he has to do. I will do the same.

"What about my phone call?"

"This isn't *Hawaii Five-O.*" He turned away.

"Wait." I was desperate. I started to say, "Don't leave me here." But I didn't. I didn't want to be that weak, that afraid, that pitiful.

He closed the door and walked away. I heard his feet echo down the corridor.

Later he came back to the sour-smelling room with food and a blanket. At least my jailer was kind. After he left, I was silent. It wasn't what I expected in the way of a jail. This was only a room with thick walls, no bars. Light green paint. On one side, behind a partition, was a toilet.

In the night they brought in two other women. I sat up and looked at them. Like me, they were Indian women. Unlike me, they had been drinking and their faces were swollen and they wore jeans and T-shirts. I glanced at them, then lay back down, pulling the blanket tight around me. One of the women cried all night. The other comforted her. I listened for a while and tears came to my own eyes from the sorrowful wailing of the weeping woman's voice. I cared what happened to her. I understood grief.

And then I must have slept because I dreamed a white whale swam above me, singing, looking with its intelligent eyes into my own with something akin to love.

The next day, they let me go. He'd traced my name and found out that I was Hannah's daughter. She'd been a frequent visitor to the jail. He verified that I was living at Tulik's, "I'm being nice this time," he said. "Just this once. But this is a lesson. Don't follow in your mother's footsteps."

It was a bright morning. I walked the distance home, worried about how I would tell Tulik and Auntie that they couldn't get the truck back until they paid the fine and bought current plates. I was certain they'd be mad at me. But instead, they were relieved to find me safe. Bush was pale with worry and she held me tight. "You gave us a scare." They even seemed, secretly, to like what I had done, although they didn't come right out and say it.

"He didn't even read me my rights," I complained.

"From now on," Tulik said to me softly, "you need to keep quiet about things. Mostly they are afraid of the longhairs from out of town. But they don't know you. For all they know, you are a trouble-maker."

The radio was on in the background. As if from a distant time and place, Tony apologized to Loretta that day and said, "Baby, I want to come home." Then they played his request, Percy Sledge's "When a Man Loves a Woman." It seemed so out of place, this love of Tony's, that I looked at Bush and said, "Did you hear that?"

"Doesn't Tony have a job?" said Dora-Rouge. "Where does he get time for all this?"

On that same day, the police had picked up one of the young protesters, taken him to a town, removed his clothing, and pushed him naked from the car. Then they arrested him for indecent exposure. We heard about this from "Indian Time." And as I listened to it that noon, I thought, the radio. Why hadn't I thought of it earlier?

Later that day, I went past the broken-down fence and up to the radio station, a little hut next to the old clinic. I told the DJ what had happened. "Okay," he said. "Let's do an interview." I felt bad doing it, not laying low like I'd promised Tulik, but I was foolish; I still believed in justice, so I told Mike Seela all about the bulldozers and lights and how I'd been arrested and the truck impounded and even that it would cost $128 to get it out of tow. I wanted everyone to know. He recorded our conversation. It would be aired the next day, so I had to be certain Tulik didn't listen to the radio that day at noon.

The next day as noon approached, I became nervous. I made a deal with Bush, Luce, and Auntie that we would get Tulik out of the house just before lunch. None of us would tell him a thing. "Oh, Tulik," I said at ten minutes before the hour, "your grandfather, Totsohi, needs for you to go to the store and buy him some milk. It's very urgent. Also, I have such a bad headache. Will you get me some Tylenol?"

"We have aspirin."

It was true; aspirin was no stranger to this household of herbs and remedies. I said, "Aspirin upsets my stomach."

As soon as he left, Bush tuned in the station and there was my voice. It sounded completely foreign to me, girlish. I was embarrassed. My cheeks reddened. "That's how I sound?" I said, incredulous.

Bush nodded.

I wasn't sure if I'd done the right thing. I asked Bush what she thought.

"I don't know," she said. I wondered if she was just being tactful, but her look was soft.

I was nervous all that day, afraid I would make trouble, afraid of being found out. I was probably ruining Tulik's plans to remain quiet until the right time came. He hadn't wanted to escalate the situation. I was sure it wouldn't be the last time we disagreed.

That evening I stood at the window, looking out at the thin road and pale horizon. I watched to see if the dozers would return. Instead, from far away, I saw a round-backed old woman walking toward us. She was very dark, small, and old. She wore a scarf on her head, one around her neck, and a red, flowered shirt. When I realized that she was coming to see us, I called out, "Look, someone's coming."

Auntie came to the window. "It's Miss Nett!"

Auntie knew exactly what to do, as if the dry old woman had visited hundreds of times before. Auntie went right to the food bin and took out a cake mix while I remained, watching the woman grow larger and closer, clouds moving across the sky toward her, traveling west to east.

Miss Nett's back was hunched, so it looked as if she stared at the ground. It was an effort for her to look up. As soon as she came through the door, she and Tulik smoked the house with cedar. Miss Nett moved her lips in quiet prayer. She and Tulik walked around the corners of the house. Right away the air felt calm and peaceful.

Miss Nett had heard about us, she said, from "Indian Time." "I heard her," she said, pointing to me. "The girl!"

Tulik glanced at me. "Angel?" He looked suspicious.

I shrugged my shoulders as if I didn't know what the old woman meant.

I couldn't tell how old Miss Nett was. She was wrinkled by snow and sun. After pointing me out as the guilty party, she was silent. The only words were Tulik's. "What did you tell them?" He looked directly at me.

I ignored his question, letting it slide.

The sweet smell of the cake in the oven already filled the room. I went over to help Auntie cut potatoes, relieved to have a job to do. "Don't walk so hard," said Auntie. "The cake will fall."

Auntie served up the food, and we sat down to eat in silence. It felt strange, sitting at the table so quietly. We were accustomed to noisy meals, with lots of talk and laughter. I looked at the potatoes and eggs on my plate.

Miss Nett said, "Do you have ketchup?"

I got up and took it off the shelf, handing it to her, still avoiding Tulik's eyes. Miss Nett nodded at me, then went back to eating.

She was thin, except for her rounded back, and when I placed the cup of black tea before her, she stared into it as if she could read the leaves and they would tell her what to say. Maybe they did, but all she said was, "Those damned men," and then she was quiet again, but we heard all the words that lived inside the spare three she'd just spoken; we knew exactly what she meant. She stirred two heaping spoons of sugar into her tea.

Miss Nett was from farther north, about ten miles from Holy String Town. She'd walked the whole distance to Tulik's. Where she was from, a good half of the land was already flooded. We knew this from Bush. Bush had gone to see it and to photograph the devastation. I'd seen her pictures of the dead caribou, the houses with water lapping against their walls.

Miss Nett spoke to Tulik mostly in words I couldn't understand. It was similar to the language of the Fat-Eaters, but a different dialect. I understood only a little.

Where she lived, where her people had lived for thousands of years, was now in ruins. NATO jets flew overhead in the sky of Miss Nett and her people, the Nanos, who lived at the Kawafi settlement. NATO jets had scared off what was left of the game and wildlife. In that place, too, they were using the land as a bombing practice range. The noise was horrifying, and now there were no deer. The fish were gone, and where the lake had been you could now cross in your boots. There was a drive to get the rest of the people off what remained of their land. They were hungry and sick. It was next to impossible for them to remain in the place where they had always lived. Some, however, like Miss Nett, had tried. Just a few days ago, the government had given them two weeks to move. The developers were already at work stripping the land, and soldiers had arrived to protect the laborers. This was why Husk hadn't been able to reach us, I realized. The soldiers were shooting at the few animals that remained, mostly hares and an occasional deer, taking potshots even at the few remaining trees.

"They are rotten shots, too," Miss Nett said, in her heavily accented English. "It's a good thing."

The people—not just us—truly were under assault. In fact, it seemed like we had it easy in comparison.

Above us and to the east, trees were being felled, the coal stripped away, and roads had been cut into every sacred site the people had grown from, known, and told stories about.

"Our children want to die," she said, looking out the window as if distance were a comfort. There were logging machines, she told us, with monstrous jaws that ripped trees out of the ground and threw them away as if they were already the toothpicks they would become. "It is too late for us," she said, thin-voiced, "so I've come to help you. Because when I heard that girl on the radio, I knew you were next." She looked at me. My face reddened. And maybe, she told Tulik, if they could stop the work here, her people could come here to live.

She looked at me with pride. "Also about your car. She told all that. Tulik, she's a girl who turned into a human. Maniki, we used to call them. Here, I have the hundred twenty-eight dollars." Miss

Nett took a roll of bills out of her sleeve and gave it to Tulik. "If you help drive me, I'll get the truck out for you." She took another roll of bills out of the bodice of her dress and counted them out, laying the softly wrinkled bills, of the same denomination and texture Agnes had mailed to me the year before, on the table beside an empty yellow plate.

Tulik hated to accept money but Auntie picked it up quickly before he had a chance to turn it down, which he surely would have done, being a leader and an overly proud man. "Thank you," said Auntie.

Tulik invited Miss Nett to stay with us—where, I could only guess—but except for that one night, she preferred, instead, to be driven back and forth. She loved her home no matter how loud it had become, no matter how devastated even with mud on the floor. According to her plan, we would pick her up—sometimes along with a few of the men from the Nanos—in the early morning, and drive them to the protests she helped plan. At night we would drive them home, past the piles of fresh earth, past the buildings made of tin, past the wounded land and the despairing people.

"Okay," said Tulik. "It's a deal."

She sniffed the air. "What kind of cake is that I smell?" Like me, Miss Nett cared for sweets.

By now it was out of the oven. "Lemon," said Auntie.

"I do love chocolate."

She ate the cake with great relish even though it wasn't chocolate. I sat and watched her take forkfuls of it into her mouth.

After that, we only made chocolate cakes. Auntie and I saw to that every day. We needed Miss Nett. We would feed her. And after that they began to call me Maniki. The name stuck. It was always, Maniki, would you bring some tea. Maniki this. Maniki that.

MISS NETT ALWAYS WORE a scarf around her neck. It kept her bones from aching, she said. She talked late into the night. She told us about the younger men from the city, those who had not grown up there, and their ideas about how things should be done. It was her way of warning us that they were careless, that some of their actions only made things worse. "Don't get me wrong. I love them," she said, "but they endanger the people." The more intelligent they believe themselves to be, she theorized, the less smart they actually were. "Us old women have had our hands full with them, trying to hold them back." She didn't smile when she said it.

Even Aurora seemed to listen to Miss Nett.

Miss Nett and Tulik stayed up talking through most of the night, if you could call it that, now that the nights were as light as twilight. Dora-Rouge stayed up, too. She listened intently as they spoke. There was so much to say, to hear. The older people wanted to catch up on recent events, but they also talked about what it had been like years before. "Remember the time," they would say. That night, playing cards with Grandson, I eavesdropped. I heard Miss Nett weeping, and then Tulik's soft voice comforting her.

Later, before Miss Nett went to sleep on the platform near me, the workers returned to sit outside Tulik's home. We heard their machines approach. This time they only sat there idling, talking among themselves, shining lights around the land and at the house. We thought it was probably because of Auntie that they'd singled us out. She was seen as a ringleader, as was Bush with her photographs and her typing. Her friendship with Charles, too, had marked her as a radical. On top of all this, Miss Nett had a bad reputation with them; they knew her to be an activist. She had fought them up at Two Thieves.

I sat in a shadowy place in the house and watched the men as they played loud music on battery radios and threw back Cokes. I studied them.

"This is what they did to us," Miss Nett said. "They did this at our place, too."

The next morning, early, Auntie packed the blue waterproof bag once again.

"Let me guess," I said, watching her pack it. "I'm going fishing?"

This time Auntie was prepared. She'd even boiled eggs for me to take along.

I picked up Aurora and bounced her while Auntie put Fig Newtons in the bag. Aurora smiled with happiness.

In a way, I truly was fishing, though I never cast a line. I was learning a new element, observing creatures unfamiliar to me, struggling with people and ideas from another world.

LUCE WAS A SOLITARY WOMAN, a reader and thinker. Dora-Rouge had been lonely with Luce, even a little hurt by her reluctance to chat. But Dora-Rouge and Miss Nett became the closest of friends. They talked together for hours, having much in common. Both were widowed. Both liked checkers and cards. They played for hours on end, Miss Nett clapping her hands, saying, "Look, I win!"

Dora-Rouge would say, "You cheated."

Or, "I raise you." Laughing.

Dora-Rouge, playing for time, would give her a look full of suspicion. "Let me see here." On occasion, she insisted on counting the cards to see if Miss Nett had some up her sleeve. Once proved innocent, and merely lucky, Miss Nett would give us all a satisfied smile, and wait for Dora-Rouge to say, "Okay. You win," and Miss Nett would chuckle, her eyes bright.

One afternoon when Tulik was out, I heard Miss Nett say to Dora-Rouge, "He holds a fire for you. A torch. I see it burning miles away."

Dora-Rouge looked at Nett's face. "Oh, come on."

In what seemed like the same breath, Miss Nett added, "I pass," and protected her hand by bringing the cards close to her chest.

I realized it was true, what she said. I had nearly missed it. Now that I thought of it, I realized I hadn't even noticed the silences from Luther, or that Dora-Rouge no longer got the faraway look on her face, never spoke to thin air.

And then one day I saw Tulik brushing Dora-Rouge's hair. Oh, he did it with such great tenderness, it nearly broke my heart, the heart filled with my own loneliness. And now, as if I turned into the gossipy, nosy old woman I was sure to become, I watched them. Sometimes, late into the night, they sat and chatted at the table and it seemed they were alone in the house. Dora-Rouge sometimes talked about Minneapolis, and Tulik would nod and say, "Just like when I went to Montreal. We got bilked, too." Or she'd talk about

Luther in the way people speak of their lost relationships before they begin a new one. "Yes, we knew each other since childhood." Dora-Rouge and Tulik had a budding romance, and the stem and flower had been growing beside us all the time and no one had noticed until Miss Nett pointed it out.

One afternoon Auntie and her father, Tulik, had a falling-out. I was on the porch sitting in the chair when I overheard her say, "She's too old! She's old enough to be your mother!"

Tulik laughed, which made her more upset.

Unlike Tulik, I hid my laughter. Imagine that, I thought, tough old Auntie, jealous!

Then one day, while "Indian Time" was on, as if fate decided to take charge of things, Dora-Rouge, trying to turn up the radio, slid out of her chair and took a bad fall, injuring her hip and hitting her head against the music box. Tulik put a cloth on her forehead and he bent at the knees and lifted her up to his bed. That completed what had started between them, I think. The same night, when I was awake, I saw that her little bed beneath the window was empty. Later, sleepless and curious, I peered behind the divider and saw that they were curled up together, Dora-Rouge in his arms, Mika at the foot of the bed, snoring.

After that, a person could feel the love they had for each other. Dora-Rouge was happier then, but sometimes still a sad look would come to her eyes and I knew she was thinking of Agnes, not of my grandfather, Luther, not anymore.

In this way, my grandfather was finally put to rest. Dora-Rouge left him alone at last. Perhaps he was relieved to be finished with flesh people, but I wondered if he was jealous. I tried to strike up a conversation with him. I called him by name. When that didn't work, I called him Grandfather. I needed the voice of my ancestors. But Luther had said all he was going to say, and now he was silent.

MOST DAYS AND SOME NIGHTS, the intruders turned on lights and moved earth, using the bulldozer or backhoe to carry it from place to place, their machines beeping. Now we learned why they had tried to intimidate us: they were rerouting a river. They wanted to make its new bed pass between Tulik's and the post. But wherever they went, we followed, blocked their roads and machines, and protested. At first we were only a small group and still we were able, at least for the time being, to keep them from Tulik's house.

On quiet nights at one of the construction sites with a temporary stay of noise and earth moving, we sat before the fire, our eyes shining in firelight, thinking about our own worlds, how we had come to this through history, how there'd been a prophecy that we would unite and become like an ocean made up of many rivers. Even though we were afraid, it was a full feeling. We thought maybe this was our time. We believed in what we were doing, and like the others, I felt hope that we would succeed, that we would be able to protect the earth and her people. On those nights the evening light turned rosy and a cloud or two rose up from water. At those times, they too, our enemy, were lost in their own worlds, worlds of girlfriends, parents, cars.

Sometimes the only sounds were voices, water, and the rare, solitary cry of a loon or a coyote. But at other times Tulik's house was filled with noise. It became something of a headquarters. Our lives were filled with activity, with planning, and talk. Young people came in and out at all hours of the day to drink coffee, rest, or listen to the radio. We were like a hive of bees, producing something sweet and golden. And always there was the sound of Bush typing. She had been smuggling our story out to newspapers in the United States and to cities in Canada. Luce edited the stories for her.

Aurora slept to the rhythm of the typewriter, the buzz of voices. "Just like Totsohi," Tulik would note. "He could always sleep." And Grandson grew hyper with all the action, running around from person to person, inducing them to swing him, inviting them to a chase. "Not now," some would say. But others would match his energy and throw a ball or dance with him, his feet standing on their feet, singing songs.

We were so busy that I barely noticed when Bush no longer spent any of her nights at the house. When I did miss her, I assumed she was at the church, or at her hidden-away campsite, or maybe with Charles. She spent much time with him, and as curious as I was, it wasn't my place to ask her about it. Even so, I watched her like a hawk for clues. As always, she was placid, calm water on the surface, no matter what fast or pulling currents were underneath.

ONE DAY MR. ORENSEN, the owner of Two-Town Post, knocked on our door.

I opened it. He stood there looking uncomfortable. "Tulik?" he said.

"Just a minute," I told him. "I'll get him."

But Tulik, seeing Orensen, said, "Come in."

"There's a phone call from the prime minister. They want to talk to you at four o'clock."

At first, Orensen resisted our struggle. I think he believed we would hurt him. It was an ancient fear, that we would retaliate for past wrongs. He remembered the old roots of these new events. There was a time when our people had killed the animals, persuaded by the Europeans who would, even then, starve out anyone who didn't cooperate. Then, when the people were hungry, the Europeans had dumped food into the lake to demonstrate their indifference to the hunger of the Indians. It is why the post had such thick walls, so no one could shoot into it. Orensen's family, however, had done well there because they'd stayed out of the problems of Indians, and Orensen learned this lesson well. But now he brought with him several bags of homemade doughnuts.

Orensen was worried about us. I think he saw what the government and corporation were capable of doing. To Tulik, he said, "The Two-Town Post is open to you and the others. It's cooler in there."

He took up our cause because the injustice was so blatant that not even one of their own could abide it. He was a fair man, and in spite of my first impression of him, I began to like him. Eventually we set up shop at the post, where there was a phone, and an electric fan on the ceiling. Many days were hot and uncomfortable, and the whirling fan felt like heaven. The presence of showers was an even greater boon. Plus, I liked having Tulik's to ourselves again, if you could call it that, with all of us squeezed in together, Miss Nett eating cake and beating Dora-Rouge at checkers or cards, Auntie watching her father and Dora-Rouge the way an osprey watches a fish. Bush came in occasionally, overworked and tired and too thin. She looked pale from spending so much time in the darkroom she'd set up in the church kitchen, watching images come into being from under chemical baths.

It was a great relief to be rid of the piles of clothing, shoes, shaving gear, and other belongings of protesters.

Mr. Orensen—Joseph, as I began to call him—was on our side. He brought in cots for people to sleep on in the back room of the post. They slept among the few remaining dried beans and peanut butter jars. There was no longer much else to store, not even the jeans with faded squares on the front thigh; all of the supplies had disappeared quickly, and now it was next to impossible to get deliveries to the post via roads or waterways.

On some evenings, Orensen himself needed to escape the crowding at the post, and came to Tulik's to sit with us. By this time I could tell he was sweet on Bush. Many of the men were interested in her, but this fact never occurred to her. It was probably a good thing, because however wise and intelligent she was in the forest and on water, that's how stupid and foolish she was about love.

THE NOMADIC PEOPLE, the hunters, showed up from time to time in between their trips into the diminishing wilderness. It was a sad thing for them to see a forest turned into rubble and stump, the land stripped of game. Now they traveled longer distances and down to the south and west to find animals; because of this, they too wanted to help us. There were stories for everything, they said. But not for this. We needed a story for what was happening to us now, as if a story would guide us.

Oh, there were stories all right, like those in *The Greater River News*, about how we "Occupied" Two-Town Post, as if we'd stolen it and taken it over by force, as if we were soldiers who knew what we were doing. How quickly we became the enemy; and we, the enemy, sat there on quiet nights, warm with hope, and no bitterness among us.

But now I know it was a story of people eating, as toothy and sharp and hungry as the cannibal clan was said to be—eating land, eating people, eating tomorrow. And memory is long about these things. It happens that in a crisis, all of the time between one history and another falls away. It disappears and the two times come together, gathered as one. Remembered.

Memory is long about other things as well; the men began to sing the oldest hunting songs. The songs made the wind rise. I felt it on my neck, my face, my hair, a cool-fingered breeze touching me.

AURORA LOOKED at the world with eyes bright enough and clear enough to see what was all around her: the old people, the shadows of birds, dragonflies that floated like the ones at Fur Island, through the air and through the house. I saw the world new again through her eyes, as if I had grown old, laid down in a common remembering, and returned once again, restored.

One evening, Tulik prepared beaver meat. He boiled off the fat and I chewed it for Aurora, then gave it to her to eat while Tulik told her a story.

"When Beaver was an infant," he said, "Crow swam into the icy water and stole her from the den. Oh, Crow tried to preen the little infant. He carried it into his nest in the trees. Beaver would help, Crow reasoned, with so many things—the cutting of tree limbs, the carrying, the making of new water and land, and when danger was near, Beaver would hit its tail against things, the earth or tree, and make a loud noise. The noise would scare away those who did not belong. It would scare away those who made dams that did not belong. Yes, Beaver would hit the surface of water." He hit the table, startling Aurora, making her laugh.

The meat had filled out her little cheeks. I looked into her mouth. "Look," I said, "she has another new tooth." I smiled at her. She leaned her head against me. Oh, she was loved, and her face showed it. "Pass the baby," people would say after dinner, as if she were sugar or salt. Everyone wanted to hold her. I wondered at times about her first half-year. Sometimes a look came to her eye and I'd think of my sister, the one who'd eaten glass and smiled at me with her bloody teeth, the splinters and crystals of glass on her lips and tongue. I'd think of my own scars, and of Hannah's body with the words of the newspaper reversed across it. "Man Injured in Hunting Accident," and "Dam Construction Begins at St. Bleu Falls."

SOON THE RAILROAD began running again. Its purpose was not for human transportation, but to carry the land and trees away. Sometimes it sounded like an earthquake as the train passed by, carrying our world.

"You've got to stop that train," Luce said.

Her words were on the mark and that's how easily it came to us, the decision to block the railroad tracks. We had been quiet up to now, and even gotten a man in canoe past the block toward the south seeking help for us, telling other tribes of our travails, mapping possible ways to enter, seeking support. It was Luce's idea.

"That's it," said Tulik, thanking her. "We will stop the trains." And that day we busied ourselves dragging, carrying, hauling, and driving things to the blockade. We blocked the tracks with whatever we could find: sawhorses, fenders. We even put Tulik's chair in the pathway, me and Auntie carrying it with more difficulty than I'd ever had carrying my old grandmother.

The young men carried pieces of pipe and dark gray stones. With Auntie's truck, Tulik pushed a rusted-out old truck to the site, me sitting inside on its cracked seat, steering, making sure it didn't go off the road. On the way, I noticed that the asphalt road was already bending and cracking.

The barricade, full of clutter and old oil barrels which the men had filled with sand and dirt, grew quickly.

And then we waited. As the first train approached our barricade, I was nervous, my hands sweating. When the train stopped, a cheer went up. I remember the joy of it, seeing the train, honking and impatient, come to a chugging halt, waiting for us to open the way.

But our victory proved to be a small one. Soon, in order to protect our blockade, we were forced to arm ourselves and stand guard. How quickly things turned. Our hearts fell as we realized the men were willing to shoot us for these dams. Bush now carried, inside the pocket of her cardigan, the small handgun that had been a gift from Husk. I didn't like the feel of how things were going, nor did Tulik, but we knew there was no going back. We had few options. We could open the railroad, which would be admitting defeat. We could lose the land without a fight, but then what would be left for the people? In any case, it seemed there was nothing to lose from fighting.

It wasn't long before a number of police cars drove into the territory and a good number of men emerged slowly from the cars, afraid of us, ready to fire, their eyes alert, their movements careful.

I studied them with a kind of objectivity new to me. They were young. Some were my age, and when they faced us, I saw that they had bony-looking throats and adolescent faces. They were dressed in uniforms that were too warm for day, not warm enough for night, and they were uncomfortable with the few lingering mosquitoes.

But mostly, I remember thinking that there was so much distance between them and this world of my people I had entered; they were boys from the city who had probably, until now, believed we no longer existed. They had long admired the photos and stories of our dead, only to find us alive and threatening. Their worries in life, too, were years and miles away from ours. And they were too young to see beyond their own skin, let alone to care about other skins, darker and older, skins that knew land, animals, and water.

As I stood there on the road that became the front line, looking at them, a light wind blew their scent toward me, carrying the odors of shaving lotion, coffee, suntan cream, and tobacco smoke.

MISS NETT loved our young men. They were warriors, she said, although they would never have called themselves that, at least not the locals, who said that only city Indians came up with names and labels for themselves, that the rest lived their way and didn't talk about it. But still they were standing up for the people, all of them, and even if we lost, they would have self-respect.

Miss Nett's eyes shone when she saw the young men, and she liked to tease them and make them blush. At the post one day, in her strong accent, she said she was going to glue their AIM buttons above the toilet seat. They laughed and looked down and loved her back for all that, because a laugh was what they needed and they knew she was in this war with them and she, like Dora-Rouge, had nothing to lose. So she could squeeze their arm muscles all she wanted, and she did.

Miss Nett and Dora-Rouge became an awe-inspiring pair. Short, dark, white-haired, bent over, tight-muscled Miss Nett pushed Dora-Rouge's chair from place to place, keeping her out of the sun, or putting her in it when Dora-Rouge wanted "real" light and energy and power. Dora-Rouge merely had to point a crooked finger and Miss Nett, as we had done in our canoes, would take her that direction. At the house, they told stories I couldn't understand, but I knew they were more than a little seamy, judging from the way they laughed. And they gave speeches to us and to the police: Dora-Rouge said to the workers one day, "We were happy before you came here. We treated the land well. We treated the animals well. Our children wanted to live."

And Miss Nett said, "The earth loves our people. Even in a hard place. The water loves us. We live in the place of its birth. This is where rivers are born and we're going to protect them."

Sometimes, too, the two women were harsh with the young men, such as the day two young men arrived at the protest. They had been drinking, and violence was always a seed the women did not want planted. As older women, Miss Nett and Dora-Rouge were able to do what the rest of us couldn't; they frisked the two men. "Let me feel that strong arm," said Miss Nett, a blue scarf around her neck. The young man had known her since he was a child. He let her. She found a knife on one of the boys, put it in her pocket, and threw their liquor out, emptying their cups on the ground. One of them cried and wanted to stop her. But she herself was crying. "No," she said. "No more."

And Bush told them gently to come back sober. "Tomorrow," she said. "We need you. We really do."

The next day they were there.

SOMEHOW WE KEPT the young police and workers from clearing the railroad track. Dora-Rouge placed her chair right in front of them. Now and then she tried to stare one of them down, as if she could transmit into them her knowledge, the sum of human emotions, as if she could speak her life to them through her eyes or send them away and show them her anger and determination. They were uneasy about her. She was old. She was in a wheelchair. And her eyes said she was willing to die. What they didn't know was that she had a pact with water and that it was signed with something deeper than pen and ink, deeper even than blood. In her, they saw only fierceness and determination; their youthful eyes missed such things as duty and obligation.

One evening, as we sat outside listening to the roaring of machines at the dam site, Bush said to me in an intimate voice, "I always wanted a chicken farm. I wanted to raise tomatoes. I wanted a kitchen painted yellow. Never did I think I'd fight soldiers and police. And look at those boys. They are so young. They don't even know history. They thought this place was barren. Now they are here. They will do as they are told. They don't have the courage not to. They are afraid and dangerous."

It was true, what she said. One wrong move, a word misspoken, and there would be war. Even now I think of this when I see young men, that they are unshaped and dangerous. And these were in terrain they didn't know, one with forces and powers and beliefs beyond their understanding.

EARLY ONE EVENING, Bush left in the rattling old truck to drive Miss Nett home. We were surprised when she returned a few hours later, with Miss Nett still in the car seat, weeping, her old hands over her face.

They walked into the house together, Bush's arm about the old woman.

Nett's territory had already been partly flooded, and now it was all gone: land, human dwellings, the river they lived by. Bush had it on film. When the pictures were developed, they were sad and tragic documents; they showed Miss Nett crying and trying to get the men to stop, her arms held out wide as if she could keep the men from passing through them. She still wore her white apron, tied at the back. An old woman with a rounded back. These were the photographs that would appear in magazines and papers, pictures that would show the world what was happening to the people.

Bush had taken one picture of Miss Nett collapsed on the ground, holding it as if to protect it. That night Miss Nett cried, "My children were born there. I was born there."

Tulik and Bush helped her into a chair. Dora-Rouge held her hand, sitting beside her. Luce wept in sympathy. Tulik boiled a bundle of bitter-smelling herbs and gave the tea to Miss Nett, who looked so pitiful I could hardly bear to look at her, and before long, the tea quieted her.

Bush seemed always to be in the thick of things when trouble started, camera in hand. She had a knack for determining where a conflict would arise. She became something of a truth teller, a journalist, and she was certain she could get the photographs to *The Nation* or *The New York Times*.

I looked at the photo of Miss Nett on the ground, the man turned away from her and looking toward the camera. He was gesturing with his hand for Bush to stop, his sharp, world-eating teeth visible, a pitiful old woman in the foreground.

A FEW DAYS AFTER one of Bush's stories and photographs were smuggled out by a man who left in a canoe, a number of Indian men arrived. They'd come through waters and forests to help us, having heard about our grassroots organizing, "swamp roots," as we called it. We needed them. They were experienced at handling these situations. Their confidence was rock-hard.

We felt more secure right away—at least I did. The leader was Arlie Caso House, a short, strong Ojibwa man who had been a political prisoner several times, once in Lompoc Prison, and had escaped from every jail that held him. Houdini, he was called. Always his arrests were for political action, never for violence; even so, he frightened people. The wardens feared him because they didn't know how he managed to pass through narrow spaces and get away. Once he'd escaped through a narrow heat duct. Some of the Indian people thought he possessed magic, that he could become invisible and vanish into sky, distance, even time, that he had the power to control matter, even his own atoms. Like the ancient people, he could cease being matter.

Arlie was a master strategist. He studied leaders like Sitting Bull, my hero; Geronimo, and Geronimo's military planner, a woman named Lozen. It was through Geronimo that Arlie said he'd learned to vanish. The Apaches, he told me, had evaded entire armies and million-dollar searches. They had a manner of vanishing completely. I was fascinated by Lozen. She was a healer, a fighter, and a locator of the enemy. She had sung a prayer: "Upon this earth on which we live, Ussen (God) has power. This power is mine for locating the enemy." Once, Arlie told me, Lozen swam a strong river upstream to steal a horse from the Mexican army in order to save another woman. She died with Geronimo and the others who carried their lives on their fingernails to prison.

When the government representatives saw Arlie, they stared, openmouthed. They recognized him. They'd thought he was in jail. And the Junior Police, as we called them, looked even more afraid when they saw these new men, mature and strong; their presence changed the terms of the struggle.

Twelve men came along with Arlie. Bush called them the Apostles. I thought about those fishers of men, how they'd followed Jesus without question. It now seemed so unlikely. I mentioned this to Bush. She said, "It's the kind of leadership we need."

Arlie was calm and careful, although I saw how he could be pushed into becoming fire, one that might rage over prairies and through forests without limit. But his burning was to change this world. He still saw how a world could be. He had beliefs, and in his living so far, he had given up nothing of himself. Unlike so many of us who were lost to weapons of the American world, their tools of television, of bottled spirits and other cruelties, he still had himself. I admired this about him. He remembered who he was, in the same way our elders still held steadfast and tight.

A few days after the appearance of Arlie, two new men came to help us out. They wore regulation shoes, even though they were dressed in plain clothes and easy to spot as informers just by their manner. Their carelessness about their shoes and their movements showed how little they knew of us. Even if they'd been meticulous, though, we would have recognized them. They had a certain set of the chin, an awkward way of moving, an invisible shell they wore as if to deflect bullets, and they, unlike us, possessed a belief that there would be bullets. All of that together put a strange and wary glint in their eyes, and made their movements exaggerated and unnatural.

Arlie knew how to handle them. Like the Pueblo leader Popé, a man who led a successful revolt against the Spanish, he always made two plans of action. One he gave to them, the other he passed on to the rest of us, so the informants were always confused and bumbling about. They would meet at a location where Arlie or one of the disciples said the Indian people would be, but no one else arrived. They would wait and then, confused, come looking for us.

WE NEEDED to cripple their other routes. Even with the railroad tracks blocked, goods were still getting out to other parts of the country by truck. Their blockades only turned back Indians and supporters, and we needed to keep out loggers, oil explorers, and dam builders. It was decided that since the long road of Holy String Town was the essential passage back and forth between towns, the road should be blocked. It would get more attention, they said, than either our peaceful protests or the blockade of the railroad, since the railroad had drawn little interest from those outside the Two-Town area.

By then, others had managed to slip past the blockade of the railroad, and some tents were set up; others slept in old cars.

Once again, we put together our own blockade. All of us together dug around for what we could use—ordinary things like an old Volkswagen and chairs from the church. We stationed ourselves at various places, and now, more sophisticated, we used a walkie-talkie to communicate with each other, to tell if anyone was coming, to see how many of us were at the road, at the railroad, and sometimes at the digging sites.

Now, however, in response to the blockade, the government sent in a special tactical unit. These "soldiers" were older than the security police and they were quiet and ready, a tension inside their skin. They wore dark clothing and bulletproof vests and, unlike the police, who seemed to be my age, these men were experienced. They had semiautomatics and moved like spiders. A few of our men, antagonistic that this special unit had been sent in, yelled "Go home!" but Tulik put a stop to the crying out. "Don't bully them," he said. Even I saw the danger, and how vulnerable we were. And worse, the appearance of these older men made the younger police feel more secure, more bold. And sometimes, when I heard the click-click of Bush's camera, I thought it was the clicking of their guns.

WE BECAME DIVIDED among ourselves after this. The squadron, the tactical unit, took us to a new depth of seriousness, conflict, and danger. There were now those of us who were against this protest. A few even reasoned with themselves now, thinking perhaps the dams would provide work for the Indian people. They thought maybe it wouldn't be so bad. They came forward and said they no longer wanted to hunt in order to survive, especially with the game disappearing so quickly. A few even believed they'd profit off the project. Or maybe it was fear; maybe they knew the governments would still war against us, might even kill us. Whatever it was, this was the hardest part, not having the people united. Tulik and Auntie were heartbroken to have to go against any of their own beloved people. And our division provided ammunition for the spokesman of the dam builders. He said, "It's them against each other." It was just what they wanted.

Arguments were only the first act of division. Then there was fear. One day a piece of black cloth had been tacked to Tulik's door. When I saw it, I stopped dead still and gazed at it. I knew nothing about it, except that it felt ominous. My skin rose up with the bodily memory of danger. I was afraid to open the door and pass through it, as if this door would open to something cold and unholy. I went to the window and spoke with Auntie. "Auntie," I said, "do you know what this means?"

She sang to it and took it down, then buried it outside the house. "It's okay now, Maniki."

Another day, there was a dying crow. Someone had captured the large black bird and before they placed it inside the door of Tulik's house they had painted one claw red, the other black, and sewn its eyes closed. I heard a sound and went toward the door and saw the crow, still alive, still fluttering, wanting to walk away on its enameled claws, but unable to see where it might go. It cried out. It was a horrible sight. I screamed.

Bush came running. "My God," she said. She chased it, picked it up. It bit her. She removed the stitches with tiny scissors, and let it fly. But the terror was inside us now, running through our veins, settling in our stomachs and chests. We were in this so deep there was no turning back. I was afraid. I wept.

Later, shots were fired into the house, a window broken. Dust flew up from where bullets left holes in the wood. Aurora screamed out in terror.

"They could have killed us!" Auntie yelled.

Much later, long after Tulik put a piece of cardboard over the broken window, we could still see bits of sky through the holes. Tulik tried to lighten up our mood. "Our air-conditioning," he called it. But Auntie, afraid she had put us in danger, moved into the post with its thick, bulletproof walls.

HARDLY ANYONE outside of Two-Town knew what was happening. There was no press, no truth telling, and whenever questioned, the officials denied any wrongdoing. "It's them against each other," they'd repeat when anyone got wind of the events, and it was true; we were reduced to that.

Then one day Lake Tanka to the northeast of us disappeared. The water was cut off, rerouted into a reservoir that had been built to the south of us. As the lake evaporated and sank into earth, we were silent.

After that, Miss Nett didn't tease the young men any longer, nor did she play cards. Her back seemed more bent than it had been. But before she'd let herself die of heartache, she said, she was going to take out some of the dam builders with her. And she said she didn't mind being unable to look up. "I love the ground," she said. "It's my God."

▼

N I N E T E E N

AT TIMES NOW I lie in bed. The room is silver with moonlight, and I think of it—of what might have happened, what could have been won, what was lost. I remember only the strongest of memories: what it felt like to persist that way in the heat and the rain, to be wet and cold, to stand up with my people. We had pride. We were in something together. We no longer allowed others to call us Fat-Eaters. We were again the Beautiful People.

I don't remember exactly when I noticed the nights were darker and longer. Time was different in the north. It seemed to happen all at once, the darker nights. But, as with the sleepers on their beautiful island, electricity did not matter so much to us. It had brought only a temporary stay of darkness, a brief light that had passed through on its way up into the black, dense universe. We didn't miss it.

Soon everything was splendidly dark, the wolves again spoke, the loons called, lovers met behind spindly trees. Tulik said, "There's a kind of light. It just isn't the visible kind."

In the midst of all this—the protest, the arguing, the fear—my heart opened as if I'd taken scilla, the plant which opens bodies in so many ways. I spent nights sitting on the ground before the fire, my heart and eyes feeling something like love in spite of the presence of police. Aurora sat on my lap or slept beside me. When awake, she watched the ghosts of trees all around us, the opening of lights and the closing of shadows. She was early learning to walk. She, so new on earth, heard the clacking of caribou feet walking over land. Once she said a word that sounded like Tulik's name and he beamed at her.

IN RARE SILENCE, even late in the season, there were still songs of frogs, although these were as endangered as they were beautiful. Sometimes, as we sat on what we called "the front lines," the women brought fried fish to us, and I began to love the women as I had come to love the land. At times I felt so joyful that I forgot our purpose. We had a kind of hope, is what I'm trying to say. All of us together had found something back in our lives, something we had forgotten to miss. And now I was one of the Beautiful People. I knew this bone-deep, in my blood. So did the others. We painted the church bright red.

Even with a few dissenters, we were a field of rich soil, growing. Once we started our act of defiance, we couldn't quit. As certain as it was that the bulldozers would move earth, it was equally certain that we would stand in their way. Because not to stand in their way was a greater loss when they were making new geographics, the kind nature would never have dreamed or wanted, ones that would open us into a future we couldn't yet know.

I MISSED BUSH. She now spent most of her time with Arlie. One day I saw Arlie put his wide hand on her bony shoulder as he passed by, and my mouth fell open. I remember having three thoughts: that LaRue would be heartbroken; that Bush wouldn't go home with us; and my last thought was one of childish jealousy, a fear that I would lose this woman who seemed most like a mother to me. "You slept with him," I said one day, accusing her as if she had betrayed me.

She only laughed, in the same way Tulik had done when Auntie accused him of a similar sin. I was as bad as Auntie.

During the lengthening evenings, while we were singing, the white people from nearby towns, workers and their wives, arrived and stationed themselves on the other side of the blockade. They yelled at us, at our singing, our needs. They chanted "Bullshit. Bullshit." This was their song. It was a song against life, against their own futures, but they did not yet know this. They wanted their jobs. They believed they were limited and could live in only one way and they wanted us to give up our way of life for theirs. They thought the land would starve them. Maybe it would. It couldn't have loved them.

We tried to sing louder, so as not to hear their voices.

The mudflats continued to grow and water fell away from where it had lived as long as anyone remembered. The migration routes of the animals were being flooded. A river disappeared.

At times, as we sat there, we were silent, each of us lost in our own worlds. It was the older people who were the most saddened. I could see it in their eyes. In these silent times, the only sound was that of water or animals in the distance, and in those silent times some of us would sing. Old songs, the kind Agnes had remembered. Some of us would stand in the way of the workers. If we were removed, others came in to take our places. "What shift are you on?" was a common question. "Swing or graveyard?" We tried to laugh because it carried us further than despair. By then we had also managed to close the filling station so the workers could not refuel their machines.

ONE SOFT MORNING, Dora-Rouge sat in her white chair on "the front line." The trees gave off a perfume in the heat. The air was still and heavy. It was going to be a warm day. But there was a tension to things. I felt anxious and didn't know why. Aurora also seemed disturbed. I stood a short distance away from Dora-Rouge, speaking with Bush, and I heard a young policeman say, "Oh, shit. It's one of those old ladies again." He trained the gun on Dora-Rouge, set his sight as if to scare her, took aim.

I ran toward him. "No!"

But Dora-Rouge looked right at him and said, "I'm not that old."

It made me love her all the more. That in a moment of danger, she would make a joke of this. But many yards away, Bush looked on in silence.

This was the day Bush began to talk to the police and soldiers. It wasn't just because she was a peacemaker at heart. It was because she saw the young man aim at Dora-Rouge that she began to speak with them. I could see why she did it, but after that, many young Indian men became suspicious of her. Tulik and Auntie stuck up for her, but by then divisions among our people came about more easily. There would be more and more splintering to follow, and even though I saw how straight Bush stood, how beautiful she was in her strength, there were times even I doubted her.

The young men who were quickest to accuse her were the ones from the city, the ones of uncertain identity who had names and categories for themselves, who wore braids like those I saw on LaRue the day he walked toward us from the direction of water, limping slightly, as if his shoes pinched his feet. In spite of his black zippered shoes, bell-bottom jeans, and the clean ribbon shirt on which his medals were pinned, I recognized him immediately. He looked so good! I couldn't help myself. I ran toward him. "LaRue!" I jumped against him, put my arms around him. He smelled of English Leather, and he was embarrassed. So was I, that for all my dislike of him, I was glad to see him. "Hey, watch it!" he said, smoothing his shirt. I was messing up his outfit.

"How'd you get here?" I asked. "Boy, am I glad to see you! How's Husk and Tommy?" He was my link to Adam's Rib. "Are the roads blocked?"

"Whoa." He put up a hand to stop me, as if we'd traded roles. "One question at a time."

Husk, he said, hadn't been well since hearing about Agnes. He and Tommy had been turned back from reaching Two-Town. Now Tommy was helping Chiquita care for Wiley, who'd had a stroke, and he was fiercely worried about me.

I took LaRue up the hill and introduced him to the others. When LaRue saw Bush, his face reddened. "How are you?" he said. His voice was softer than usual.

"Good." Hunched over the typewriter, she hardly looked at him.

But Rue was transparent in the way he looked at Bush, and later, when he saw her with Arlie, he tried to seem indifferent. But I knew better. I saw how his expression changed. I felt a little sorry for Rue. I'd come to like him the way a wayward brother is liked.

Soon, LaRue's presence became another source of division for the people. I believe it started when he stood up in a meeting and said, "I'm a warrior and a soldier," and it wasn't long before he began to tell some of the younger men what to do. They followed. Not the ones who were with Arlie, not the ones who worried about the land and animals, but the ones who wanted something different, another way of life, who pushed toward a monetary settlement.

"LaRue," I said to him one day. "I can't believe you think this way."

"It's logical," he said. "It's rational."

Even a few of the younger men who'd followed Arlie respected LaRue because he had been a soldier, because he had what looked at times to their young eyes like worldliness, and because of the medals on his chest. They were inspired by his aggressive manner, the very thing Bush hated about him. After that, her dark eyes sent him sparks of anger. The conflict between them, the differences of opinion, grew. A wide space opened between them, as far apart as the pieces of land that had split open when Pangaea had separated from itself.

And with Bush's angry reaction to LaRue, the younger men thought again about this woman. You could see it in their eyes, how their suspicions grew. But LaRue said to them, "That's just her way," and hitched up his pants, and no one looked more surprised at his words than Bush.

ONE DAY it was dark and cold, the sky thick with rolling clouds of rain. Sometimes it was a heavy, male rain that descended on us, turning everything to earth-colored mud. At other times it was light and soft, but even then the wet ground could not absorb it all. It fell for three days and water ran everywhere across the surface of earth, settled into pools that reflected the pewter gray of sky. Nevertheless, where they could, on a rocky mound, the men set up a few tarps and a tent and we remained at the site. One evening, after the hardest rain, two women came with hot rice broth and fresh berries. "It hits the spot," said Dora-Rouge, the wheels of her chair sinking into soft, wet earth.

Work came to a temporary standstill. Frustrated by the weather and lost wages, the workers left. Some of our own water-soaked people dispersed and went home to be dry and warm.

During these days of rain, one of the bulldozers was vandalized. Two young men were taken in for questioning. Dora-Rouge thought the workmen had done it themselves in order to bring the confrontation to a head. Whichever way it was, the next day, at Tulik's, with the dog curled at my feet, a blue-eyed man in a dark suit came and stood outside the door, beneath an umbrella, to try to convince us we were wrong. He tried to "reason" with us, he said. I eyed him, his large coat, his pant hems muddy. He came to talk about a settlement.

"Be sensible," he said, adjusting his sleeve, looking around at the little house, uncomfortable.

But after a while, Tulik turned off his hearing aid and stopped listening. He took a jar of aspirin out of his pocket and swallowed two without water, and he didn't look at the man in the suit again.

"SHE'S LOOKING GOOD, just good!" Tulik said of Aurora. She had put on weight and in spite of her narrow bones she had a fat, cheery babyness. She was a relaxed child and she laughed often, joyfully. We could all tell Aurora would grow up beautifully, and we called her "Our Future," as Dora-Rouge had called me. She held a fullness we longed for.

AFTER THE DAYS of rain there was heat, and soon the earth seemed scorched and the trees began to dry out. The place where water had once been smelled like old fish, rotting. Soon it dried into tiles, sunbaked and curling up at the edges. I kept Aurora inside the post to keep the sun and insects, born of the recent rain, from her. I took Agnes' coat to the post for her to sleep on, and its closeness seemed to calm her.

We were singing old songs, newly revived, the day we heard Tulik's name being called from the distance. A man came running toward the post, yelling, "Tulik!" He clattered up the steps. "It's your house!" But Tulik had already seen the smoke. He jumped to his feet, and the two men ran together toward the house, trying to talk as they ran, the wind blowing against their words, the smoke rising ahead of them.

Quickly I picked up Aurora and followed behind them.

When we reached Tulik's house, flames were shooting out of the roof and dark smoke filled the sky. Tulik's little wood house was an easy meal for hungry fire. We could see that it was a lost cause. There was no reason to get water, even if water had still been there. We could only watch as Tulik's world became a charred black ruin. Tulik, now and then, ran in close to the fire, coughing, yelling, "Mika. Mika." He moved toward it again and again, searching for the dog, seeing if anything could be salvaged, but he couldn't get close for the heat and smoke. He coughed, holding his arm over his mouth, his eyes watering.

I realized in that moment what we'd been fueling. I knew instinctively that it was a set fire. I knew no dog would come out of that inferno. I knew our lives, too, could disappear like the smoke, becoming invisible and thin, rising up to the sky. I prayed silently, "Please, God, whatever you are, help us."

Aurora cried.

"Shh," I said to her. "It's all right." Lying.

Smoke drifted toward me and I stepped out of its way, holding Aurora so tightly she whimpered. Suddenly I was very tired and I sat down on the ground. Aurora stood on her chubby legs and held on to me, my arm about her. She stared at the fire the way we did, helplessly as the raging flames dwindled down to black wood and smoking embers. Then the charred black house collapsed and everything became cinders. By then, Arlie and the others were there, Auntie with them, crying, trying to comfort her father.

Arlie circled the house to see what evidence he might find.

"Look," he said to Tulik.

I saw them, too, what he pointed at. All around the house were wolverine tracks. A chill went up my spine. Tulik thought at first it might have been his dog, but looking closer, he said, disheartened, "No, it can only be human mischief. Someone wanted me to think it was a witch come here."

Even before it was cool enough, Tulik went through the rubble, poking at everything with a stick, as if the dog would be dug in somewhere, alive and panting, tongue hanging out from the heat.

When the fire cooled, other men, too, poked at the debris, smothered the remaining hot spots, searched out smoke and cinders. All that was left in the ashes and black wood were some traps, a glass jar of instant Lipton iced tea, a few black pans, and the rake that had been leaning against the house. Some dishes with smoke stains were on the ground. I looked at the tracks that circled the dark haze, smelled the strong, smoky odor of the house. And then, not knowing what else to do, I sat on a rock and watched Tulik rake and sweep the wolverine prints away. He worked as if he believed he could sweep trouble off our backs. He didn't notice that he'd burned the soles off his shoes and that his feet were blistered in places.

"THEY BURNED DOWN Tulik's house," Dora-Rouge said. She repeated it over and over. "They burned it." This broke Tulik's heart even more. He closed his hand over hers. She leaned against him. She looked tiny and gray, her sharp bones poking through her skin.

For several days, on his sore feet, Tulik walked the land and called for Mika, searching in the trees, walking through Holy String Town, even through the workers' settlements. After that, he seemed bent and tired. He had hopes that the dog had run away in fear. At every moment, I half-expected Mika to come out from between trees. Mika, strong and old, pale-eyed, long-legged.

A little at a time, we tallied all our losses. Things we'd barely noticed when they existed were suddenly heavy with meaning, as were the important things: the sleeping potion, the photographs, the amber. What we all missed most was Mika. Ek's book was gone, too, the one with the beautiful drawings of plants on bark. Now Luce had no magnifying glass, nothing to read words with. After that she was forced to be patient while someone else read to her. So much, Tulik said, was only junk, but not the sealskin clothing he had traded for in 1937 and the salmon-skin coat he so prized for its tiny, waterproof stitches. With all that gone, Tulik hardly missed the radio he'd so valued before the fire. Its importance faded next to the loss of Mika and Ek's book.

I, at least, had Agnes' coat.

I had loved Tulik's house, the way thin lines of light came inside it like long fingers of gods and spirits, touching the floor in slants and angles of warmth.

And now I became more aware of our danger. Even now, they would send death with its long white hair. Like Eron saw before he killed my mother. Its white ragged clothing and its red, bloody hands.

LUCE SAID there were witches who turned themselves into wolverines. "I saw it once with my own eyes," she said.

Auntie said she'd been going to sleep the afternoon of the fire, but something had told her to get up and go to the church.

"It must have been your guardian spirit that sent you there," said Miss Nett.

Auntie looked pale.

"It saved you."

Miss Nett agreed with Luce. "Yes, it is true there are witches who turn themselves into wolverines in order to do their work, just like the old people always said. Like Wolverine, they make themselves invisible. They can pass right by you and you'll only feel a chill or catch the smell of them. Old Wolverine is just a mask. There's a man or a woman underneath the mask, wearing it, you see. That person can walk on all fours, and has learned to be sly. They move so soft, like a whisper, and all you see is a shadow."

"Like the agents in their shoes over there!" Luce said. She could still see far into the distance. "Do you see them?"

Miss Nett said, "Did you ever see a wolverine with a pair of shoes? That's how you know."

"No," said Luce. "I've never seen a wolverine at all."

People came from all around to offer condolences to Tulik, and in hopes of seeing the wolverine tracks.

Perhaps they were hopeful it was the trail of a spirit they could follow. As one woman said, "We want to know if it was the feet of Mondi." Because it was Mondi, Wolverine, who'd made the world and the sun and the moon. They wanted to follow Wolverine's spirit path, but at the same time they were afraid of the tracks.

One day, listening to them talk about Mondi, I realized why Wolverine had destroyed the food of humans. It came to me like lightning out of the sky. It was so simple, I wondered why I hadn't thought of it before. Others knew this, I was sure. Wolverine wanted the people to leave, he wanted to starve them out of his territory, his world. Just as quickly, like thunder following the lightning, a plan sprang to my mind: I would starve out the soldiers and police.

I told my plan to no one; I couldn't risk it. I knew they would say it was foolish and dangerous.

Quietly one night, in the brief hours of northern darkness, I slipped out of bed, pretending to be Wolverine, thinking inside myself the way a wolverine might think. Once the floor creaked and I stood still, to see if anyone woke, then I walked down the mound of land near the church, going unseen across the lines of their territory, straight toward their food supply. I knew Wolverine and his destruction perfectly well. Without words, I, like Wolverine, would tell the men to leave our world. Without words, I, like Wolverine, would speak, would destroy their food so they would grow hungry, so they would have to leave. I could hardly breathe for my nervousness and excitement. I knew it would work.

I planned to make only one trip, but their food store was so large and ours so thin that I decided to return and take more. It was easier than I imagined to pass through their quarters and into their kitchen. I went in, first through the window, afraid, catching my foot on a nail. I took away what I could inside my clothing on that first trip; chipped beef, eggs, potatoes, canned fish, coffee.

I took the tins and packages to the trees behind the post and camouflaged them as best I could in the shadows of night. Then I went back to the Quonset hut for a backpack and returned once more to their kitchen. But on my second trip, as I moved about in the shadows of their kitchen, someone came inside the door. I froze, hiding behind a stack of flour bags. The light of a flashlight moved about the room, and before I ducked I saw a young man looking for a snack, perhaps, or stealing extra rations for a girl he might have in String Town. No one had been able to get food into the area, and many girls flirted with the men for food. I could hardly breathe for fear. My breath sounded loud as the ocean, but soon he turned off the light and I heard him walk away. After my eyes adjusted once again to the shadows of the room, I filled the backpack, and then, as Wolverine would have done, I poured out the flour, ripping the bags open with a knife. I poured their bottled water on top of it so it couldn't be scooped up and salvaged, angry all the while that they'd ruined our water and brought in their own. Then I opened the bags of sugar and poured them out, as well, and when I left, with my pockets and the backpack full, I made a trail of white footsteps, the path of a ghost.

I'd learned this kind of thinking from Arlie. But my teachers were different. While his lessons came from Indian leaders, like Geronimo and Popé, mine came from stories. They came from the animals. From Wolverine.

The only thing Wolverine would have done that I didn't was to pee on all the food he left behind.

TULIK AND AUNTIE seemed like different people once they were moved into one of the Quonset huts on Church Mound. Tulik began to close up in a way. Auntie became more angry. Against the advice of Bush and Tulik, she joined up with the young men who believed most strongly in violence. Not Arlie's disciples, but the younger ones, the ones who were suspicious of Arlie's group, believing even the emphasis on peace to be suspect, believing they might be traitors.

One day Auntie yelled out to a soldier she suspected of starting the blaze, "You son of a bitch!" Another day she tried to run over a group of soldiers with her red truck. They scattered like chickens, which pleased her, I could tell. With fondness, the young men called her "Hurricane Auntie."

But now a conflict grew between Auntie and Bush, and one day Auntie said to Bush, "You're too passive." Bush said, in return, "You are out of control, Auntie." It was a lost friendship.

And it was true, Auntie's anger ruled her. It was another danger-ous fire.

Bush, afraid for us, tried hard to be diplomatic and to meet with the enemies. Not to have peace, she believed, was to invite violence. She recalled the gun aimed at Dora-Rouge.

I worried for Bush. She was an outsider. Maybe she was wise, and maybe she knew how fear worked, but there were ancient animosities she didn't know in that place, old memories and rage.

SOMETIMES, I think now, the thing in life that turns toward you, looks at you with cold eyes, eyes that shine in the night and blink and open and take you in the way night-shining eyes of animals glare for a moment and then look away. Sometimes it is loving, sometimes indifferent and chilling. What was done to our world was not right, and all of us saw the eyes of that monster. It was not true that wind had four corners like a room, that it was contained. It was not true that I helped fashion a bomb, although I would lie if I said I hadn't wanted to. It was not right, having the world pulled away from us unable to catch it. I wanted my eyes to turn it over, to set something right, the way it happens between the lens and the brain, the way it happened one evening as I sat at the window and watched a bonfire burning on the hill and thought of Tulik's house, black embers looking like hundreds of black crows flying away, crows that remembered the trees their ancestors once sat in. Like us, crows forget nothing.

I remember these events like an illness, and I wish I could forget what men do for small and pitiful power. And there are nights I lay awake and think of what we were in danger of becoming. Our lives in that place were being taken from us, the people removed from the land, water, animals, trees, all violated, and no one lives with full humanity without these elements.

And there was the day, caught in a web of anger and fear, that I walked toward the soldiers, a rock in my hand.

Bush laid her hand on me.

I turned my head and looked at her in all her quiet strength. I did not throw the rock. I know now what a single thrown rock would have done. Just one rock.

So easily, we could become a little society like their larger one. We argued strategy. We fought among ourselves. Within our own ranks, there were divisions as quick and malignant as cells. Some of our young men broke the windows of cars. They carried guns and hunting rifles.

One day, I supposed, the police would return to solving crimes rather than creating them. One day, no matter what happened, no matter who possessed the land, no matter whether there were dams or not, all of this might sink to the bottom of a sea or dissolve in rain. Perhaps fire would turn the land to glass and it might catch light and shine and reflect the sun back to itself. In time, all things would break and would become whole again. The soldiers would grow old and die and be placed in the ground with small white markers. The permafrost would melt, seasons would change.

By now, everything had a shining darkness about it. The days had become shorter, the light slowly faded. The lake, at times, looked red as blood. The world seemed to be breaking open. Husk would have said it was like the beginning of a universe. We did not know what would come from this unfolding.

DECISIONS ARE MADE in a person's life by small moments of knowing, each moment opening until, like pieces of a quilt, one day everything comes together in a precise, clear knowing. It enters the present, as if it had come all of a piece. It was in this way that I began to understand who I was. Every piece of myself was together anew, a shifted pattern.

For my people, the problem has always been this: that the only possibility of survival has been resistance. Not to strike back has meant certain loss and death. To strike back has also meant loss and death, only with a fighting chance. To fight has meant that we can respect ourselves, we Beautiful People. Now we believed in ourselves once again. The old songs were there, came back to us. Sometimes I think the ghost dancers were right, that we would return, that we are still returning. Even now.

"There are still people who go to the past," Tulik told me one day. "They know the road there and when they return it is with something valuable, a flint, a story, or a map. "It is what we are always looking for, we who were at the place of old rocks, worn and gray, at islands emerging and falling.

One day, one of the Indian men said he was so sorry but he'd taken a job at the Tip River, a new dam site. "I have to feed my family," he said. "Please forgive me." I could see just by looking at him how hard this decision had been.

Bush was a fair and compassionate person. "I understand," she said. She knew he told the truth, that his children were growing thinner. But the younger men were angry. They saw the Indian laborers as traitors.

Two men, his cousins, rushed toward him in anger.

"Let him go," Bush said, her voice soft, quiet.

"You stay out of this! This isn't your fight."

The two men attacked the laborer. Bush, small as she was, tried to push her way between them.

"So, death has not yet abandoned us, I see," said Dora-Rouge.

ONE RAINY DAY, as if to mirror our division, a piece of land split off from all the rest and moved through the rain down toward the new river. When I see it now, in my dreams, it is noisy, that separation of land from land, but that day it floated away, moving without a sound except for the falling rain. As we watched it, I remembered what Husk had once said about the creation of the moon, how it split off from earth, leaving an ocean behind, salt tears. The moon left the body of its mother, both of them knowing there would be no return.

Some bushes floated away with that land. It was frightening and sad to see, but there was also a kind of defiance in that splitting, one that couldn't be spoken except in the language of the earth, and it was a sign we couldn't decipher, a meaning not known to us. LaRue leaped on it, as if to pull it back or save it. No one knew why he did that. He looked as surprised as the rest of us. But once he was on that swirling island, he could not get off and he was carried away by the muddy surge of water. He went with the land, past the sentries, to other places. How far he went we couldn't know. But it made us think of a strategy, that we could take down a piece of dam, float parts of it away, and return the river to its natural course.

· · ·

IT WAS no longer summer. The days were shorter now. Air and water had a different smell. Peat smoke breathed out from the houses. I was ready to return to Adam's Rib, to see Tommy. Sitting beside Tulik, I dreamed of Tommy's touch, his large warm hands, his dark eyes.

"You need your strength. Eat this." Tulik handed me a bologna sandwich. I did as he said. The food tasted good in my mouth, bologna and ketchup on white bread. He poured a cup of coffee out of the thermos. He was always feeding other people. As I ate, I saw how the shadows were now longer, how some of the trees were already tinted by fall. The workers wouldn't be able to work in winter when the cold stopped machines, so they worked quickly now, day and night, to get as much done as possible.

Gathered around the fire, we were silent. It had been a nerve-racking day. Now some of the women were hunched down, asleep, dead tired, and it was silent outside.

And then we woke to harsh, searching lights and the brash noise of helicopters. That day they brought in assault rifles, tanks, machine guns, and even APCs. And they, these men that came with such weapons, were really just boys who not long before talked about music and girlfriends. Yet they crossed a line. And now they were in a position to kill us. Already they'd cut through the edges of the world we'd known.

That day a bulldozer started up with a dark cloud of gas and tumult, and ran over rocks and into a clothesline and tree, over oil drums and an outhouse and the bedsprings that sat outside it and they came toward the post.

"We've got children in here!" one of the men yelled out.

Already I was crying.

"They're shooting!" I heard someone shout and I heard the popping sounds of a gun.

They shot Mr. Orensen's dogs, afraid they would attack them. It took so little. Within fifteen seconds, perhaps less, the course of things changed forever.

Then the trees that were still there were run over and folded like nothing, broke and bent beneath their will. I could not read the expression on Tulik's face. He knew something true, that's all I could tell. I think he knew that this fight would be forever, that it would never end, but he knew, also, that he was in it and would always be.

Dora-Rouge sat unmoved in her chair, shook her fist, and cried. "They shot the dogs!"

They even shot at the geese, the opening of wings as they rose up, afraid, into the sky. Guns in soldier's hands, Bush would say, always shoot precious things. It was true, like one of Husk's rules of physics. It wasn't their heads that shot, or even their minds. I am trying to say they were not bad people. They were common as sons and brothers and that made it all the more frightening.

ONE MORNING, like a ghost in the early dawn fog, a wolf was standing in the shadows. It was thin. It was silent. "Grandmother," I said to it. I thought it was Agnes. It stood and watched awhile, then walked toward the soldiers. "Don't go," I willed it. I could hardly breathe. I squeezed my eyes tight. But it went. I heard shots and my heart ached with a swollen feeling, as if something had set itself right in the center of it, between all the chambers, and whatever it was, it would remain, it would never come out again.

That afternoon, tear-gas canisters were thrown and fired. But the wind, the one we knew so well, changed direction, and some of the police and soldiers were the ones who had to run. We were happy to see that the wind was on our side. But the next morning Aurora was sick. She was feverish, her eyes tearing. Throughout the day she worsened. I sat beside her, gave her a corner of a wet rag to suck on. I wiped her forehead with a cool cloth. Her skin was sensitive. She cried when I touched her.

"It must be the tear gas," I said to Tulik. "Do you think we could get a doctor past the soldiers?" We were inside the post. Orensen heard me. "No," he said. "We'll have to take her out. That way we won't risk the doctor coming in here with a gun." He was right. The doctor's drinking had left him erratic; he wasn't to be trusted.

By then, everyone was concerned about Aurora. Her fever had shot up and while at first she had screamed, now she was dull-looking, feeble.

Bush washed Aurora with cool water.

Orensen knew they wouldn't shoot at him even if he wasn't on their side, so he was the one who went out and talked to the soldiers.

When he came back, he said, "Come on." In a hurry, he pulled on my hand. "Let's go." He was pale and I could see that he was frightened. In spite of his anxiety, we moved slowly, uncertain whether we would make it past the lines.

"Bush, too," he said. "Come on. In case she needs you."

I was afraid for Bush. "Are you sure we're safe?" I asked.

"Just come."

When we walked outside, I expected them to shoot. My muscles were tight, my heart beating too fast. The light was bright. I froze. Bush touched my arm. To my relief they let us through. Then Orensen put gas in the tank from a can and started the car. Bush, Aurora, and I sat inside it and were still.

But when we reached the turn to the doctor's clinic, Orensen kept going.

"Stop," I said, afraid, suddenly not trusting him. "Where are you going?"

At first he didn't answer. Then he said, "The doctor here won't help her. I already know this. I'm getting you out of here." He looked directly at Bush. "You have to go. It's going to get rough here. And they don't trust you."

I looked to Bush for support. She nodded at me. Orensen was right.

"I'm having Charles meet you," he said. "We're going to pick you up with the mail plane."

But I argued. "The baby needs a doctor. Now."

Bush looked at Orensen, then at me. "He's right," she said, but I could see she felt the same fear I felt.

As we waited for Charles to arrive, I thought how he, too, was now a suspect by both sides. Like Bush, he was another person in the middle, not to be trusted.

Bush put her hands on Aurora's forehead. "She'll be all right," she said, trying to reassure me.

What happened after that, we only heard later. A railroad bridge was burned, transmission towers damaged. With bolts removed

from them, they collapsed. It was as if the old warrior spirit, the Wolf
Society, was resurrected. The people vowed to fight to the death before allowing the food, water, medicines, and burial grounds to be
flooded, before allowing the wildlife to be killed, the fish poisoned.

Theirs was the job of healing the river, breaching a dike, letting
water flow in its own way.

Later I would feel guilty for leaving, but that day as we left, I was
relieved. We, at least, had somewhere to go. As outsiders, we were
the ones fortune changed clothes for, the ones for whom she wore
more than one dress.

Bush wiped Aurora's drawn face with a cool cloth, to break her
fever. I looked at this strange woman from the island, dressed in
jeans and workshirt, holding in her arms the child of a child she had
both loved and feared in another time, another place.

Then there was the familiar sound of the mail plane, the sound
of propellers, the shaking of it. And then we were gone. From the
noisy plane, I looked back, and as we left, I saw how the place
where I'd first stepped into the territory of my people, the Fat-
Eaters, the Beautiful People, was now dust, the plants covered by
it, so the land looked dull, and already the original road was beneath the water. Flying in a growing darkness, I saw the thin line of
road that was String Town, like a necklace of artificial gems opened
out along the land, the lights emerging from transformed water. It
was against the will of land, I knew, to turn rivers into lakes, lakes
into dry land, to send rivers along new paths. I hoped the earth
would one day forgive this breach of faith, the broken agreement
humans had with it.

It wasn't long before the plane landed near Pinetown.

"We have a sick baby. Where's the hospital?" Charles asked a
man at the landing strip.

"Up there." He pointed. We could see it.

We rushed toward it.

At the clinic, Bush rang the bell. Someone looked outside, but
didn't open the door. I held up the baby for them to see. Still, the
door remained locked. "She's sick!" I yelled out, but they wouldn't
treat us. As we were turned away, I screamed at them. "Why don't

you help us?" I went back and banged my fist on the door. "Help us!"

"Don't fight them," Bush's voice sounded flat as she pulled me away. "It scares them."

"I don't care! How cowardly!" I accused her.

"They'll arrest us. They'll keep us from getting help."

"She's right," Charles said. "It's useless, your anger. Save it."

It was only later that I realized how much they feared us, our darkness, our coming from the site of the dams.

"We'll go to Chinobe," Bush said.

Already Charles, now carrying Aurora, was running toward the water. We would have to travel by canoe, he told us.

"Where are we going to get a canoe?" I asked, but I knew we would steal one. Our list of crimes was growing.

At the dock, there was a rack with several canoes. Charles took out a large one. Then he broke into a boathouse and found paddles, and with haste we went to the edge of water and set off. Between us there was only one life jacket. For Aurora, I thought, in case something happened to us. She'd live. She'd come in from water like Loretta, Hannah, and me.

While Bush wrapped Aurora tight against the chill and held her, Charles and I paddled quickly across the muddy waters. Aurora was silent. We were swift. I didn't know a canoe could move so quickly. It frightened me, as if we'd leave water and enter sky. My breathing was loud.

Then Bush took over and I held Aurora close to my heart, praying. Hurry! I kept thinking. Hurry! as if the words themselves, like traditional people know, were supernatural beings and would speed us along like light or cloud.

It must have been several hours to land. When we reached it, Charles told us to wait by a stone road. The heel had come off my shoe, and tiny nails poked up into my foot. I put some leaves in the shoe. Before long, Charles returned in a wreck of a car, another man beside him.

"My cousin," was all he said by way of explanation. "Hurry." In no time the cousin left and we were in the car. A window was missing; it was covered with taped plastic. Duct tape. It was a rattling machine and I didn't hold out much hope that it would get us to Chinobe, but at least the radio worked. At first it was a diversion. Then, I could hardly believe my ears, there was Loretta telling Tony to come home. I turned it off.

Bush slept in the back seat with Aurora on her stomach. I touched Aurora's face. She was burning up. My own arms were shaking with fatigue.

It was still a few hours to Chinobe, to the nearest hospital. Rain fell. It was my turn to drive. I drove quickly over the dirt road and once, when we hit pavement, the car hydroplaned, spinning around. Bush sat up, covered Aurora, protecting her. Charles yelled, "Lift your foot." I did as he said and the car came to rest in a ditch, then I drove out of the ditch and went on as if nothing had happened. It was only later that I realized the danger we had been in. I thanked Fortune, the one who had changed clothing for us.

After that, the road was straight and flat. We headed south in silence with only the hypnotic movement of the car, the road, the sound of tires, and Aurora's breathing. There was an occasional animal at the side of the road, a coyote or a rabbit.

We were low on gas, uncertain how many miles to Chinobe. I reassured myself, thinking maybe there was a gas can in the trunk.

Even through my fear, I saw beautiful meadows.

When we came to Chinobe, we were all relieved to see the sign: "Indian Health Service Hospital." They would help us; they had no choice.

Charles and I took Aurora inside like her parents, with Bush following. It was a sterile white place with its smells of alcohol, bandages. I watched the doctor's every move.

"She's going to be fine," the woman said after the IVs were in place.

I breathed then.

THAT NIGHT we slept in the car in the hospital parking lot. Once or twice a security guard drove by and shone his light on us but he didn't make us leave. Before I fell asleep, I watched the quick movements of bats in the sky. It seemed so peaceful—the trees, the silence, the round white moon—so comforting.

I was stiff the next morning. I went into the hospital to see Aurora.

She slept peacefully in the little crib. Her fever was gone.

We drove into town. We stopped for coffee in a little restaurant with red tables and the smell of pancakes and bacon, and as we sipped a terrible excuse for coffee, the Indian waitress asked us, "Where did you come from?" She was young. She wore a heart on a chain around her neck.

"String Town," I said.

"Oh, is that right?" she said mostly to Charles, not to me. It was the first time I'd noticed he was good-looking. "What's going on up there?"

I didn't hear all that Charles said to her. Instead, I went into the bathroom and washed my hair in the sink with hand soap. Outside the bathroom door, in the dingy hallway, there were notes on the bulletin board: "Massage Therapy." "Canoe for Sale." "Used Fur." How far away all this seemed to me now, having traveled down from the north, a child folded inside my life, my heart. As I stood there it seemed like seeds and chaff swirled away to a future far away from the mother plant. Which future, I couldn't yet know.

When we left, the waitress said, "I hope they win. The Indians, I mean." She fingered the heart absentmindedly, smiling at Charles and then at Bush.

"Me, too," Bush said.

▼

T W E N T Y

BEGINNINGS, I know now, are everything. And when Bush and I returned to Adam's Rib, I knew we walked into another day of creation, a beginning. Perhaps my own return began long ago, in a time before I was born, when I was held inside the bodies of my ancestors. What a fine savagery we had then, in the dark stirrings of first life, long before the notion of civilization. We knew the languages of earth, water, and trees. We knew the rich darkness of creation. For tens of thousands of years we spoke with the animals and they spoke with us.

And perhaps it was flood from the start of my first going there, or maybe there has always been something coming toward us that sweeps away things both familiar and strange, swallows them in its path. Whatever it was, when Bush, Aurora, and I returned to Adam's Rib on Tinselman's Ferry, the place seemed unfamiliar. Little by little, the land had been sinking, diminishing. Before we'd left for the far north, the water level had been low, but now, because of the diversion of rivers, the closing of floodgates, now it was high. While we'd been at Two-Town, caught up in the battle over water at its source, the flooding of this place had already begun. It was the result of the damming we'd witnessed at the Fat-Eaters', the result of the stopped rivers to the north. It was the result of our failure to end the first phase of the project.

As we stepped off the ferry, the sign that read "Auto Parts, Boat Repair" was just above water, the wooden building half-submerged, the water still rising slowly. Of the houses that sat next to the lake, only the tops and roofs were still dry. Levees were breached, overtopped. One river that had emptied into Lake Grand had flooded the surrounding land. A red plastic tablecloth from some water-filled kitchen had floated off a table or out of a drawer and risen to the surface of the water. It was opened, as if welcoming guests to a meal. Dead fish lapped against the walls of buildings, and I could see drying racks, hoists, and old cars beneath the water, and the water was still rising and going to rise.

Soon the four remaining white pines trees would turn slowly into white skeleton trees, half under water, and graves would be covered. All this from the destroyed lands above us. In this flood, there would be no animals escaping two by two, no one to reach out for those who wander gracefully and far on four legs, to take hold of the wading birds with their golden claws at the bottom of water, to carry to safety the yellow-eyed lynx, the swift dark marten.

Bush carried Aurora as we walked toward Agnes' house. And Aurora was about all we carried. We'd left everything but our cash at the Fat-Eaters'. Aurora slept peacefully, her head against Bush's shoulder. A few inches of water covered the lower part of Poison Road, that first road I'd walked on over a year ago, returning to Agnes and Bush and Dora-Rouge. Now water spread out through the grasses and brush and it neared the doors of low-lying houses.

We were silent, looking around us, our shoes wet.

When we reached Agnes' worn brown house, the door was as wide open as if it had never been closed since the time we left. I half expected to see Agnes standing waiting there in welcome, her glasses with light on the edge of them. Or to hear her voice saying, "Look at you, you are a woman."

When Bush and I entered her house was when I missed her the most. I looked at the cot, the table, the stove. All were dusty. Leaves and mouse droppings were on the cot. Bush brushed it off, then laid Aurora on a blanket. We looked around. John Husk was not there. He hadn't been there for some time, I could see. Inside the house a layer of dust was laid down on everything, as if no one had inhabited the place in all the time we'd been gone.

"Where do you think he is?" I asked Bush, half afraid he was dead.

Bush said nothing.

I went outside and sat quietly in the red chair for a few moments, remembering Agnes. I wanted to call out her name and see her come toward me, walking in from the lake.

After a while, Bush came to stand beside me. "It's terribly lonely here, don't you think?"

"Yes. We should go find Husk." I was half afraid that he had died of grief, having lost Agnes.

"Aurora's sleeping. I'll wait here," Bush said. "I'm tired."

But as tired as she was, Bush tied back her hair and began dusting the stove and table as if we would move into this little house. She cried as she cleaned.

I knew that she wanted to be alone, and I was anxious to go to the Hundred-Year-Old Road to see Tommy and Husk, so I left Aurora and Bush.

As I walked uphill toward the Hundred-Year-Old Road, Tommy stood inside my inner eye and I could see him clearly— dark eyes, compassionate face. Slowly and without words I moved toward him. I felt his presence as if he walked beside me, smelled the odor of his skin. When I reached Wiley's place, Tommy was standing just outside the door as if he'd known I was coming, standing just like the image of him inside my eye. Lean, large-handed, he stepped toward me. I went to him, nearly floating as if I had no feet, and we held each other. I felt my heart grow large. We were quiet, breathing, loving, holding each other in the silence of deep love.

We walked into the trees and sat on the ground in the thin shade of two birches.

Later I told him all that I'd done, how I'd stolen food and almost thrown a rock at the men with guns.

"Do you still love me?" I asked him.

He said, "I love you even more," and took my hand.

We are small, I thought, touching Tommy's forehead, neck,

chest with its few brown hairs. We are awake in the gone forest, stepping out of clay. We are precious as earth, as diatoms shaped like mystery itself in the blooming seas.

WHEN WE WENT INDOORS, I asked for Husk. He beamed when he saw me. "Angel," he cried out, but he looked poorly, his pants baggy, his shirt wrinkled, and one eye drooped. He had moved in along the Hundred-Year-Old Road and he, along with the others, had put up a long fight against the flooding. They had fought their own battle in Adam's Rib, and lost, and now the water was rising and the people were simply tired. The fatigue showed on all of them.

A FEW DAYS LATER, as the water continued to rise, Bush and Husk gathered up Agnes' things—the kettles, the boxes Dora-Rouge had left behind, the blankets folded on the cot.

Husk looked better on this day. He even wore permanent-press slacks, as Agnes had suggested. "We should let it all go," said Husk, as we prepared to pack the back of his truck with the toaster and pans and dishes. He sat down, tired. We would take everything up the rise to the Hundred-Year-Old Road, hoping that place at least, as the engineers had promised, would be spared.

Bush waxed the old, dirty linoleum.

"What are you doing?" I asked.

"I'm making this place presentable for water."

I said to Bush and Husk, "What Agnes wanted all along was to be eaten by the animals. Did you know that?"

"Yes, she told me that when no one was listening," Husk answered.

THE NEXT DAY we crossed from Adam's Rib to Fur Island. Water was still rising and motorboats moved across it, seeking out confused animals, some trying to swim. Many had already drowned. A wooden ironing board floated up. We saw all this while Bush and I paddled. The waters looked suddenly vast.

Fur Island, like all the other broken pieces of land, had begun to shrink. We wanted to salvage the plants, the corn, whatever could be taken away. As we set to work in what was already mud, we saw the water level rise. It wasn't long before the white stones of the path were nearly invisible, jutting out of water like small icebergs in a line. The turtle bones, somewhat higher, were not yet covered.

And then LaRue barged through it all in the dark gray *Raven*, cutting through the reflection of sun as if he'd crossed sky instead of water, loud and urgent. In spite of herself, Bush was happy to see him. He had come to help us. She wanted to know where he'd gone after we'd seen him float away from the place of the Beautiful People on the new, muddy island of land, but she didn't ask. Nor did she accuse. This, I thought, was a good sign.

Soon the water would approach Bush's house, enter the door as lightly and easily as if it were an invited guest. We saw it coming, the slow rise of it, as we worked hard, muddy and wet, trying to save the plants Bush had cultivated, taking the seeds of some, digging others up by the roots and wrapping them in cloth to replant later, at the Hundred-Year-Old Road.

We worked for days, and were still hard at work when Tommy arrived with his traps. Some of the animals that couldn't swim he trapped or snared, carried off to Adam's Rib, and let go. From water's edge I watched as he and LaRue roped a deer that couldn't swim and, with the rope around its neck, took it across water to the mainland. It was a stranded deer that had come across on ice and been unable to return.

We worked ourselves into exhaustion, the rich loamy-smelling soil on us, wanting not to be claimed by water. But water, I thought, wanted all things equal, level, contained.

LaRue and *The Raven* towed the island of spiders, with its silken weavings and shimmering strands, to the mainland and secured it there. We didn't want to lose that little broken-off raft of land in all the greedy, hungry water that was, through the acts of men, laying claim to everything it once created.

The next day, the house of black stones, the House of No, filled up with frogs and mud. We watched the water continue to rise, and in spite of our heartache, it looked peaceful, all the water laying itself down across our world. From *The Raven* we watched the turtle bones that Bush had assembled. Water was taking back the turtle. And as the four of us left Fur Island for good, we sat in *The Raven* and watched. The turtle was lifted. First the water came over it slowly, like a lover, then it rose a little at a time, until finally the turtle came loose and began to float. For a moment I saw it whole, the bones of a great thing returning to water, where it would move once again inside water's darkness. Bush turned to LaRue with a look of defiance, but he, too, looked jubilant and she said nothing.

The Hungry Mouth of Water closed. It took in nothing else. Instead, it was taken in, like the turtle, along with the beluga, the snowmobiles, skinned animals, and Frenchie's Helene.

Then, even the floorboards of the house rose, a few at a time, and Fur Island, with its house made of ballast, fell to the bottom of water as if by design. So did the organ pipes and the blasted milkstone and the shed filled with old rusted traps.

ONE DAY I went to see LaRue. He'd been crying. He tried to hide this from me, but I said, "What gives?" I looked about that place of scorpions, snake spines, and pinned butterflies in cases.

He looked at me. To gauge my seriousness. "Come here," he said.

I followed him into the smelly dark basement of bones and hides and glass eyes. There, on a table, was an animal with nearly green fur. Beautiful beyond anything I had seen: large dark eyes shaped like almonds; a face soft as velvet with thin whiskers; a thin, lithe body; a long tail. It lay there like a tendril, the first rise of a fern, that's how delicate and beautiful it was.

"What is it?" I asked.

I pieced together what he said. The animal had been killed by a hunter in a far forest. One of his regular customers. It was the last of this kind of creature, according to the man who'd shot it, and he was proud for taking it. Take, I thought then, what a strange word it is. To conquer, to possess, to win, to swallow.

By then I knew so much about crying that I held Rue's hand. "Talk to me," I said. He cried for the animal, for us, our lives, and for the war he'd endured and never told about. He changed after that, inch by inch. Another person might not have noticed, but I saw it. And so did Bush. She was moved by his new openness, his lack of skin. Tears have a purpose. They are what we carry of ocean, and perhaps we must become sea, give ourselves to it, if we are to be transformed.

▼

TWENTY-ONE

IT WAS NEARLY A YEAR later when I saw Tulik. A hot city day. I was standing on a corner thinking how pavement was only a thin shell on earth, that the plants would outlast it and grow over it again, and then I saw him. He was asking directions of a tall man in a suit. He looked tiny, vulnerable, and very old there in the city with the traffic racing about, the large buildings rising up behind him. The passing people were dressed mostly in dark, trim clothing. Although I knew he was a strong man, Tulik looked nearly feeble in the city. He wore a light blue shirt and his sharp bones showed through it. It looked as if the walls of buildings, the street signs, the electric lights, the markets could have swallowed him, the way they had swallowed land. People stared with curiosity, as if he'd walked out of an ancient history they'd all but forgotten. It seemed now that his wisdom was nothing more than a worn-out belief that had no place in this new world where the walls themselves came from the lost lives and worlds of men like Tulik.

I was happy to see him. "Tulik!" I yelled, running to catch up.

He'd been growing his hair; now it was tied in a ponytail down his back, and it was still black as crow wings.

"Tulik!" I hurried toward him.

He stopped as though no one had ever spoken his name before.

The streetlight changed to yellow. A man behind Tulik bumped into him, then stepped around him, quickly passing. Tulik turned and looked straight at me. "Angel!" he cried out. "Maniki! Look at you! You're so good!"

He touched my face and held me, then he said, in a very businesslike way, "Come with me. I have to find the barbershop."

"Barbershop? You always said they were a waste of money."

"I want the judge to listen to me. I'll have to look like one of them."

But at the barber's, as I sat and watched the feathers of black hair fall to the floor, I thought he looked ridiculous. He knew it, too, this man who had always been so proud of his appearance.

Then, with his respectable hair, we went to a restaurant and had coffee and American pie, as Tulik called the apples baked in a skin.

I asked, "How is Dora-Rouge?"

"She's fine. She sends you her love. And, oh, I have this for you." He reached into his pocket and took out a container, the last one, of sleeping potion.

Later that day at the courthouse, Tulik said, "I've been meditating. But I don't have inner peace. I can't find it again. I think it would be better to have never had it than to lose it this way." He shook his head, sad. "But then why should the inside be different than the outside? This is what happens to humans when their land is destroyed. Don't you think so, Maniki, that they lose their inside ways?"

I brushed the black hair off his shoulders and straightened his collar and we entered the marble halls of justice.

WHEN IT WAS EVENING, the day of court over, Tulik said he longed to take Aurora on his lap and rock her. We went to the kitchenette Chiquita, Wiley's wife, and I had rented, and Tulik lifted Aurora and made her light up. "She's so big!"

"You still have the gift," I said to him with pride in my voice. You'd never have thought she could remember him from so long ago, but she did. She had eyes only for Tulik. And she toddled toward him and called his name while I boiled water in a pan and stirred instant coffee into two cups.

Tulik called the courthouse the House of Units, Measures, and Standards, because the questions asked there were how many, how much, how often. How many fish did you catch two years ago? How many did you catch last year? He knew well that the worth and weight of things was now asked in terms of numbers, dollars, grams. His testimony was always direct and honest. "Are there less than there were?" they'd ask, and he'd say, "I never counted, but it seems like there are. By at least half."

They asked Tulik and some of the other men about their traplines, the places where they'd found moose, how many they'd killed in a year, what their income was. Had they lived off the land?

The sessions started daily at nine. There were few breaks in the testimony. I was overwhelmed with the exhaustion of sitting all day.

"Please answer the question." The voice was strong-sounding.

"I'm trying to answer."

Aurora's eyes followed it all. Inside, she seemed to be listening to the testimony. Outside, she looked at the large buildings with the sun on their windows.

In the evenings, after his testimony, Tulik looked gray and tired. It wore on him, on all of them, to be treated with derision and ridicule. To others, we were such insignificant people. In their minds we were only a remnant of a past. They romanticized this past in fantasy, sometimes even wanted to bring it back for themselves, but they despised our real human presence. Their men, even their children, had entered forests, pretended to be us, imagined our lives, but now we were present, alive, a force to be reckoned with.

Those with the money, the investments, the city power, had no understanding of the destruction their decisions and wants and desires brought to the world. If they'd known what their decisions meant to our people, and if they continued with this building in spite of that knowing, then they were evil. They were the cannibals who consumed human flesh, set fire to worlds the gods had loved and asked the humans to care for.

There was little press coverage. But one day there was a small photo in the bottom corner of a page. It was a newspaper photo of Tulik and the other distinguished men and women, brilliant ones, standing on the front steps of the courthouse. The caption read, "On the Warpath Again." I hid the paper from Tulik. I tried, as he had done with me earlier, to keep him from pain.

I think of him now sitting there with all his beauty turned into some kind of homeliness contained in the cold halls of stone that came from the illegal quarries of our world. He sat quietly, and listened.

IT TOOK MORE THAN A YEAR before the building of the dams ceased and Tulik did not live long enough to see us win. He would have liked that, even though so much change had already fallen on the land. It was too late for the Child River, for the caribou, the fish, even for our own children, but we had to believe, true or not, that our belated victory was the end of something. That one fracture was healed, one crack mended, one piece back in place. Yes, the pieces were infinite and worn as broken pots, and our human pain was deep, but we'd thrown an anchor into the future and followed the rope to the end of it, to where we would dream new dreams, new medicines, and one day, once again, remember the sacredness of every living thing.

In all of this, something was stripped away from me. Like a snake I emerged, rubbing myself out of my old skin, my old eyes. I was fresh, I was seeing clearly.

One day, in the city, I looked up. It was going to rain. I couldn't see the stars, but I knew they were there.

There are such cruel tricks I have wondered about in nature, the way a whale must surface to breathe in the presence of its waiting killers, the way the white tails of deer and rabbit are so easily seen as they run from danger. There is something, too, in some human beings that wants to die, that drives us to our own destruction. There is something that makes us pretend to be less than we are, less than the other creatures with their grace and dignity. Perhaps it is this that makes us bow down to an angry god when we might better have knelt at the altar of our own love.

And sometimes I sit and think about those who took apart this land, our lives. When they pull back their covers in the morning, I wonder, do they rise from sleep with joy? For all this, is there happiness and peace? Are they singing as they sit beneath the light of a lamp, or loving each other? I might as well ask if infinity has bitten off the end of its circular flight.

SO OFTEN I think of Hannah. She is always at the edge of my dreaming, at the periphery of wakefulness and sleep. Anything can bring her to mind—an icy wind on a hot day, a day with a bad feel to it, a newspaper account of an injured child.

My mother walked out of the rifles of our killers. She was born of knives, the skinned-alive beaver and marten and the chewed-off legs of wolves. She hurt me because I was part of her and she hated herself. I think of her last name, Wing, as if she could fly, weightless as a bird catching a current of air. Or, like the wolverine on the rock paintings, perhaps her wings were invisible until they were wet, and then they opened, full and strong. I hoped she lived in a place where she could open those wings with a love she'd never known in her life.

Tulik once said there are still those of us who can travel to the past and return with something of value, a knowing, a cure, or a song. I wanted to be one of those, to return from the far regions having retrieved a song, a sacred bundle, a box of herbs, anything I could take to the future. But I wasn't. I had to leave the songs behind with their owners, leave the herbs beneath water, the bundles in their caves and trees alongside bear skulls that had been watching us from hidden places. For a time, I thought that all I'd found were sharp sticks with skins and rags over them. Something like the things Old Mother, the first woman, had used to create her children. Maybe I had not gone far enough, or maybe, as in the stories of the creation of first woman and first man, I only needed the right song to sing to the sticks so they would come alive, take shape, and begin to breathe and move. Lately I hear something like a voice inside my ear, whispering to me. "Get up," the voice says in the morning. "Offer cornmeal to the morning people." I do it. "Be slow," it says. I do this, too.

And I could tell about my own passing through doors not of this world, how my soul travels at times to the middle of rivers where doctors named stone reside, how I search for the plants of my grandmothers. Since then I have stood in the way of fireballs, begging them to fill me. There are other mysteries, too, ones lost men and women cannot find because the ancestral markers are taken away. There is no map to show where to step, no guide to tell us how to see. But maybe, as Dora-Rouge once said, maps are only masks over the face of God and we are the lost ones; it is not that the ways are lost from us but that we are lost from them. But the ways are patient and await our return.

I've shaped my own life, after all. Like a deer curled into grasses, or the place a moose slept.

ONE DAY BUSH, Husk, and I received a note card from Dora-Rouge. It was an invitation to her death. I dreamed we should go, but Bush, as painful as this was for her, could not travel. She could leave neither the old people we now lived with, nor the plants she was propagating, so I went alone. This time I took the train, watching the land pass the coyotes. Standing between the cars of the noisy train, everything seemed fragile and temporary.

When I arrived at what had been Two-Town, I was stunned. The tracks I traveled along now ended in water. There were submerged buildings, sediment rising up, dark and silty. I didn't have to dive to see any of it. I knew the terrain by heart. Miles covered, pictographs, rivers drowned, even a dead moose floating. A fast river had become nothing but a pond, green with algae, stagnant, a desperate place except for the dragonflies above it. There were floating trees, pines, fish. The wood of old walls floated to the surface, fence posts, a piece of tree bark carved in the shape of a heart; maybe it carried the initials of Tony and Loretta.

Walking from the train, I asked a man, "Where is Tulik's house?" Even though Tulik was gone, he was remembered, and the man pointed me to a new, government-built house.

When I knocked on the door, Miss Nett answered, her curved back forcing her to strain to look up at me. Filled with emotion, she hugged me, saying nothing, just holding me tight. Then, rosy-cheeked, she turned to Dora-Rouge, who was inside. "Ena. It's Maniki!" she said.

As I entered the room, Dora-Rouge said, "Oh, darling, I can

barely see you." I held her close. I could smell sickness on Dora-Rouge and she was bonier than before. "Nobody will come to my death," she said.

"I'm here," I told her gently.

"Yes, you are, Maniki, a true human being."

I went inside and sat down on a wooden chair beside her, re-membering a story Tulik had once told me about the men, the human people, who wanted what all the other creatures had. They went to the large bird and said they wanted to fly. They were granted this wish. They went to the mole and said they wanted to tunnel, and this they were able to do. Last, they went to the water and said, We must have this unbound manner of living. The water said, You have asked for too much, and then all of it was taken away from them. With all of their wishes, they had forgotten to ask to be-come human beings.

"I had such a rough night. I couldn't sleep," Dora-Rouge said. Her wild white hair and the dark circles under her eyes showed it. "Do you have any of that potion left? Did you find those plants?"

"No," I said. The truth was, I had not looked. I'd been so busy salvaging everything from the flooding and helping the people at Adam's Rib, I'd forgotten all about the plants. But I vowed to my-self that I would keep looking. I didn't tell Dora-Rouge about the world she'd lived in for so long at Adam's Rib, now flooded. Now there was no need for her to know, no reason to add weight to her grief.

"I know it's out there, that plant. I feel it." She pointed toward the north.

I hoped she was right.

"Where's Bush?"

"They are so sorry." Then I told her that we had moved to the Hundred-Year-Old Road and that the people needed Bush.

Dora-Rouge was sorry to hear this, but still she was cheered by my presence.

I decided to stay for a while with Dora-Rouge and Miss Nett. I thought I'd search out the plants. I sent word to Tommy that I would stay for a few weeks, and the two women settled me into a folding cot. I didn't complain.

One day I went out searching for the plants. I thought I might have a chance of finding them, if only Tulik were with me. I wished I had Ek's book, too, with its maps to certain plants, but with the terrain so changed, the maps would have been of no use. Now the river below us was trying to learn its new home, its new journey. It wasn't doing very well. Nor was the dry land that had been under water, now exposed to air, not yet with new grasses sprouting from it.

Early one morning I dreamed that Dora-Rouge was alone in the woods. That morning, when I woke, I found her missing. "I don't know where she went," said Miss Nett. "How could she have gotten away?"

I went to the place of my dream. It was near the place of the three-leafed plants Tulik had taken me to visit. On the pathway was her chair, a knot and tangle of wicker turned on its side, the name Mother Jordan still visible beneath the paint. It was strange-looking, overturned that way with the grasses beneath the webbing and weaving of it. But Dora-Rouge was not in sight.

I found her on a bed of moss just off a path in the remaining forest. She was surrounded by ferns, mosses, and the deep green of spring. Although she was white-haired and withered, she was curled up like an infant waiting to be born.

"Grandmother," I said. "How did you get here?" I knelt and touched her shoulder.

"I have my ways."

"All this way?"

"This is where I want to die." She was on her side, smiling up at me.

"You came all this way without anyone seeing you?"

"All this way." She looked proud of her accomplishment, but she was weak.

I sat beside her on the ground. She smiled into my eyes. "Look. The rain cloud. How beautiful." She looked at the sky.

I lay next to her on my back and looked up. There was not a cloud in the sky. It was a clear blue day. When I looked back at her, she was gone, not in the hard way that I have seen in other deaths, no death rattle or struggle to breathe, no fighting. She died easily, soft as a leaf falling from a tree that knew new leaves, branches, and roots would unfold, a tree that had the power of its belief that spring would one day come.

And though it was cloudless, it began to rain, a soft female rain. It fell over us. I sat with her body, rocking her in my lap. Above the cloudless rain was the sun, meteor showers, and cosmic dust. I was small, sitting there, rocking death. I sang an old song. It had been Dora-Rouge's song. It was the animal-calling song. And while I sang, the animals came to where she lay. I didn't see them with my eyes, but I knew they were there. Wolf, thin and old, stood back away from us in the trees. He kept his distance. Who could blame him? And there was Eagle with watchful eyes. The sound of a bear, snuffling, moving through the brush, and another shadow behind him. Wolverine, I thought, come to pay last respects.

THE NORTH is not always cold and white. Some mornings it is warm and the wind stirs, a gentle hand touching the world and people. On these mornings, the shadows of leaves are beautiful on the ground. Light comes slow and languid, as if the sun is hesitant to rise above earth, as if earth has slowed in its spin to a lazy, gentle curve. And some nights when moonlight casts a spell, it is clear enough to see the shape of Fish in the sky. Next to it are Wolf, Badger, and Wolverine. Though I have never seen that constellation, I know it is there. Sometimes the aurora borealis moves across night, strands of light that remind me of a spider's web or a fishnet cast out across the starry skies to pull life in toward it. At other times it reminds me of the lines across a pregnant woman's belly. It leaves me thinking that maybe our earth, our sky, will give birth to something, perhaps there's still another day of creation, and the earth is only a little boat with men and women, slugs and manta rays, all floating in a shell across the dark blue face of a god.

ONE NIGHT, at his home, I asked LaRue, "Say, whatever happened on that river when you escaped?"

"You think I did that on purpose?" I could see he was reverting to his old self. "I was scared shitless. I thought, This is it. You saw that river. It was wild." But just then LaRue looked at the window,

"Oh my God," he said. "It's a wolverine." He jumped up, half-screaming, grabbed his gun, and went to the door.

"Don't shoot it," I yelled after him but already I started to laugh. When he came back in, I held my belly and said, "It was you." I could hardly talk for laughing. "Your reflection."

He looked beaten in some way, but he said, "I *thought* it was too ugly for a wolverine."

When I told Bush, she laughed and softened even more. I told her he had holes in his socks and that I'd seen him cry.

She said, "I'm starting to like that man."

LOVE OPENS its eyes that way. When I am with Tommy, I have no words, and together we are awake in a still-unnamed forest. One night, together, Tommy and I held Aurora up at the traditional dances, in our hands, raised her above Tommy's head and showed her off to the people. Together we danced the dance where songs were dressed in sunlight, where they walked silver and thin out of sky, out of a distant past. There were songs that helped rain fall.

We danced the dance of our own marriage, two become one. I was grateful for the love of Tommy. I believed Tommy and I were our ancestors reunited in their search for each other and we loved deeply, in the way they had loved. I thought how gods breathe on people and they come to life. Something had breathed on us.

Or maybe it's the way light comes from wood and becomes sun once again, passing through whispers of a hundred past years.

EVEN NOW the voice of Agnes floats toward me. I hear her say, "Once the whole world was covered in water." I hear her sing, stepping out of the fog the way she did that day when I first saw her. And sometimes Dora-Rouge touches me. It's her, I know. I can tell by the bony finger, the familiar feel of her hand on my shoulder. At times she brushes back a strand of my hair like she had always done, in order to see my beautiful face. There are times I would think her hand was the wind, but in another brush of her hand, I hear her say that a human is alive water, that creation is not yet over.

If you listen at the walls of one human being, even if that one is yourself, you will hear the drumming. Older creatures are remembered in the blood. Inside ourselves we are not yet upright walkers. We are tree. We are frog in amber. Maybe earth itself is just now starting to form.

One day, when the light was yellow, I turned to Bush and I said, "Something wonderful lives inside me."

She looked at me. "Yes," she said. "The early people knew this, that's why they painted animals on the inside of caves."

Something beautiful lives inside us. You will see. Just believe it. You will see.